"I hear you have a warning for the king," he said boldly. "You may speak it to me."

"My orders are to speak only to the king himself," Miranda said. "It is a matter of some delicacy."

"I am Oban, Master of Security. You'll speak it to me, or not at all," he huffed.

Miranda looked at Gin, who flicked his ear in the ghosthound equivalent of a shrug. "I suppose we have wasted enough time," she said. "I am here on behalf of the Spirit Court by order of the Rector Spiritualis, Etmon Banage. Yesterday morning we received a tip that the known fugitive wizard and wanted criminal Eli Monpress has been sighted within your kingdom. It is our belief that he is after an old wizard artifact held in your treasury. I am here to offer my assistance to keep him from stealing it."

There was a long pause, and Miranda got the horrible, sinking feeling that she had missed something important.

"Lady," the Master of Security said, shaking his head, "if you're here to warn the king about Eli, then you're a little late."

Miranda scowled. "You mean he's already stolen the artifact?"

"No." The Master of Security sighed. "He's stolen the king."

By Rachel Aaron

The Legend of Eli Monpress

The Spirit Thief
The Spirit Rebellion
The Spirit Eater

THE SPIRIT THIEF

The Legend of Eli Monpress Book 1

RACHEL AARON

orbit

www.orbitbooks.net

Copyright © 2010 by Rachel Aaron
Excerpt from *The Spirit Rebellion* copyright © 2010 by Rachel Aaron
All rights reserved. Except as permitted under the U.S. Copyright Act of 1976, no part of this publication may be reproduced, distributed, or transmitted in any form or by any means, or stored in a database or retrieval system, without the prior written permission of the publisher.

Book design by Giorgetta Bell McRee

Orbit
Hachette Book Group
237 Park Avenue, New York, NY 10017
Visit our website at www.orbitbooks.net

Orbit is an imprint of Hachette Book Group. The Orbit name and logo are trademarks of Little, Brown Book Group Limited.

Printed in the United States of America

First edition: October 2010

10 9 8 7 6 5 4 3 2 1

For Travis. All the really good ideas are his.

THE SPIRIT THIEF

CHAPTER
1

In the prison under the castle Allaze, in the dark, moldy cells where the greatest criminals in Mellinor spent the remainder of their lives counting rocks to stave off madness, Eli Monpress was trying to wake up a door.

It was a heavy oak door with an iron frame, created centuries ago by an overzealous carpenter to have, perhaps, more corners than it should. The edges were carefully fitted to lie flush against the stained, stone walls, and the heavy boards were nailed together so tightly that not even the flickering torch light could wedge between them. In all, the effect was so overdone, the construction so inhumanly strong, that the whole black affair had transcended simple confinement and become a monument to the absolute hopelessness of the prisoner's situation. Eli decided to focus on the wood; the iron would have taken forever.

He ran his hands over it, long fingers gently tapping in a way living trees find desperately annoying, but dead wood finds soothing, like a scratch behind the ears. At last, the boards gave a little shudder and said, in a dusty, splintery voice, "What do you want?"

"My dear friend," Eli said, never letting up on his tapping, "the real question here is, what do *you* want?"

"Pardon?" the door rattled, thoroughly confused. It wasn't used to having questions asked of it.

"Well, doesn't it strike you as unfair?" Eli said. "From your grain, anyone can see you were once a great tree. Yet, here you are, locked up through no fault of your own, shut off from the sun by cruel stones with no concern at all for your comfort or continued health."

The door rattled again, knocking the dust from its hinges. Something about the man's voice was off. It was too clear for a normal human's, and the certainty in his words stirred up strange memories that made the door decidedly uncomfortable.

"Wait," it grumbled suspiciously. "You're not a wizard, are you?"

"Me?" Eli clutched his chest. "I, one of those confidence tricksters, manipulators of spirits? Why, the very thought offends me! I am but a wanderer, moving from place to place, listening to the spirits' sorrows and doing what little I can to make them more comfortable." He resumed the pleasant tapping, and the door relaxed against his fingers.

"Well"—it leaned forward a fraction, lowering its creak conspiratorially—"if that's the case, then I don't mind telling you the nails do poke a bit." It rattled, and the nails stood out for a second before returning to their position flush against the wood. The door sighed. "I don't mind the dark so much, or the damp. It's just that people are always slamming me, and that just drives the sharp ends deeper. It hurts something awful, but no one seems to care."

"Let me have a look," Eli said, his voice soft with concern. He made a great show of poring over the door and running his fingers along the joints. The door waited impatiently, creaking every time Eli's hands brushed over a spot where the nails rubbed. Finally, when he had finished his inspection, Eli leaned back and tucked his fist under his chin, obviously deep in thought. When he didn't say anything for a few minutes, the door began to grow impatient, which is a very uncomfortable feeling for a door.

"Well?" it croaked.

"I've found the answer," Eli said, crouching down on the doorstep. "Those nails, which give you so much trouble, are there to pin you to the iron frame. However"—Eli held up one finger in a sage gesture—"they don't stay in of their own accord. They're not glued in; there's no hook. In fact, they seem to be held in place only by the pressure of the wood around them. So"—he arched an eyebrow—"the reason they stay in at all, the only reason, is because you're holding on to them."

"Of course!" the door rumbled. "How else would I stay upright?"

"Who said you had to stay upright?" Eli said, throwing out his arms in a grand gesture. "You're your own spirit, aren't you? If those nails hurt you, why, there's no law that you have to put up with it. If you stay in this situation, you're making yourself a victim."

"But..." The door shuddered uncertainly.

"The first step is admitting you have a problem." Eli

gave the wood a reassuring pat. "And that's enough for now. However"—his voice dropped to a whisper—"if you're ever going to live your life, *really* live it, then you need to let go of the roles others have forced on you. You need to let go of those nails."

"But, I don't know..." The door shifted back and forth.

"Indecision is the bane of all hardwoods." Eli shook his head. "Come on, it doesn't have to be forever. Just give it a try."

The door clanged softly against its frame, gathering its resolve as Eli made encouraging gestures. Then, with a loud bang, the nails popped like corks, and the boards clattered to the ground with a long, relieved sigh.

Eli stepped over the planks and through the now-empty iron doorframe. The narrow hall outside was dark and empty. Eli looked one way, then the other, and shook his head.

"First rule of dungeons," he said with a wry grin, "don't pin all your hopes on a gullible door."

With that, he stepped over the sprawled boards, now mumbling happily in peaceful, nail-free slumber, and jogged off down the hall toward the rendezvous point.

In the sun-drenched rose garden of the castle Allaze, King Henrith of Mellinor was spending money he hadn't received yet.

"Twenty thousand gold standards!" He shook his teacup at his Master of the Exchequer. "What does that come out to in mellinos?"

The exchequer, who had answered this question five times already, responded immediately. "Thirty-one thousand five hundred at the current rate, my lord, or approximately half Mellinor's yearly tax income."

"Not bad for a windfall, eh?" The king punched him in the shoulder good-naturedly. "And the Council of Thrones is actually going to pay all that for one thief? What did the bastard do?"

The Master of the Exchequer smiled tightly and rubbed his shoulder. "Eli Monpress"—he picked up the wanted poster that was lying on the table, where the roughly sketched face of a handsome man with dark, shaggy hair grinned boyishly up at them—"bounty, paid dead or alive, twenty thousand Council Gold Standard Weights. Wanted on a hundred and fifty-seven counts of grand larceny against a noble person, three counts of fraud, one charge of counterfeiting, and treason against the Rector Spiritualis." He squinted at the small print along the bottom of the page. "There's a separate bounty of five thousand gold standards from the Spiritualists for that last count, which has to be claimed independently."

"Figures." The king slurped his tea. "The Council can't even ink a wanted poster without the wizards butting their noses in. But"—he grinned broadly—"money's money, eh? Someone get the Master Builder up here. It looks like we'll have that new arena after all."

The order, however, was never given, for at that moment, the Master Jailer came running through the garden gate, his plumed helmet gripped between his white-knuckled hands.

"Your Majesty." He bowed.

"Ah, Master Jailer." The king nodded. "How is our money bag liking his cell?"

The jailer's face, already pale from a job that required

him to spend his daylight hours deep underground, turned ghostly. "Well, you see, sir, the prisoner, that is to say"—he looked around for help, but the other officials were already backing away—"he's not in his cell."

"What?" The king leaped out of his seat, face scarlet. "If he's not in his cell, then where is he?"

"We're working on that right now, Majesty!" the jailer said in a rush. "I have the whole guard out looking for him. He won't get out of the palace!"

"See that he doesn't," the king growled. "Because if he's not back in his cell within the hour..."

He didn't need to finish the threat. The jailer saluted and ran out of the garden as fast as his boots would carry him. The officials stayed frozen where they were, each waiting for the others to move first as the king began to stalk around the garden, sipping his tea with murderous intent.

"Your Majesty," squeaked a minor official, who was safely hidden behind the crowd. "This Eli seems a dangerous character. Shouldn't you move to safer quarters?"

"Yes!" The Master of Security grabbed the idea and ran with it. "If that thief could get out of his cell, he can certainly get into the castle!" He seized the king's arm. "We must get you to a safer location, Your Majesty!"

This was followed by a chorus of cries from the other officials.

"Of course!"

"His majesty's safety is of utmost importance!"

"We must preserve the monarchy at all costs!"

Any objections the king may have had were overridden as a surge of officials swept down and half carried, half dragged him into the castle.

"Put me down, you idiots!" the king bellowed, but the officials were good and scared now. Each saw only the precipitous fall that awaited him personally if there were a regime change, and fear gave them courage as they pushed their protesting monarch into the castle, down the arching hallways, and into the throne room.

"Don't worry, Your Majesty," the Master of Security said, organizing two teams to shut the great, golden doors. "That thief won't get in."

The king, who had given up fighting somewhere during the last hundred feet, just harrumphed and stomped up the dais stairs to his throne to wait it out. Meanwhile, the officials dashed back and forth across the marble—locking the parlor doors, overturning the elegant end tables, peeking behind the busts of former kings—checking for every possible, or impossible, security vulnerability. Henrith did his best to ignore the nonsense. Being royalty meant enduring people's endless fussing over your safety, but when the councilors started talking about boarding over the stained-glass windows, the king decided that enough was enough. He stood from his throne and took a breath in preparation for a good bellow when a tug on his robes stopped him short. The king looked down incredulously to see who would dare, and found two royal guards in full armor standing at attention beside the royal dais.

"Sir!" The shorter guard saluted. "The Master of Security has assigned us to move you to a safer location."

"I thought this *was* a safer location." The king sighed.

"Sir!" The soldier saluted again. "With all due respect, the throne room is the first place the enemy would look, and with this ruckus, he could easily get through."

"You're right about that," the king said, glowering at

the seething mass of panicked officials. "Let's get out of here."

He stomped down the steps from the high marble dais and let the guards lead him to the back wall of the throne room. The shorter soldier went straight to an older tapestry hanging forgotten in one corner and pushed it aside, revealing, much to the king's amazement, a small door set flush with the stonework.

"I never knew this was here," the king said, genuinely astonished.

"Doors like these are standard in most castles this age," the guard said, running his gloved hand over the stones to the right of the door. "You just have to know where to look." His fingers closed in the crack between two stones. Something clicked deep in the wall, and the door swung open with a soft scrape.

"This way, sir," the soldier said, ducking through.

The secret passage was only a few feet long. This was good, because it was only a few inches wide, and the king was getting very claustrophobic sliding along sideways between the dusty stone walls, especially when the second soldier closed the door behind them, plunging the passage into darkness. A few steps later, they emerged into the back of another large tapestry. The soldier pushed the heavy cloth aside, and the king was amazed to find himself in his own drawing room.

"Why did no one tell me about this?" he said, exasperated, watching as the second soldier draped the tapestry back into place. "It will be fantastically useful the next time I want to get out of an audience."

"Over here, sir," the shorter guard said, waving toward the wide balcony that overlooked the castle garden. The king didn't see how a balcony was much safer than a throne room, but the guard seemed to know what he was doing, so the king followed quietly. Perhaps there was another secret passage. The king frowned, regretting all those times he'd chosen to go hunting rather than let the Master Builder take him on that tour of the castle the man was always so keen on. Well, the king thought, if the Master Builder had put more emphasis on secret passages rather than appreciation of the flying buttresses, perhaps he would have been more inclined to come along.

The balcony jutted out from the drawing room in a large semicircle of pale golden marble. His mother had had it built so she could watch the birds up close, and the handrails brushed right up against the leafy branches of the linden trees. The king was about to comment on how peaceful it was compared to the nonsense in the throne room, but the shorter of the two soldiers spoke first.

"I'm really sorry about this."

The king looked at him quizzically. "Sorry about wha—" His question was answered by a blinding pain at the back of his head. The trees and the balcony swirled together, and then he was on the ground with no notion of how he'd gotten there.

"Did you have to hit him that hard?" The soldier's voice floated above him.

"Yes," answered a voice he hadn't heard before, which his poor, aching brain assigned to the tall soldier who hadn't spoken while they were escorting him. "That is, if you want him to stay quiet."

The shorter soldier took off his helmet, revealing a young man with a head of dark, shaggy hair. "If you say so," he said, tucking the helmet under his arm.

The shorter soldier trotted to the edge of the balcony, where the trees were thickest. Spots danced across the king's vision, but he was sure he saw what happened next. One of the trees moved to meet the soldier. The king blinked, but the tree was still moving. It leaned over as far as it could, stretching out a thick branch to make a nice little step up off the railing. So great was his astonishment, the king barely felt the bigger soldier heft him over his shoulder like an oat sack. Then they were up on the tree branch, and the tree was bending over to set them gently on the ground.

"Thank you," said the shorter soldier as they stepped onto the grass.

And the king, though his ears were ringing horribly, could have sworn he heard the leaves whisper, "Anytime, Eli."

That thought was too much for him, and he dove into unconsciousness.

CHAPTER
2

The ghosthound appeared at the gates of the royal city of Allaze without warning. One moment, the guards were standing beside the gatehouse playing divel shanks and speculating on what all the noise in the palace was about, the next they were on their backs, staring up at an animal that only lived in stories. From the way it was showing its teeth, the guards would rather it had stayed there. Twice the size of a horse and built like a racing dog, it had to swivel its head down to look them over. The great orange eyes, each the size of a dinner plate, twinkled with amusement, or perhaps hunger. But most horrifying of all was the way the white patterns on the animal's silver fur moved like night clouds in a high wind, forming terrifying, shifting shapes above its dagger-sharp teeth.

"Excuse me," said a voice, "but I need you to open the gates. I have an urgent message for King Henrith."

The guards cowered on the sandy ground. "Great powers," the left one muttered. "I never knew they could talk."

There was a long sigh, and the beast lay down in a fluid motion, bringing the woman on its back into view. She was very well dressed in a handsome green riding suit with a crisp white shirt and tall boots. Red hair hung in a cascade of curls around her pretty, girlish face. Overall, she had a very striking look that was entirely out of place for a woman who rode a monster.

When she was sure she had their attention, the woman said, very slowly and with a charming smile, "My name is Miranda Lyonette, and I am here on behalf of the Spirit Court with a warning for your king. Now, I'm on a very tight deadline, so I would appreciate it very much if you would open the gate and let me on my way."

It was the older guard who gathered his wits first. "Um, lady," he said, picking himself up off the ground, "we'd like to help, but we can't open the gate without the Master Gatekeeper, and he's been called off to the castle."

"Well," she said, "then you'd better run and get him."

The men looked at each other, then back at the woman. She made a little shooing motion, and the guards ran off, falling over each other as they rushed the tiny gatehouse door.

When they were gone, Miranda slid down the hound's back and began to stretch the last few days out of her joints.

"I could have just jumped it," the hound growled. It eyed the two-story wall and snorted dismissively. "Saved us some time. I *thought* you said we were in a hurry."

"We *are* in a hurry," Miranda said, shaking the road dust out of her hair as best she could. "But we're also trying to make a good impression, Gin. Mellinor has a reputation for not liking wizards."

"Good impressions are wasted on this lot." Gin shook himself vigorously, raising a small cloud of grit from his ever-shifting coat. "We should have just jumped and saved the act for the king."

"Next time I'll just leave the negotiating to you, then." Miranda stepped clear of the hound's dust cloud. "Why don't you worry less about the schedule and more about keeping your nose sharp? He has to be skulking around here somewhere."

Gin gave her a withering look. "My nose is always sharp." His long ears twitched, then swiveled forward. "The guards are coming back, and they brought a lot of other clanky metal types with them." He flopped down, resting his chin on his paws. "So much for doing things the quick way."

Miranda ignored him and put on a dazzling smile as the two guards, and a small squad of spearmen, marched through the gatehouse.

The gate guards had had no trouble finding the Master Gatekeeper. He was in the throne room, standing in a rough clump around the empty throne with every other official in Allaze.

"Sir," the older guard said, tapping him on the shoulder. "We have a situation outside."

"I'm a bit busy," the Master Gatekeeper snapped.

"But, sir," the guard said, clutching his metal cap, "it's really something I think you should—"

"There's a wizard at the east gate!" the younger guard burst out, and then shrank back as the older guard and the Master Gatekeeper both snapped their heads around to glare at him. "It has to be a wizard," he said sheepishly. "Ain't no one else can ride a monster like that."

"Did you say wizard?" The Master of Security pushed his way over to them. "Was it a dark-haired man? Young looking?"

"No, sir." The young guard saluted. "It was a lady wizard, sir. Redheaded. Said she had a warning for the king."

The Master Gatekeeper and the Master of Security put their heads together and began arguing quietly. Whatever it was they argued about, the Master of Security must have won because he was the one who started barking orders. Three minutes later, the two gate guards were back at their post, only now with a squad of royal guard and the Master of Security between them and the monster, which lay with its long chin rested on its paws, watching.

The woman appeared completely unruffled by the sudden arrival of a large number of spears pointed in her direction. If there were any remaining doubts about her being a wizard, the large, ostentatiously jeweled rings covering her fingers put those to rest. She watched patiently, gently tapping her nails against the large ruby on her thumb, which was beginning to glow like an ember in the bright sun. Several of the men started to ease back toward the gatehouse, their spears wobbling, and the Master of Security decided it was time to take control of the situation.

"I hear you have a warning for the king," he said boldly. "You may speak it to me."

"My orders are to speak only to the king himself," Miranda said. "It is a matter of some delicacy."

"I am Oban, Master of Security. You'll speak it to me, or not at all," he huffed.

Miranda looked at Gin, who flicked his ear in the ghosthound equivalent of a shrug. "I suppose we have wasted enough time," she said. "I am here on behalf of the Spirit Court by order of the Rector Spiritualis, Etmon Banage. Yesterday morning we received a tip that the known fugitive wizard and wanted criminal Eli Monpress has been sighted within your kingdom. It is our belief that he is after an old wizard artifact held in your treasury. I am here to offer my assistance to keep him from stealing it."

There was a long pause, and Miranda got the horrible, sinking feeling that she had missed something important.

"Lady," the Master of Security said, shaking his head, "if you're here to warn the king about Eli, then you're a little late."

Miranda scowled. "You mean he's already stolen the artifact?"

"No." The Master of Security sighed. "He's stolen the king."

Three hours later, Miranda was seated at the foot of a small table in a cramped office in the lower part of the castle. Oban, Master of Security, the Master of the Exchequer, and the Master of the Courts were crammed together at the other end of the table, as far from her as possible. Other than Oban, none of them had told her their names, and they all looked equally displeased at being cornered in a small room with a wizard. Still, this was a step forward. An hour ago, she'd been sitting in the throne room with all forty masters of Mellinor, whom she guessed were the local equivalent of the standard governing body of lords and appointees that most kingdoms this size seemed to favor, staring daggers at her. It was only after much official argument that these three had stepped forward to speak for the whole, but from the way they were glaring at her, Miranda didn't think she'd gotten off any easier. In fact, she was beginning to regret telling Gin to wait at the gate. Miranda knew from experience that a large set of teeth on one's side tended to make these bureaucratic talks much easier.

Still, for all their pomp, the men across from her seemed to be in no hurry to get things started. After several minutes of waiting, compounded by the hours already wasted while the Mellinor officials decided who was going to deal with her, Miranda came to the conclusion that civility could get one only so far in life, and she cut straight to the point.

"Gentlemen," she said. "This would be much easier if you just told me the whole story."

The two nameless officials sneered, but Oban, at least, had the decency to look embarrassed. "There's not much to tell," he said. "We caught Eli this morning trying to get the king's prized stallion out of the stables. The horse made a racket and the Master of the Stables caught him red-handed. The thief gave up immediately, and as soon as he told us his name was Eli Monpress...Well," Oban said and shrugged, "who hasn't heard of him? I was called in and we locked him up in our strongest cell. Now, of course, we're sure the horse business was only a ploy to get inside the castle proper, because no sooner had we put him in the cell than he was gone, and shortly after that, so was our king."

"If you knew he was a wizard," Miranda said slowly, "why did you leave him alone?"

"Well," Oban said, wiping his bald head with a hand-kerchief, "as I said, it was our strongest cell. We took everything off him that looked magical. He didn't have any rings or gems, nothing like that." He shrugged his shoulders. "Of course, as soon as we knew the thief was out, we tried to get the king to safety. His Majesty was with us all the way to the throne room, and then he vanished. We searched all the secret passages, all the hidden stairs. By that point, the grounds were crawling with soldiers and every exit was watched. No one saw a thing."

"This is our only clue," said the small man to his left, the Master of the Exchequer. He took a small white card from his pocket and slid it across the polished table. "We found it in the rose garden shortly after the king vanished."

Miranda picked up the card, holding it delicately between her thumb and forefinger. It was cut from a heavy white stock, like a calling card, and at the center, engraved in gold ink, was an extravagant, cursive *M*. Miranda scowled and flipped the card over. On the back, someone had written *Forty thousand.*

That was it, no instructions, no threats, just the number written out in small, neat capitals across the lower left corner. Miranda scowled and slid the card back across the table. "I assume he means forty thousand in council gold standards." She smiled. "A king's ransom, indeed."

"We can't pay it," the Master of the Exchequer groaned, clutching his bony hands together. "That's an entire year's revenue for a small country like ours. We don't even have that much cash on hand in our own currency, let alone Council standards."

"But we must have our king back, whatever the cost," Oban said, landing his fist on the table. "King Henrith is young. He has yet to take a wife or produce an heir, and he's the last son of House Allaze. We've never had any kings other than House Allaze. There's not even a protocol for this sort of thing. If he vanished, our country would fall into chaos, and that would cost us far more than forty thousand standards."

Miranda tapped her finger against the polished arm of her chair. "A difficult problem," she said, "and one that could have been easily avoided. It seems that Mellinor is paying the price for its long unfriendliness toward wizards."

"It is the law," said the solemn old man to Oban's right, the Master of the Courts. "The oldest law in Mellinor, decreed by our first king, a law that we are breaking, I might add, by talking to you."

"But your first king was a wizard, wasn't he?" Miranda leaned forward, enjoying the pinched look on their faces. Ruffling stuffy politicians was one of the best perks of her job. "Come now, gentlemen, you can hardly expect an agent of the Spirit Court not to be up on her magical history."

"If you know that much," the Master of the Courts growled, "then you already know why he closed Mellinor to your kind. King Gregorn was disgusted by the misuse of power he witnessed at the hands of greedy, arrogant wizards, and he sought to create a country where people could live without fear, where no wizard would threaten us. For that purpose, he led his family and followers to the edge of what was then a great inland sea. In a tremendous act of magic, King Gregorn banished the sea and created a new land, made by magic, yet free of wizardly corruption. This act of selfless bravery took his life. That is why, for four hundred years, we have honored his sacrifice by upholding his law." The old man closed his eyes. "For Gregorn's direct descendant to be held for ransom by some wizard thief"—he took a shuddering breath—"it's only slightly worse than enlisting a wizard to rescue him." He lifted his chin to face Miranda, glaring snowstorms at her from under his bushy eyebrows. "Rest assured, young lady, were we not in such dire straits, you would never have made it into this castle."

"Had I been in this castle," Miranda said dryly, "you wouldn't *be* in such dire straits."

All three men glowered, and she gave them a scalding look. "I think you'll find that wizards have changed in the years since your country was founded. The Spirit Court exists to maintain a balance between the power of man and spirit, and to prevent wizards from abusing their gifts. So, as you see, the Spiritualist's purpose and your Gregorn's dream are dissimilar in method but not in substance. We both want to keep the world safe from people like Eli."

The overdressed men shifted uncomfortably, and Miranda saw her chance. "Here's my offer," she said. "I will get your king back for you, and, in exchange, you will let me work unhindered. When I return your monarch, you must promise me that he will allow envoys from the Spirit Court and consider welcoming our Spiritualists into his kingdom."

The officials put their heads together for a moment, and then the Master of the Courts nodded. "You drive a hard bargain, Miss Lyonette, but we do not have the luxury of time. Your terms are acceptable. We must have our king."

Miranda stood up with a triumphant smile. "In that case, gentlemen, let's get to work."

An hour later, when Miranda had wrung almost every provision she wanted out of the old men, they adjourned. After being shown to her room, she threw down her pack, grabbed a handful of bread off the dinner tray, and went to find Gin. This proved an easy task, for he was lounging in the afternoon sun right where she'd left him, surrounded by a gawking circle of stable boys at the main entrance to the castle.

Miranda approached with a grin, scattering the boys like sparrows. "Time to work, mutt."

Gin sat up slowly, stretching his paws. "You're in a good mood."

"There may be hope for this country yet." She smiled.

The dog snorted. "What about that artifact thing Banage made us rush down here for? Find out anything about that?"

"The bureaucrats didn't mention it, so I felt no need to bring it up," she said. "Gregorn's Pillar is only dangerous to wizards, and the only one of those we have to worry about is off having a slumber party with the king. Besides, I don't think I could have spoken ill of their honored founder and lived to tell about it. Though, mind you, I could tell them a few things about their precious *Gregorn* that would set their hair on end."

"So why didn't you?" Gin yawned, showing all of his teeth.

"Telling people what they don't want to hear gets us nowhere," Miranda said. "My duty is to catch Eli before he can mess things up more than he already has, not force old men to change their prejudices. *That's* the unhappy job of whichever poor sap Master Banage promotes to Tower Keeper of Mellinor when we're done." She flopped down on the marble step with a sigh. "So long as Eli isn't interested in Gregorn's Pillar, I'm not either. There's no point in trying to convince a panicked kingdom to let us poke around in their treasury if we don't need to. Besides, if we play our cards right, Mellinor will be crawling with Spiritualists by year's end. We'll have a Tower and a court envoy with plenty of time to talk the king into giving the Spirit Court all the pillars and artifacts and whatever else Gregorn left lying around. Right now, we focus on catching Monpress, and speaking of which"—she leaned forward—"what did you find?"

"His smell is everywhere." Gin's nostrils flared. "He was probably scouting the palace for days before he let himself get caught. The smells are all knotted together, though, so I can't tell where he made his final exit."

"So much for doing things the easy way," Miranda said and sighed, running her hand through her curly hair. "All right, we'll do this by the book. I'll start with the throne room and work my way down. You check the grounds and try not to scare anyone too badly."

"Shouldn't you get some rest?" Gin said, eyeing the sinking sun. "I can take two days of hard travel, but we don't want you flopping over like last time."

"That was an isolated incident." Miranda said, bristling. "No breaks. We're finally in the same country as that thief, possibly the same city. I'm not going to risk letting him slip away again, not when we're this close."

"You're the boss," Gin said, trotting across the courtyard. "Don't get carried away."

"That's my line," Miranda called after him, but the enormous hound was already slinking away behind the stables, sniffing the ground. Miranda shook her head and fanned out her fingers, nudging her rings awake.

"Time to get to work," she muttered, smiling as the stones began to glow. With a final look at the setting sun, she turned and tromped up the castle stairs. With any luck, she'd have Eli by the time it rose again.

CHAPTER
3

Down below the stable yard, quivering away from the ghosthound's fearsome scent, a rat darted through a narrow crack in the castle's foundation and made a break for the wall. It bounded through the ornamental gardens as if all the cats in Mellinor were on its tail, though nothing followed it in the dim evening light. What terrified the rat was not behind it, but inside it, pressed like a knife against its brain. It hit the castle battlements at full speed and began to climb the rough white stone, running vertically as easily as it had run along the ground. The knot of guards at the castle gate didn't notice as the rat crested the wall behind them and, without so much as pausing for balance, launched itself into the air. For a terrifying moment, the rat scrambled in free fall, then, with a clang that made the guards jump, landed on a drainpipe. The rat clung to the pipe, stunned for a moment, and then the pressure was back, the inescapable voice pressing down on its poor, fright-addled mind, and it had to go on. The rat scurried down the drainpipe to the cobbled street. Keeping to the gutters and dark places people forget to sweep, it made its way through the tangled streets of Allaze, following the sewer ditches away from the castle, down and west toward the river, into the darker parts of the city.

Scooting between the tilting wooden buildings, the rat threaded its way through the blind turns and back alleys to a ramshackle three-story nestled at the end of a row of identical ramshackle three-stories. Without missing a beat, the rat jumped on a gutter pipe and, quick as it had climbed the castle wall, scaled the pipefitting to the building's third floor. The window had been left open for it, and the rat tumbled inside, squeaking in relief that the horrible journey was almost over. It landed on the floor with a scrambling thud, but the momentary triumph was pushed from its mind by a wave of pressure that thickened the air to syrup. The attic room it had landed in was scarcely bigger than a closet, and the slanted ceiling made it smaller still. Broken furniture and discarded rags were stacked in dusty piles, but the rat's attention was on the figure sitting in the far corner, the source of the pressure.

The man sat slumped against the wall, rolling a black ball in a circle on his left palm. It was the size of a large marble, black and shiny like a wet river stone. He was thin and long, with matted blond hair that hung around his face in a dirty curtain. For a moment, the man didn't move, and then, slowly, lovingly, he slid the black sphere into his pocket and beckoned the rat closer. The pressure spiked, and the rat obeyed, crawling on its belly until it was an inch from the man's bare foot.

"Now," the man said, his whisper humming through

the room, resonating against the pressure that threatened to crush the rat's mind. "Tell me what you saw."

The rat had no choice. It told him everything.

Crouched on the floor in the hall with his eye pressed against a crack in the baseboard, the boy had to cover his mouth to keep from shouting. The blond man who rented the spare room had always made him nervous, which was why the boy took it upon himself to spy on him. He'd told his father over and over that their renter wasn't right in the head. He'd seen him talking to the walls, the floor, even the junk in the room as though they could answer back. Every time, his father had told him to lay off and leave the renter be. The blond man had come with the house when they'd moved in last year, and his money kept the family in shoes and off the street when times were hard. But this time was different. This time, the boy had actually seen the blond man open the window for a rat. His father was a butcher who kept his shop on the first floor. Once he told him the renter was letting vermin into the house, his father would have to throw the crazy man out, money or no. Grinning fit to break his face, the boy got to his feet and started to tiptoe toward the stairs. Before he took two steps, a strange sound stopped him. It was coming from the rented room, and it took the boy a moment to realize that the renter was laughing.

The door to the renter's room burst open, and the blond man was on him before he could run. Still laughing, the man grabbed the boy by his patched collar and dragged him up with surprising force.

"Young man," he said in a smooth voice, and something cold and heavy slid into the boy's shaking hand.

"Take this. Find whatever passes for a tailor in this pit and bring him here. If you're quick, I'll give you another."

He dropped the boy as suddenly as he'd grabbed him. The boy landed on his feet and immediately looked at the object in his hand. It was a gold standard. His eyes went as wide as eggs, and, for a moment, he forgot that he disliked the strange blond man. "Yes, sir!" ·

"Tell your mother to bring some hot water up as well," the renter called as the boy tumbled down the stairs.

The child began to bellow for his mother, and the blond man stepped back into his rented room. The rat lay twitching in the corner where he had left it, and he kicked it aside with his foot. Such weak spirits were only useful once. He'd need something else. He turned his attention to the dusty wall beside him and grinned as the timbers creaked in fear.

"Find me another spy."

A fine cloud of grit fell from the ceiling as the wall shuddered its response. "Yes, Master Renaud." The room began to buzz as the order spread through the building, asking for a new rat.

Renaud slumped against the dusty piles of junk and stared out the open window at the last glow of the setting sun as it lit up the tall towers of castle Allaze, just as white and beautiful as he remembered from his childhood. Now, finally, after eight years of shame and banishment, eight years of watching for a chance, *any* chance, fate, it seemed, had paid out in spades.

He began to chuckle, and it was all thanks to a simple wizard thief.

His chuckle became a full-fledged cackle, and Renaud

doubled over, his shoulders shaking. He laughed like that until the butcher wife's timid knock interrupted him.

There was much coming and going at the butcher's house that night, enough to attract the neighborhood's attention. Contrary to his usual nature, the butcher wasn't talking, and that just made the whole thing more interesting. Down the road in the raucous Merrymont Tavern, men with missing teeth made wagers about what was going on. Some put money on a murder; others said it had to do with the ruckus up at the castle. One man was blaming wizards, though he was a bit unclear about what exactly he was blaming them for. This led to more betting and speculation and, in their excitement, no one noticed the swordsman sitting at the corner table quietly nursing the same drink he'd been on for hours.

On a less interesting night, a swordsman would have been a fine topic of conversation. Especially this one, with the wicked scar he bore over the left side of his face, but with the mystery at the butcher's and rumors of a wizardess riding up to the castle on a dog the size of a house, the people had no breath left to spare for a swordsman. For his part, the swordsman didn't seem to mind the lack of attention. He simply sat in his corner, swirling his drink and listening. As the night dragged on, the talk began to go in circles. Finally, after the same theory was brought up three times in a quarter hour, the swordsman stood, laid his coins on the table, and, carefully tucking his wrapped sword into his belt, slipped out into the night.

He walked north for several blocks, ducking in and out of buildings almost at random. Only when he was sure no one was following him did he turn around and begin walking purposefully toward the butcher's house.

Renaud was fastening the starched cuffs of his new jacket when he heard it, an icy, blood-thirsty whine that grated against his thoughts. He froze. The butcher's wife stood in the corner, her eyes roving, looking at everything except him, just as they had for the last four hours. She gave no sign she heard anything.

"Get out," Renaud said.

The woman jumped and hastily obeyed, closing the door behind her. Renaud resumed working on the small buttons at his wrists. Outside his tiny window, the night was drifting toward morning, and in the faint gray light he saw the man's shadow seconds before he heard the window scrape.

"If you're going to sneak up on someone," Renaud said coldly, turning to face the man who was now crouched on the windowsill, "learn how to keep your sword quiet."

The man smiled, but the scar across his cheek warped the expression into a leer as he sat down on the window ledge and laid his gloved palm against his sword's wrapped hilt. The wailing stopped, and Renaud let out a relieved sigh.

The man's smile widened. "So it's true," he said. "There *is* a wizard in Mellinor."

Renaud did not move, but somehow his slouched posture shifted from bored to threatening. "Who are you? What do you want?"

"First answer"—the man leaned back against the window's bowed frame—"my name is Coriano, and I'm a bounty hunter. Second answer, I was curious. You've caused quite a stir."

"A bounty hunter?" Renaud laughed. "I'm afraid you've found the wrong wizard. The one you want has already struck and gone."

Coriano's good eye narrowed. "On the contrary, you're exactly the wizard I wanted to find, Renaud of Allaze."

Renaud's hand slipped into his pocket and gripped the glassy black sphere that lay hidden at the bottom. "How do you know that name?"

"It's my business to know," Coriano said dryly. "But don't worry, I'm not here to threaten you. In fact, I'd like to make you an offer."

Renaud's fingers eased their grip. "And what could you offer me?"

"Something that will help you reach your goals."

Renaud arched an eyebrow. "What would you know of my goals?"

"I told you," Coriano said. "It's my business to know."

"All right," Renaud took his hand from his pocket and folded his arms over his chest. "I'm listening."

Coriano, grinning, hopped down from the windowsill. Renaud gave the sooty, warped glass a warning look, and the window slammed itself shut with a terrified squeal, locking the men's words away from the brightening sky.

CHAPTER
4

When King Henrith opened his eyes, he knew he was dead. A few blinks later, the certainty hadn't changed, but he was starting to feel a little upset about it. However, what happened next put all of that out of his head, for the great nothingness he had been staring into, the endless void that lies beyond human experience, stood up and began stirring the fire. As his eyes adjusted to the sudden light, he saw it was a girl. Or, at least, that was his best guess. All he could see at this angle was a tangle of short, black hair and a bit of pale forehead. The rest of her was lost inside an enormous coal-black coat that, he now realized, had been the void covering his head.

The sudden knowledge that he was, indeed, not dead was further underscored by the extreme discomfort of his position. He was lying on his side on a dirt floor, his hands and feet tied behind him so that he was bent belly out. The fire the girl tended was far too large for the small stone hovel they were in, and the heat pressed down on him as tightly as the ropes.

Finished poking at the fire, the girl walked over to the woodpile, pushed up her sleeves, and, despite the suffocating heat, began tossing more logs on. The fire accepted them reluctantly, shrinking away from her thin, pale hands. In the flickering light, Henrith caught the dull gleam of silver at her wrists, and he leaned his head slowly to the side for a better look. They weren't bracelets. The dull, thick metal was badly scuffed, and it was wrapped tightly around her bony wrist, like a manacle. His hopes began to rise. If she was a prisoner as well, maybe she could help him escape.

But before he could get her attention, the rickety wooden door burst open, flooding the small hut with blinding sunlight as two men stomped in. The first, medium height and gangly, was carrying a huge stack of wood. "Nico!" he shouted, craning his neck over the logs. "Are you trying to burn us to crisps?"

The girl shrugged and then turned and glared at the fire. The flames shuddered, and the fire shrank to half the size it had been only seconds before. A cold terror ran up the king's spine, but the man carrying the wood only sighed and started adding his armload to the woodpile. The second man, a towering figure with cropped sandy hair, carried two rabbits over one broad shoulder and what looked to be a sharpened six-foot-long iron bar over the other. The rest of him, from shoulders to calves, was covered in blades. He wore two swords at his waist, another sideways across his lower back, and knives of every size poking out of his belt, boots, and sleeves. Two long braces of throwing knives were strapped across his chest, with two more around his thighs. Anywhere he could strap a sheath, he had one, until it was difficult to tell what color his clothing actually was beneath the maze of leather sheaths.

The king cringed, terrified, as the swordsman walked past, but the man didn't even glance the king's way. He stepped nonchalantly over the scorched dirt the bonfire had vacated moments before and sauntered over to the small table set against the far wall, where he began to skin the rabbits. He kept all of his blades belted on as he did this, paying them as little mind as another man would pay to his jacket. The sword-shaped iron bar he leaned against the table beside him, keeping it close, like a trusted friend.

Not wanting to draw the attention of anyone so fond of sharp objects, the king focused his efforts on lying as still as possible. However, the girl looked at him, watching him with her head tilted to the side as the men worked. A few moments later, she announced, "The king's awake."

"Is he?" the man at the woodpile said and whirled around. "Wonderful!" The next moment, he was crouching beside King Henrith, a huge grin on his face. "Hello, Your Majesty! How have you enjoyed your kidnapping so far?"

The king looked up at him, noting the shaggy dark hair, thin build, and boyish grin that, in any other circumstance, would have been infectious. He looked just like his wanted poster. "Eli Monpress."

The grin grew wider. "You've heard of me! I'm flattered!"

At that, the king's fear was overwhelmed by indignation. "Of course I've heard of you!" the king blustered, blowing the dirt out of his beard. "We caught you trying to steal my horses this morning!"

"Yesterday morning, actually." Eli looked sideways across the fire at the knife-covered man. "I'm afraid Josef may have hit you a little too hard."

"I hit him perfectly," Josef said, not looking up from his rabbits. "He's not in pain, is he?"

Eli looked down at the king. "Are you?"

Henrith paused, considering. His head didn't hurt. He remembered being hit and the shooting pain on the balcony, but now he felt nothing, just uncomfortable from the ropes and the strange position. He looked up at Eli, who was still waiting for his answer, and shook his head.

"See?" Josef said. "Perfect."

Eli sighed dramatically. "Well, after that display, I suppose I'd better introduce my associates." He reached down and took the king's head in his hands, turning him toward the tall man with the blades. "That man of perfection you see mutilating the bunnies for our supper is our swordsman, Josef Liechten, and this little bundle"—he turned the king's head to the left, toward the girl, who was back to poking the fire—"is Nico."

That was apparently enough for introductions, for Eli let the king's head go and plopped down in the dirt beside him, leaning on his elbow so his eyes were level with the king's.

"Why are you doing this?" the king whispered, wavering between rage and genuine bewilderment.

"I'm a thief." Eli shrugged. "I steal valuable things. What could be more valuable than a king to his country?"

"Why me, then?" Henrith wiggled himself semi-upright. "If money is what you're after, why not go after a larger country, or a richer one?"

"Trade secret," Eli said. "But since you're being such a good sport about all this, I will tell you that we're not working for anyone. There's no great scheme, no big plot. Just pay our price and we can all go home happy."

Henrith supposed that was a relief. "What's your price, then?"

"Forty thousand gold standards," Eli said calmly.

The king nearly choked. "Are you mad? We can't pay that!"

"Then I guess you'll just have to lie here forever." Eli gave him a little pat on the shoulder, and then stood up and walked over to where Nico was poking the fire, leaving the king to wiggle futilely in the dirt.

"Of course," he added, almost as an afterthought, "you wouldn't have to pay it all at once."

"What," the king scoffed, "set up an installment plan? Would you leave a forwarding address, or should I just send a company of armed men every month?"

"Nothing so complicated." Eli walked over and kneeled down again. "How about this? You write a letter to your Master of the Money, or whatever you call him, and tell him to put aside a mere five thousand gold standards. Surely even Mellinor can gather such a small sum without too much difficulty. We'll make a switch"—he waggled his long finger at the king—"you for the money, and the rest of the debt can be pledged to my council bounty."

Henrith's face went blank. "Pledged to what?"

Eli gawked down at him. "The Council of Thrones' bounty account." He leaned down, looking incredulous. "Do you even know how bounties work?"

The king started to answer, but Eli rolled right over him. "Of course not, you're a king. I doubt you've even been to a council meeting. You've probably never even left your kingdom." He sat down again, muttering under his breath, "Council of Thrones, pah. More like Council of Junior-Adjuncts-No-One-in-Their-Own-Kingdom-Wanted-Around.

"All right," Eli said when he was settled. "So you know the Council of Thrones takes care of things no single kingdom can handle—large-scale trade disputes, peace negotiations, and offering bounties on criminals wanted for crimes in more than one kingdom." Eli reached into the pocket of his faded blue jacket and pulled out a folded square of paper, which he shook out proudly. It was his wanted poster, the same one the king had seen in the rose garden back when Eli had been his prisoner, and not the other way around.

Eli held the poster up. "Only the biggest criminals, those considered to be a danger to every member kingdom of the Council, are listed on the Council wanted board, and that means the bounties have to be in amounts that can get the attention of whole kingdoms, not just small-time bounty hunters.

"As you see," he said, tapping the numbers under his portrait, "my head, dead or alive, is currently worth twenty thousand gold standards. This price is guaranteed by five countries, each of which pledged a little of its hard-earned money to entice men like yourself to try and catch me. Since you've made such a fuss over how you can't pay the whole amount of your ransom at the moment, I'm going to cut you a deal. All you have to do to buy your freedom is top what those countries have offered by pledging your ransom to my bounty. Minus, of course, the five thousand in cash we'll be taking with us. Still, that means the kingdom of Mellinor will be responsible for the remaining thirty-five thousand only in the unlikely event of my capture. Now," he said, folding the poster back into a square, "I think that's more than fair. What do you say, Mr. King?"

The king didn't have much to say to that, actually. This was either the worst kidnapping in history or the best Council fundraiser he'd ever seen.

"So," he said slowly, "Mellinor pledges the thirty-five thousand to your bounty, we give you five thousand in cash, and you let me go. But," he said and paused, desperately trying to find some sense in what was happening, "that will bring your bounty to fifty-five thousand gold standards. It doesn't make sense at all. You're a thief! Won't having a higher bounty make stealing things more difficult?"

"Any thief worth the name can *steal*," Eli snorted. "I, however, am not just any thief." He straightened up. "I'm Eli Monpress, the greatest thief in the world. I'm worth more gold dead than most people will see in two lifetimes, and this is only the beginning." He leaned down, bringing his eyes level with Henrith's. "A bounty of fifty-five thousand puts me in the top ten percent of all criminals wanted by the council, but so far as I'm concerned, that's nothing. Child's play. One day," he said, smiling, "I'll be worth one million gold standards."

He said it with such gravity that the king couldn't help himself, he burst out laughing. He laughed until the ropes cut into his skin and his throat was thick with grit from the dirt floor. Eli just watched him convulse, a calm smile on his face.

At last, the king's laughter receded into gasps and hiccups, and he slumped to the floor with a sigh. "One *million*?" he said, chuckling. "Impossible. You could buy the Council itself for that much. You'd have to kidnap every king in the world!"

"If they're all as easily gotten as you were," Eli said with a grin, "that won't be a problem." He gave the king a pat on the head, like he was a royal puppy, and stood up. He stepped over the sprawled king and crouched down behind him, where the king's hands were tied.

The king wiggled, trying to get a look at what Eli was doing. But the thief put his boot on the king's side, keeping him still while he reached down and brushed his fingers over the rope at the king's hands and ankles. "Thank you very much," Eli said. "You've been most helpful. I think he's got the point, though, so you can let him go now."

Henrith was about to ask who he thought he was talking to when the rope at his hands wiggled like a snake. He jumped as the rope untied itself and fell into a neat coil at his side. Eli reached down and picked the rope up, leaving the king slack-jawed on the floor.

"Good-natured rope," the thief cooed, holding the coils up. "It's always such a pleasure to work with."

He left the king gaping in the dirt and went over to a corner where a small pile of leather packs leaned against the wall, well away from the fire. He tucked the rope carefully into the pack on the top and began to dig through the others, looking for something.

Henrith sat up gingerly, squeezing his hands to get the feeling back and trying not to think too hard about what had just happened. By the time he got the blood flowing in his fingers again, Eli was back, this time shoving a pen nib, ink pot, and a sheaf of slightly dirty paper into the king's hands.

"All right, Your Majesty," he said, grinning. "If you would write a letter detailing what we talked about, I'll make sure it gets sent to whoever deals with this sort of thing. Be sure to stipulate that you will not be returned until I see my new wanted poster—that part is key. With any luck, this will all be over in a few days and we'll never have to see each other again."

He clapped the king on the shoulder one last time and stood up. "Nico," he said. "I'm going to find someone who wants to carry a letter. Would you mind watching our guest? I want to make sure he doesn't get any ideas that might come to a sad conclusion."

The girl nodded absently, never looking up from the fire. Eli gave the king a final wink before opening the cabin door and walking out into the sunlight. The swordsman, who had long finished skinning his rabbits, picked up his iron sword and followed, leaving the king alone in the small, dark hut with the girl.

Her back was to him, and King Henrith flexed his newly freed hands again. The door was only a few feet away.

"Whatever you're thinking, I wouldn't suggest it."

The sudden edge in her voice nearly made him jump backward. He froze as she turned to look at him. When her brown eyes locked with his, the feeling of oblivion came roaring back. Suddenly, it was very hard to breathe.

"Write your letter," she said, and turned back to the fire.

He took a shuddering breath and spread the paper

out on his knee. With one last look at the girl's back, he leaned over and began to write his ransom note.

"That was stupid," Josef said, closing the rickety door behind him.

"Why do you say that?" Eli asked, scanning the tree-tops. They were standing in the small clearing outside of the forester's hut that Eli had "repurposed" for this operation. High overhead, sunlight streamed through the treetops while hidden birds called to one another from their branches. Eli whistled back.

Josef scowled, leaning against the small trees that shielded their hut from view. "Why did you put that part in about seeing the poster? This job has dragged on long enough already. We'll be here forever if we have to wait on Council politics."

"You'd be surprised how sprightly they can be when there's a lot of money involved," Eli said, and whistled again. "The Council gets a percent fee on capture for every bounty posted, and fifty-five thousand is a lot of money, even for them."

"It wouldn't be so bad if there was something to do," Josef said, stabbing his iron sword into the patchy grass at their feet. The battered black blade slid easily into the dirt, as though the hard, rocky ground were loose sand. "There's no challenge in this country. The city guards were a joke. The palace had no swordsmen, no wizards. I don't understand why we even bothered to sneak in."

"A job finally goes smoothly," Eli said, "and you're complaining? All we have to do is lounge around for a few days, collect the money, get my new bounty, and we can be on our way."

"Smooth jobs are boring," the swordsman grumbled, "and you're the only one who enjoys lounging."

"You might like if you tried it," Eli said.

Josef shook his head and Eli turned back to the leafy canopy, whistling a third time. This time something whistled in answer, and a small falcon swooped down to land on the moss beside him.

"You needed a break anyway," Eli said, kneeling down. "You're too tense these days."

"I'm not tense," Josef said, pushing himself off the trees with a grunt. "Just bored."

He yanked his sword out of the ground and walked off into the forest, tossing the enormous blade between his hands as though it were made of paper. Eli watched him leave with a mixed expression, and then, shrugging, he turned back to the falcon and began talking it into taking a message to the castle.

CHAPTER
5

Miranda stood at the center of the empty prison cell, her bare feet resting on a springy bed of new moss that spread out from the moss agate ring lying in the middle of the floor. The heavy door to the cell was open, though it would have been useless even if closed, owing to the gaping hole in the middle where the wooden boards should have been. The boards themselves lay in disgrace a few feet away, piled against the far wall of the cell.

She could feel the moss humming under her toes as it crept across the stone, feeling for slight changes in the dust. "He's very light-footed; I'll give him that," the moss said. "It feels like he spent most of his time by the door, but"—Miranda got the strange sensation that the moss was frowning—"every spirit here is dead asleep, mistress. If he used any spirits, he was uncommonly quiet about it."

Miranda nodded thoughtfully. "What about the door?"

"That's the strangest bit." The moss crept over the pile

of boards, poking them with thousands of tiny rootlings. "The door is sleeping soundest of all."

"Thief nothing," Miranda said, rubbing her palms against her temples. "That man is a ghost."

The cell was only the latest in a long line of failures as night turned to morning. "Well," she said, "Eli's not a Spiritualist. Maybe he used something else."

"Enslavement, you mean?" The moss wiggled with displeasure. "Impossible, mistress. Enslavements happen when the wizard's will completely dominates the spirit's until it has no choice but to obey. It's *not* a subtle thing. Why, even a momentary enslavement just to open the door would spook every spirit within earshot. They'd be moaning about it forever. But this room is so relaxed even I'm feeling sleepy. If you hadn't told me otherwise, I would have guessed these idiots hadn't so much as smelled a wizard in a hundred years."

"Why do you say that?" Miranda sat down on her heels. "If he didn't do anything flashy or dangerous, like enslavement, I doubt these rocks would notice a wizard standing right on top of them. Most spirits won't even wake up enough to talk to a wizard unless we stand around making a racket for a few hours. Remember how long it took me to get *your* attention, Alliana?"

Alliana ruffled her green fuzz. "Spirits might not always respond, but we always notice a wizard. You're very distracting."

"You mean we're loud and obnoxious," Miranda said. "But then why did no one notice Eli?"

"Sometimes, spirits choose not to notice," the moss said wistfully. "There are some wizards it's better not to look at."

"What do you mean?" Miranda leaned closer to the moss's fluffy green surface. "Is Eli one of those?"

"I wouldn't know," Alliana said with a huff. "I've never seen him."

"Then what—"

"It's no use asking any more questions, mistress," the moss said. "I can't say it any clearer. It really is too bad you humans are spirit blind. It's so hard to explain things like this when you can't see what I'm talking about."

Miranda blew the hair out of her face with an exasperated huff. Spirits were eternally complaining about the human inability to the see the spirit world, as if humans chose to be blind out of sheer stubbornness. As always, she tried to remind herself that it was very hard on spirits. All humans had the innate ability to control the spirits around them, though only born wizards could actually hear the spirits' voices, and thus actually use their power. But this power came with a price, for, wizard or not, no human could see as the spirits saw. It was as if the whole race lacked a vital sense, and this lack was a source of endless frustration for both sides. It wasn't that Miranda didn't appreciate the difficulty. She did, really. For Alliana to explain how a wizard was distracting would be like Miranda trying to describe the color red to a blind person. Even so, it was impossibly frustrating when, every time she got a little closer to finally understanding, the spirit would pull the whole "Well, you can't see, so I can't explain" cop-out. Her spirits might serve her willingly, but sometimes she got the feeling she didn't really understand them at all.

"Let's move on," she said. "Go ahead and wake up

the door. You said Eli spent all his time beside it. If he's as powerful as Master Banage seems to think he is, the wood should have noticed something."

The wood was not cooperative. First, it took thirty minutes of Alliana's poking to wake it up. Then, as soon as the wood recognized the moss as a wizard-bound spirit, it shut itself down in protest. Even after some direct threats from Miranda herself, the most she could get out of it was that Eli had been a nice and helpful human, with a strong implication that she was not. After that, the door buried itself in a sound sleep and nothing Alliana did could wake it.

Miranda threw herself down on the cell's narrow bench with a frustrated sigh and began to tug her socks back on. She still didn't know how Eli had escaped, but at least the door had mentioned him. Her attempts in the throne room had been a disaster. The officials had trailed her every step, muttering suspiciously, while the spirits remained sleepy, distant, and decidedly unhelpful. Ten hours wasted, altogether, and nothing but frustration and an attack on her personality to show for it. It was enough to make her spit.

She called Alliana and the circle of bright green moss began to shrink, returning to the moss agate ring that lay on the floor. When the moss was completely gone, Miranda bent down and picked the ring up. She ran her fingertips lovingly over the smooth stone, soothing the moss spirit into a light sleep. When Alliana was quiet, Miranda slipped the ring back onto its home on her right pinky finger.

"What are you doing now?" a perky voice behind her asked. "Did you find anything?"

Miranda's smile vanished. She'd almost forgotten about the girl.

Of course, Mellinor, a country that had built a long and proud tradition out of hating wizards, wasn't about to let one roam around alone. When it became clear they couldn't follow her all night, the masters of Mellinor had insisted on providing a "guide" who stayed with her at all times "for her convenience." Unfortunately, because of that long and proud tradition of hating wizards, volunteers for the position of wizard watcher had been scarce. Finally, the masters had given the job to the only person who actually seemed to want it, an overly inquisitive junior librarian named Marion.

Marion peered through the doorway, her round face beaming. "Are you done growing moss?"

"In a manner, yes." Miranda leaned back against the cool stone.

The girl poked around the cell, growing more excited by the moment. "Amazing! The moss is gone! Was that a spell?"

Miranda rolled her eyes. A spell? No one had talked about magic in terms of spells since before the first Spirit Court. "The moss was my servant spirit," she said, and she held up her hand, waggling her fingers so the rings glittered in the torchlight. "She was very helpful, but, unfortunately, we're no closer to finding where Eli took the king. I'd like to try—"

"Did the spirit cast a spell?" The girl looked hopeful.

Miranda pressed her palm hard against her forehead. "Marion, this would go more smoothly if you wouldn't ask questions."

The girl's face fell, and Miranda immediately felt

awful. *Fabulous effort at making a good impression*, she thought. *The one person in the whole kingdom who doesn't think you're the living incarnation of all that's wrong in the world, and you yell at her.*

"Look, Marion," Miranda said gently, "how much do you know about wizards?"

"Not much, really," Marion said sheepishly, tugging at her long, formless tunic dress, which Miranda had come to recognize as the Mellinorian librarian uniform. "All the books about wizards were destroyed generations ago." She reached furtively into one of her cavernous side pockets and pulled out a slim leather book. "This was all I could find. I've practically memorized it."

The book looked ancient. Its leather cover was cracked and worn and missing chunks in several places. Miranda took it gently and stifled a groan when she read the title, Morticime Kant's *A Wizarde's Travels*. Of course, the one book the Mellinorian purge missed would be the most ostentatious, misinformed plague on wizardry that had ever stained a page. If you wanted someone to get the wrong idea about magic, this was the book you would give them.

Out of morbid curiosity, she flipped it open to a random page and started reading a section labeled "On the Dress and Manner of Wizardes."

"A wizarde is easily separated from his fellow men owing to the Presence of his Person. Often he will carry the Fragrance of Old Magic, gained from his years over the cauldron brewing his fearsome Magical Potions. If you do not wish to step close enough to determine his odor (for doing so may put you in his thrall, beware!) you may determine his demeanor from a safe distance, for all

wizardes wear, by oath, the marks of their Station, namely
the ever present flowing Robes of State, the flashing Rings
of Enchantment, and the long-pointed, elegant cap of a
Master of Magicks. Further more—"

Miranda snapped the book shut in disgust. Whoever
had purged the library had probably left it on purpose.

"Well," she said, handing the book back, "that explains
much."

The girl cringed at the scorn her voice, and lowered
her head until the thick woolen veil that covered her
blonde hair slid down to hide her face as well. "I did not
mean to offend, lady wizard."

"Spiritualist," Miranda corrected gently. The girl
peeked at her quizzically, and Miranda tried again. "Let
me explain. Wizards don't do magic—at least, not like
the book describes it. What Kant calls 'magicks' are
actually spirits. The world we live in is made of spirits.
Mountains, trees, water, even the stones in the wall or
the bench I'm sitting on"—she rapped the wood with
her knuckles—"they each have their own souls, just as
humans do. The word 'wizard' is just a catchall name
for a person who can hear those spirits' voices. Now,
it's possible for anyone to hear the spirits if they are
seriously injured or dying. Death brings us as close as
humans can get to the spirit world. What makes a wizard
different is that wizards hear spirits all the time, even if
they don't want to. But a wizard's real power is not just
hearing the spirits, it's control. Wizards can exert their
will over the spirits around them and, if the wizard's will
is strong enough, control them. Though, of course, this
control must always be used responsibly and only with
the spirit's consent."

She looked at Marion to make sure this wasn't more explanation than the girl was willing to listen to, but the librarian was practically leaning on to Miranda's shoulder in rapt attention, so the Spiritualist continued.

"Not all spirits are the same, of course. There are Great Spirits, a mountain, for example, and small spirits, like a pebble. The larger the spirit, the greater its power, and the stronger a wizard's will has to be to control it, or even just get its attention. Almost any wizard can wake up a small, stupid spirit, like a pebble, or that door you saw me yelling at earlier, but it's how they treat the spirit once they've woken it that determines what kind of wizard they are."

Miranda pointed at her rings. "I am a Spiritualist. Like all wizards, I have the power to dominate spirits and force them to do my bidding, but I don't. The Spirit Court does not believe in forcing the world to do our will. Instead, we make contracts. Each of these rings contains a spirit who has willingly entered my service." She wiggled her fingers. "In return for their work and obedience, I share my energy with them and provide a safe haven. That's the way a Spiritualist works, give and take. Often, it's a good deal for both wizard and spirit. Born wizards often have large and powerful souls, and spirits love to share that power that is often greater than their own. In return, the wizard gets a powerful ally, so it works out both ways. Still, service is always by choice. We never force a spirit to serve us against its will. Any wizard who does is not a Spiritualist, and thus not someone you want around." She pointed at the only ring on her hand without a jewel, a thick gold signet on her left ring finger stamped with a perfect circle. "This is the mark of the

Spirit Court. The only legitimate wizards are ones who show this ring proudly. It is a sign of the vows Spiritualists make to never abuse that power, or the spirits who depend on us."

"I see," Marion said, her blue eyes widening until her wispy eyebrows were lost under her square bangs. "But there are wizards who aren't Spiritualists, right? Who can dominate any spirits? Could those wizards dominate another person?"

"No," Miranda said. "A wizard can move mountains if her will is strong enough, but no wizardry can touch another human's soul. Brush it, maybe, press upon it, certainly, if the other soul is sensitive to spirits, but no power I have could force you to act against your wishes. I could make trees dance and rocks sing, but I couldn't even make you bow your head if you wanted it straight. Does that make sense?"

Marion frowned thoughtfully. "I think so, but—"

"Good." Miranda stood up with a smile. "Then today hasn't been a complete waste." She looked dolefully around the small cell. "I don't think there's much more I can do here. We need a change of scenery." She took a small leather folder out of her bag and began to flip through a neat stack of papers.

Marion looked quizzical. "Scenery?"

"Ah-ha," Miranda said and smiled triumphantly, holding up a small, tattered note. "Looks like we're going for a walk to the west side of town."

A horrified look spread over Marion's face. "Why?"

"I'm getting nowhere around here." Miranda stuck the folder back in her bag and slung it over her shoulder. "Either Eli is a much more powerful wizard than I anticipated, which is unlikely, or he's got some trick that lets him march around unnoticed. Either way, I need to learn more about him, so we're going to see an expert."

Marion's look of horror deepened. "An expert? But what kind of—lady!" She had to scramble to keep up as Miranda swept out of the room, past the prison guards, and up the narrow stairs. "Lady wiz...Spiritualist! Lady Miranda! Wait!" She chased her through the maze of narrow passageways and caught up just as Miranda pushed open the outer door, where the prison let out below the stable yard. With a gasp, she threw herself in front of the Spiritualist. "Wait!" she said, panting. "The west side of the city isn't exactly, that is, I have to alert the guards. You'll need a security squad and—"

"Security squad?" Miranda pushed past her with a grin. "Gin!"

He must have been waiting for this, because the ghosthound appeared with a speed that surprised even Miranda. Gin slid to a halt right in front of them, grinning toothily, while the misty patterns flew over his coat in a way that meant he was feeling extraordinarily pleased with himself. Miranda shook her head and turned to the librarian. Marion was almost sitting on the ground in her scramble to get away from the monster that had not been there a second before. It was all Miranda could do not to reach down and shut the girl's gaping jaw for her.

"I don't think a security squad will be needed," Miranda said, vaulting onto Gin's back. "Coming?"

The girl had barely nodded before Gin swept her up with his paw and tossed her on his back. The stable dogs howled as the ghosthound loped across the castle grounds, fast as an icy gale. He took the castle gate in two leaps and hit the city street running, sending the well-dressed townsfolk screaming in all directions.

"Did you find anything?" Miranda asked.

"Of course not." Gin sighed. "So, do we have a destination, or are we just putting on a show?"

"West side of the city, and slow it down a little." She glanced over her shoulder at Marion, who was clinging to the ghosthound's short coat with everything she had. "We have a delicate flower with us."

The ghosthound slowed just a fraction as he took a narrow alley westward, downhill toward the river.

CHAPTER
6

If looked at from the sky, Allaze, the capital and only walled city of Mellinor, was a thing of beauty. It lay like a sun-bleached sand dollar on the grassy banks of the river Aze, circular and white with the spires of the castle as the star at its center. Low, undulating hills, spotted with split wood fences and fat cattle, rose around it, so that the city was a bump at the lowest point of a soft, green bowl.

Along the city's northern wall, the bushy edge of the king's deer park met the city in a mash of green oaks and tall pines. Only a thin strip of grass and the taller than usual northern parapets kept the trees out of the city proper. Within the walls, a charming, if confusing, knot of streets twisted outward and downward from the castle hill. Following the king's example, the citizens had also arranged themselves vertically, starting at the top with impressive, stone mansions pressed right against the castle's outer perimeter and moving down to the sprawling ring of flat-roofed timber houses leaning against Allaze's edge, where the white stone outer wall ran in a nearly perfect circle around the city. Nearly perfect, but for one slight flaw.

In a fit of architectural rebellion, a small section of the city's western edge deviated to form an unsightly bulge. It was as if the stones in that part of the wall had tried to make a break for the river, only to fail halfway and rejoin the circle a quarter mile later in sullen resignation. If this building irregularity had a purpose, it was long forgotten, and the western bulge was now a pile of ramshackle buildings on top of what had been a swamp, but was now home to some of the least reputable businesses in Mellinor.

Gin trotted to a stop in front of one such establishment, a ramshackle building with the words MERRYMONT TAVERN painted in fading, uneven block letters across the shuttered upper story.

"This looks like the place," Miranda said, sliding off Gin's back. Marion followed timidly, wincing as her nice court slippers hit the muddy road with a wet slap. The wooden buildings here tilted in every direction, leaning on each other like drunks until it was difficult to tell where one ended and the next began. The smell of stagnant water and unwashed bodies hung in a haze over the narrow streets, but there was no one to be seen. Every window was dark and empty, projecting gloom and decay until even the noon sunlight seemed dimmer. Miranda surveyed the empty streets, her face set in her best imitation of the Rector Spiritualis at a Council meeting, equal parts nonchalant superiority and honed indifference to the opinions of others. If growing up in the enormous city of Zarin had taught her anything, it was that empty streets hid the most ears of all.

"Gin," she said loudly, "if anyone gives you trouble, don't bother asking permission, just eat them."

Gin responded by lazily stretching his forelegs out in front of him and yawning, revealing a mouth of yellow, glistening teeth as his ears swiveled for any hint of sound.

Satisfied that no one would bother them after that little display, Miranda marched up the rickety stairs of the Merrymont and pushed aside the muddy blanket that served as a door. The barroom was narrow, dark, and stank of the river. It was also just as empty as the street outside, though the mugs scattered on the warped tables told her it hadn't been that way a few moments ago. Large, stained barrels took up most of the room, their taps dripping something that smelled faintly of rotting bread and vinegar. The only windows were papered over with advertisements and notices, including a large, peeling poster featuring a pair of girls wearing outfits that made Miranda blush. Looking away, she selected a cleanish table near the center of the room and sat down so that she was facing the main entrance. Marion, white as new cheese and twice as wobbly, took a seat beside her.

The librarian eyed the empty tables and the trash scattered across the warped floor boards. "I don't think your expert is here," she whispered.

"He will be," Miranda said, setting her bag in the chair beside her. "The Spirit Court pays its informants very well, and bounty hunters thrive in trash heaps like this."

"Such words of praise," a deep voice purred behind them. "You'll make me blush, little wizardess."

Marion fell out of her chair with a series of squeaks, but Miranda stayed perfectly still.

"Well met, Mr. Coriano," she said calmly. "You seem to be living up to your reputation." Without turning, she motioned to the chair on the other side of the table. "Since you have time to sneak around and scare young women, surely you can spare a few moments."

She felt more than heard him stalk around the table. As he came into her line of vision, Miranda did not waste her first look at the infamous Gerard Coriano. He was shorter than she'd expected, with black hair that he wore tied in a ponytail. His clothes were plain, brown cloth and leather, and his face had a sharp, hawkish handsomeness to it that was pleasant enough save for the long, thin scar running down the left side. It started at his temple, split his eyebrow, and ran down his cheek and over his lips, stopping just above his jaw. His left eye was discolored and murky where the scar crossed it, but it followed her movements just as well as his right, which was cold and flat gray-blue. He wore a sword low on his hip, but the guard and hilt were wrapped in thick felt that only hinted at their shape. Judging from the way he took his seat, however, Miranda harbored no illusions that the wrapping would slow his draw.

Coriano leaned on the table, gloved hands steepled in front of him and a small smile tugging at the edge of his thin mouth. "That was quite a display you put on outside. Normally, I prefer a note left at the bar, but I should know better by now than to expect subtlety from a Spiritualist."

"I would have contacted you more discreetly if I had time to wait in seedy taverns," Miranda said. "We

Spiritualists lack the copious amounts of leisure time you bounty hunters seem to enjoy, Mr. Coriano."

His smile broadened, and he leaned back in his chair. "How may I help you?"

"You've been tracking the wizard thief Eli Monpress for months." Miranda leaned forward. "Both of our last tips came from you. I want to know how you do it."

Coriano glanced pointedly down at her rings. "What, can't root him out with your little menagerie? I thought that was one of the Spiritualist's specialties."

Miranda didn't bother to hide her annoyance. "With any other rogue wizard, yes, but Eli hides his tracks very well. You, however, always seem to be right on his heels." She reached into her bag and pulled out a heavy sack that jingled invitingly when she laid it on the table. "That's double the normal payment. It's yours if you tell me how to find him. More, if you lead me there."

Coriano glanced at the money, then back at her. "If I knew how to find Eli and his companions, do you really think I'd be wasting my time here?"

"Maybe, if you're as smart as the rumors say." Miranda moved her hand slightly, maneuvering her rings to catch the dim light. "You might be a great swordsman, but you can't take Eli on your own. You need a wizard to fight a wizard, or why else would you endanger your prize by tipping off the Spiritualists?"

"How do you know we're after the same prize?" Coriano said, tapping his fingers on the table.

"Because Eli is the prize everyone is after," she said sweetly. "Even us. If I catch Eli, his Council bounty belongs to the Spirit Court. Twenty thousand standards would be quite a boon to our budget. However"—Miranda leaned forward and lowered her voice—"there are things we value far more than money. If you help me, perhaps we can come to an arrangement. I have the authority to be very generous in this affair, Mr. Coriano."

Coriano leaned forward to match her. "Banage must be desperate indeed if he's stooped to making deals."

Miranda jerked back. "The Rector Spiritualis does what is best for the harmony of the Spirit Court," she said coldly. "Eli Monpress's rising notoriety threatens the good reputation we've spent the last several hundred years building."

"More valuable than gold indeed." Coriano smirked. "Can't have Monpress playing the wolf when the good Rector Spiritualis is busy trying to convince the world he's leading a flock of sheep."

"You will not find me a docile lamb," Miranda said flatly. "Will you help us, or am I wasting my breath?"

"Oh, you're not wasting anything," Coriano said. "This has been quite a charming chat. Sadly, I'm afraid I can't offer you my services this time around. I have a prior engagement. Besides," he smiled, "I don't think our methods would mesh."

"What kind of prior engagement is worth jeopardizing your good standing with the Spirit Court?" Miranda scoffed. "Master Banage has spoken so highly of your services, he would be most disappointed if you didn't help me now."

"How dreadful," Coriano said and arched his scarred eyebrow. "In that case, let me give you some advice, as one professional to another." He leaned in close, lowering his voice to an almost inaudible whisper. "Don't underestimate Monpress. He's a wizard, true, but not as you are, and he's been doing this for a long time. That twenty thousand bounty he carries isn't an exaggeration. Monpress has stolen enough gold from the Council Kingdoms to live like a king for five lifetimes, but the only records we have of him spending it are on setups for ever-larger thefts. Some of the world's best bounty hunters have chased him for months and caught nothing but stories, others simply vanished. This has led some experienced hunters to dismiss him as a wild chase, but that is because they have failed to understand Monpress's only constant: his pride in his vocation. Eli Monpress is a true thief. He steals for the joy of it. He doesn't make a show unless he wants you to see, and he never runs before he's gotten what he came for. He may act the charming fool, but he has a goal to everything he does. Find out what he really wants, and then position yourself so that he has to go through you to get it. Make him come to you. That's the only way you'll catch him.

"Now," he said, holding up the bag of money, which Miranda hadn't seen him take, "I've told you how to find him, so I'll be taking the payment as agreed."

He stood up in one smooth motion and bowed courteously, slipping the bulging coin purse into his pocket. "Forgive me, ladies, I must hurry to my next appointment. I'm sure we'll meet again."

He left the way he had come, disappearing as quietly as a cat behind the empty bar. Miranda gave him to the count of twenty before pushing her chair back with a clatter and stomping out of the decrepit tavern.

"Complete waste of time," she muttered, shoving the dirty blanket out of her way. "For all the information he gave us, I might as well have interrogated the door a few more times."

Marion followed meekly, eyes on the dusty corners in case any other mysterious swordsmen were waiting to make an entrance. "What did he mean 'a wizard not as you are'?"

"How should I know?" Miranda said, marching down the creaking stairs. "I don't think he understands what comes out of his mouth any more than we do. We'll just have to expand the search. There's got to be something I'm missing. Whatever Coriano says about Eli's skill, Monpress can't do what he's doing without a spirit's help, and he can't use spirits without leaving some trace. He's been lucky so far, but as soon as I can figure out his gimmick, I'll wring his—" She stopped short.

The street outside was just as empty as it had been when they'd arrived. Gin was where they had left him, slouched on the ground. His large head rested on his paws, one of which had something squirmy pinned in the mud beneath it.

"You have a visitor," he said, tail twitching. "He didn't want to wait until you were done with your meeting, but I convinced him otherwise."

"Gin," Miranda said through gritted teeth. "Let him up."

The ghosthound lifted his paw, and Miranda hurried to help the man. Even covered in mud, the royal messenger's livery was recognizable. He wobbled a bit, like his knees wouldn't support him, and Miranda had to position herself between him and Gin before he could get his message out.

"T-the Master of Security s-sent me to f-find you, lady," he stuttered. "A letter just arrived from the king."

Miranda's face lit up. "A letter from the king? How long ago?"

"Master Oban sent me as soon as it came," he said, keeping his distance from the Spiritualist and her monster. "Ten minutes maybe? Twenty?"

That was all Miranda needed. She hooked her arm over Gin's nose and he lifted her up onto his waiting back.

"Lady!" Marion cried. "Where are you going?"

"To the castle, of course!" Miranda shouted. "Eli's made his move, and I'm not about to let him get away so easily this time."

Marion opened her mouth to say something else, but the ghosthound dashed behind her and Miranda swept the girl up onto his back. Gin whirled, patterns flashing wildly over his fur, and dashed up the hill, pouncing in silent bounds toward the castle.

The moment the ghosthound was out of sight, the neighborhood started pouring out of its hiding places. Men, women, and grubby children flooded the muddy street, and the royal messenger found himself surrounded by gawking, dirty people. One look at the knives some of the men wore in their boots and the messenger decided it was time to return as well, and he followed the ghosthound up the hill toward the castle at a dead run.

CHAPTER
7

Oban, the Master of Security, was waiting for them at the castle gate with a roll of parchment in his hand.

"Lady Miranda!" he shouted, running toward them as Gin slid to a stop.

"Is that the letter?" Miranda hopped down.

"Yes." He shoved the parchment into her hand. "Read it quickly."

She shook the paper open and read, muttering along as she went. "*King is safe...Send riders to the Council... Mellinor shall pledge an additional thirty-five thousand to Monpress's bounty*"—her eyebrows shot up—"*and five thousand in cash*—these demands are ridiculous!" She shook her head as she finished reading. "'*Raise a white flag from the second tower when you receive the new bounty notice from the Council and await further instructions.*' Why that greedy little thief, what is he playing at?" She thrust the note back at Oban. "You said the king wrote this?"

"Yes," Oban said, "under much duress, we fear."

Miranda gave him a flat look. "He has very good handwriting for a king under duress."

"Oh, this isn't the original." The Master of Security ran a nervous hand over his bald head. "It's a scribe copy."

"Well, that won't do." Miranda put her hands on her hips. "Where is the original? I need it now." Time was precious. If she got it soon enough, the faint, weak spirits in the ink might still remember the ink pot they'd lived in. That would give her a direction at least, maybe even a relative distance, but only if she got to them before they fell asleep completely and forgot that they'd ever been anything except words on a page.

The Master of Security blanched. "I'm afraid I can't get it, lady. The situation's, um"—he clutched his hands—"changed."

"Changed how?" Miranda's eyes narrowed.

"Go to the throne room, and you'll see." He sighed. "They don't know I let you see the note, lady, but I couldn't let you go in there without some information at least. Good luck." He bowed slightly, then whirled around and disappeared into the stables.

"He stinks of fear," Gin said, his orange eyes on Oban's retreating back.

"Do you know what this is about?" Miranda asked Marion, who was still working her way down off the ghosthound. The girl shook her head.

Miranda stared up at the white castle, which looked much more forbidding than usual. "Ears open, mutt," she muttered. "Be ready if I call you."

"Always am," Gin huffed, sitting down in the middle of the stable yard.

Miranda nodded and hurried up the castle steps, Marion keeping close behind her.

The entrance hall was quiet and empty. Miranda frowned, glancing around for the usual clusters of servants and officials, but there was no sign of them. She quickened her pace, trotting across the polished marble to the arched doorway that led to the throne room. As she rounded the corner, what she saw stopped her dead in her tracks. The entire servant population of castle Allaze, from the stable boys to the chambermaids, was crammed into the great hall that led to the throne room. They were crowded in, shoulder to shoulder, filling the hall to bursting.

Miranda stared bewildered at the wall of backs blocking their way. "All right," she sighed, slumping against the wall, "I give up. What is going on?"

Marion hurried forward, tapping the shoulder of a man at the back of the crowd wearing a blacksmith's leather apron to ask what was happening.

"Didn't ya hear?" the man said. "Lord Renaud's back."

Marion's face went white as cheese. She thanked the man and hurried back to Miranda. "Lord Renaud is back," she whispered.

"So I heard," Miranda said. "But let's assume for the moment that I know nothing about this country. Who is Lord Renaud?"

"King Henrith's older brother."

"*Older* brother?" Miranda frowned in confusion. "Is he a bastard or something?"

"Of course not!" Marion looked mortified.

"Then why did Henrith become king, and not him?"

None of the research she'd done on Mellinor had mentioned any variance in the normal lines of succession. Of course, she hadn't had time to do much research in her rush to beat Eli.

"Lord Renaud was first in line for the throne, but then there were, um"—she glanced pointedly at Miranda's rings—"problems."

"I see," Miranda said quietly, following her gaze. "You know, in most countries, having a wizard in the royal family is considered a blessing." Marion winced at the coldness in her voice. "He was banished as a child, then?"

Marion shook her head. "That's usually the way, but not this time. You see, no one knew he was a wizard until a few days after the prince's sixteenth birthday. The old king was furious when he found out, of course, and he banished Lord Renaud to the desert on the southern edge of Mellinor."

"Sixteen is far too old for a manifestation," Miranda said, drumming her fingers against the stone doorway. "A wizard child can hear spirits from birth. It's obvious by the time they can talk that something is off. A prince, especially an heir to the throne, is hardly raised in obscurity. How did no one know?"

"The queen covered up for him," Marion said sadly. "It was no secret that she loved him the most. She wouldn't let the servants near him. She took care of him herself, dressed him and mended his clothes, prepared his meals, and so forth. We assumed it was because Renaud was the crown prince, since she never did any of that for Henrith. Now, of course, we know the real reason."

Miranda arched an eyebrow. "So how did it come to light?"

"The queen had a weak heart," Marion said sadly. "It got worse as she grew older, and finally there was nothing the doctors could do. She died on Renaud's birthday. They say the prince went mad with grief after that, his mother had been his whole world, and with him going on like that, there was no hiding what he was. He was banished before the week was out, and Henrith was made crown prince in his place." Marion leaned on the wall beside Miranda. "Of course, this all happened years ago, well before I came to the palace. I've seen Lord Renaud only once, when the king drove him out of the city."

Miranda eyed the packed crowd. "The return of a banished prince, no wonder everyone's making such a fuss. Well," she said and straightened up, "strange goings on or no, I need to get my spirits on that note or we'll be right back where we started. Follow me."

She walked up to the wall of backs and, without fanfare, began to elbow her way through. Marion wiggled along behind her, apologizing profusely to the angry people in their wake.

"I could have asked them to move," she huffed, squeezing between two guardsmen. "Despite the circumstances, you *are* a guest of the masters."

Miranda shook her head. "From what I've seen of Mellinor, announcing I'm a Spiritualist would be the same as shouting 'fire.' I don't want to cause a stampede."

As they neared the throne room doors, the press of people grew even tighter, and Miranda's and Marion's progress slowed to an agonizing crawl.

"This is ridiculous," Marion gasped, pressed against Miranda's shoulder by a pack of guardsmen. "We'll never get through."

Miranda pursed her lips, thinking, and then her eyes lit up. "Let me try something."

She closed her eyes and slumped forward slightly, letting her body relax. With practiced ease she retreated to the deepest part of her mind, the well of power her spirits sipped from, the well that was usually kept tightly shut. She breathed deeply, relaxing her hold just a fraction. The effect was immediate.

The crowd around them shivered and stepped away. It was only a step, but it left just enough room for her and Marion to push through all the way to the golden doors. As soon as they reached the throne room's threshold, Miranda clamped down again. The small knot of people behind them gave a slight shiver and pressed in again as if nothing had happened.

Marion looked over her shoulder with wide eyes. "What did you do?"

"I opened my spirit," Miranda said.

"Opened your..." If possible, her eyes got wider.

That was all Miranda had meant to say, but, after that awed display, she couldn't help showing off just a little. "Opening the spirit reveals the strength of a wizard's power," she whispered. "Remember when I told you that a wizard's true power is control? That's because all wizards are born with more spirit, more energy than normal people. However, that energy is generally locked away shortly after birth by the child's own self-defense mechanisms. Having your spirit wide open all the time makes you vulnerable. Spirits are attracted to power, you see, and not all of them always mean you well. With training, wizards can learn to open their spirits, sometimes a little, sometimes all the way, depending on how much power you need to display. This is a vital part of getting a spirit's attention when you start really working with them."

"But," Marion said and frowned, thoroughly confused, "I thought you said you couldn't control people?"

"Well," Miranda smiled smugly, "what I just did is more of a trick on my part than any kind of real magic. Normal people can't feel a wizard's spirit even if it's open full blast—not consciously, anyway. However, I've found that with just the right feather touch even the most spirit deaf will feel a slight pressure without knowing they feel it, and step away."

"So," Marion shivered, "that feeling just now, like someone was stepping on my grave, that was you?"

"Yes," Miranda said, nodding. "A bit unconventional, but dreadfully handy."

"Must be," Marion said. "What would happen if you opened it all the way?"

"Let's say it would be very uncomfortable for everyone involved." Miranda smiled. "Come"—she grabbed the librarian's hand and pushed through the last line of people separating them from the throne room—"let's do what we came here to do. We've wasted too much time as it is." She tallied the time inwardly and winced. The note was probably dead asleep by now. Still, any clue, anything at all, and this would all be worth it.

Though the crowd was better dressed, the throne room was every bit as packed as the hall outside, and buzzing just as intently. Miranda stood on tiptoe, looking around for the Master of the Courts or anyone who could help her, when she heard the solemn sound of metal on stone. It must have been a signal, for all at once the whispers died out and the crowd fell silent. All attention was now on the tall, slim figure climbing the steps of the dais. When he was one step from the empty throne, he stopped and turned to face the crowd. As his face came into view, Miranda caught her breath.

After Marion's story, she wasn't sure what she was expecting. A bitter, weather-worn exile, perhaps, or a smug, spoiled prince enjoying his triumphant return. Whatever she'd expected, the man standing on the dais was nothing like it. He was, however, undoubtedly a prince. Tall and handsomely dressed in a dark-blue coat, he projected the confidence of someone used to being obeyed. A waterfall of golden hair hung down his back, swaying gently as he bowed low to the crowd. His fine-featured face was almost feminine in its beauty, and Miranda swallowed despite herself. He certainly didn't look like someone who'd spent the last ten years exiled in the desert.

The golden prince looked out over the sea of people, a benevolent and humble expression on his lovely face. He held up his hands in a welcoming gesture. Miranda could almost feel the crowd leaning forward to drink him in as he began to speak.

"Citizens of Mellinor!" His voice rang out through the enraptured room. "I come before you as a criminal and an exile. Many have asked me how, seeing this, I come to stand before you today, and so, first, before you all, I must confess. Eleven years ago, I was banished for being born a wizard, in accordance with the ancient law. Yet, despite this, and because of the deep love I bear this country, for the past eight years I have disobeyed my father's order and lived among you. For Mellinor's sake,

I have lived nameless, a pauper among paupers. I was here four years ago when my younger brother, Henrith, took the throne, and I cheered him in the streets alongside you, without jealousy or malice. Until yesterday, I was content to live forgetting the duty I was born to and denying the curse that took my crown if that was what was needed to stay here, in my home. But yesterday, when I heard of the atrocious crime that had been committed, not just against the throne of Mellinor, but against my own flesh and blood, I could stay silent no more."

Renaud leaned forward, his ringing voice heavy with contempt. "You have heard by now that the wizard thief Monpress, wanted throughout the Council Kingdoms for a list of crimes too long to read here, has kidnapped our king. This crime must not go unanswered."

A great cry rose up at this, and Renaud leaned into it, letting it grow. When the noise reached a fevered pitch, Renaud threw out his arms, and silence fell like a knife.

When he spoke again, his words were choked with sorrow. "My friends, I come to you with no expectations, no pleas, nothing but the offer of my service. It was my wizardry that forced this burden upon my younger brother. Let it be my wizardry that ends it. As I was once your prince, I beg you now, let me face this criminal and help save my brother, the only family I have left. Let me serve him as I could not serve you, and I swear to you, I swear on my life that Mellinor will have her king again!"

He threw his fists in the air, and the crowd erupted. The nobles around Miranda clapped and cheered, but their polite noise was drowned out by the crowd in the hall, who hadn't seen such drama in years, if ever. Even the somberly dressed masters were milling about looking impressed despite themselves, and some of the younger ones were cheering just as loudly as the servants.

Marion bounced up and down on her toes. "Oh, isn't it exciting?"

"Quite." Miranda scowled. Something about Renaud's smile as he shook the waiting masters' hands didn't sit well with her. Marion gave her a quizzical look, but Miranda had already begun elbowing her way through the well-dressed crowd.

She ran to catch up. "Lady! Where are you going?"

"To hold him to his words," Miranda said, pushing past a pair of old ladies waving their lacy handkerchiefs at the prince. "He says he wants to help, so I'm going to make him give me that note."

Marion shrank from the nasty looks they were getting, but before she could start apologizing, a boy in page's livery popped out of the crowd right beside Miranda.

"Lady Spiritualist," he said, bowing nervously. "Lord Renaud wishes to meet you right away."

"Well," Miranda said. "That saves some trouble. Lead on."

The page turned and led them away from the crowd to a small door just off the back half of the main throne room. This opened into a small, richly decorated parlor. As soon as they were inside, the page vanished back into the crowd, letting the door close softly behind him.

"Well," Miranda said, dropping into one of the silk couches, "that was all very neat. We were swept up and tucked away before we could cause trouble." She glanced at Marion, who was still standing by the door, looking slightly dazed. "Your Renaud seems to have gained quite a bit of influence in a very short time for a banished wizard prince. His speech wasn't *that* good."

"Prince is the key word there, I think." Marion sighed, padding across the carpet to take a seat on one of the straight-backed, carved wooden chairs under the window. "With the king gone, Mellinor's been headless. Since our founding, we've never been without a king for more than a day. There's no precedent at all, so it's no wonder the masters are in a panic. I shouldn't say this, but they'd probably follow the king's dog at this point if it could prove a royal lineage." She glanced at the door. "Lord Renaud sure picked the right time to come back. Only in a situation like this could his status as a prince outweigh his stigma as a wizard."

"How very convenient for him," Miranda said thoughtfully.

Marion paled. "Please don't take offense, lady. Stigma's the wrong word. I—"

"It's fine." Miranda smiled. "Don't apologize. You've given me a lot to think about."

"It's just…" Marion pulled at her dress. "I've never had to think about things from a wizard's—Spiritualist! Spiritualist's point of view, and—"

She stopped midbabble and sprang out of her chair. Miranda looked at her, confused, but Marion shook her head fiercely and pointed at the door before dropping into a low curtsy.

A second later, Prince Renaud himself swept into the room.

CHAPTER
8

He was alone, which struck Miranda as unusual, and he bowed as graciously as any servant as the door drifted shut behind him.

"Lady Spiritualist," he said, "I've very much looked forward to meeting you."

Miranda stood up and bowed as well, hoping Mellinor had no special deviations from common court etiquette. "Lord Renaud, I appreciate your taking the time to see me. There are several things—"

"Shouldn't you be resting?" Renaud said, rolling right over her. "The masters told me you've been up since you got here."

Miranda stiffened. "I appreciate your concern, but time is of the essence. If we are to save your brother, I must have access to the king's original ransom note."

"Oh, it's far too late to question the spirits, if that's what you're after." Renaud smiled sweetly.

"I'll make my own decision on that," Miranda said

flatly. "The spirits in that note are our only connection to Eli. If you will not give it to me, then tell me where to find it and I will fetch the note myself, but do not waste my time, or your brother's, with assumptions about my methods."

Renaud's smile did not waver. "I'm afraid that simply won't be possible."

"Excuse me?" Miranda's glare seemed to lower the temperature in the room. Lord Renaud continued as if nothing had happened.

"The court of Mellinor was in a panic when you arrived, and the officials you bullied into permitting your free reign of this kingdom had no right to grant you the freedoms they did. Now that I have restored order, I'm afraid your assistance in this matter is no longer needed."

"Forgive me, prince," Miranda said, "but it is not your place to decide my duties. Panic or no, my aid was requested by officials acting on the king's behalf. My duty lies with Henrith now, and only his rescue or death can relieve me of it."

"Your dedication is admirable," Renaud said. "But Mellinor will deal with Mellinor's problems."

"A bold statement." Miranda eyed him. "But how will you go about it? A wizard dangerous enough for a twenty thousand gold bounty is not one to be taken lightly. No matter what boasts you make, you are going to need my help if you plan to face him."

Renaud paused and flicked his eyes pointedly to Marion. The girl, who was trying to make herself as small as possible, froze. He made a slight shooing motion with one finger, and Marion, palace trained as she was, leaped to obey. After a series of overly polite curtsies, she hurried past him and out of the room. Only when the door was shut completely did Renaud continue.

"That's better." Renaud smiled. "As I was saying, your statement might be true, *if* we intended to fight him. The masters and I went over the ransom note as soon as it arrived, and we found Eli's demands to be quite reasonable."

Miranda stared blankly at him. "You're joking."

"I can assure you I am not," Renaud said, meeting her gaze levelly.

"Five thousand in cash and thirty-five in bounty pledges? In what world is that reasonable?"

"Is my brother not worth five times as much?" Renaud's glare sharpened.

"You can't just give that, that *thief* what he wants!" Miranda sputtered.

Renaud sighed. "You see, this is precisely why we cannot accept your help. How could we trust our king's life to someone who values it so cheaply?"

Miranda flinched, getting a firm grip on her rage. "It's not about the money," she said, calmly now. "Don't you see this is exactly what he wants? Think about it: by demanding you pledge thirty-five thousand to his bounty, Eli ensures that Mellinor has a hefty stake in keeping him uncaught. He's using this country as a safety net. If you just give in like this, think about what kind of signal you'll be sending other would-be thieves. Eli is an innovator, but he's not the only wizard thief. If he is successful, others will surely follow his lead. Doing this could make Mellinor a target for years to come, and your policy against wizards leaves you helpless."

"But you forget," Renaud said, folding his hands behind his back, "Mellinor has its own wizard now."

"Being born a wizard doesn't mean you have the skills to fight one. What if Eli double-crosses you? Did you think about that? If he decides to take the money and not return your king, do you really think you could stop him?"

"Your concern for our well-being is touching," Renaud said, "but such matters are no longer yours to worry about." He walked casually to the door and held it open. "You'll find whatever provisions you need in the kitchens. If that dog of yours is half of what they say, you should be able to make it over the border by nightfall." His smile didn't reach his eyes. "I sincerely suggest you make all haste. I might not feel so generous tomorrow, should you be caught on our lands."

Miranda stood her ground. "I am not one to be dismissed so easily."

"But you are a member of the Spirit Court," Renaud said, "and you are bound by your oaths not to interfere in internal kingdom affairs. You could be stripped of your position if you push this much further." His smile turned cruel. "Isn't that so, lady Spiritualist?"

It was all Miranda could do not to strangle the smug lordling with his own flowing hair. Her spirits picked up her tension and began to murmur in their gems. For a wild moment, she was on the edge of opening up and showing him the difference between a Court-trained Spiritualist and a self-taught brat. Slowly, methodically, she clamped down on the impulse. She turned and walked out of the room, but when she reached Renaud, she stopped and whispered in a low, cutting voice, "This isn't over."

"No," Renaud whispered back. "I believe it is."

Miranda stomped past him and into the still-crowded throne room, boot heels clicking angrily against the marble. The waiting masters scrambled to get out of her way, which made her feel a hair better, until she heard Renaud politely call after her: "Good day, Spiritualist."

She didn't give him the satisfaction of looking back.

Renaud waited until the Spiritualist was completely out of sight before he shut the door. "Are you sure that was wise?" asked an amused voice from the corner.

Renaud jumped before he could stop himself. "Must you do that?"

Coriano was already sitting on the silk couch when the prince turned, his boots propped up on the low table and his wrapped sword laid across his knees. He gave Renaud a smile and waved at the chair across from him. "Sit."

Renaud remained standing. "You were saying?"

Coriano shrugged and put his hands behind his head. "I was just asking if you didn't come across a little too brash with the whole 'I might not feel so generous tomorrow' bit. I gave you all the information you'd need to trap her with her own vows. There was no need to push her further. Old man Banage taught her how to put up a cold front, but anyone can see she's got a mean temper inside. After that display, I wouldn't be surprised if she really did leave tonight, just to spite you."

"She won't," Renaud said. "One thing I do know about Spiritualists is that they all share the same debilitating sense of duty. If she's been sent here to do a job, she won't leave until it's done." He eyed the man cautiously. "Why do you care? I thought all you wanted was Eli's swordsman."

"Yes." Coriano's bored voice hid a dangerous edge. "But that will be hard if you flub your part sporting with something as volatile as Spiritualist pride." The swordsman's gloved fingers drifted gently along the wrapped hilt of his sword and he gave the prince a sideways look. "You're not the only one who's been waiting for his chance, wizard. If you play games with this, we will gut you before you see us coming."

"Everything is on schedule," the prince said, the words grinding through his gritted teeth. "You mind your end and I'll mind mine."

"Fair enough." Coriano stood up. "We're about to have company, so I'll take my leave. I'll be back when the flag flies, so have my fee ready. Double rate, of course, but considering you'll be the one collecting Eli's bounty when this is over, it hardly matters."

"What are you talking about?" Renaud said. "You told me Josef Liechten had a ten thousand gold bounty of his own."

"He does," Coriano said, walking toward the servant's door, his boots quiet as cat feet on the stone. "But that's only if he's brought in alive." He gave Renaud a feral grin. "Some things are worth more than money, prince."

"There, at least, we agree," Renaud said, straightening his cuffs. When he looked up again, the swordsman was gone, the servant's small door swinging shut behind him. A second later, a soft knock sounded on the door connecting the parlor to the throne room.

Renaud gathered his patience and opened it before the second knock landed. When he faced the waiting crowd of masters, his smile was the picture of sad sincerity.

"Gentlemen," he said, "forgive me for making you

wait. I had a lot to consider. I am sad to report that, for reasons of her own, the Lady Miranda has declined to aid us further."

"You must be mistaken!" Master Oban elbowed his way to the front of the group. "She promised to help us!"

"The Spirit Court is a single-minded organization," Renaud said gravely. "They care only for their laws and those who break them, not for the victims left behind. Honestly, we should have expected no less."

"But," the Master of the Exchequer clutched his ledger, "what are we to do?"

"There is only one solution," Renaud said, "in order to save my brother. I will meet Eli and make the exchange without her."

A swell of conversation erupted as everyone turned to his neighbor to remark at the selfless nobility of this gesture.

The Master of the Courts alone remained calm. "And, my lord, should the thief betray you?" He glanced at the Master of the Exchequer. "The bounty request has already been sent, and Council law says we cannot change it for any reason once our pledge has been entered in the official records. Your bold claim is noble, but Mellinor can hardly afford to lose our king, our prince, and forty thousand standards in one swoop."

"That will not happen," Renaud said, glaring at the old master. "The Spirit Court may be willing to gamble a country's safety to catch a thief, but I am not one of their pet wizards. Though I was banished, I am a prince still, and my goal is the preservation of Mellinor. That is why, in all the world, I am the only wizard you can trust."

A cheer erupted at this, and the old Master of the

Courts was overwhelmed by the waving hands of the younger masters, who thought this was all very grand. Master Oban caught the eye of the Master of Courts and the two of them quietly retreated to a corner of the throne room.

"The tide in Mellinor is shifting," the Master of the Courts said with a sigh when they were safely away. "I wonder if we shall like where it takes us."

"Wizard or no, he's a prince of House Allaze." The Master of Security shrugged. "In four hundred years, they've never led us wrong. It'll work out in the end, old friend." He said, "You'll see."

The Master of the Courts stroked his gray beard thoughtfully. "I pray you are right." He turned his eyes to the empty throne, standing high and alone on the marble dais. "We must all pray."

CHAPTER
9

Miranda stormed into the stable yard, scattering the crowd of boys who had gathered to watch Gin eat the pig he had helped himself to from the swine pen.

"We're leaving," she said. "*Now*."

Gin looked sadly at the pig, then pulled away with a sigh, licking his mouth clean as he trotted over. Miranda stuffed the bag of traveling food that she'd frightened out of the kitchen staff into her rucksack and slung it into position over Gin's neck. Gin lay down with uncharacteristic meekness as Miranda clambered into her riding position.

"Get us out of here."

The hound rose swiftly, but before he could spring forward a familiar voice called out: "Lady Miranda!"

Miranda looked up in surprise as Marion jumped down the castle steps and hit the stable yard at a dead run. She didn't stop until she reached Gin, slamming into his foreleg rather than taking the time to slow down.

"Here," she gasped, and thrust her hand out. Miranda reached down and plucked the creased slip of paper from her fingers. As she unfolded it, her face lit up. "How did you get this?"

Marion grinned from ear to ear. "All important papers go to the library for storage. Sometimes being a junior librarian does have its advantages."

"Won't you get in trouble?" Miranda frowned. "You know I probably won't be able to get this back to you before they notice it's gone."

Marion shook her head violently. "So long as the king comes back, I don't think they would care if I raided the whole treasury."

Miranda smiled. "Thank you," she said. "I won't forget this."

Marion waved and pushed off the ghosthound's leg.

Waving back, Miranda gave Gin the go-ahead. The ghosthound sprang forward, leaving the boys gawking as he disappeared over the gates in a cloud of dust.

"How convincing should I be?" Gin said as they jumped the final gate of the city.

Miranda glared darkly at the rolling countryside as it streaked by. "And what makes you think we're not actually leaving?"

She could feel Gin's chuckle through his fur. "You don't normally lose this gracefully. The castle isn't on fire, so far as I can see."

"Smart aleck mutt." Miranda smacked him good-naturedly. "You're right, we're not leaving. I'll give up my rings before I let that jerk have his way."

"What jerk?" Gin panted.

Miranda gave him the short version of her meeting

with Renaud. When she finished, Gin growled thought-fully. "Politics and gold are human vices, so maybe there's something here I don't understand, but I have trouble believing that an exiled prince like Renaud is really that concerned over the recovery of the little brother who took his throne."

"My thoughts exactly." Miranda leaned over to scratch his ears.

"What are we going to do, then?"

"That part is simple. We're going to find Eli first." She pointed to the left, where a thick line of shaggy conifers separated two fields. "Duck into that copse."

Gin picked up the pace, and a few seconds later they were hidden behind the small stand of pines. Miranda jumped down and, after checking the area for any stray watchers, pressed her thumb against the fat, smooth sapphire on her right index finger. "Allinu, wake up, I need you."

A moment later, a small, white spout of pure water bubbled happily out of the ring, forming a small pool in Miranda's cupped hand. When the water was up to her thumb, Miranda shoved the ransom note in. "Find this ink's source."

"Yes, mistress," the water whispered, and began to churn.

Miranda kept her fingers pressed as tightly as she could, though she knew it was not needed. Allinu was a mountain mist. She could stay together in a sieve if she needed to. Still, it made Miranda feel better when the water was splashing in all directions like it was now.

A few moments later, the note floated to the top, per-fectly dry.

"I'm sorry, mistress," the water said. "The ink's been dry too long. It doesn't remember anything."

"I figured as much," Miranda said, shifting the water to one cupped hand and plucking the note out. She looked at it once more before stuffing it into her pocket. So much for that.

"The paper was a bit more helpful," the water added, almost as an afterthought.

Miranda's head jerked up. "The what?"

"The paper," Allinu said again. "I noticed a few rips on one side, so I asked it what had happened. Once it realized I wasn't going to drown it into pulp, it told me about the bird. Apparently, your thief had the note delivered by falcon. In the falcon's talons, actually, which the paper did not appreciate. Claws are very hard on paper, and—"

"Yes, of course," Miranda said. "Did the paper say anything else?"

"I was getting to that," Allinu sloshed, insulted. "It said, 'At least the trip was short.'"

"How short?"

"Two, three minutes from when the falcon grabbed him until the falcon dropped it on some guards," Allinu bubbled.

"That's more like it." Miranda grinned. "Thank you, Allinu."

The water rose in a white mist, swirling and then vanishing back into the sapphire, leaving Miranda's fingers damp and cold.

"Two minutes," Gin said. "That's a pretty big area."

"Not everything's as fast as you are," Miranda said, wiping her hand on her trousers. "Coriano did say Eli wouldn't run far. Besides, if he wasn't close by, how could he see the signal when they meet his demands? He specifically told them to fly it from the second tower, which is barely visible above the wall." She smiled at the castle rising over the city, less than a mile behind them. "Look, you can hardly see it even at this distance. He must be close, and when they give the signal, he'll need to send another note to set up the trade and deliver the king. When he does that, we'll be ready."

She reached into the neck of her shirt and pulled out a silver pendant of delicate spirals wrapped around a large, white pearl. It was a lovely piece of work. She'd had it made especially for the spirit she kept inside, before she caught him, which wasn't the normal order of things, but Eril had been worth it. The number of Spiritualists who kept wind spirits could be counted on one hand. Wind spirits were almost impossible to catch, and nearly as impossible to control if you did catch one. That was why she'd chosen a pendant to house him. It kept him close. A Spiritualist never forced her spirits to serve, but some spirits required more supervision than others.

"Eril," she said, holding the pendant out. "I need you."

At first, nothing happened. Miranda stood stone still, eyes on the pendant, until a soft breeze tangled the wispy hair around her ears. "You called?"

Miranda grimaced inwardly. Talking to a wind spirit was uncomfortably like talking to thin air. Eril, of course, took full advantage of this.

"I need you to keep an eye on the castle and all surrounding land for the next few days," she said, careful to keep her face in the determined but slightly bored expression that worked best with flighty spirits. "You're watching for a white flag from the second tower. The moment it flies, you'll be looking for a bird, likely a falcon, but it could be anything, with a note in its claws. I'll want to know where it came from, where it goes once the note is delivered, plus anything else of interest you might see."

"Bird watching?" Eril said and sighed dramatically, blowing Miranda's hair into her eyes. "That sounds so *boring*. Can't I do something else?"

"No," Miranda said firmly. "Don't forget to keep an eye on *all* the surrounding territory—the city, the countryside, and the forest to the north where the king keeps his deer. I'll want reports on everything."

"All right, all right, I heard you the first time," he huffed. "Never get to have any fun," Miranda heard him mutter as the wind began to die down.

Miranda stayed frozen even after the air was still, a scowl etched on her face.

"He's gone," Gin said.

"Good," Miranda said, giving herself a little shake. "He likes to hang around sometimes, just to see what I say about him. Gives me the jeebies."

The hound snorted sympathetically. "How did you catch him in the first place if you couldn't see him?"

"I used smoke," Miranda said, untying Gin's pack and dropping it on the ground. "But even when I could see, it took me a solid month before I managed to catch hold of a wind spirit long enough to convince him to join me."

Gin shook his massive head. "I will never understand how you humans manage to get through your short lives being spirit blind. That's probably why the Powers gave your kind the ability to command spirits. It's a survival mechanism."

"We get by well enough." Miranda pushed aside the thick branches for a better look at the castle. "It might have been a little much, sending him so early. The riders won't even reach the Council city until late tomorrow, and that's if they ride through the night. Then there's the wait while the bounty is approved."

"So what?" Gin flopped down on the thick carpet of pine needles. "I could use a break."

"Lazy mutt." Miranda grinned. Still, he was right. Ever since they'd gotten Coriano's tip that Eli was in Mellinor, they'd been constantly on the move. She hadn't had more than three hours of sleep in one stretch since she'd left the Spirit Court.

"All right," she said, slumping down next to him, "you win. But since you got to sleep while I was searching the castle, you get first watch."

Gin snorted, sending pine straw everywhere, but he moved to the edge of the clearing where he could lounge and watch the road at the same time. When he was settled, Miranda lay back, looking up at the deep blue sky through the tree tops. Eventually, they'd need to find a better hiding place, but this would do for now. Anyway, the sun was warm here. She closed her eyes. When Eli made his move, they would be ready. The thought made her smile, and with that, she fell asleep.

CHAPTER
10

Josef glared at his opponent, watching for an opening. The smallest twitch could show the weakness that would turn his defeat into victory. A few feet away, Eli lounged in the sunlight, leaning against the branches that hid their tumbledown stone shack and grinning like an idiot.

The thief's eyes flicked down, and Josef saw his opening. "Match and raise," he growled, tossing two gold standards on the grass in front of him.

Eli's grin faltered a fraction, and he picked up a pair of oblong coins from his own stack. "You're showing a knight," he said, pointing at the face-up card by Josef's foot. "That's five points at least. Maybe you're confused, but in Daggerback, it's the *lowest* hand that wins." He paused, twirling the coins between his long fingers, seemingly oblivious to the danger of taunting a man whose daily dress included over fifty pounds of edged weaponry. "You can take the bet back, if you want," he said, his voice positively dripping with generosity. "I won't mind."

"No." Josef crouched behind his cards. "You're not getting me with that again."

"Have it your way," Eli said, tossing his coins into the pot. "Let's see who was right."

Josef threw his hand down, adding a bearded man with a staff and an old geezer with a crown to his gallant knight in the grass. "Bachelor party: wizard, king, knight. That's ten points," he said, grinning.

Eli smirked and deftly flipped his cards like a fan. "Wizard, king, and my lovely lady." He scooped up the queen card he'd laid face-up in the grass after the first round of bets, and his smirk became intolerable. "Nine points."

Josef glowered murderously as Eli rubbed his hands together and reached out to gather his winnings.

"Grand sweep," Nico said quietly, and the two men froze. "Hunter, weaver, shepherdess." She named each card as she laid it in the grass. "Three points."

Eli sighed and shoved the pile of gold toward Nico. Now it was Josef's turn to grin. "Too bad, Eli," he said, leaning back against one of the mossy trees that ringed their tiny clearing. "Next time, you should worry less about bluffing me and more about not losing your shirt."

"I don't mind losing to Nico," Eli said, tossing her the last of the coins. "She's a much better winner than you are."

Josef grunted and nodded over his shoulder in the direction of the castle, where the spires were barely visible through the thick trees. "Speaking of winning, have those idiots gotten back to us? We've been sitting here for almost a week, and if I have to spend another day playing Daggerback with you lot, the name might start to sound like a good suggestion."

"Actually, the flag went up fifteen minutes ago," Eli

said casually. "I just wanted to see if I could win the rest of your gold before telling you."

Josef jumped to his feet. Sure enough, a large flag dangled from the top of the second tower, its white folds lying limp against the slate shingles, twitching in the breeze.

Eli winked at Josef's murderous glare and walked whistling into the hut.

The king was lying on the dirt floor, looking miserable as always. Eli had left him under the watchful flicker of the fire, which, in exchange for Eli keeping Nico outside for most of the day, was willing to make sure their royal prisoner didn't escape. Eli skirted the edge of the hearth and poked the king's shoulder with the toe of his boot.

"Almost done, your royalness."

The king sat up stiffly, and Eli handed him a tiny pot of ink and a pen nib attached to a stick, which he produced from somewhere in his pockets. "All you have to do now is write exactly what I say, and we'll take you home."

The king looked defiant for a half second and then he nodded glumly and began to copy Eli's demands word for word.

Josef was gone when Eli emerged ten minutes later, the king's letter rolled in a tight tube and ready to go. Nico, however, was where he had left her, arranging her newly acquired gold in shining patterns across the scrubby grass.

"Don't worry," she said without looking up. "He's just gone to scout the meeting place."

"Why?" Eli said, laughing. "We haven't even told them where it is yet."

Nico shrugged. "He said you would say that, and he said to tell you that you can't make assumptions about anything." She paused thoughtfully. "He also said to tell you that if he does find any traps he's going to make sure you stand on them."

"Marvelous." Eli sighed. Why did swordsmen have to be so competitive about *everything*? "The good king was kind enough to write another note for us," he said, twirling the roll of paper in his hands. "I'm setting the trade-off for this evening, an hour before sunset. That should give them plenty of time to prepare, and us plenty of leeway should things go off course."

Nico turned back to her coins. "Do you expect things to go off course?"

Eli shrugged. "Does anything we do ever go as planned?"

Nico looked up at him and shrugged back.

"Anyway," Eli continued, holding up the note, "I'm going to find a bird to take this to the palace. If Josef gets back before I do, make sure to tell him that if his trap finding is as good as his card playing I'll gladly stand anywhere he tells me."

Nico's mouth twitched, and if Eli hadn't known better, he would have said she had just suppressed a laugh. Shoving his hands in his pockets, he turned and walked into the forest, whistling a falcon call.

An hour before the appointed time, Josef made everyone move out.

"You can't be serious," Eli said from his comfy spot in the grass.

Josef just shook his head and strapped another bandolier of throwing knives on top of his already impressive personal arsenal. "Last to a fight, first in the dirt," he said, hooking his short swords into place, one on each hip. When those were set, he grabbed his enormous iron sword from the log beside him and slung it over his shoulder. "Let's go."

He turned and walked out of the clearing, his heavy boots surprisingly quiet on the leaf-littered ground. Nico followed just behind him, moving over the fallen logs like a shadow. Eli lounged for a moment longer. Then, with a long sigh, he heaved himself up and went into the hut to get the king.

They walked single file through the forest. Josef went first, stalking through the tree shadows like a knife-covered jungle cat. Eli strolled a good distance behind him, leading the king by his rope like a puppy. Nico trailed at the back, her enormous coat pulled tight around her despite the warm afternoon, and her eyes glued to the thick undergrowth.

"You'll never get away with this, you know," King Henrith said, trying to keep some of his dignity as he stumbled after Eli. "As soon as I'm back with my own men, I'll put my entire army after you. You won't even reach the border."

"Splendid!" Eli said, ducking under a low branch. "At least things won't be boring. After this last week, an army on our heels sounds like a welcome vacation."

"Don't you understand?" the king sputtered, shaking his bound fists at the thief's back. "I'll have you drawn and quartered! I'll hang your innards up in the city square for birds to pick at, and what's left, I'll throw in the river for the fish!"

"That doesn't sound very sanitary." Eli pressed his finger to his lips thoughtfully. "Still, it's the thought that counts." He looked over his shoulder, a heartfelt sunbeam of a smile lighting up his face. "I'm so happy we got to know each other like this. That's the best part about this business: You meet so many interesting people!"

The king turned purple with rage, but before he could think of a proper comeback, Eli came to an abrupt halt, causing the king to run face first into his back. A few feet ahead, Josef had stopped and was watching the trees, one hand hovering over the short sword at his hip.

They were at the edge of a small gap in the trees, not really a meadow but a rare sunny space where bushes and wildflowers had taken root. The forest around them looked just like every other bit they'd spent the last twenty minutes walking through, a mix of midsized hardwoods and thick undergrowth. The only sounds were the cries of far-off birds and the wind rustling the leaves high above them.

"What is it?" Eli whispered, creeping toward the swordsman.

Josef stayed perfectly still, with his hands on his swords. "We're being followed."

As soon as he said it, a monster launched itself out of the undergrowth. It moved like mist over water, gray and cold and canine, with enormous teeth, which Josef managed to dodge barely a second before they would have sunk into his leg. He landed hard on his knees beside Eli, rolling to his feet as soon as he touched the ground, his short sword flashing. Eli pulled the king and Nico close behind him, backing them into the center of the small clearing to give the swordsman room to maneuver. Josef crouched low beside them, both short swords out now, and readied himself for the creature's next charge.

However, the charge never came. As soon as they were all bunched together, the trap sprang.

CHAPTER
11

The ground erupted at their feet, sprouting four enormous walls that grew ten feet before they could react. At first, the walls appeared to be made of dirt, but as soon as they reached their full height, the dirt shifted and became solid, slick stone, caging them in on all sides save for a tiny, open square of sky at the very top. Then, as suddenly as the walls had grown, they stopped, leaving the king and his kidnappers squashed together like fish in a square, stone barrel.

"Eli," Josef whispered. "Please tell me this is one of your spirits."

"No such luck," came a voice from above. A shadow fell over them, and the captives looked up to see a redheaded woman smirking down through the opening.

"Eli Monpress," she said, "I am Spiritualist Miranda Lyonette. You are hereby under arrest by order of the Rector Spiritualis, Etmon Banage, for the improper use of spirits, treason against the Spirit Court, and, most recently, the kidnapping of King Henrith of Mellinor. You will surrender your spirits and come quietly."

"Now wait a minute," Eli yelled up at her. "Treason against the Spirit Court? Don't you have to be a member of something to commit treason against it? I don't recall ever joining your little social club."

The woman arched her eyebrow. "The Spirit Court preserves the balance between human and spirit. When you used your abilities to ruin the reputation of all wizards by turning to a flamboyant life of crime, you committed treason against all spirits and the humans who care for them. Does that answer your question?"

"Not really," Eli said.

"Well, we'll have plenty of time to talk about it later," Miranda said, smirking. "Will you surrender the king and come quietly, or must I ask Durn here to march you all the way to the Spirit Court's door?"

The stone prison jerked several feet to the left, knocking its occupants in a pile on the dusty ground.

"You make a strong argument, Lady Miranda," Eli said, untangling himself from the king. "But I'm afraid there's a slight problem."

"Oh?" Miranda leaned forward.

"You see, we already had his royal dustiness here order his people to write a letter pledging thirty-five thousand gold toward my bounty. You know how the Council is; they never go back on something once it's been through the system, so you must agree it would be frightfully rude of me to just go off with you and forfeit all of Mellinor's money to the Spirit Court, especially considering the country's general aversion to practitioners of the magical arts."

"I fail to see how that is my concern, Mr. Monpress."

Miranda waved her hand dismissively. "Why don't we wait and ask the Rector Spiritualis what he thinks?"

"Ah," Eli said. "That sounds lovely. Unfortunately, I must refuse. You see, I have a pressing prior obligation to take his highness home and pick up a rather disgusting amount of money."

"You might find that difficult, considering the circumstances," Miranda said, patting the wall below her. "I don't know how you charm your spirits, sir, but Durn here only answers to me, and he says you're coming with us."

"Really?" Eli rapped his knuckles against the hard stone. "Let's see if he won't have a change of heart. Nico, if you would?"

Nico nodded and stretched out her hand, pressing her long fingers delicately against the stone wall. For a moment, nothing happened. Then her eyes flashed under the shadow of her hat, and the wall beneath her fingers began to vanish. Not pull back, not crumble, but vanish, as if it had never been there to begin with.

After that, things happened very quickly. The stone walls of the prison collapsed with a thundering scream, falling over in an avalanche of rubble, including the wall Miranda had been so confidently perched on only seconds before. Suddenly without purchase, the female Spiritualist fell tumbling to the ground with a sickening thud.

The giant hound sprang forward with a terrifying roar, landing in a protective crouch above his motionless mistress. "Monster!" he roared, his patterns whirling through the thick cloud of dust and grit. "What did you do?"

"I'm sure we don't know what you're talking about," Eli said, dusting himself off. "We were the ones attacked by a mon—"

Gin didn't give the thief a chance to finish. He leaped forward, almost too fast to see, his claws going straight for Nico's throat. He would have struck true if Josef's blade hadn't been there. The swordsman parried the hound's swipe at the last second, but the impact took them both to the ground. Josef rolled and came up sword first. The hound pushed off the grass in a shower of dirt and wheeled around, narrowly dodging the swordsman's counterswipe with a well-timed leap.

"Stand aside, human," Gin snarled, his hackles bristling as he circled for another charge. "It's not you I want now. Rest assured, I'll eat you later for what you did to my mistress."

"Growl all you want, pup." Josef flipped his swords with a toothy grin, and pointed both tips at the ghost-hound's nose. "I'm no wizard, so if you have something to tell me, you'll have to say it in a language I understand."

The ghosthound clawed the ground and launched forward, teeth snapping in readiness to crush the swordsman's skull, but before he had gone more than a few feet, something extraordinary happened. On either side of the charging hound, enormous roots burst out of the ground. They flew like spears, shooting out of the dirt and over the ghosthound in a tall arc. Then, with a whip crack, they slammed down hard, pinning the dog beneath them. Howling, Gin clawed and tore at the ground, foam flicking from his mouth as he fought to get free, but it was no use. The roots were young and strong, and, as much as he struggled, they would not let him go.

Josef stared in confusion for a moment and then glanced over at Eli, who looked to be in deep conversation with the stand of oaks on the far side of the clearing, and his face fell.

"Powers, Eli, did you have to?" He slammed his swords back into their sheaths. "Things were finally getting interesting."

Eli finished thanking the trees and turned to scowl at his companion. "Don't worry, I'm sure he'll still want to kill you later, but we don't have time for this right now. You were the one who said we should be early."

Josef grunted and turned away. "Nico," he called, "grab the king."

Nico nodded and reached down. The king shied away from her with a terrified squeak. On her next grab, she didn't give him the chance to dodge. She took hold of his collar and dragged him up. Then, as easily as a thresher lifts a bag of chaff, she roped her arm around his middle and hoisted him onto her shoulders. She looked at Josef, who nodded, and they began to walk slowly in the direction they had been going before the disturbance.

Eli didn't follow immediately. Instead, he walked over to the struggling ghosthound and knelt just out of claw range, so that he was eye to enormous eye with the beast.

"I asked the trees to hold you until nightfall," he said, watching in amusement as the hound tried to snap at him. "You're no servant spirit, are you? I've never heard of a Spiritualist keeping a ghosthound in a ring, and no member of the Spirit Court would enslave a spirit against its will. So, I'm curious, why do you follow her? Did she save your life? Pull a thorn out of your paw?"

"Come a little closer," the hound growled, "and I'll tell you."

"Maybe later." Eli stood, brushing the dirt off his

knees. "I'm sure you'll be able to find us easily enough when you do get out, but I would suggest you look to your mistress first." He glanced over at the Spiritualist's crumpled body. "We humans are so fragile."

"Miranda is no weakling," Gin snapped. "She would not forgive me if I let you escape, especially now that we've seen the company you keep."

"Nico? Don't worry about her. We've got things well in hand on that count. Besides," he said, grinning, "she's our companion, as I suspect that Spiritualist is for you. Companions don't leave each other in the lurch."

He turned and started to jog after the others. "Think on what I said," he called over his shoulder.

Gin growled and snapped at the wizard's retreating back until he disappeared into the brush. When Eli was well out of sight, the hound flopped against the dirt, panting. The roots snickered above him, and he snarled menacingly, which just made them snicker harder. Gin laid his ears back and flicked an eye over at Miranda. She was still lying where she had fallen, crumpled on her stomach, face down in the dirt. She wasn't moving, but her shoulders rose and fell slightly, and that gave him hope. Gin watched her for a moment more and then, with a sigh, he began the long process of digging himself out.

Miranda woke up slowly, one muscle at a time. Everything hurt. There was dirt in her eyes and, she grimaced, her mouth. She coughed experimentally and immediately regretted it as the bruised muscles along her rib cage seized up in protest. She lay still for a moment, with her eyes clenched shut, concentrating on breathing without pain. The world was strangely still around her. She heard nothing except the normal sounds of the forest, crickets and frogs croaking in warm air and the evening wind in the trees high overhead. Gritting her teeth, she raised her hand and began wiping away the dirt. When she had cleaned as much as she could hope to, she cautiously opened her eyes.

Gin's face filled her vision and she jumped in surprise, waking a whole new round of aches. The ghosthound's eyes widened at her string of mumbled expletives, and he bent closer, his hot breath blowing more dirt into her face. She coughed again, wincing. Gin gave a low whimper and, to her great surprise, gently licked her face. Miranda couldn't stop her grimace as his wet tongue slipped over her cheek, but it helped with the caked-on dirt and she knew better than to complain over a rare show of affection.

"Thanks," she muttered.

The ghosthound flicked his ear and nudged his nose under her, helping her up.

"Thanks again," she said, sitting up slowly. Then she got her first good look at her companion, and her eyes went wide. "Powers, what happened to you?"

Gin was filthy. His front paws, muzzle, and stomach were black with dirt, and the rest of him was so covered with dust and debris she could barely see his patterns moving.

"The wizard trapped me," he said simply, "and I got out."

Miranda looked confused. "Trapped…"

Gin shifted to one side, and Miranda stared in amazement at what had been their neat, quiet, ambush-friendly clearing. It looked like a tree had exploded. Roots stuck out of the ground in every direction, some torn wide open, others in large knots. At the center was a deep ditch where the ground was furrowed with long claw marks. A

Gin-sized pile of dirt rested against the trees to her left, and Miranda began to put the picture together.

"No wonder we both look like a dirt spirit decided to give us a hug," she said. "You never could learn to dig cleanly."

"Ghosthounds aren't made for digging," Gin growled.

Miranda shook her head and dug her fingers into the dirty fur at his neck, pulling herself slowly to her feet. "Any idea where the king is?"

"West somewhat." Gin flicked an ear in that direction. "They're waiting for something."

Using Gin as a prop, Miranda bent over with a wince and picked up a piece of her stone spirit off the ground. "I'm surprised Durn hasn't reformed himself," she said, clutching the stone to her chest. "That girl must have given him quite a scare."

"You know what she is, then?" Gin asked, surprised.

Miranda nodded. "What kind of Spiritualist would I be if I didn't know a demonseed when I saw one? Especially after it tried to eat one of my servants. This might be my first time actually meeting one, but Master Banage made absolutely sure we knew what to do if we did."

Gin crinkled his dirty nose. "And what is that?"

"Nothing," Miranda said, stepping away.

"What!" Gin roared. "I don't know what kind of demonseeds he's talking about, but the kind I know, the kind that just took a chunk out of Durn, those eat spirits like I eat pigs. 'Nothing,'" he snorted. "The next time I see her..." He snapped his teeth.

"Don't even think about it, mutt," Miranda said, hobbling slowly around the clearing, picking up Durn's broken pieces. "Demonseeds are League business. If we want to stay in the Spirit Court, we don't interfere with the League of Storms. Besides," she said smiling sadly, "it's not like a Spiritualist could do much against her. Like you said, demonseeds gain their strength by eating spirits. If I did decide to fight her, the only weapon I have is you lot, and I'm not risking my spirits like that."

"You think so little of us—"

"Quite the opposite," Miranda said, shaking her head. "I'm sure that, if you put your mind to it, you could make her fight full force to defend herself, but look at it this way: If the girl can still maintain her human form, the demonseed inside her must still be small. However, if we offered it the chance to devour a larger spirit, say, a certain hot-headed dog, it might be enough to awaken her demon, and then where would we be?"

Gin bared his teeth. "Say what you want, but if I see a chance, I'm taking it. Any demonseed, no matter how small, is a danger to all spirits. Even the sleepiest, stupidest of us will try to kill one when we see it. I'm surprised Eli can talk to spirits if they know she's around. You'd think they'd want nothing to do with him."

"He must be hiding her somehow." Miranda frowned, piling the last bits of Durn in a circle on the ground. "You didn't sense her until she took a bite out of Durn, and your nose is sharper than most." She shook her head. "A wizard thief who uses only small-time spirits to kidnap kings, but travels with a hidden demonseed strong enough to damage my spirits and a master swordsman fast enough to counter your bite. This whole mission is one big knot of curiosities." She stood and dusted off her hands. "But it doesn't really matter. Next time I find that thief, I'm not going to take chances. I'm just going to fry him from behind. We'll see how he wiggles out of that."

Point made, she spread her hands over the collected pile of rubble that had been one of her most powerful spirits and closed her eyes. Durn's ring, a square of dark, cloudy emerald set in a yellow-gold band that took up the whole bottom joint of her left thumb, began to glow dully as she forced her own spirit energy through the stone. The energy flowed freely through the orderly pattern of the gem, calling gently to Durn's core. She felt his answer, weak and frightened, but there. Miranda sent a wave of power in response, the pulses repeating the pledge she'd made when she first bonded him—the exchange of power for service, strength for obedience, the sacred promise between spirit and Spiritualist that neither would ever abuse the other. With each pulse, the ring vibrated gently and began to glow. The rocks at her feet shook in answer, and then, at last, rolled together, matching their cracked edges and reforming until Durn himself sat crouched in front of her, his black, shiny surface dented but whole, and looking as ashamed as stone allowed.

"Forgive me, mistress," he rattled. "I failed you."

"There is nothing to forgive," Miranda said gently, running her fingers over his jagged edges. "I sent you into danger neither of us could have foreseen. You did well in the job I assigned you. Now it's time to come home."

Durn sighed against her skin, and then, with a sound like slag falling down a cliff, began to disintegrate. He broke first into small boulders, then gravel, and then dust that glowed silver in the afternoon sun as it drifted up into Miranda's open hands. She gathered him bit by bit into his ring, using her own spirit as a guide to fold him into the gem. When the last tendril of dust vanished, the emerald flashed faintly before dying out altogether as Miranda pushed him into a deep sleep.

"He'll recover," she said and sighed, twisting the ring over so the dark stone was against her palm. "But it'll be weeks before he's fit for anything except sleeping."

"It could have been worse," Gin offered, but she cut him off with a raised hand.

"I don't want to think about it. Let's focus on doing our job. Which way did they go?"

"This way." Gin stood up and turned with a swish of his tail, hopping over the remains of Eli's root trap.

Miranda hobbled after him, gritting her teeth against the pain in her bruised legs and side. "How far?"

"Less than a mile," Gin said, looking over his shoulder.

Miranda grabbed a broken root and, leaning her weight on it, hobbled faster. "I'm surprised you're not stalking them if they're that close. I could have caught up."

He gave her a long look as she limped forward pathetically. Then, with a sigh, he jumped back over the roots and flopped on the ground beside her. "Get on already, you're making me hurt just watching you."

Miranda grinned and tossed her improvised crutch aside, climbing up his back as fast as her aching muscles allowed.

"Anyway"—Gin lowered his head to his paws, which suddenly required his immediate attention—"I preferred to wait."

Miranda hid her smile in his fur as she made her way to her usual seat behind his ears. When she was settled, she nudged him with her boot. Gin rose and, together, they slunk westward through the trees.

In another world, a door opened in a white room. Or, rather, that was incorrect, for to say a door opened implies that a door existed. Nothing here existed if she did not will it, and she was not expecting the door. Still, it opened just the same, and a tall, angry man stepped into the perfect white nothing she lounged in, watching her sphere.

Her white eyes flicked over him, and a delicate sneer appeared on her flawless white face.

Why do you come when you are not summoned?

The angry man did not answer. He crossed the blankness with long strides and stood beside her, arms folded over his chest.

"He's doing it again." His voice was like distant thunder. "You have to put a stop to this."

What should you care?

The man's face grew even angrier, and his long fingers gripped the blue-wrapped sword at his hip. She smiled coyly. It was times like these, when his rages got the better of his sense, that she remembered why she treasured him still, despite his presumptions.

"With respect," he growled, "you created me to care. I spared your favorite's companion when he took in the demonseed. I even turned a blind eye when he gave her that triple-damned coat, but this is too far. The whole League just felt her attack a stone spirit, and yet you give no order to attack." His voice rose with each word, and small tongues of lightning began to crackle from the hand that gripped his sword hilt. "How am I to fulfill my purpose if you block me at every turn for the sake of your pet thief!"

He had barely finished when the empty whiteness pressed in around him, grabbing him in a vise of air and lead. The woman's coy smile never faded, but her anger thrilled through the emptiness until he felt the light itself burning his skin. Even then, he did not move, and his scowl did not change.

Eli is mine. The words were glass shards grinding through his mind. *You are not to go near him.*

"And should the demonseed awake?" he said, choking against the unrelenting pressure. "Am I to watch her devour the world and your precious Eli with it?!"

I have spoken!

The man staggered under her anger, dropping to one knee. Her white face softened, and she reached out to lay a snowy hand on his dark hair.

There, there, she cooed. *It will not come to that.* She slid her hand down his cheek and tilted his head up, her sharp nails digging into the tender flesh of his throat. *Have faith in me, my Lord of Storms.*

The dark-haired man shivered as his silver eyes locked with her white ones, unable to look away. Slowly, she leaned across the emptiness and laid a kiss sharp as broken ice on his trembling lips.

Now go. She pushed him away. *And do not return until summoned.*

Released from her grip, the Lord of Storms struggled to his feet, but the white woman's attention had already strayed back to the sphere that floated in front of her. It hung in the white nothingness like a rain drop frozen in the moment before it lands, and inside, a tiny, flat map of greens and blues, snowy mountains and glinting seas, revolved in absolute perfection under a cloud-strewn evening sky.

"As you ask," the dark-haired man said, bowing low, "Benehime." With those words he vanished from the white, empty world, leaving the lady to her delights as the door that was not a door closed behind him without a sound.

In the inmost chamber of a great stone fortress that stood alone on a sea cliff hundreds of miles from the nearest city of men, a thin, white line appeared on the soot-blackened wall, drowning the sputtering light of the oil lamps with snowblind brilliance. The man waiting there sprang to his feet, his long black coat falling around him like wings as the Lord of Storms stepped through the cut in reality and into his office.

The unworldly light had barely faded before he grabbed the sword from his side and flung it as hard as he could against the iron armor chest on the far wall.

"Damn that woman's moods!" he roared, and whirled to face the man who had been waiting for him. "Do you believe it, Alric? A blatant attack on a spirit and she still refuses to let me go anywhere near that thief and his damned demon!"

"But the seed has already eaten her down to skin and bone," Alric said, crossing the room to retrieve his master's cast-off sword. "With food like that, and unlimited time to consume it, the seed could reach full maturity before awakening. If that happens, we might not have the numbers to stop it, and it will be the Dead Mountain fiasco all over again."

"It won't come to that," the Lord of Storms said and began to pace the tiny room. "Have the League put up a watch for a hundred miles around the area where we felt the girl attack. Even if that blasted coat hides her when she's passive, it can't hide her when she uses the demon."

"You think she'll use it again in so short a period?" Alric handed him his sword. "Monpress has been very careful about that."

"It doesn't matter what the thief does." The Lord of Storms sat down on his desk and laid his sword across his knees. "No matter how careful he tries to be, the truth doesn't change. If he keeps letting the girl use her demon powers, then, sooner or later, the balance will tip. Once the awakening starts, nothing can stop it. Eventually, the demonseed will turn on him, and that infatuated woman will have no choice but to give the order."

"You say that," Alric said, frowning, "but a fully awakened demon is no small matter. We'll have to be extremely thorough if we want to keep the seed from regressing and switching hosts. What of the thief or his swordsman should they get in the way? They seem very attached to the demon's human shell."

The Lord of Storms unsheathed his sword with a ring of steel. "Killing the demon is all that matters," he said, admiring the blue silver blade with a bloodthirsty smile. "Everything else can burn to ash."

"Everything?" Alric arched an eyebrow.

The Lord of Storms swung his sword, his silver eyes lightning bright as he watched the air spirits flee before the blade. "Despite her whims, there are some rules even the Shepherdess can't afford to break, and the lady always finds a new favorite in time."

Alric bowed low. "We shall be ready. The League of Storms moves at your command."

The Lord of Storms nodded, and Alric slipped quietly out of the room. Closing the door behind him, he set off down the narrow hall to ready the League for the hunt.

CHAPTER
12

Josef leaned against the tall boulder that marked the outer ring of the clearing that he'd chosen as their trade-off point, sharpening his dagger. It didn't need the sharpening, but it was a good way to kill the time, and he had plenty of time to kill. Nico and the king were a few feet away, Nico looking thoughtful, the king looking terrified, standing at the very end of his tether. Eli was around the other side of the boulder, as he had been for the past half hour, talking to it animatedly. Josef ignored him when he could, focusing on the sound of the blade as it slid over the stone. Finally, the boulder rumbled gently, and Eli came around to Josef's side, looking very pleased with himself.

"Are you done gossiping with the scenery?" Josef said, holding his knife out in front of him to check the edge.

Eli rubbed his hands together. "For your information, I've just created a foolproof escape."

"From what?" Josef said sullenly. "There's nothing here. Are you sure your bird even made it?"

"Of course," Eli said, leaning on the rock face next to him. "The falcon told me he dropped it straight into a guard's dinner. They're just late. I'm sure the ransom will be showing up any moment now. In the meanwhile," he reached into his jacket pocket, "who's for a nice, friendly game of—"

"No." Josef's dagger landed with a thunk in the dirt less than an inch from Eli's boot. Eli glanced at the dagger, still quivering from the impact, and then back at the swordsman.

"You're oversharpening those."

Josef bent down to retrieve his knife. "I don't tell you how to wizard, so don't tell me how to fight."

Eli's eyebrows shot up. "I don't think you can use 'wizard' as a verb like that."

"And I don't see how your little tea party with a rock is going to cover our escape," Josef said, slamming the dagger back into his boot. "I guess we'll just have to trust each other."

Eli took a deep breath, preparing to point out all the ways that grammar and wizardry were different, but a look at Josef's expression told him it could be a bloody argument, mostly his blood, and he decided to leave it at that. Thankfully, that was the moment the riders appeared at the opposite edge of the clearing.

"Nico," Josef said, tightening the iron sword on his back as he and Eli took the forward positions. "Make sure his highness doesn't get any ideas."

Nico nodded and yanked the rope, knocking the king to his knees.

As Eli had the king specify in his instructions, there were only five riders. Three of them rode in a point

formation while the other two hung back, riding as a pair,
with an iron-bound, triple-locked chest slung between
their horses. Eli's grin widened. When they reached the
clearing's edge, one of the forward riders, a thickset balding man in polished armor, stood up in his saddle.

"Majesty!" he shouted. "Are you hurt?"

The king sprang up, jerking his tether. "Oban!"

Nico gave him a hard tug, and the king quickly sat
down again. "I'm fine! Just don't do anything stupid."

"We had no intention to, Henrith," the man at the point
of the formation said flatly, removing his helmet to let his
blond braid swing freely down his back. "This situation's
idiotic enough as it is."

The king stopped straining against Nico's hold.
"Renaud?" he whispered. All at once, he lunged forward,
fighting against the rope. "Renaud!" Nico slapped him
hard behind the knees, and he tumbled to the ground,
but his eyes were still on the blond rider. "What are you
doing here, brother?"

Eli glanced back. "I didn't know you had a brother."

"Not many outsiders do," Renaud said. He sat back on
his skittish horse, looking them over. "You must be Eli,
the thief."

"The very same." Eli smiled courteously, nodding
toward the reinforced chest. "And unless you're planning
on setting up house in the woods, *that* must be my gold."

Renaud raised his hand. At his signal, the soldiers
dismounted and began unlocking the chest. It took a full
minute to undo the locks and the three chains before the
soldiers threw back the lid and stepped aside. Eli licked
his lips. The chest was filled to the brim with sparkling,
oblong, golden coins.

"Five thousand council standards," Renaud said flatly. "As agreed."

"Ah," Eli said smiling. "And the other part of our bargain?"

Renaud took a tightly rolled scroll out of his saddle-bag. "It arrived by special courier this morning," he said, unfurling the paper. "The first one, straight from the Council's copy rooms."

Stretched between his hands was a bounty notice bearing an enormous likeness of Eli's face at its center and his name in block capitals across the top. Best of all, however, was the number stenciled across the bottom in thick black blocks: fifty-five thousand gold standards. Eli let out a low whistle.

Renaud rolled the notice back into a tube and tossed it casually on top of the piled gold. "Everything you wanted, exactly as promised. Now give me my brother."

"Gold first," Eli said, putting his hand on the king's rope.

Renaud nodded, and the third rider, a dark-haired swordsman with a scar across one side of his face, dismounted. He took the reins of the chest carriers and led them out to the center of the clearing, twenty feet from either party. There, he cut the straps, and the chest fell with a thud onto the dusty grass. He led the horses back to their riders and took his place again beside Renaud.

When he stopped completely, Eli nodded to Nico, and she released her death grip on the king's tether. Eli picked up the slack and twisted the rope around his arm until it was tight. Then he put his hand on the king's shoulder and, tied together, they started the slow, silent walk to the center of the circular field.

Five feet from the gold, Eli stopped. "All right," he

said slowly, "I'm going to let him walk forward. Any funny moves on your part, and"—he tugged the rope, nearly taking the king off his feet—"Got it?"

Renaud nodded, and Eli unclamped his hand from the king's shoulder. The king walked forward. As soon as he passed the gold, Eli reached for the chest.

He heard the spirit almost too late, and he jumped back just in time as a bolt of blue lightning shrieked inches from his face. He fell backward, tugging hard on the rope. The king came flailing after him, and they landed in a heap a few feet from the chest.

"That's enough," said a cold voice. The thick brush at the edge of the clearing rustled, and the enormous ghost-hound stepped into view, Miranda sitting high on his back. They were dirty, and Miranda looked like she was having trouble staying mounted, but the hand she pointed at Eli was steady as a stone, and the blue lightning arcing from the large aquamarine on her right middle finger was nothing to be flippant about.

Gin padded silently across the open ground. "I don't know how you dodged Skarest," Miranda said, and the lightning on her arm crackled angrily, "but the next shot will kill you before the girl can move." She shot Nico a glare before turning it on Eli. "Step away from the king and put your hands out where I can see them."

"What do you think you are doing, Miss Lyonette?" Renaud said, reining in his nervous horse.

"The Spirit Court is done playing politics, Renaud," she said. "My orders were to placate the local officials only if it did not interfere with my primary mission." She gave him a cold look. "Mellinor is free to deal with Mellinor's problems, prince, but this thief will answer to us.

Now," she continued and turned her glare back to Eli, and the lightning arced high above her head, "release your hostage and put out your hands, Mr. Monpress."

Eli got to his feet, smiling cockily. "And if I don't?"

"My orders are to apprehend you and bring you to the Rector Spiritualis." She smiled right back at him. "But they didn't specify what condition you had to be in when you got there."

Eli opened his mouth to reply, but Miranda never got to hear it, for at that moment, her lightning spirit discharged.

It happened instantly, as if some giant hand had plucked the lightning off her finger and hurled it across the clearing. The world became very still, and she could do nothing but watch in horror as Skarest arced through the air with an ear-ripping crack and struck the center of the king's chest. King Henrith convulsed and toppled to the ground, a thin wisp of smoke rising from his open mouth. Lightning sparked on her fingers as Skarest returned to his ring, and the spirit's fear racing through their connection made her blood run thin.

"Mistress!" he crackled. "He was too strong, mistress. I couldn't fight him!"

"Who?" Miranda shouted, but the spirit had buried himself in his ring.

The Mellinor group was frozen in shock, and even Eli was gaping at her. Only the prince kept his composure, turning on her with a look of triumphant hate.

"Foul murder!" Renaud shouted, breaking the stunned silence. "The Spiritualist has killed our king! She'll stop at nothing! Soldiers, attack! We won't let her sacrifice our king to catch her mark!"

His words were like a match in a hayloft, and they

were barely out his mouth before a wave of spearmen wearing House Allaze blue poured out of the brush behind him and charged the center of the clearing.

Master Oban started to ride with the charge toward his fallen king, but Renaud grabbed his horse's reins. "No, Oban! I'll handle this! Get back to the castle and tell the others!"

Oban shouted curses, but he turned his horse and rode madly back into the woods, parting the line of archers that was forming up on the clearing's edge.

"Kill them all!" Renaud shouted, waving the soldiers forward. "Avenge our king!"

The first volley of arrows launched with a ringing twang, and Miranda ducked low on her hound's back. "Gin!" she shouted. "Get to the king!"

"You sure?" he panted, launching forward as the arrows sailed over their heads. "I don't think it will do any good."

"Henrith's our only hope of salvaging this situation," she said, and her hand shot to her throat, clutching the pendant through her shirt. "Eril! Give us some cover!"

Even a wind spirit understands a real emergency, and Eril set to work with no backtalk, raising a thick dust storm in a matter of moments.

As soon as the lightning struck, Eli knew he had to get the money. He rolled the fallen king over and felt his throat. There was a pulse, erratic but strong, and he decided that was good enough. He stepped over the king and made a dash for the chest, reaching it just as the first wave of soldiers crashed into the clearing.

"Nico!" he shouted, ducking under the arrow that whizzed by his head. "Josef! Get to the boulder!"

He dropped to his knees and grabbed the chest, but as soon as he touched it, his stomach sank. The iron-bound chest was heavy, but not nearly heavy enough. He popped the three locks and flung it open, plunging his hand inside. His fingers barely made it past the top layer of coins before they hit the wooden false bottom. For a moment, he just sat there, staring, as the soldiers charged forward. Then, while more arrows struck the ground beside him, Eli carefully folded the bounty notice and put it in his pocket. When that was done, he slammed the trunk's lid and sprang forward, running toward where he'd last seen Renaud as an enormous, spirit-driven dust storm covered everything.

"Eli!" Josef shouted, squinting into the swirling dust. Get to the boulder? At this point he'd be lucky to find it. Voices shouted all around him, and he could hear the arrows whizzing overhead, but everywhere he looked, all he saw was dust. He didn't have to be a wizard to know the cloud wasn't natural. He just wished he knew which wizard it belonged to.

He felt someone behind him and whirled around, drawing his blade as he spun, only to find himself facing Nico. She pressed her pale lips together, cocking her head to peer quizzically at the sword point hovering beside her unguarded throat. "Jumpy?"

Josef sighed and lowered his sword. "How many times do I have to tell you not to do that? One day I might not stop in time, you know."

"I trust you," she said.

"Glad to hear it, but that doesn't change"—he chopped an arrow out of the air just before it struck her shoulder—"the situation."

A soldier loomed out of the dust behind her, his sword already falling. Without looking, Nico dropped to the ground, letting his overbalanced swing tip him forward. When he was halfway down, she shot up again, plunging her elbow into his unguarded stomach. The blow caught him right under his ribs, and he fell wheezing to the ground at Josef's feet.

"This is getting ridiculous," Josef said, kicking the fallen soldier's hands out from under him when he tried to get up. "Eli's probably already got the money. Let's just find him and—"

He froze. Nico looked up, confused. "And?"

With a whisper of steel, Josef drew his second sword. "Nico," he said quietly, "go find Eli. I'll catch up."

He caught her dark eyes and held them until she nodded and stepped away, disappearing instantly into the dust. He brought his swords up and turned to face the person he knew was standing there.

"Good guess," a voice said, floating on the swirling dust.

"Guess nothing," Josef said, stepping into a defensive stance. "I could follow a killing intent like yours blindfolded. Something you pick up when you live your life on the sword."

The swordsman with the scar across his face stepped out of the swirling dust. "I should have expected nothing less from *the* Josef Liechten." He laid his hand on the wrapped sword at his hip. "My name is Gerard Coriano," he said casually, as if they were meeting in a tavern rather than a battlefield, "and this"—he unhooked the wrapped sword, sheath and all, from his belt—"is Dunea. We are here to kill you."

"Is that so?" Josef said. "Why bother telling me your name then?"

"A final courtesy." Coriano smiled. "A true swordsman would want to die knowing the name of the man who killed him. Remember it well, Josef Liechten."

Josef's face broke into a feral grin. "I only remember things that deserve to be remembered. So, if you want me to remember your name, you'll have to make it worth my while."

Coriano held his wrapped sword out before him, the blade still in its wooden sheath. "When you're ready."

Gin led them straight through the dust to the fallen king. Miranda jumped down, gritting her teeth as the impact's force shot up her spine. The king was on his back, caked in yellow-brown dust. She kneeled beside him, pressing her fingers against his throat.

"He's alive," she said, her voice hoarse with relief. She slid her arms under his shoulders. "Help me get him up."

Gin lowered his head, and she rolled the king onto his long nose. When he was balanced, Gin lifted the unconscious man and, with Miranda's help, laid the king gently across his back.

She was getting ready to climb up herself when Gin growled low in his throat. He caught her eye, and she knew why.

"Lord Renaud," she said, turning around. "You're faster than expected."

Renaud stepped out of the swirling dust, a cocky smile on his handsome face. "Look at it from my perspective, lady. I see my brother's murderer stealing his body, is it so surprising I should hurry to stop her?"

"No, but not for the reasons you give." She brushed her fingers over her rings, calling her spirits awake. "Your brother is still alive, but I imagine you knew that, seeing how you were the one who flung Skarest at him."

"Skarest?" Renault folded his hands behind him. "Was that the little lightning bolt's name?"

Miranda's eyes widened. "You don't deny it?"

"Why should I?" Renault shrugged. "I am a wizard, controlling spirits is my right."

Miranda clenched her fists. "What you call your right we call enslavement, and it is an abomination. No spirit, human or otherwise, has the right to dominate another! Even if you hadn't tried to kill your brother, what you did to Skarest is crime enough to bring the whole Spirit Court down on your head!"

"Enslavement?" Renaud chuckled. "You Spiritualists were always very fond of giving things names, anything to set yourselves apart, to label your magic as right and everything else as wrong."

"Considering enslavement destroys the soul of the spirit it commands, I'd say it's a pretty clear-cut division."

"And what do I care for their souls?"

Miranda took a step back at the disgust in his voice, but Renaud stepped closer, ignoring Gin's warning growl as the prince closed the distance between them.

"We have our own souls to think of," he whispered, almost in her ear, and the cold hatred in his voice made her shiver. "In nature, it is the strong who dominate the weak, the strong who survive."

"Those rules don't apply to us, Renaud," Miranda said. "We're not animals! Only humans have the power to dominate another spirit. We have to—"

"It was the spirits who dominated me for most of my life!" Renaud snapped, eyes flashing. "It's because I was born with their voices talking in my ears that I lost everything to that idiot," he said and pointed to Henrith's smoking body sprawled on Gin's back.

"That's different."

"No!" Renaud roared. "No difference! I will take back tenfold what was taken from me. A hundredfold! It was the world that decided to make my will a weapon, Spiritualist, and I will use it bluntly, as it was intended. No rings, no pretensions, only my strength against the spirit's, my boot on its neck until it cries for mercy." He stepped closer still, clenching his fists beneath her chin. "I will take Mellinor from its weakling king," he growled. "I will take my inheritance with these hands, and then I will take dominion of the spirits from your weakling Court. I will return the world to its natural balance, with the wizard on top and the spirits below, and you"—he looked at Miranda with disgust—"you, with your hobbled power and your foolish pledge, will go down with the trash you've tied yourself to. A fitting end for a wizard who would not take her power."

Miranda jerked back, eyes flashing, but when she spoke, her voice was cold and sharp. "Bold words, enslaver," she said, holding up her right thumb, which was wearing a knuckle-sized ruby that was glowing like an ember. "But it will take more than the raving of a jilted prince to make me forget the truth of the vows I serve." She thrust out her hand, and the ruby began to smoke on her finger. "Perhaps you'd like to try your speech on another of my spirits? You'll have to speak quickly, though, because I don't think he'll listen as patiently as I did. Will you, Kirik?"

When she spoke the name, the wind around them died out completely. A flame winked to life above Miranda's fist. It hovered there for a split second, sputtering like a candle, and then, with a deafening roar, it exploded upward, growing into an enormous column of fire that reached the sky. Any dust it touched vanished, burned to cinders in an instant. The column surrounded Miranda on all sides, the heat pouring off it in waves until even Renaud was forced to step back and put up his hands to shield his face.

"What's the matter, enslaver?" Miranda crowed from behind the wall of flame. "Weren't you going to put your boot on his neck?"

If Renaud answered, it was lost in Kirik's crackling laughter. Grinning triumphantly, Miranda raised her voice to command the attack.

Just before she spoke the words, the prince fell to his knees. Miranda squinted against Kirik's bright light. No, Renaud hadn't fallen; he'd sunk up to his thighs in the sandy ground. As she watched, more sand poured up his chest, pinning his arms and pulling him toward the ground. He struggled frantically, but for every handful of sand he tossed away, five more took its place. Within seconds he was buried up to his shoulders, completely trapped in the shifting, buzzing ground.

"So sorry," said a smug voice.

Miranda whirled around, her eyes wide and astonished as a gangly, dark-haired figure stepped out of the dust. "Can't have any of that." He snapped his fingers and a torrent of water shot up from the ground at his feet.

Miranda had no time to react, no time to do anything except stare stupidly as the water arched through the air and struck her fire spirit full on. Kirik roared and steamed, but there was nothing he could do against the endless deluge. The column of flame shrank to an ember in the space of a breath, and Miranda barely managed to pull him back into his ring before the water extinguished him altogether.

For the next few moments, Miranda was so furious she couldn't do more than sputter and clutch the dimly glowing ruby on her thumb. When she did find her voice, however, she made up for lost time.

"What do you think you are doing?!" she roared so violently that even Gin flinched back.

Eli raised his hands. "Easy, Lady Spiritualist, I couldn't let you bake him just yet. You see"—he glared down at Renaud, still pinned by the dirt—"this man still owes me some money."

If possible, Miranda looked even angrier. "He tried to kill his brother, enslaved my spirit, threatened the entire spirit world, and you're worried about *money*?"

"Of course." Eli looked at her innocently. "I'm a thief. What else is there for me to worry about?"

"You could start worrying about your hide," she growled, "because I'm about to flay it off you."

"Charming!" Eli said, grinning. "But give me two seconds first. I need to make a point." He crouched down in the dirt beside Renaud. "Hello, Lord Whoever-You-Are. I don't know if you've heard of me, but I'm Eli Monpress, the greatest thief in the world."

Eli put his arm around Renaud's sand-covered shoulder. "I'm going to let you in on a secret. I didn't get to be the greatest thief in the world by letting hack wizards like you cheat me out of my hard-earned money. However,

I'm a generous man, so I'm going to offer you a choice: Either you give me my money or I take it from you. Now, while five thousand may seem like a hefty sum, please take my word on this"—he smiled sweetly—"you don't want me in your treasury."

Renaud's eyes widened. "Aren't you the pair?" he said, spitting the sand out of his mouth. "The thief and the officer of the Spirit Court working together."

"We're not together!" Miranda shouted. "Enough of this nonsense! Gin, bite the thief's head off."

Gin charged forward, but all he got was a mouthful of sand as the ground in front of Eli sprang up to protect him.

"An impressive spirit, Mr. Monpress," Miranda said as Gin coughed up dirt.

"Oh, it's not mine," Eli said, grinning. "This particular stretch of ground was getting frustrated that a certain Spiritualist's wind spirit was whipping bits of it up into the air. I simply offered to help it stop the wind if it helped me."

Miranda stared at him in disbelief. "You offered? What, you mean you just had a chat with the ground, without opening your spirit or having a servant spirit to mediate, and it listened, just like that?"

Eli shrugged. "More or less."

"Don't be stupid," she scoffed. "You can't just sit down and talk to the ground."

"Some of us don't need slaves or servants to get things done," he said.

Miranda sputtered, but Renaud burst out laughing. Miranda and Eli both turned to stare at him, but the prince paid no mind, laughing until he was nearly choking on the sandy dirt.

"That's it?" he said when he could speak again. *"That's* the famous Eli's great secret that every bounty hunter is after? You just asked?"

Eli arched an eyebrow at him. "I don't see how it's so hard to believe. Most spirits are very obliging when you're not trying to crush them into submission. But you wouldn't know much about that, from what I hear." He straightened up. "Now, are you going to play nicely, or do I need to ask the dirt for another favor?"

The ground around Renaud began to snicker, but the smile on the prince's face did not change. "As grateful as I am to you for the opportunities you've given me, I'm afraid my thanks are all you're going to get, Mr. Monpress."

"Oh?" Eli crossed his arms over his chest. "Does that mean you choose the 'Eli takes the money from you' option?"

Renaud's smile widened. "Let me show you how a true wizard works."

Still chuckling, he closed his eyes and, for a moment, nothing happened. Then Renaud opened his spirit, and everything changed.

This wasn't the controlled opening Miranda had done earlier. Renaud threw his spirit wide for the world to see, and the strength of it was wholly unexpected. Miranda barely had time to register what was happening before it hit her. She fell to her knees, gasping for breath as the full pressure of Renaud's soul landed on her. Her rings cut into her fingers as her spirits writhed under the weight. Behind her, she heard Gin whimpering as he fought it, but even the ghosthound was forced to the ground in the end. Miranda gritted her teeth and focused on dampening the panic shooting up the link she shared with her spirits, but they were already beaten down. Another wave of pressure hit, and she gasped as it slammed her into the ground.

Spitting out dirt, she forced her head to turn, and she caught something out of the corner of her eye. Eli was still standing beside her, arms crossed just like before, as if nothing was happening, but the cocky smile on his face had vanished.

The sand trapping Renaud burst outward, the grains cutting Miranda's skin. The prince stepped calmly out of the crater he had made and looked over to where Gin lay pinned with the king's body still slung over the arch of his back. His hand went to his pocket, and when he spoke, his words pulsed through his opened spirit, battering over Miranda like iron waves.

"I've been saving this since I left the desert and returned to Allaze. I was waiting to use it on my brother, if I ever got the chance." He grinned at Eli. "Now that you have made me king, I won't be needing it anymore. Such a pity." His mad grin grew deadly. "I will miss collecting your bounty."

Eli glared at him. "And why's that?"

"Because once I'm done cleaning this clearing, there won't be enough of you left to turn in."

"Sounds like a stupid waste of fifty-five thousand standards to me," Eli said. "And if that false-bottomed chest was any indication, you could use the gold."

"Yes," Renaud cackled, "but as another of your kind once told me, there are some things that are worth more than money."

His eyes flicked away from Eli's incredulous expression and came to rest on Miranda, who was still fighting to raise her head. "Watch and learn, Spiritualist," he whispered, holding out his clenched fist. "*This* is how you master a spirit."

He opened his fist and a small, dark, glittering sphere dropped from his fingers. At first, Miranda thought it was a kind of black pearl, like the pearl she kept Eril in, but as it fell, the ball began to disintegrate, and as it broke apart, the sphere began to scream.

CHAPTER
13

Josef struck hard and fast, bringing his twin blades down one after the other so that there was no pause between strikes. Coriano blocked each blow on his sheathed sword, his scarred face bored and impassive. Josef tried striking low, high, and both sides at once, testing for weaknesses, but every blow was knocked aside with the same easy indifference, no matter how fast he struck. Finally, Josef tried a wild attack, striking high and low simultaneously while leaving his middle deliberately unguarded. The other swordsman ducked the high blow, slid the low off his wooden sheath, and ignored the easy opening all together. After that, Josef lowered his swords and stepped back.

"I'm sorry," he said, wiping the sweaty dust out of his eyes with the back of his hand, "but if we're going to fight, you have to do more than block. It also helps if you draw your sword, I'm told."

Coriano planted his sheathed blade in the dirt and

leaned on it. "I'll draw my sword when you draw yours."

"I don't get what you mean," Josef said, swinging his twin blades in a whistling arc.

"Well," Coriano said, straightening up. "If that's the case, I'm going to have to start breaking your toys until you do."

Josef opened his mouth to say something rude, but before he had taken a breath, Coriano was there, his sheathed sword pressed deep into Josef's stomach. Josef went sprawling in the dirt, and only years of training brought his swords up in time to block the next blow before it landed on his head. If Coriano's blocks had been fast before, his blows were in another category altogether. The next one fell before Josef realized the scarred man had lifted his blade, and the force slammed Josef into the ground. A cloud of dust shot up at the impact, and a long crack appeared in the wooden sheath of Coriano's sword. Sprawled on his back, Josef brought both swords in a cross over his chest, blocking the next blow on both blades, inches from his face. Coriano's cracked sheath shattered on impact, sending wood flying in every direction, and Josef found himself staring down the blade of the most beautiful sword he had ever seen.

It was pure white from tip to guard, unembellished, except for a slight wavering shimmer along the sharpened edge that glittered like new snow in the dusty light. The hilt was wrapped in blood-red silk, but the bright color paled beneath the sword's cold, dancing light.

"River of White Snow," Coriano whispered. "Dunea."

He pushed down, and the shimmering white edge cut through Josef's crossed blades like paper to bury itself in the swordsman's chest. Pain exploded where the blade bit down, darkening his vision, and Josef gasped, forcing his lungs to work. Coriano only smiled and pushed his blade farther, clearly intending to pin Josef to the dirt like a butterfly on a board. With a desperate heave, Josef flung the hilt of his broken blade at the swordsman's face, aiming for his scarred eye. Coriano jumped back, and Josef scrambled to his feet, clutching his chest with one hand and the remaining broken blade with the other.

It was still hard to see, and every breath hurt like another stab, but Josef forced himself to be calm. The cut was small but deep, sticking right below the sternum. It hadn't hit his heart, and it hadn't hit his lungs, but it was bleeding in a torrent down his shirt.

Coriano looked him over casually, the white sword balanced perfectly in his hands. "No time for licking wounds," he said, and lunged.

Josef tossed his ruined sword on the ground and drew a short blade from his belt just in time to parry. However, his parry turned into a rolling dodge as Coriano's white sword snapped the knife neatly in two without losing speed or direction. The white edge simply cut through the metal like it was not there.

Josef rolled to his feet again and shakily drew another blade from his boot. Coriano gave him a scornful look.

"Come now," he said. "Surely you don't intend to keep insulting us with your dull blades?" He whirled his sword, and Josef could almost hear the snowy blade singing as it cut the air. "You must have realized what she is by now. Why do you not draw your sword?"

Josef's hand went to the hilt of the great iron sword on his back. Coriano's grin grew delighted, and he brought

Dunea back to her ready position as Josef's hand gripped the wrapped handle. As he began to lift the iron blade, his fingers turned deftly and his hand flew out, flashing silver. Coriano sliced the first knife out of the air, but he was a hair too slow for the second. The throwing knife grazed his shoulder as he dodged, leaving a long, bloody gash.

Josef straightened up with an enormous grin on his face and three more knives fanned between his fingers. "Not yet," he said, tossing a knife and catching it in his free hand. "I'm not out of things to throw at you."

Coriano gritted his teeth, but as he leaned forward for another lunge, his posture changed. Just before kicking off, he stopped and shivered like a cat dipped in cold water. Josef lowered his knives a fraction and watched in confusion as the other swordsman clutched his sword to his chest like it was a frightened child. The wizard wind driving the storm around them died as suddenly as it had begun, and the dust fell to the ground with unnatural speed, as if something was pressing it down.

"That idiot," Coriano whispered, clutching his sword as the white light flew in wild patterns across the blade. "That short-sighted, power-drunk fool."

Josef shifted his weight, easing the knives between his fingers, waiting to see what kind of ruse this was, but the scarred swordsman lowered his sword and gave a little bow. "We'll have to finish this another time, Mr. Liechten," he said with annoyance. "Things are about to become very unpleasant. If your Eli has an escape set up, I suggest you use it."

"You can't be serious," Josef said. "You can't run now; we were just getting started!"

Coriano smiled back at him. "I have tracked you for a very long time, too long to waste my one chance on a wizard's stupidity. Don't worry, we'll meet again very soon. Then, Mr. Liechten, I promise, I will make you draw the Heart of War."

"Wait," Josef called out, but Coriano was walking away through the falling dust. Josef hurled his knife into the dirt a finger's width from the scarred man's feet. "I said wait!"

But Coriano kept walking, disappearing like a shadow into the trees at the clearing's edge. Josef ran after him for a few steps, but the pain was too much. Clutching his burning chest, he reached into his pocket with a grimace and pulled out one of the long strips of cloth he kept for occasions like this. He wrapped it around his chest, binding the wound as tight as he could. The angle was awkward, but it stemmed the bleeding for now. He could have Nico redo it later, if there was a later. The wound was quickly dropping down his list of priorities. There was a ringing growing in his ears, a high-pitched wail just out of his hearing. It reminded him of the dull buzzing he heard in Eli's voice whenever the wizard talked to rocks or trees or whatever he wasted his time with—only this was more frantic, and it was getting louder.

As the dust cleared completely, he could see Nico on the other side of the circular clearing standing over a pile of groaning soldiers. She was looking away from him, watching something. He followed her gaze and saw Eli. Their thief was standing over the downed Spiritualist and her dog, who looked to be out of the fight, but Eli's attention was on the tall, blond leader of the Mellinor troops, who was the only other person besides themselves still standing as the dust settled. The man was saying something, but all Josef could hear was that high-pitched whine, more like a pressure than a sound. Then the man opened his fist and everything went to hell.

The scream shot through her, driving everything else from Miranda's mind. Only the sharp pain of her bruises and the feel of grit in her mouth told her she was writhing in the dirt. Still, her eyes were open, and she watched in horror as the screaming sphere broke apart completely, becoming a black cloud of glittering particles. A cloud that was growing.

"Miranda," Eli said, his voice cutting cleanly through the panic. She barely felt his hands as he grabbed her shoulders and dragged her to her feet, but his voice was clear and commanding. Somewhere in her garbled mind, she realized that he was speaking to her like she was a spirit. "Leave right now."

He let her go, and she nearly toppled over. Only Gin's cold nose pressed into her back kept her from falling.

"He's right," the hound whined, ears flat. "That thing is insane. We leave now."

Miranda opened her mouth to protest, but Gin didn't give her a chance. He ran for the forest with Miranda clutched like a pup between his teeth and the still-unconscious king bouncing on his back. Miranda was screaming something about Eli, but the hound didn't stop, and he never once looked back.

As soon as the ghosthound disappeared into the woods, Eli turned and ran as hard as he could in the other direction, nearly colliding with Josef and Nico.

"What are you doing?" Eli yelled, grabbing them both. "I told you to get to the boulder!" He did a double take when he saw the bloodstain across most of Josef's shirt. "What happened to you?"

"Never mind that!" Josef shouted. "Where's the gold?"

"I'll explain later!" Eli shouted back, yanking them both toward the rock at the clearing's edge. "Just run!"

Josef nodded and started running. If the situation was serious enough for Eli to abandon cash, then this was not the time to argue. They tore across the clearing, ignoring the growing roar behind them. Even Josef could hear it now, a high-pitched screaming that rubbed his nerves raw. It was like an injured child's scream, but there was nothing human in this sound and it did not stop for breath. Josef shuddered and kept running.

Eli was shouting at the rock even before they reached the clearing's edge. However, the rock didn't seem to be answering, because Eli slid to a halt just in front of it and started to gesture frantically as a dark shadow fell across them.

Josef whirled around, grabbing one of his remaining knives just so he didn't have to face whatever it was empty-handed. But even a blade in his hand didn't make him feel better when he saw what was behind them. Across the clearing, an enormous tower of black cloud loomed over the blasted ground where Renaud had been standing only moments ago. Billows of dark dust, black and glistening like volcanic glass, spun impossibly fast in the windless sky, rising in great swirls that blotted out the sun. As if it had been waiting for him to turn around, the cloud's wailing reached a frantic pitch, and it began to move forward.

"Eli," Josef said over his shoulder, "whatever you're doing, could you do it a little faster?"

Eli gave him a biting look before turning back to the boulder. Josef backed up a step, pressing Nico into the stone. The cloud was not heading at them directly. Instead, it skirted the edge of the clearing, keeping close to the forest. The trees leaned back when the billowing black dust came near, lifting their branches high in the air, as if they were trying to get out of its way. Then the screaming storm touched a tree that had the misfortune of growing too far out, and Josef saw why. As soon as the spinning black gusts connected with the branches, they disintegrated. The cyclone passed over the tree as if it were not there, reducing it to sawdust without effort or notice, and without slowing its progress toward the huddled group by the boulder.

"Eli," Josef said again, "now would be good."

"Got it!" Eli shouted. "All right, *go*!"

"Go where?!" Josef yelled frantically. The cloud was almost on top of them, filling his vision from ground to sky. That was the last thing he saw before the rock swallowed him.

CHAPTER
14

Miranda didn't realize she had passed out until she woke up sore, stiff, dirty, and uncomfortably damp. She was propped on Gin's paw, and as soon as she moved, his long snout filled her vision.

"How are you feeling?"

Miranda thought about it, and winced. "Like someone's beaten me, eaten me, and thrown me up again."

She ignored his disgusted look and pulled herself up by his fur. "That went well," she muttered, cleaning the grit out of her mouth with a less dirty corner of her riding coat. "Somehow, I'm not surprised Coriano was there. I'd love to know what that enslaver's paying him to make him toss out his good reputation with the Spirit Court."

"I don't think it's always about money with that one," Gin said thoughtfully. "He smells more of blood than gold to me."

Miranda grimaced. "Well, that's a problem for later," on top of the mountain of problems they already faced.

"Right now, we've got to figure out what we're going to do about Renaud."

Gin laid his ears back. "Men like that don't deserve to be wizards. Sandstorms may be stupid, but no spirit deserves what he did. It's even worse than being eaten by a demon. At least then you're just dead rather than jabbering insane and balled up in some maniac's pocket."

Miranda looked up. "Is it still around?"

"I can't hear it, but that's no guarantee he didn't put it back in his pocket."

Miranda groaned and rubbed her temples. "An enslaver with an ax to grind and a throne to grind it on, it doesn't get much worse than that."

"Wait," Gin said. "What about that Banage thing? The thing he sent us here to stop Eli from getting?"

Miranda blanched. "Gregorn's Pillar..." She put her knuckles to her mouth, thinking madly. "No," she said at last. "I don't think he knows about it. Gregorn's Pillar is a pretty obscure piece of wizarding history. Banage wasn't even sure Eli knew about it, but it was the only thing he could think of that Monpress would want from Mellinor. Anyway, Renaud was a jilted wizard in the castle for sixteen years. If he knew about the Pillar, he would have enslaved his way to it years ago, wouldn't he?"

"I'd think so," Gin said. "But can we count on that? I mean, I'm pretty good against enslavers usually, but Renaud had me down in the dust before I knew what was happening. He's got a strong soul, and he's not afraid to use it full tilt. Now, that's bad enough, but if that pillar is half of what Banage made it out to be, Renaud really will be able to put the spirit world under his boot if he gets his hands on it."

"That may be true," Miranda said and nodded, pulling

herself up by his fur. "But Renaud getting the pillar is not a possibility we can handle, so there's no point in dwelling on it. Let's just focus on getting him off the throne quickly before he figures out what's in his treasury."

"It should be simple enough," Gin said. "Jump the gates, eat the prince, and get out." He snapped his teeth. "An enslaver is only human, after all."

"Out of the question." Miranda shook her head. "We'd just get flattened again if we tried a direct attack."

Gin snorted, and Miranda ignored him, pacing little nervous circles around the hound's paws. "What we need is help," she said. "But there's no time to send to the Spirit Court for backup, and with all of Mellinor thinking I murdered their king, we'll get no aid from—" She stopped suddenly, looking around. "Wait a minute, where *is* the king?"

"He's here," Gin said. "He's actually been awake for some time. I didn't want to bother you, so I asked him to wait."

Miranda stared, confused. "You asked him to wait?"

"Yes." The hound grinned, showing all of his teeth. "Nicely."

Miranda put her aching head in her hands. "Gin, let him up."

Gin feigned innocence for a few more seconds and then lifted his back rear paw, allowing the king, who at this point looked more like a pig farmer with a good tailor than royalty, to wiggle his way to freedom.

"Honestly," Miranda said and sighed, giving her companion a final glare before running to help the dirt-caked monarch. "As if things weren't bad enough."

Gin lowered his head and began cleaning the mud off his paws, completely unconcerned.

The king's clothes were nearly black with dirt, and if he'd had a jacket, he'd lost it somewhere, leaving him with nothing but the thin, dirty remains of a white linen shirt that had a large burn mark down the center where Skarest had hit him. Miranda winced at that, and at the marked resemblance between him and his brother. There hadn't been time to get a good look at him in the clearing, but now that the king was crouched in front of her, the family connection was painfully obvious. The two men had the same long build and blond hair, though Henrith's was nearly brown with dirt at this point. Also, the king's face was much rounder than the prince's, a trait that was emphasized by the dusty, overgrown beard that covered nearly all of his lower face after a week away from the royal barber. When he looked up to see who was helping him, his eyes were the same as Renaud's. The fear that shone in them, however, was new.

As soon as he recognized her face, he bolted for the trees.

"Wait!" Miranda shouted, jumping to block his way.

The king made a break in the other direction, but Gin stuck his leg out at the last moment, sending the king sprawling into the dirt yet again. Miranda ran to help him up.

"Your Majesty," she pleaded, helping him turn over. "I am Miranda Lyonette of the Spirit Court. I'm here to help!"

"Help?" the king sputtered, smacking her hands away. "*Help*!? You shot me!"

Miranda winced, but held her position, standing so that the king was stuck between her and Gin. "I know how this sounds, but you must believe me when I say that that was not my lightning bolt."

"Really?" the king shouted, pointing at his singed chest. "It felt real enough to me!"

"Just listen," Miranda said, crouching down to a less threatening height. "That was my lightning spirit, but he wasn't acting on my command. Your brother, Renaud, is an enslaver, a kind of wizard who uses the raw strength of his soul to force weaker spirits to do his bidding. He took my lightning spirit to make it look like I tried to kill you and he is now using the situation to usurp your throne."

The king looked at her blankly. "An ensla-what?"

"An enslaver," Miranda repeated. When comprehension failed to dawn on the king's face, she added, "A bad wizard."

Gin chuckled at the simplification, and the king, assuming the noise was aimed at him, went scarlet. "And I suppose it was Renaud who told your dog to sit on me," he said, pointing accusingly at Gin's nose.

"Unfortunately, that was his own idea," Miranda growled. "But it was for your own protection!" she added quickly.

The king crouched in the dirt, eyeing her suspiciously. Carefully, Miranda sat down across from him, trying to look as meek and harmless as she could.

"I know you don't have much cause to like wizards right now," she said gently, "but I will swear any oath you like that I am on your side."

"My side?" the king snapped. "You wizards ruined everything! How can you expect me to believe that you could possibly be on my side?"

Miranda answered honestly. "Because in this situation the fact that I'm a wizard makes me your greatest ally." She held up her dirty hands where her rings still glittered dully. "I'm a member of the Spirit Court. That means I took an oath to preserve the balance between spirit and man, and to do all I could to prevent the abuse of either. Without the Spirit Court's rules to guide him, your brother has turned to enslavement, forcing his will on the world and doing permanent damage to the spirits he abuses. By my oaths, by my life, I cannot let him continue."

She finished, looking as earnest as possible, and the king scratched his dirty beard thoughtfully. "It's that serious, is it?"

"Let me put it this way." Miranda leaned a little closer. "I was sent here on express orders to stop Eli before he did anything to ruin the reputation of wizards any more than he already has. But if it came down to bringing Renaud in to stand trial or catching Eli red-handed, I'd take Renaud in a heartbeat. I would be stripped of my spirits if I didn't."

The king eyed her suspiciously. "I'm still not convinced, but let's just say I don't find your story of Renaud's betrayal all that unbelievable."

Miranda bit her lip. "I understand it is difficult for you to hear these things of your brother—"

"Not so difficult as you might imagine." The king sighed, plopping down in the dirt. "You forget, I grew up with the bastard. He was mother's favorite, no question, and he knew it. Father had nothing to do with us before we were old enough to hunt, so Renaud ran things for most of my childhood. It's safe to say I don't find it hard to believe that he misuses his magic."

Miranda's eyes widened. "You knew he was a wizard?"

"Oh no, not in the beginning," Henrith said, waving dismissively. "But when it came out, I wasn't surprised.

He was always going on about his birthright and his inheritance and the proper way of things, but he never seemed very interested in the business of being king. Father didn't quite know what to do with him. Frankly, I think my brother scared him a little. It's always been my suspicion that he was secretly relieved when Renaud turned out to be a wizard and gave him a chance to reorder the succession." The king gave her a long wink. "I was always father's favorite."

Miranda suppressed the urge to roll her eyes.

"Anyway, I'm not surprised that he was so quick to come in and take command, either," the king continued. "Ever since father died, I've been hearing rumors that Renaud was hiding somewhere in Allaze. It's been my theory for years that he would appear the moment he saw a chance."

"And Eli handed him that chance on a string," Miranda said hotly. "You may be more right than you realize. Renaud was in the palace the day after you were taken. That's suspiciously fast, even for an ambitious opportunist. I'll bet Eli was in on this from the beginning."

"No," the king said, vehemently shaking his head. "Renaud and Monpress are not the kind who would work together."

"But how can you know?"

"Believe me," the king answered. "I spent twelve years as brother to one and a week as prisoner to the other. Both stints were plenty long enough for me to know that much at least."

Miranda sighed. "If that's true, then Eli's actions are almost worse. If he was working for someone, that would at least show some forethought, but to just charge recklessly into a country and overturn the balance of power like this, with no attention to the consequences…" She shook her head. "He's lucky Master Banage wants him alive, or I'd kill him myself."

The king nodded approvingly at that sentiment. "Well, if you are on my side, what do we do now?"

Miranda tapped her fingers against her chin thoughtfully. "Let's look at our situation. I saw Oban get out, so I think we can safely assume that everyone at the palace thinks you're dead, and that I killed you. Your brother's control of the castle depends on them continuing to think that. That screaming black cloud was his way of erasing the evidence, but I'd bet Eli's bounty that he's taken steps to make sure there's a plausible story in place, just in case you did survive."

"That'd be easy enough," the king said. "All of Mellinor's heard the same stories about wizards. They'd never believe I wasn't a phantom you conjured if we tried to gather allies."

"A phantom?" Miranda frowned. "Where did you get *that* idea?"

"It was in a book," Henrith said. "It's banned, but everyone's read it. *Morticime's Travels* or something."

Miranda suddenly had a splitting headache. "Morticime Kant's *A Wizarde's Travels*?"

"Yes," Henrith said, laughing, "that's the one! Oban's son and I used to sneak it around under our armor and read it when our tutors thought we were studying. I haven't thought about it in years."

Miranda didn't have the energy for the rage she could feel building, so she put the whole affair out of her mind and focused instead on her spirits. Eril had come racing back the moment Renaud had opened his spirit, but he was curled up in his pearl in a deep sleep and traumatized beyond usefulness. Skarest had locked himself away, Durn was still recovering, and Kirik was little better than an ember. Her resources were looking grim indeed.

"You have no idea how much I hate to say this," she said slowly, "but I think we need some outside help."

The king frowned. "You mean send a message to an ally country? Get your spirit-whatever to send more wizards? But that will—"

"Take too long, I know." Miranda stood up. "That's not the kind of outside help I had in mind." She looked over at her companion. "Gin?"

The ghosthound glanced up from his grooming. "If you're asking what I think you're asking, the answer is yes, back the way we came."

"Good." She walked over and began pulling herself onto his back. "Let's be quick about it, then. We've wasted too much time already." She settled herself on his neck and patted the fur behind her. "Climb up, Your Majesty, time is wasting."

The king looked at the hound in horror. "Climb?"

The word was barely out of his mouth before the ghosthound lurched into action. Gin moved like lightning, plucking the king off the ground with a long claw and tossing him in the air. He landed in a heap on the hound's back, and Miranda righted him just in time as Gin set off through the woods at a full run. The king clung to the shifting fur, yelping in terror as the trees flew by, too busy trying not to fall off to ask where they were going. That suited Miranda just fine. As hard as this was for her, it was going to be ten times worse for him. Better to explain it when they arrived and he couldn't get out of it. She grimaced and gripped Gin's fur tightly. No matter how she sliced it, this was going to be some bitter bread to swallow indeed.

The sun had dropped to the horizon by the time the rock spit Eli, Josef, and Nico in a tumble on the dusty ground. Nico landed gracefully. Eli landed on top of Josef.

"I don't believe it," Josef grunted, shoving Eli off. "*That* was your great escape plan? Hide inside a rock?"

"It worked, didn't it?" Eli snapped back. "Besides, do you have any idea how hard it was to convince that boulder to hide Nico in the first place? *Before* the other nonsense sent it into a panic?"

"Maybe if it wasn't such a stupid idea to begin with, you wouldn't have had so much trouble pulling it—*ow*." Josef snatched back the fist he'd been hammering on the ground to make his point. "What the—?"

Nico took his hand before he could mangle it further and deftly pulled a long, glass splinter out of his palm.

"Where did that come from?" He glared at the glass, then at Nico. Nico just shrugged and nodded over his shoulder. Josef turned, and his eyes went wide. The forest, the piebald grass of the clearing, the injured soldiers, the broken weapons, the arrows—they were all gone. The three of them were at the center of a smooth, black dust bowl that bore no resemblance at all to the clearing they had left just a few hours earlier. The dust lay in undulating patterns, ground so fine that the slightest breeze stirred up a miniature tornado. Other than their rock, nothing else remained, not even the natural slope of the ground.

A hundred feet back from its original position, the forest started again, but the new tree line was unnaturally straight. Some trees were missing limbs; others had entire sections of their trunks ripped away. The damage was surgically clean, as if some giant had taken a razor and simply cut away a circle of the forest using their rock as a center mark.

"I take it back," Josef muttered. "The rock was a great idea. How did you know it would be the only survivor?"

"I didn't," Eli said, leaning in to examine the stone's face.

The boulder itself looked worse for wear. Long, sharp-edged gashes pitted the stone's surface. When Eli brushed his hand over them, a shower of glass dislodged and toppled to the ground, raising a sparkling cloud that sent them all into painful coughing fits.

When he could speak again, Josef asked, "What was that thing, anyway?"

"A sandstorm spirit," Eli wheezed.

"I've never seen a sandstorm that could do this."

"Normally, it couldn't," Eli said, covering his mouth with his hand. "But this one wasn't in its right mind. Did you see that Ronald guy drop the sphere?"

"Renaud," Nico corrected, casually pulling glass splinters out of her coat.

"Whatever," Eli said. "That ball wasn't a gem or anything you normally store a spirit in. It *was* the spirit. He used his will to overpower the sandstorm, like a bully crushing ants together. He forced it to press itself down into that tiny ball, and what do you get when you put sand under high pressure?"

Nico held up one of the dark glass shards.

"Exactly," Eli said and nodded. "Compressing it into a size he could carry around completely altered the spirit's form. Considering the color, he's probably had it like that for a very long time." He frowned, and his next words were uncharacteristically gentle. "It must have been very painful for the storm."

"Well, if it hurt so much, why didn't the spirit just escape?" Josef said, leaning over to knock the glass dust out of his hair. "I've never been clear on all this wizard talk, but a sandstorm's a lot bigger than he is. Couldn't it have just up and run?"

"It's not that simple," Eli said. "A sandstorm isn't a whole spirit to start with, not like other spirits. A rock, for example, has been a rock for a long time. It may have been part of a mountain in the past, but it's always been stone. The rock's spirit has a strong sense of identity. It's fully developed. Sandstorms are different. They're born when air spirits and sand spirits rub each other the wrong way, kind of like a spirit brawl. As the sand is thrown up into the air, both spirits merge into one violent storm. Eventually, they blow their anger out and the sand falls back down, separating the spirits again, but while they're fighting, the sand and air spirits together are a sandstorm spirit. Believe me, neither side is very happy about it. Storms like that are impossible to talk to.

"Unfortunately," Eli continued, "storms like that are also very stupid. Both spirits are battling for control of the storm, so there's a lot of raw spirit power, but no control. That's probably why Renaud was able to dominate it so completely. It didn't have the presence of mind to resist."

"So where is the storm now?" Josef said. "Did he roll it back into a ball and take it with him?"

"No," Eli said, shaking his head. "If there's anything left, we're standing on it." He nudged the sand gently with his foot, stirring up a small cloud of glitter. "Once a spirit degrades that far, it's only good for one last blow. Renaud knew that, so he used the last of its self-control as a leash to sic it on us, and then left it to blow itself out, taking all the evidence of his double cross with it." Eli ran his finger delicately over one of the long scars on the rock face. "It would have worked too, if not for my brilliant plan."

"Very brilliant," Josef said stiffly, pressing his injured chest. "Where's Renaud now, then?"

"Back at the palace, I'd say." Eli nodded toward the spires that poked above the treetops, dark and flat against the evening sky. "Princes who have just overthrown their brothers probably have better things to do than wait around for the likes of us. Maybe we should—"

He stopped as a strong wind blew across the clearing, swirling the loose glass dust into a biting whirlwind. Eli, Josef, and Nico huddled in the lee of the stone, trying not to breathe.

"Well, I think that does it," Eli wheezed when the wind finally died down. "Cowering in a glass dust bath with no gold, no king, and no easy way to get either. This is, officially, our worst job ever."

"It was your idea," Josef said. He dug out one of his spare bandages and tied it over his mouth. "Here," he said and handed one to Nico and another to Eli. "Let's go."

They secured the cloth over their faces and began their trek out of the dustbowl. It took much longer than it should have, for the dust was knee deep in places and so fine it got under their improvised masks within minutes, caking anywhere there was moisture. The bloody front of Josef's shirt was black with it, and even Nico grimaced when it got in her nose. The dusty circle was deathly silent. In the forest ahead, crickets chirped and evening birds called out, but inside the clearing the only sound was the shuffle of their feet sliding through the dust and the wheezing of their own labored breathing.

"Faster," Eli mumbled, trying to speak without opening his mouth. They picked up the pace, and by the time they reached the forest's edge, they were almost running.

As soon as they reached the trees, they tore off their masks and collapsed panting on the ground.

"There should be a stream or something around here," Eli said, spitting the dust out of his mouth. "If I don't get this mess off me soon, I'll be Eli jerky."

A leather canteen flew through the darkness and landed with a wet slap as his feet. Eli jumped back with a sound that was half obscenity, half squeal. Josef whirled in the direction the canteen had come from, blades out. In the last dim light, a pair of amused orange eyes flashed down from the shadows.

Eli recovered in the blink of an eye, slouching into a carefully nonchalant pose. "How long were you waiting?"

"Long enough," Miranda said, not fooled for a moment by his sudden cool attitude. Below her, Gin choked back a laugh. "You can call off your pet swordsman. My intentions are peaceful for the moment."

Josef looked nonplussed at his new title, but he put the knives away. Eli just grinned. "Such assurances!" He waved at the king sitting behind her. "Hello, Your Majesty! Couldn't live without us, could you?"

The king went scarlet and opened his mouth to protest, but Miranda cut him off. "You will refrain from harassing King Henrith any further, Mr. Monpress." Her voice would have frozen a boiling pot.

Eli gave her a wink and reached for the canteen. "So, Miss Spiritualist, to what do we owe the honor of this peaceful chat?"

Miranda folded her arms over her chest. "I want to know what your plans are for fixing this mess you've made."

"I'm afraid I don't know what you are talking about," Eli said, and took a long drink. "I'm just a thief."

"Just a thief?" Miranda gave him an incredulous look. "You kidnapped the king of a council kingdom."

"I was going to give him back," Eli said, splashing a handful of water on his face. He took another swig and then passed the canteen to Josef. "Actually, that makes me better than a thief, since they don't normally return what they steal." He grinned. "I guess I'm moving up in the world."

"I don't care what you were *going* to do. I care about what you *did*." Miranda leaned forward, resting her elbow on Gin's forehead. "Did it not cross your mind, even for a second, what kidnapping a king might do to his country?"

"For your information, I chose Henrith very carefully. How was I supposed to know he had a crazy wizard brother?"

"If you used half the time you spend talking on research, you would have known Mellinor's entire family tree," Miranda snapped. "Now, because of your shameful incompetence, that 'crazy wizard brother,' who also happens to be an enslaver and an attempted murderer, is in spitting distance of the throne, and it's All. Your. Fault."

"Now hold on," Eli said. "You can't blame all that on me."

"By the Powers, I can!" Henrith yelled. "Everything was fine before you came! Even Renaud stayed in line. Then you appear and turn things upside down and expect us to let you walk away?"

Josef finished his swig and handed the canteen to Nico. "I understand Dusty's concern." He nodded to the king, who fumed. "But I don't understand why you're involved." He fixed his eyes on Miranda. "You were sent here to catch Eli, right? So why aren't you attacking us and leaving the king to fend for himself? Mellinor doesn't even like wizards. Why should the Spirit Court care who's on the throne?"

"Because an enslaver king is bad for everyone," Miranda said. "He cannot be allowed to secure his power."

"Seems to me like you've already got the answer to that." Josef looked at the king.

"It's not that simple," Miranda said. "Renaud wouldn't take a chance on this brother surviving without some kind of cover. Henrith tells me that Renaud has probably already convinced the masters that anyone resembling Henrith who approaches the castle is a phantom I've summoned to trick them."

"A phantom?" Eli cackled. "Where did they get *that* idea?"

"Don't ask," Miranda grumbled. "Anyway, suffice it to say the direct approach is out of the question, but the Spirit Court cannot allow an enslaver access to a kingdom's power. We learned that lesson with Gregorn. Master Banage would back Henrith's claim, but the people of Mellinor would never believe it wasn't a Spiritualist trick. Whatever way we go, Mellinor will be thrown into conflict either with the Spiritualists, the Council forces, or itself. War is bad enough, but war with an enslaver involved?" She shuddered. "Imagine rivers used as soldiers, armies of trees, an infantry of bonfires, and all of them left mad at the end, no matter which way the fighting went. That mad sandstorm was nothing compared to what Renaud could do if he had the reason. We can't let that happen."

"Well, that sounds dreadful," Eli said. "I'm still failing to see what this has to do with us."

"It has everything to do with you!" Miranda shouted. "Who do you think started all of this? Everything in Mellinor was perfectly fine for four hundred years. Four hundred! That's four centuries without a coup, a rebellion, or any problems bigger than a trade dispute, until you three showed up."

"That's a bit unfair," Eli said and frowned. "We only—"

"I don't care!" Miranda rolled right over him. "I don't care what you wanted or how it was supposed to turn out. No matter what spin you put on it, this whole country is about to go to hell because of *you* and *your* stupid plan to bilk forty thousand gold standards by destabilizing a peaceful kingdom. So, what I want to know, Mr. Greatest-Thief-In-The-World, is what do you mean to do about it?"

Eli looked from the fuming Spiritualist to the king and back again. He turned to Josef, who shrugged, then Nico, who was trying to get the last drops of water out of the canteen, and his shoulders slumped.

"All right," he said. "I admit that things might not have gone exactly as I would have liked, but perhaps we can come to an arrangement." His smile was back as he looked up at Miranda. "Say I agree to help you, what exactly would you be asking us to do?"

"Our primary objective is to apprehend Renaud," Miranda said, nodding toward the castle, which was now lost in the evening gloom. "After that, returning Henrith to his throne will be easy."

"And you'd want our help on the apprehending part," Eli said, tapping his finger against his belt idly. "That's a tall order. Renaud's pretty strong."

"Strong, yes," Miranda said, "but surely a man with a fifty-five-thousand-gold bounty on his head is plenty strong in his own right."

"Such flattery is dangerous for a humble man like myself." Eli grinned, and Josef rolled his eyes. "But I'm a thief, Miss Spiritualist, not an assassin. Robbing him blind is one thing, but confronting him outright?" He shook his head. "I'm afraid you'll have to sweeten the deal."

"How do you mean?"

Eli put on his best innocent look. "I do feel somewhat responsible for the current state of affairs in Mellinor, and I am a man who takes his responsibilities very seriously. That's why I'm going to offer you our services at a very reasonable rate."

Miranda's eyes narrowed. "I'm not going to pay you to do what you should be doing in the first place."

"Oh, not money." Eli waved his hand. "Nothing like that. Just a small trade of favors. I help you, you help me."

"If you want me to talk to the Council about your bounty—"

"Powers, no!" Eli laughed. "You couldn't change a

thing even if I did want it. My favor is much, much simpler. You see, right now I'm wanted by both the Spirit Court and the Council of Thrones for different infractions. Two posters, two listings in the bounty roster, two payouts. It's all very impractical. All I want you to do is convince the Spirit Court to combine its reward of five thousand standards with the Council's. No extra money needed, just a tiny administrative change."

Miranda kept her eye on him as she went over the words in her head, looking for the catch. "But that would raise your bounty to..."

"Sixty thousand." Eli reached in his pocket and pulled out his new wanted poster. "It's really too bad," he sighed, unfolding it. "They just copied out all these new ones. I think it's their best likeness of me yet."

He tried to hand the poster to Miranda, but she held up her hand. "Stop. You're up to something."

Eli blinked innocently, but Miranda leaned forward on Gin's head, keeping her eyes pinned on his. "Asking Mellinor to pledge money, I can understand. That gives them a thirty-five-thousand-gold stake in making sure you don't get caught. But the Spirit Council won't stop chasing you no matter what it costs. You know this, so why raise your bounty? Don't you realize that every gold standard draws another ten bounty hunters out of the woodwork? Sixty thousand is enough money to bankroll a small war. Your own mother would turn you in for half as much."

"I don't doubt she would." Eli's grin grew wicked. "But you're missing the point, Lady Spiritualist. It's not about the bounty hunters or extorting countries. It's about the bounty. It's about a little boy's dream!" He threw out his arms. "Sixty thousand is nothing. Chump change! My goal is to be worth one million gold."

Miranda's eyes widened. "One million? Are you crazy? There's not that much money in the world! The Council's war with the Immortal Empress didn't cost half so much, and they're still paying it off. Even if you kidnapped a king a week, you'd die of old age before you got your bounty that high."

"Well," Eli said, "if that's how you feel, how can you object to a trifle like moving the Spirit Court's five thousand?"

Miranda hunched over Gin's head, glaring suspiciously at the grinning thief. "Why a million?"

Eli shrugged. "Seemed like a good number. No one's ever had a million-gold bounty."

Miranda gave him a scathing look. "It can't be that simple."

"I never said it was, but you're free to make up your own reasons if it'll make you feel better." He shoved his hands in his pockets and looked up at her, his face unbearably smug. "Time's ticking, Miss Spiritualist. Do we have a deal or not?"

Miranda knotted her hands in Gin's fur, thinking. Henrith shifted uneasily behind her while the hound kept a close eye on Nico, who hadn't done anything except sit on the ground and watch the show. Finally, the Spiritualist gave a long sigh.

"All right," she said. "I'm sure I'll regret this, but you have a deal, Mr. Monpress. If you help apprehend Renaud *and* put Henrith safely back on his throne, I will talk to the Rector Spiritualis about transferring our bounty on you to the Council. However"—she stabbed her index finger at him—"even though, at the moment, I'm looking the other way for the sake of the greater good, my orders to bring you in have not changed. When we are done here, I'm not going to stop chasing you."

Eli smiled graciously. "I expected nothing less."

Miranda blinked, thrown off balance by his sudden sincerity. "Well, that's settled then."

Josef pushed himself off the tree. "If you two are done chatting, we'd better get moving. Sitting out in the dark on the edge of the clearing where we were almost killed isn't a good place to talk strategy. Besides"—he slapped his neck—"I'm being eaten alive out here."

Now that he mentioned it, Miranda could feel them too. "Lead on," she mumbled, slapping one of the biting midges off her hand.

When she looked up, the swordsman was already stalking off through the trees. The demonseed girl followed a few steps behind, silent as a shadow. Eli strolled along at his own pace with his hands in his pockets, whistling something off key.

Miranda exchanged glances with the king. At last he gave a resigned nod, and she nudged Gin with her toe. The ghosthound rose soundlessly. Quiet as his namesake, he slipped through the trees, keeping abreast with the swordsman but well away from the girl who followed him. High overhead, the moon was beginning its climb through the black sky, illuminating their winding path through the rocky hills and steep gullies of the deer park with her clear, white light.

CHAPTER
15

*T*his is where you were hiding?" Miranda gaped, sliding off Gin's back. The moonlight that filtered through the treetops was just enough for her to be able to make out the tumbledown walls and gaping roof of the small hunting shack. "You could barely spend a night in this."

"It's a bit run down," Eli admitted, "but"—he leaned over and pointed through a gap in the surrounding trees— "you can't beat the location."

Looking where he pointed, she could just spot the white walls of the city glowing silver through the trees, barely half a mile away.

"I don't believe it," Miranda said.

"First rule of thievery," Eli said, grinning, "only run if you're not coming back." He thumped his heels on the hard ground. "The last place a man looks is under his feet."

"All this time you've been hiding in the king's deer

park?" She was almost laughing now. "You're putting me on. I had Eril search this area days ago."

"Spirits don't see everything," Eli said. "Besides, I had some excellent camouflage." He tilted his head back. "Ladies?"

The pleasant purr of his spirit voice reverberated through her. High overhead, a chorus of sighs answered, "Eli!"

Miranda took a step back as the trees behind the cabin, a clump of young hardwoods taking advantage of the tiny clearing's sunlight, shook themselves to life. They bent down, giggling like geese, and surrounded Eli in a nest of branches. He said something low, and they giggled harder before lifting away and settling lightly over the ruined roof. They rustled madly, fluffing their broad leaves over the gaping holes and forming a sort of net over the fire hole to diffuse the smoke. When they stopped moving at last, Miranda's eyes widened. The young trees covered the hut perfectly. In fact, had she not seen them move, she would have sworn that the hovel was just another rocky outcropping, and that the trees had always been that way.

"Welcome," Eli said, slipping between the branches with practiced ease and opening the rickety wooden door. Josef followed him, clutching his injured chest and grumbling under his breath the whole way. Nico went into the hut last, pulling her coat tight around her and her hat down over her eyes as she squeezed between the branches. Only when they were all inside and she saw the first sparks of a fire being struck did Miranda begin to untie her own bag from Gin's back.

King Henrith had just made it to the ground. He

looked at the hut with no small amount of panic in his eyes. "What should I do?"

"For now, go in," Miranda said, struggling with the leather straps. "We have a deal, and I don't think he'll go back on it. After all, you're no profit to him now."

The king grimaced. "That's supposed to be comforting?"

"With a thief like him, it's the most comforting thing you'll hear. Go in, I'll follow in a moment."

The king hovered a moment longer and then timidly made his way into the hut.

"Can't really blame him," Miranda said as the king's shadow joined the others' around the infant fire. "It's not exactly a place of pleasant memories, considering what he's been through."

Gin snorted, sending a wave of dead leaves scurrying across the grass. "What kind of wizard starts a fire with rocks?"

"The same kind who flirts with trees, apparently." Miranda worked the pack free at last and set it on the ground beside her. "No wonder he was so hard to track. Half the spirits in this clearing are in love with him. It's like that stupid door all over again."

Gin rolled his eyes, but stayed oddly silent. Miranda walked over to his head and began to scratch his ears. "How does he do it?" she murmured. "How does he get them to just, I don't know"—she shrugged—"do what he says?"

"There's something about him," the ghosthound said quietly. "He's got a sort of brightness."

Miranda kept scratching, listening carefully. Spirits, even talkative ones like Gin, almost never talked about the spirit world. She'd tried to cajole information out of him on uncountable occasions, but every time he refused, saying it would be too difficult, like trying to describe the color red to a blind child. Some things, he would growl, you just had to see for yourself.

When he didn't continue on his own, she tried a delicate prompt. "Brightness? Like sunlight?"

"No," Gin said, "not like light through the eyes. Bright, like something beautiful." He shook himself and stood up. "Leave off, I'm no good at this. He's just got a light around him, all right? And spirits are attracted to light. Interpret as you will. I'm going to get some food. Be back in a few hours."

Then he was gone. It happened so quickly, she barely felt his fur slip between her fingers before he vanished into the night. Miranda stood for a long while where he had left her, looking up at the full moon with her eyes closed tightly, trying to imagine what light not like light through the eyes looked like. Only when Eli yelled something about dinner did she finally go into the cabin.

"All right," Eli said, rubbing his hands together. "What's the plan?"

They were seated in two factions on either side of the fire, Miranda and the king against one wall, Eli against the other. Josef was lying flat on his back in the far corner, gripping the hilt of his iron sword while Nico hovered over him, treating the nasty gash in his chest. She had finished cleaning the glass sand out of it by the time Miranda entered and was now stitching the skin back together. From Josef's bored expression, she might as well have been doing needlepoint next to him rather than *in* him, and Miranda was impressed in spite of herself.

Eli's question seemed aimed at no one in particular, but when no one answered, Miranda took it upon herself. "A frontal assault is out of the question," she said. "Renaud will be on high alert. He also has a master swordsman, as we saw, so there's that to think about." She nodded slightly at Josef, who either didn't notice or didn't care. "I just wish we knew what other enslaved spirits he had."

Eli shrugged. "Well, he can't have too many enormous, mad spirits just lying around."

"We can't count on that," Josef said. "I'm not a wizard, but even I can tell the man's obviously powerful. I mean, no offense, Miss Spiritualist, but he had you squirming in the sand the minute he got serious."

Miranda blushed scarlet. "Do not postulate where you do not understand, swordsman," she snapped.

Josef looked at Eli, who was doing his best not to laugh. "Don't be prickly, Miranda," Eli said. "He didn't mean anything by it. Do you want to tell him, or should I?"

Miranda looked away, fuming. "I don't see why it needs to be explained at all. He won't understand it."

Josef's glare matched her own. "Try me."

Miranda tugged a hand through her hair. "Fine," she growled. "It's not exactly a secret." She held up her hand so that her rings glittered in the shaky firelight. "Wizards can impose their will over spirits. That's one of the basic principles behind magic. The other, of course, is that our control does not extend over other human souls. That's why most people feel only a slightly uncomfortable pressure when a wizard opens their spirit, no matter how strong the wizard is. Spiritualists, however, are different, because we maintain a constant bond through our rings with our servant spirits. Each of my spirits siphons off a small, steady stream of energy from my soul as per our agreement when they became my servants."

"Power for service," Eli said, with mock seriousness. "Strength for obedience."

Miranda ignored him. "Most of the time, this connection is one way. But sometimes, for example, when a powerful wizard opens his spirit full tilt right in front of them, my servant spirits are affected like any other spirit, and that can cause feedback through our connection."

"So what does that mean?" Josef said.

Eli beat Miranda to it. "It means normal humans may feel a bit queasy when a wizard's open soul is pressing against them, but it can't hurt us, so we don't go all weak at the knees about it. Spiritualists, however, are tied into their pet spirits waking and sleeping, and when those spirits are squashed under a strong wizard's will, like Renaud's, the Spiritualist," he said and made a squishing motion with his hands, "goes right down with them."

Miranda shook her head, but Josef nodded. "Hell of a weakness. How does the Spirit Court fight an enslaver, then?"

"A strong, loyal fire spirit is usually enough," Miranda said. "They're so chaotic that most enslavers can't get control before they're burned. My Kirik would have been perfect had *someone*"—she glared murderously at Eli— "not doused him."

"How was I supposed to know he'd go out so quickly?"

Josef shook his head. "Well, that's out. Is there any other way around the problem?"

"No," said Miranda.

"Yes," said Eli.

She whirled to face him. "What do you mean?"

Eli shrugged. "Your rings are what give you trouble, right? So take them off. Seems simple to me."

"*Take them off?*" Miranda looked incredulous. "I can't just take them off!"

"Well, how else do you think you're going to be able to come into the castle with us?" Eli said.

"Maybe you can get by sweet-talking trees and doors," she huffed, "but I'm not leaving my spirits. I'll be defenseless!"

"Can't be worse than what happened before," Josef said. "I'm sure your wiggling on the ground really intimidated Renaud. Might and majesty of the Spirit Court and all that."

"There's no other way, Miranda," Eli cut in. "We need your help in this, and we can't go in if we can't count on you not to fall over when things get sticky."

Miranda looked at the king, who looked thoroughly lost in all this spirit talk. When he saw her looking, he smiled trustingly, and she heaved a long sigh. With great difficulty, she reached down and pulled off her rings one by one, laying them gently on the ground in front of her. She pulled Eril's pendant over her head and added him to the pile. Lastly, she slipped the Spirit Court signet off her left ring finger and laid it reverently beside the others, the heavy gold glowing warmly in the firelight.

Next, she dug around in her knapsack for the doeskin bag all Spiritualists kept for just this purpose. Her fingers felt uncomfortably light and naked as she dropped her rings one at a time into the soft leather pouch. It was a tight fit—no Spiritualist expects to have to remove all of their rings at once—but after a few tries she managed to wedge everything in and knot the bag closed with a red silk cord. Out of the glittering pile of rings, she'd kept only one. A small opal band, almost like a child's promise ring, remained on her left pinky. Her glare dared anyone to comment as she tucked the bulging doeskin bag back into her knapsack.

"Okay," Eli said, rubbing his hands together as Miranda settled back into her spot by the fire. "Now that we're serious, here's the real plan."

CHAPTER
16

The throne room of castle Allaze was as dark and forbidding as its prisons. The sun had set hours ago, but the lamps were still not lit. No one had let the servants in to light them. At the base of the dais stairs, below the empty throne, the masters of Mellinor stood in a loose circle around a balding man whose dust-streaked armor matched his tear-stained face.

"Friends," Master Oban said, his strong voice wavering, "as many times as you have me tell it, the story won't change. I saw with my own two eyes the Spiritualist's lightning strike our king. I watched him fall!"

"I thought the lightning was pointed at the thief?" an official in the back called out, sparking a new torrent of comments.

"Impossible!"

"Master Oban, are you sure you saw—"

"The real issue here—"

"—waited far too long—"

"—always said it was a trap—"

"—greatest tragedy of our times, that's what they'll say, and on our watch—"

"Enough," said the old Master of the Courts. "Leave Master Oban be."

The masters' chatter stopped immediately, and the dark room fell silent as the elderly master motioned for Oban to step aside. The Master of Security made way immediately, and the Master of the Courts took his place at the center of the circle. "We can't deny it any longer," the Master of the Courts said. "We have to accept that the Spiritualist used us. Perhaps it is as Lord Renaud theorized and she was in league with the thief from the very beginning, or perhaps not. Whatever the circumstances, we are to blame."

"It was awful convenient, her showing up not an hour after the king's disappearance," said a young, minor official, elbowing his way forward. "I for one always believed she was up to something. Why would a wizard come to Mellinor, except to cause trouble?" He glared at the old men. "The only wizard we can trust is Lord Renaud. Even banished, he tried his best to save his brother!"

"But where is the body?" another official shouted back. "Where is our king?"

This raised a new round of shouting, and it was several minutes before the Master of the Courts regained control. "Silence," he growled, staring down the younger members who were still miming punches at each other. He looked pointedly at Master Oban, who nodded, then at Master Litell, the thin Master of the Exchequer, who looked away. Satisfied, he spoke the words they'd all been waiting for. "In the four hundred years since her founding, Mellinor's succession has never once been compromised. After hearing your opinions, divided as they may be, I think we can all agree on one point: If tradition must change, it will not be with us."

The masters began to murmur again, but the Master of the Courts silenced them with a wave of his hand. "The discussion is over, send him in."

A young official broke from the circle and ran to the side parlor. His knuckles had barely touched the wooden door before Renaud flung it open. He was already clothed from chin to toes in mourning black, and his pale face seemed to float through the darkened hall of its own accord. The circle opened up as he approached, until only the Master of the Courts stood between him and the empty throne.

The Master of the Courts watched Renaud warily. For a moment, he seemed on the verge of sending the prince away again, but in the end, the Master bowed his head.

"Prince Renaud," he said, "it is with a heavy heart that we call you here, but in times of uncertainty the kingdom must not be even one day without its ruler. Therefore, it is the agreement of this emergency council that the crown should pass from father to son, brother to brother, as it has always been."

Renaud bowed solemnly, but there was a twinkle of delight hidden in his blue eyes. When he stepped forward, however, the Master of the Courts held up his hand.

"Yet," the master said, and Renaud's eyes darkened, "in the absence of King Henrith's body, you must understand our predicament. Should, by some miracle, King Henrith be found alive, all titles will revert immediately to him, as is his right."

"I would expect nothing more," Renaud said, laying his hand gently on the old man's shoulder. "Henrith was my brother and my king as well, as dear to me as my own flesh, even in my exile. Still"—his eyes moved gravely across the circle of faces—"we must not let false hope take root. Miranda Lyonette is a powerful Spiritualist, and the Spirit Court is not an organization to leave such things to chance. I have long speculated that her initial goal was to kill King Henrith in the hopes of bringing me to the throne. She, no doubt, believed that a fellow wizard would be more sympathetic to the Spirit Court's demands. Only when I rebuked her for the cruel murder of my kinsman did she realize her mistake. Now, I fear she may try to conjure up a phantom of my brother to trick you and turn us against each other, throwing Mellinor into confusion so that the Spirit Court's agents can sneak in."

Master Oban went pale. "You mean, it's not a story? Wizards can really do that? Create apparitions?"

Renaud nodded gravely. "False images, but real enough to touch." He grabbed the Master of Security's shoulder with his other hand, and the older man shrank away, shivering. "Our only defense is watchfulness," he continued, looking each master in the eyes in turn. "I have sent word to the outposts, but I am sure she will try to strike at the castle, where she's had success before. If you or any of the people below you see anyone resembling the late king, he must be brought to me immediately. The Spiritualist must not be allowed to spread fear and uncertainty among us."

The officials mumbled to each other, sometimes agreement, sometimes displeasure, but no one dared speak up. Renaud silenced them with a look. "We begin the seven days of mourning at sunrise. Go and make your preparations."

The circle scattered, but as they walked away, Renaud added. "Master Litell, another moment, if you please."

The elderly Master of the Exchequer froze and looked timidly over his shoulder. Renaud beckoned, and Litell returned without further protest. A few of the younger officials hung back, trying for a few words with their new king, but he waved them away, and they left the throne room like rejected puppies. When the last one shuffled through the great, golden doors, Renaud turned and gave the Master of the Exchequer his most pleasant smile.

"I need you to let me into the treasury."

"Now?" Litell rubbed his hands together nervously. "If my lord wishes to review the books, I have the country's balances in my office. I can wake my assistant—"

"I trust your accounts," Renaud said. "But what I need to see can be found only in the treasury. You have the key, do you not?"

"Entrusted to me by your father," Litell said, clutching the heavy chain at his neck. "But I'll have to call someone to help with the doors..."

"Do it," Renaud said. "There is something I need to confirm as soon as possible."

Master Litell jumped at his sudden sharpness, but did as he was told. Renaud followed him out of the throne room and down the steep stairs that led to the oldest part of the castle. Neither man noticed the shadow that followed silently behind them.

It took half an hour and twenty guardsmen to get the treasury open. Master Litell spent the entire time apologizing.

"I am so dreadfully sorry for the delay," he puffed, standing back as the soldiers heaved again. "That door hasn't been opened in thirty years at least, not since your mother's dower was added. Your father and brother never cared much for the historical pieces."

They were standing in a long hall deep beneath what was now the prison, but once, hundreds of years ago, had been the heart of the palace Allaze, built by Gregorn himself. The smoke-stained walls were still covered in undulating mosaics that, in the unsteady light of the guards' lamps, seemed to rise and swell like black waves on an underground sea. Renaud, however, saw nothing except the solid slab of iron as wide as the hall itself, set flush against the bare stone. The great treasury door was triple barred, each man-sized lock marked with the deep graven seal of Mellinor.

At last, with a bone-crunching scrape, the team of guards twisted the last great lock open. Unbound, the door swung slowly inward, picking up momentum as its weight dragged it into the blackness of the long-sealed room. Master Litell sprang forward, taking a torch from the guard captain and holding it aloft at the gaping entry. The glitter of gold bounced back to meet him.

"Everything looks to be in order." Master Litell handed the torch back to the guard and walked over to Renaud, taking a large stack of papers from a waiting page. "Your Majesty will of course want to see the inventory. Now, everything in the treasury is sorted by date, but you'll need this list…"

His voice faded as Renaud marched past him.

"That won't be necessary, Master Litell." The new king seized a torch of his own from one of the guards. "I know what I'm looking for. Wait here."

With that he turned and walked into treasury, leaving

Master Litell and the guards to watch from the threshold as Renaud's torch bobbed out of sight behind the maze of ancient trunks and dusty gold.

Coriano sat in the shadows for a long time, pondering what to do. Following Renaud to the treasury had been easy enough, so had slipping past the guards gawking at the entrance. But now Renaud, after walking past cabinets stuffed with silks, chests of gold, and racks of ancient weapons, had stopped in front of what was perhaps the least interesting part of the whole affair, and he had been staring at it for the last twenty minutes. They were at the center of the treasury where the shelves opened up to make room for what looked to be a support pillar. The pillar, however, failed in that regard, for it stopped ten feet short of the cavernous ceiling. Its knobby, uneven surface glittered dully where Renaud's torchlight landed. Otherwise, it was completely unexceptional, rising without fanfare from the undecorated stone floor.

Patient as he was, Coriano was growing bored. Also, there was something in the air here. Maybe it was being so deep in the earth, close to the great, sleeping spirits on which the world rested, but the room felt thick with dormant energy. It made him uncomfortable, and the sooner he got out to cleaner, younger air, the better he would feel. After another minute of watching Renaud watch the pillar, Coriano decided it was time to make himself known.

He stepped forward, deliberately scraping his boots against the smooth, dusty floor. Renaud stiffened and whirled around, holding his torch aloft. When he saw Coriano, his eyes narrowed. "You."

Coriano leaned against a heavy trunk that skirted the

edge of the empty space around the pillar and gave the new king a dry smile. "Me."

Renaud's scowl grew more menacing. "How did you get in here? Why have you come back?"

"How I got here isn't important, because I could do it twenty times again, each time a different way." Coriano's voice was dry as the air. He picked up a small gold lion from the case beside him and examined it with bored interest. "As for the why, I wasn't aware our bargain was complete. You got what you wanted, but I seem to have come up short."

"You must be mistaken." Renaud smiled politely. "I paid you before we left."

"The money is incidental," Coriano said, putting the lion down again. "I mean our real bargain."

"Our agreement was that you would take care of the swordsman if I prevented Eli's interference, which I did," Renaud said. "If anything, I should be the one complaining. I gave you Josef Liechten on a platter. You were the one who decided to run away."

"I would hardly call a three-minute fight in a dust storm followed by the release of a mad spirit 'on a platter,'" Coriano said, sneering. "But I wasn't the only one who let his quarry escape, was I?"

Renaud stiffened. "If you're talking about my brother—"

"Your brother?" Coriano shook his head. "No, no, I'm sure you've got that quite under control. I'm talking about Eli."

"Eli?" Renaud started to laugh. "You think I'm worried about that hack thief? The one who trades favors with dirt spirits? For all his posturing, he ran at the first sign of trouble. I'm only sorry I bothered to put any gold in the chest at all."

Coriano wasn't laughing. "You've been planning this for a long time, Renaud. You watched for weakness and jumped with both feet when you saw your chance. I respect that, so let me give you some advice. Eli didn't get to where he is now by being a fool, and he didn't get there by letting ambitious idiots like you cheat him."

Renaud's face grew murderous in the torchlight. "Such praise." He spat the words, "If I didn't know better, I would think he was your real target, not the swordsman."

"Eli is the one who makes Josef Liechten difficult to pin," Coriano said, laying his hand on his sword. "Only a stupid man doesn't respect his opponent's strengths, and if there's one thing Eli is good at, it's never showing up when you want him and always showing up when you don't."

"Sounds like someone else I know," Renaud said.

"Really?" Coriano's mouth twitched. "Then consider what I'm about to say very carefully. I was able to sneak into the castle, past all your guards, right into your treasury, where I waited twenty minutes for you to notice me. Had I struck at any point, you would have been dead before you felt the blow, and all this treasure would be mine." He slammed his hand down on the cabinet beside him and the resounding crack echoed through the cavern. "If I could do all this," he said in the silence that followed, "Eli could do it. Only he could do it faster, quieter, and with more backup. So think very hard before you dismiss either of us, Your Majesty. Because in this entire kingdom, I'm the only one who can protect you from what you started the moment you decided to cheat Eli Monpress."

"You," Renaud said, scowling, "protect me? What

would you do, sneak up behind him and make a speech? That seems to be your only real talent—"

The last *t* of "talent" had barely left his lips before something sharp and unbearably cold crushed into his neck. Renaud hadn't even seen the swordsman move, but all at once Coriano was right on top of him, pressing the bare white blade of his sword against the king's throat. The torch clattered to the ground as Renaud gasped for air. He flung open his spirit and desperately swung his will against the blade's edge, trying to overpower the metal's spirit, but the sword was like a glacier against his throat, and no matter how hard he fought, it would not move.

"Your tricks may work on dull, unsuspecting spirits," Coriano whispered, inches from Renaud's ear, "but an awakened sword is different. Now"—the swordsman's voice scraped against Renaud's opened soul like a razor—"listen, and listen well. I don't care why you took this kingdom, and I don't care if you keep it. I don't care what kind of wizard you are or what you're planning here in the dark. I am here for the Heart of War, nothing else. Now, if you do exactly as I say and help me corner Josef Liechten, I can give you victory. You might even live to reap the benefits of all your years of plotting. Do we have a deal?"

Eyes bulging, Renaud held out a moment longer before nodding frantically. As fast as he'd lunged, Coriano stepped back, and Renaud sank to his knees, gasping and clutching his bruised throat.

"All right," Coriano said, sheathing his white sword as he kept his good eye on the king. "The original bargain still stands. I will fight Josef Liechten without interference."

Renaud glowered from the floor, still rubbing his neck. "And what would my part entail?"

"You will arrange your forces exactly as I tell you," Coriano said, "and then we wait. Without Josef, the girl will leave and Eli will be vulnerable. You should have no trouble dealing with him then. In any event, after I have defeated the Heart of War, you'll never have to hear from me again."

"That would be a relief." Renaud rubbed his throat one last time and pushed himself up, turning back to the pillar. Almost at once, his sour glare faded, and his face relaxed into a warm smile. He reached out to touch the pillar's dull surface with his bare hands, and when his fingers brushed the stone, Coriano felt a tremor through his boots.

"How long would this plan take?"

Coriano eyed him warily. "That depends on Eli. Probably not more than a day, maybe two. Monpress moves quickly when he needs to."

"More than enough time," Renaud said, reluctantly withdrawing his hand from the pillar. "Follow me."

He whirled and marched out of the treasury, shouting for his guards. Coriano shot one last glance at the strange pillar before following the king into the hall. Whatever Renaud was planning down here, Coriano had a feeling it was larger than Mellinor. He would need to keep his wits about him if he was going to face Josef before it happened. After that, Coriano smiled, Renaud could bring the whole world crashing down for all it mattered to him. Dunea sang in agreement, and Coriano gripped her hilt.

Somewhere in the darkness behind them, the pillar quaked in response.

CHAPTER
17

The morning mists hovered thick and wet over the forest. Deer, the king's own stock, had come out to feed on the delicate new leaves sprouting in the scattered open spaces, but they shied away from the tiny clearing by the stone hut, and for good reason.

Gin lay by the door with his head on his paws, his orange eyes half open. The door to the hut creaked and a growl rumbled up from deep in the ghosthound's chest as Josef stepped out into the gray morning with Nico close behind him.

The swordsman was shirtless, but the wide swath of bandages wrapped around his chest kept the mist off him. For the first time Gin had seen, he was unarmed save for the enormous iron sword that he held in one hand.

The swordsman and the girl walked a short distance through the forest, stopping at a spot where the trees were farther apart, not quite a clearing, but room enough for their purposes. Nico took a seat on a fallen log while

Josef took up position at a wide spot between two young poplars. When he judged he had enough space, he held out his arms and, very carefully, raised his black blade. He brought it up in a slow arc until it was over his head. His shoulders tensed as the barely healed cut under his bandages stretched, but his face remained calm and serious as he brought the blade down again.

When he had lowered the point all the way to the leaf litter, Nico spoke. "Will it do?"

Josef let out a pained breath. "The stitches held," he said. "That'll have to be enough. It's not like we have time to lie around."

Nico stood up and went around to his back, adjusting the bandages to sit higher. As she reached up to get his shoulders, the wide sleeves of her enormous black coat fell away from her scrawny arms revealing the scuffed silver manacles she wore clamped tight on each wrist. A dozen feet behind them, Gin's growl grew louder.

"What is he going on about?" Josef grunted, rolling his shoulders to test the new bandage arrangement.

"The usual," she murmured.

Josef scowled. "I can make him stop if it's bothering you."

Nico shook her head. "Eli needs them for his plan, and things like that stopped bothering me long ago, after you found me." She reached into her coat and pulled out a clean shirt, which she held out to the swordsman.

Josef took it and pulled it over his head, ignoring the pain in his chest. "I'll talk to Eli about it, then. You shouldn't have to put up with that idiocy just so he can get another ten thousand on his bounty."

"I'd put up with more for less," Nico said. She caught

his eye and gave him one of her rare smiles. "The higher we make his bounty, the better the bounty hunters get. Soon you'll have the kind of fights you've been searching for."

"Fights seem to find us no matter what Eli's bounty is," Josef grumbled, but he was grinning when he looked at her. "Still, that Coriano and his awakened blade will be a challenge worth remembering. If the higher bounty attracts more of that sort of opponent, all of this stomping around in the woods will be worth it." He paused. "Which isn't to say I'll agree to another of your idiot kidnapping ideas, Monpress."

He turned around and folded his arms over his chest. A moment later, Eli stepped out of the underbrush with an enormous sigh.

"Too much suspicion will lead to an early grave," he said, strolling over to stand beside Nico.

"I would argue it's the other way around," Josef said. "So, did you need something, or did you just come out here to bother us?"

Eli made a great show of looking hurt. "For your information, I came out to see if you were all right. Nico was still putting your chest back together when I drifted off last night, so when you weren't in the hut when I woke up, I decided to investigate. Now I'm glad I did. What's this about an awakened blade?"

Josef plunged the Heart of War into the soft ground and leaned on it. "The swordsman I fought had an awakened blade."

"Must be a good one considering it put a hole in your tough hide," Eli said. "Good thing yours is better. We'll make short work of him if we see him again."

"I'm not going to use the Heart," Josef said solemnly.

"Josef, not this again," Eli groaned. "You're the swordsman; you decide how you fight. I respect that, but every time you get this way, half your blood ends up on the ground. If things go down the way they're looking like they will, we're going to have to make a quick exit, and that's hard enough without Nico having to drag your sword-riddled carcass across the countryside. The Heart of War chose you for a reason, and it wasn't to get carted around the world on a strap. Can't you just smash the swordsman and take the easy win for once in your life?"

"An easy win is meaningless," Josef growled. "If I'm going to get stronger, I have to defeat Coriano on my own, the right way."

"Nonsense!" Eli smiled. "We think you're plenty strong already, don't we, Nico?"

Nico stared at him. "Do you think your bounty is plenty high?"

Eli's grin faded. "Point taken." He shook his head. "Fine, do whatever you want. Just don't do something stupid like die on us, all right?"

Josef snorted. "Who do you think I am?"

"For the sake of our friendship, I'm not going to answer that." Eli met Josef's glare with a wry grin. "Now, I'm going back to the hut to mind our guests. Can you two handle getting the costumes?"

"Shouldn't be a problem," Josef said, pulling his iron sword out of the ground and resting it on his shoulder. "The real question is, will the Spiritualist follow orders?"

"Oh, yes," Eli said, nodding. "She's in this neck deep now. When Renaud showed his true colors, he put her duty to Spirit Court doctrines on the line. She'd break just about any law to keep her oaths to the spirits. So while she may try and moralize us to death, I think we can count on her not to flub the plan."

"Just make sure you actually *have* a plan this time," Josef called as he walked back toward the hut for the rest of his weapons.

Eli folded his arms over his chest, glaring at the swordsman's bandaged back. "Do you believe that?" he grumbled. "And after all the scrapes I've gotten him out of."

Nico shrugged. "With all the scrapes you get him into, I think it works out about even."

"Don't you start, too," Eli sighed. "In the year you've been with us, have I ever let us down? Don't you trust me yet?"

"Josef trusts you," Nico said, starting toward the hut as well. "That's enough for me."

Eli sighed again, louder this time, but Nico didn't look back. Shaking his head, he jogged after her, stopping a moment to say good morning to Gin, who was still growling, before joining the others in the hut.

"You know this is a terrible plan," Gin growled.

"Yes," Miranda said, pulling the long tunic dress over her head. "You've told me so every ten minutes since sunrise."

They were in the tiny space behind the forester's hut, wedged between the trees and the crumbling stone. Gin was slouched by the hut's corner, his body blocking the opening to the clearing so Miranda could have some privacy while she changed into the costume Josef had shoved into her hands a few minutes ago, when he and Nico had finally returned from wherever they'd been. She'd never been so happy to see them. A whole morning alone with the king and Eli had almost been more than she could stand.

"Disguise yourselves and sneak into the castle?" Gin snorted, making the low-hanging branches dance. "How are you going to get through the doors with no spirits? Wait for the thief to charm them all? And he didn't say a thing about what you'd do when you actually got in. I'm telling you, it's never going to work."

"I wouldn't be so sure about that," Miranda said, finding the opening for her head at last. "Eli's terrible plans have an interesting habit of working out."

Gin rolled his eyes. "Because his kidnapping plan went *so* well."

"Up until us, yes it did," Miranda said, giving him a sharp look. "I don't like this any more than you do, mutt, but we're in deep now, so we might as well do our best."

Gin kept grumbling, but Miranda ignored him. She smoothed the bulky dress over her shift with a final wiggle, and then, reaching awkwardly behind her, tied it with the strings sewn into the back. Next, she reached up and pulled her hair as tight as she could, knotting it in place at the base of her neck with a bit of twine. She grabbed the thick veil from a waiting branch and draped it over her forehead, letting the rest hang down her back so that her red hair was completely covered. Last of all, she fixed the small cap at the crown of her head with a long stickpin that held the whole affair in place. She gave her head an experimental shake to make sure the veil wouldn't slide off. When it stayed put to her satisfaction, she turned around.

"There," she said, putting her hands on her hips. "How do I look?"

Gin eyed her up and down. "Like a librarian."

"Such flattery!" Miranda folded her hands over her chest dramatically. "Be still, my trembling heart!"

"What? That's the point, right?" Gin said, getting up.

Miranda grinned at his confusion and tucked her discarded clothes under her arm before pushing her way through the giggling trees. Gin padded after her, muttering under his breath.

The tiny clearing outside the hut that served as Eli's hideout had become quite crowded since Nico and Josef had returned. Most of the space, however, was taken up by the new additions. Laid out on a ratty blanket, two men and a woman, dressed only in their underclothes, were sleeping peacefully in the tree-dappled sunlight—castle servants, the sources of the costumes. King Henrith was crouched beside them, his hands moving in worried circles on his knees. He had traded out his filthy silk clothes for what looked like a set of Josef's spares, though it was hard to tell without the knives. The bad fit and the king's dour expression as he hovered over the unconscious servants made him look like a refugee from a tragedy play.

"I don't see why you had to knock them out like this," he muttered.

"It was the simplest way to get the sizes correct," Josef said in a bored voice. He was lounging beside the hut, with his back propped against the ever-present camouflage thatch of branches provided by Eli's arboreal admirers. His enormous sword was stabbed into the ground beside him and a pile of throwing knives was spread out in the grass at his feet. His normal array of cross-belted sheaths was gone, and in their place he wore the chain and blue surcoat of a House Allaze royal guard, which, judging from the gaps at the shoulders, had recently belonged to the narrower of the sleeping men. "They'll wake up soon enough, no worse for wear."

"And you'll be here, sire," Eli chimed in, fastening the cuffs of his valet's coat. "A free evening off work and a touching reunion with their monarch. I'd say we're doing them a favor."

"What I don't understand," Miranda said, kneeling beside the distressed king, "is why we're stealing costumes to sneak into the castle when Josef and Nico already snuck into the castle to grab these three."

"We did nothing of the sort," Eli said. "Every servant doesn't live in the palace, you know. Josef spotted this lot walking into town from the outlying village. He merely gave them an involuntary night off. Oh, don't look like that." He waved his hands at Miranda's horrified expression. "If Josef says they'll be fine, they'll be fine. He's a professional. He does this all the time."

Josef nodded sagely at the pile of knives he was polishing. Somehow, Miranda failed to find the gesture comforting.

"Of course," Eli put his hands in his pockets, "the real question here is why we had to resort to this in the first place. I thought you said you had a contact in the palace?"

Miranda shook her head vehemently, making her veil fly. "There's no way I'm letting you drag Marion into this, not after she already stuck her neck out for me once. Just look what you did to one of her coworkers." She pointed at the unconscious girl, whose librarian uniform dress Miranda was now wearing. "Besides," she muttered, "I spent a good deal of time correcting her ideas about wizards. I don't want her meeting you lot and getting the wrong impression all over again."

"You cut me to the bone, lady," Eli said, clutching his

chest. "Are you implying that I blacken the reputation of wizardry?"

Miranda cocked an eyebrow at his theatrics. "The Rector Spiritualis wouldn't have sent me out here if you were doing it a benefit, Mr. Monpress."

"Ah yes, the great Etmon Banage." Eli smiled. "How nice of him to draw the line between good wizard and bad wizard so clearly. Truly a civic-minded man."

"Master Banage is twice the wizard you are, thief," Miranda hissed, leaping to her feet. "How dare you even mention—"

A black blur shot in front of her face, and Miranda flinched as the long, pitted blade of Josef's sword came into focus an inch from her nose. The swordsman was lounging against the hut with his arm extended, holding the enormous blade between Miranda and Eli with one hand.

"Children," he said, "not now."

Miranda blinked nervously. The sword hung in the air in front of her. This close, she could see the deep gouges from a lifetime of battles that ran like canyons along the blade, though the sword's surface was like no metal she had ever seen. It was blacker than pot iron, and dull as stone. Its cutting edge was uneven, splashed here and there by a redder darkness, like old blood that could never be scoured off. The blade looked impossibly heavy, but Josef's arm was firm as an iron beam, and the sword did not once waver in his grip.

His point made, Josef plunged his blade back into the moss beside him and calmly resumed cleaning his knives as though nothing had happened.

Miranda turned to Gin as much to get away from Eli's

triumphant grin as to fix the small bag containing her rings to the rope around his neck.

"I could eat him for you," Gin growled in her ear, his eyes on the swordsman. "It wouldn't be any trouble."

"No," Miranda said, adjusting the small bag, her fingers lingering over the familiar shapes outlined through the soft doeskin. "Without you around, we'll need someone who can look threatening. Besides, he'd probably give you indigestion."

"Without me?" Gin snorted. "I'm going with you."

"No, you're not. We've been over this." Miranda pulled his head down, bringing his orange eyes level with her own. "If there's one thing we do know about Eli, it's that he's a master thief. If he says he can get us in, then I believe him, but even Eli can't work miracles, and that's what it would take to sneak your fluffy face past the walls. No, your job is to stay and guard the king. The Powers know he can't guard himself."

Gin glanced over at the king, who was prodding the passed-out guard with his finger, and gave a mighty sigh. "All right," the dog growled and shuffled over to sit next to Henrith, who looked none too pleased by this turn of events, "but I'll be listening."

"I'll call if I need you," she said.

Gin snorted, but left it at that.

"All right," Eli said. "If the girl and her puppy are finished saying their good-byes, let's get a move on."

Josef nodded and stood up, his ill-fitting armor clanking loudly. Since his outfit didn't have room for his usual arsenal, he had been forced to make do with a knife in each boot, one behind his neck, and one at his waist. Still, he could almost pass for a normal soldier. Almost, that is, until he ruined the whole look by fastening his black sword across his back with a leather strap.

"You can't wear that," Miranda said, pointing at the blade. "What's the point of wearing disguises if you're just going to give it away by carrying that monstrosity around? I mean, if I left my rings, surely you can go an hour without your sword?"

Josef looked her straight in the eye and pulled the strap tighter. "If the Heart stays, I stay."

"I hate to admit it, but she does have a point," Eli said, frowning. He went into the cabin and came out a few moments later, carrying a few sticks and a leather sack. "Just a second," he muttered, laying his materials carefully on the dirt. He kneeled beside them and began to talk in a low, soft voice. Miranda tried to listen, but it was impossible to get close enough to hear what he was saying without making it obvious that that was what she was trying to do. At last, he scooped up the shortest stick and, with a few more words, bent the wood into a circle as easily as one would coil a length of rope.

Miranda watched in amazement as Eli laid the loop of wood and the two remaining straight sticks on top of the leather bag.

"When you're ready," he said.

No sooner did the words leave his mouth than the bag sat up. With a lively wiggle, the leather sack undid its seam and began wrapping itself around the wood, forming a tube around the two longer sticks. When the leather had wrapped itself as far as it could go, it pulled itself tight, and the thread from the seam stitched itself lengthwise up the edge of the long, leather tube. When it was finished, Eli held up a long, but otherwise perfectly normal-looking, spear quiver, the exact size and shape to hide the Heart of War.

Eli thanked the quiver several times before handing it to Josef, who slid his sword into the leather with his own nod of thanks.

"How did you…" Miranda pointed a limp finger at the quiver that had been three sticks and a bag less than a minute ago.

"Easy enough," Eli said. "I've had the bag for a while. He always had higher ambitions than luggage, so he was happy to help. The sticks were greenwood, and they love any chance to move around a bit before they dry brittle." He walked over to Josef and examined his handiwork. "It's too bad we don't have any spears to really complete the effect."

He kept talking, but Miranda's mind was too dumbfounded to make sense of it. She was still processing the enormous list of impossible things she'd just watched him do like it was nothing, like he did this every day. Talking to trees was one thing, but to make something new, just by talking, it was unbelievable. Not even the great shaper wizards could craft spirits without opening their own souls at least a little. This was like the wood and leather had decided to do him a favor, just because he asked. If she'd tried to do something like that without getting one of her servants to act as a middleman, the wood would have ignored her completely. Yet it did what Eli asked joyfully, as if he were the one who needed impressing, and not the other way around. She watched Eli as he talked, his long hands moving in elegant circles, and, not for the first time, Miranda caught herself wondering just what he really was.

"Are you feeling all right?"

Miranda jumped. Eli was looking at her quizzically. "You were staring and not listening."

"It's nothing," Miranda muttered, fighting down her blush at being caught. "Let's just get going."

Eli shrugged and turned to follow Josef as he led the way toward the castle. Nico joined them at the edge of the clearing, fading out of the woods like a ghost. Miranda jumped when she saw the girl, half because of her sudden appearance, and half because she hadn't noticed Nico was missing in the first place. Then she realized that Nico didn't have a disguise.

"Wait, doesn't she need—"

"No," Nico said, without stopping or looking back.

Gin padded back over to her, his eyes on the girl. "Watch yourself," he growled, "and don't forget what she is. Demons can't be trusted."

"Duly noted," Miranda said, and she gave his fur a final ruffle before jogging into the forest after Eli and the others.

Though they were only half a mile from the city, it took over an hour to reach the wall. This was mostly because Josef led them in a crazy zigzag through the brush. They crossed back over their path more than once, and he insisted on keeping to the tall undergrowth and away from the game trails, so that with every other step Miranda had to beat back a branch or untangle her skirt from a nettle bush. To make things worse, Eli stopped every five minutes or so to murmur quietly to this tree or that rock. She made it a point to listen covertly, but so far as she could tell, his little talks were of the most mundane kind, an exchange of pleasantries, maybe a comment about the weather, like a country wife chatting with her neighbors. As he talked, he would do them little favors, flicking an ant away or scraping some moss off the peak of a rock so it could feel the sunlight. That was strange enough, but the truly amazing thing was the way the sleepy spirits perked up as soon as he spoke to them. Miranda could almost feel them leaning forward, eager to tell him anything he wanted to know. Whatever brightness Gin had been talking about, it seemed to have a universal effect.

Miranda expected Josef to complain about the seemingly meaningless stops, but he accepted Eli's little chats with bored inertness, as if he had long since argued every point of the process five times over and couldn't be bothered to care anymore.

At last, they had reached the edge of the forest, where the king's deer park met the city's northern border. The trees ended a good twenty feet from the wall, leaving a broad swath of open ground carpeted with overgrown grass and saplings. Josef made them crouch in the scrubby bushes at the edge of the clearing as he scouted ahead. While they were waiting for the swordsman to come back, Miranda took the opportunity to satisfy her curiosity and she crept over to where Eli was crouched in the grass.

"Okay," she whispered, "I give up. Is the weather talk some kind of code?"

"What?" Eli's eyebrows shot up. "No, no, I'm just building good will."

Miranda gave him a confused look. "Good will?"

"It's a harsh world," Eli said. "You never know when you'll need a little good will from the local countryside."

Miranda was skeptical. A mossy rock didn't seem like

much of an ally. "So you weren't doing reconnaissance or anything?"

"Sorry, no," Eli said, shaking his head.

Miranda frowned. "But—"

"Quiet."

Miranda and Eli both jumped at the sudden command. Josef was kneeling in the tall grass not a foot away from them, glaring icily. Miranda hadn't even heard his approach.

"We move now," he said.

"Wha—" Before Miranda could even form her question, Josef took off for the city wall at a dead run, Nico and Eli right on his heels. Miranda took a deep breath and charged after them, covering the space of open ground between the trees and the city wall faster than she had ever moved in her life. She slammed into the wall and dropped to a crouch just in time. No sooner had she reached the stones than a small troop of guards appeared out of the woods only a few feet from where they'd been hiding just moments before.

Miranda clapped her hands over her mouth as the soldiers fanned out. They patrolled the edge of the forest in a wide sweep, poking their short spears into the underbrush. Finding nothing, the leader waved his hand, and the unit faded back into the woods. Only when the sound of their boots had died to a whisper did Miranda release the breath she'd been holding.

"That was lucky," she said.

"Luck's got nothing to do with it," Josef said in a low voice, peering at her through the grass. "Those patrols have been sweeping the area all day. If it wasn't for the fact that the forest doesn't want them to find us, all the luck in the world wouldn't have gotten us this far."

Miranda started, and Eli winked at her from his hiding place farther down the wall.

Josef gave Miranda a look of grudging approval. "Nice sprint, by the way."

"Thanks," she muttered. "What now?"

"Now we have to find that panel," Josef said, turning to the wall. "It should be close."

"It's here." Nico's quiet voice made Miranda jump. Nico was crouched on Josef's right, one small white finger sticking out of her voluminous sleeve to point at the iron square, barely larger than a laundry chute, set into the wall beside her.

"What is it?" Miranda asked, leaning in for a better look.

"A bolt hole," Eli said, crawling over to crouch beside Nico, "in case the royalty need to make a fast exit. Very common in cities like this." He gave the iron door an experimental push, but it didn't so much as rattle. He tried again, harder this time, but he might as well have been pushing the wall itself. "Hmm." He frowned. "This one seems to be locked."

Miranda gave him a puzzled look. "Isn't this how you got in last time?"

"Of course not," Eli said, looking insulted. "First rule of thievery, never use the same entrance twice."

Miranda rolled her eyes. "How many 'first rules' of thievery do you have?"

"When one mistake can mean your head on a pike, every rule's a first rule," Eli said cheerfully.

The thief ran his long fingers along the door's edge, which was set flush against the stone. Miranda watched with growing uncertainty. There wasn't even a keyhole, so far as she could see. When he had tapped every inch of the metal, Eli leaned back, brow knit in thought.

"Can't you just talk it open?" Miranda asked, moving a little closer. "Like you did with the prison door?"

"I could," Eli said, "but—" He reached into his coat pocket and drew out a small leather case, monogrammed in gold with an ornate capital *M*—"sometimes a simpler solution suffices."

He flipped the case open, revealing a startling selection of lock picks. Carefully selecting the longest and thinnest, he leaned down until his nose brushed the door. He held out his hand, and, without further prompting, Josef handed him a knife. Eli expertly wedged the slender blade into the hair-thin crack between the iron and the stone. Then, using the blade as a lever, he carefully lifted the door out of its niche. It opened just a fraction before sticking again with a soft clang.

"Lever and padlock," Eli muttered, switching out the thin lock pick for a slightly longer one with a crooked head. "Josef, if you would."

Josef took the knife from him and held it where Eli pointed, putting just enough pressure on the lever to keep the opening as large as possible without snapping the blade. Eli took a pair of delicate, extremely-long-nosed pliers out of his case and, using both hands, neatly slipped the pliers and the lock pick through the knife-thin crack.

He gripped with the pliers and began to deftly maneuver the lock pick, wiggling it right, then left, then right again, like he was trying to hook something. At last there was a loud click. Eli released the pliers and a muted crash came through the iron as the padlock hit the ground on the other side. He tucked his tools back into their leather case and opened the door with a flourish. The whole operation had taken less than a minute.

When he caught Miranda gawking, Eli's grin became unbearably smug.

"What were you expecting?" he said, still grinning. "I'm the greatest thief in the—*ow*!" He yelped as Josef punched him in the arm.

"Enough bragging," the swordsman grunted. "Inside, quick. The patrols move in a circle, you know."

Still rubbing his injured arm, Eli slid feet first into the dark bolt hole. Nico went next, casually wedging herself, bulky coat and all, through the narrow opening.

"You next," Josef said, looking at Miranda.

She swallowed. Suddenly, the bolt hole looked impossibly narrow and abysmally deep. However, she had an image to maintain as a Spiritualist, and that image did not include being afraid of holes, no matter how narrow or deep they might be. She sat down stiffly and began easing herself in, feet first. Just when she'd managed to convince herself it wasn't going to be that bad, she heard the crunch of men moving through the forest. She looked frantically over her shoulder in time to see the first patrolman reach the edge of the forest. She was about to whisper a warning when Josef shoved her, hard. Miranda yelped and lost her balance, sliding the rest of the way down the bolt hole. She landed in a pile on a cold, hard-packed dirt floor. A second later, Josef landed on top of her. The iron door clanged shut above them, and the room plunged into darkness.

CHAPTER
18

The next few seconds were a confused, painful scramble as Miranda did her best to get out from under Josef. The man was amazingly heavy and, she grunted as she cracked her ribs against his elbow, full of sharp edges. It didn't help that the ground was horribly uneven. Just when she'd finally managed to untangle herself from the swordsman, a soft, yellow glow winked to life. Miranda's relief was almost physically painful as the darkness resolved itself into familiar shapes. They were in a root cellar. Other than the four of them being in it, it was a very normal root cellar, with potatoes, apples, and turnips rolling across the floor where Miranda and Josef's landing had knocked them loose from their bins.

Eli held up a tiny blackout lamp, one shutter cracked just a fraction, the source of the unsteady light. "Nice landing," he said with a grin.

"I would have been fine if someone hadn't pushed me," Miranda hissed, hurling a potato at Josef.

"If I hadn't pushed you, we would have been spotted," Josef said, catching the potato in midair, "and that would have been that."

"Well, now that we're all here and uncaught," Eli said, swinging his lamp toward the squat wooden door half hidden behind a large bin of potatoes, "let's get on with it."

Miranda stood up, slipping a little on the rolling tubers. "Where are we?"

"Under the city, inside the walls," Eli said, popping the crude lock on the wooden door with a wiggle of his lock pick. "I told you, we're in the bolt hole. Most castles would have their own tunnel to safety in case of invasion, but Allaze is so close to the river, a deep tunnel would flood, so it looks like they had to make do with linking a bunch of cellars together."

"Lucky thing for us, in any case," Josef said, walking through the door Eli held open and into the next cellar.

Nico followed close behind him, stepping between the rolling potatoes as if she had no problem seeing in the dark. Miranda tried to mimic her path, but ended up slipping on her second step. She fell with a stifled yipe, catching the demonseed's shoulder at the last minute. The strange, thick material of the girl's coat shifted like a living thing under her fingers, and Miranda jerked her hand away. Despite the Spiritualist's full weight landing on Nico's shoulder, the smaller girl had not so much as stumbled. She turned to meet Miranda's horrified look.

"Go ahead, Spiritualist," she said, her pale face impassive. "The lamp's more for you than for us."

Had that sentence come from Eli, Miranda would have brushed it off as bluster, but the strange glitter in Nico's eyes left no doubt in her mind that the girl spoke the truth. With a muttered thanks, Miranda slipped by, pressing herself against the grimy wall to make sure she didn't brush the strange, moving coat again, and hurried into the adjacent cellar where Eli was already popping the next door.

After that, Miranda kept as close to Eli as her pride could bear, desperate to stay in the tiny circle of light. The next door led to another cellar, which led to another. Sometimes they would walk through a short tunnel, crossing under a road, Miranda guessed, and then it was on to another door and another person's hoard of vegetables. Mostly, the cellars were pitch black, but a few times they would open a door to see light streaming through the floorboards above their heads. When this happened, Eli would close the shutter on his lamp and they would scurry to the next cellar like mice in a larder.

One room, however, was nearly disastrous. After a long series of dusty, empty cellars, Eli had picked up the pace. Then, after finding a door that wasn't locked at all, he opened one right next to cook picking out vegetables for supper. They all froze in the doorway, and Miranda was sure their game was up. However, nothing happened. Minutes passed, and the cook just kept sorting through vegetables, singing in an off-key, nasal voice, not a foot away from them. Finally, she finished picking her potatoes and, still singing, tromped up the ladder, her swollen ankles wobbling unsteadily as she swung her armful of tubers in time to her song, and Miranda realized the cook was sodden drunk.

"Thank the Powers for cooking wine," Eli said when the cook closed the door behind her. "Let's go."

After almost half an hour of navigating the endless

maze of doors, the cellars took a noticeable turn for the affluent. The floors shifted from hard-packed dirt to laid stone, and there were wine casks and brandy stores as well as the standard potatoes and beets.

"Getting close now," Eli whispered, lowering the shutter on his small lamp until it gave off only a splinter of light.

As they passed from cellar to cellar, Miranda began to wonder how they would know the castle door when they saw it. Every cellar they entered now seemed to have two or more locked doors leading off it. It wouldn't surprise her if the nobles had their own network of secret tunnels down here, running from house to house to facilitate liaisons and any other secret activities the rich indulged in. As each cellar led to another just like it, she began to get the panicky feeling that they were lost in the underground maze of passages, going around and around in circles forever. Then, Eli opened a triple-locked door, and Miranda realized she needn't have worried.

At the end of the next cellar was a heavy iron door. It was the same size as the other cellar doors, but the stone wall it was set in looked both older and sturdier than the walls around it. At the door's center, set so deep Miranda could have stuck her finger up to the first knuckle into the grooves, was the seal of House Allaze.

Josef snorted. "I thought this was supposed to be a secret entrance."

"Secret from outsiders, yes," Eli said. "But you don't want some maid or delivery boy coming down here and opening it by mistake."

"No chance of that." Miranda shook her head. "How do we get it open?"

"Leave that to me," Eli announced. He reached into the small leather bag he wore under his valet coat and pulled out two small glass bottles filled with clear liquid. "Two weak acids," he said, holding the bottles up, "used in metal working to etch patterns. Normally, it would take either of these a month to go through that much metal. However, these particular bottles of acid happen to hate each other."

"Hate each other?" Miranda frowned. "How did that happen?"

Eli swirled the bottles innocently. "I might have played the gossipmonger a bit too well. You see, acid spirits, though volatile and dangerous, aren't very bright. They are, however, very quick-tempered." As he spoke, the liquid began to slosh. Just a little at first, so that Miranda thought it was because of Eli's swirling, but by the time he finished speaking, the acids were practically boiling in their bottles.

"Now," Eli said, shaking the bottles violently, "we just have to get them good and mad, and—" He hurled both bottles at the door, landing them smack on top of each other. The glass shattered, and the acids fell on each other with a roar, sinking through the iron door like boiling water through fresh snow.

"A good fight does wonders for them!" Eli shouted over the din of the spirits' war.

"That's horrible!" Miranda shouted back. "Using a spirit's feelings like that, it's abusive!"

"Not at all." Eli looked hurt. "I'm treating them like living things, which is a lot more than I can say for the blacksmith I bought them from. Look, it's even waking up the door."

The acids' fight was indeed getting the door's attention. It squealed and ground on its hinges, trying to get away from the brawl that was eating through its core. The din was deafening, and Miranda clapped her hands over her ears. Eli cringed at the worst of it, but otherwise seemed content to watch the show. Josef just stood there, watching the door with bored interest. Nico crouched closer to the hissing metal than Miranda would have dared, staring in fascination as the hole in the door grew wider.

Finally, the acids fought themselves out, leaving a warped, melted hole in the iron just large enough to fit a small fist through. The door whimpered, and Eli rubbed it gently, whispering apologies and promising to have it recast as soon as possible. Whether he meant it or not, the words seemed to put the door at ease, and as it drifted back to sleep, Eli reached his hand through the melted hole and popped the lock on the other side.

"Swordsmen first," Eli said, swinging the door open.

Josef put his hand on his sword hilt and eased his way into the black tunnel.

"All clear," he whispered, and the rest of them hurried through the doorway, mindful of the spots where the last remnants of the acids were still steaming.

The hall on the other side was smaller than the cellar it joined. In fact, it was barely larger than the door itself. They walked single file, with Josef leading the way, absently twirling two knives in his hands. Miranda went next, followed by Eli, with Nico trailing behind as usual. For her part, the Spiritualist kept to the absolute center of the hall, as far as she could get from the cobwebby walls. Here and there, small roots had pushed through the ceiling, and she realized they must be under the palace grounds. Unseen things scuttled in the dark behind them, making Miranda's skin crawl. Apparently, Josef didn't like the scuttles either because he stopped suddenly, causing Miranda to nearly run into him.

"What now?" she whispered, regaining her balance.

Josef threw up his hand to silence her. She glowered at the command, but said nothing. Behind them, something skittered again, and Josef turned on his heel. Miranda didn't see the knife leave his hand, but she heard it hit. A squeal erupted behind them, and the skittering stopped. Eli whirled around, holding his lamp high. The light fell across their dusty footprints and, right at the edge of the glow, was a squirming, dying rat with Josef's knife sticking out of its side.

"Getting paranoid?" Eli muttered, lowering the lamp. "It's not like you to kill the wildlife."

"It's not paranoia." Josef walked over to reclaim his knife. "Have you ever seen a rat act like that?"

"What are you talking about?" Miranda said.

"Rats are scavengers and foragers," Josef said. "This one's been following us since the first cellar. What kind of rat leaves a cellar full of food to follow people into an empty hallway?"

Miranda hurried over to the dying animal and hovered her hand over its head. Sure enough, she could feel the faint echo of Renaud's spirit slipping away as the rat's movement stilled. She snatched her hand back.

"Josef's right," she said.

"If he has control of the rats, that could be a major problem," Josef said, looking at Eli. "Even you can't sneak past rats."

"He can't control all of them," Miranda said, rubbing

her hand on her skirt. "Controlling lots of small spirits is harder than controlling one large one."

"He wouldn't need to control all of them," Eli said thoughtfully. "Rats talk among themselves, and two wizards aren't exactly inconspicuous. Two or three informants would be enough."

Josef pushed past them and began walking in quick, impatient strides down the dark hall toward the castle. "We'll just have to assume Renaud knows we're down here," he said. "And that means we need to be somewhere else."

Miranda hurried after him. The dark, dirty tunnel was the last place she wanted to face another of Renaud's mad spirits. The swordsman set a grueling pace, not running but walking so fast they might as well have been. The tunnel around them was growing lighter or rather, less dark. She still couldn't see anything beyond the lamplight, but the tone of the darkness was shifting to something friendlier, more human. Even so, the tunnel seemed to go on forever, and Miranda's legs were beginning to ache. The gardens hadn't seemed this long when she was aboveground. As the tunnel went on and on, she started to wonder if this wasn't some new trap they had stumbled into.

At last, she saw real light up ahead. Josef slowed his pace a fraction and then came to a complete stop. Eli held up the lamp, revealing a wrought-iron gate kept closed with a simple chain and padlock. The chain had rusted long ago, and Josef was able to reach through the iron bars and yank it off without difficulty. The gate swung open with a creak, and they piled into the final room of their journey.

"Great," Miranda said, "more potatoes."

"Ah," Eli countered, "but these are royal potatoes! We're here."

Miranda looked around skeptically. The stone cellar, with its bins of root vegetables and its cold, earthy smell, was uncomfortably like every other wealthy cellar they'd tromped through. On the opposite wall, dim light shone through the cracks of a squat wooden door. Eli blew out his lamp and set it on the lip of the potato bin. He put his finger to his lips and then, slowly and silently, opened the door.

The hallway beyond was lit with indirect firelight from the room at its end. Distorted voices echoed up and down its length, and Miranda could make out the shadows of servants as they sat around the hearth. Eli craned his neck out as far as he could, then pulled back, grinning.

"All right," he said, brushing the last bits of cobweb off his valet's jacket, "time for phase two. Ready, Nico?"

The girl nodded and pulled her coat tighter.

"Wait," Miranda whispered. "What's phase two?"

Eli shook his head and put his finger to his lips before stepping out into the hall. Miranda made a rude gesture at his back and crept after him.

CHAPTER
19

Something's not right," Josef muttered.

"You've got a point," Eli said, thunking his slab of bread against his wooden plate. "This bread's two days old at least."

Miranda hunched over her stewed beef and said nothing. The three of them were crowded around a small table in the kitchen surrounded by a crowd of servants who were all eating their dinners with determined efficiency. So far, phase two had consisted of sneaking into the kitchens and blending in with the other servants for the dinner rush. No one had noticed them, but they weren't getting any closer to Renaud, and, even worse, Nico was nowhere to be seen.

"We're wasting our time," Miranda grumbled, shoving her plate away. "There was no need to get food as well."

"Nosunse," Eli said around his enormous mouthful of beef. He swallowed with gusto. "A servant who rejects food? Now *that* would stand out. Besides, why let it go to waste?" He took another bite.

"They have only two guards at the door," Josef went on, ignoring them both, "and no one checking the servants. The cooks didn't even look sideways at us."

"Maybe they don't know we're here," Eli said. "The spying rat we caught could have been the only one. Or maybe they know we're in the castle, but they weren't expecting us to come to the kitchens. Or maybe my plan is actually working. The whole point of breaking in at dinner was to catch the shift change so no one would notice three newcomers."

"Or maybe they're just incompetent," Miranda said, remembering how the castle had reacted when she'd arrived for the first time. "Renaud may be in charge, but Mellinor is still Mellinor. Common sense seems to be as forbidden as wizardry in this country."

"You have a point," Josef said, leaning back in his chair and pretending to drink while he scanned the room. "But this was too easy even for incompetence. Mellinor may be slack, and I don't know about Renaud, but Coriano isn't someone who would leave an opening like this, not unless he was planning something."

"Coriano?" Eli wiped his mouth with a greasy napkin. "Didn't he run off?"

"He's a swordsman; he only retreated. Besides"— Josef dropped his hand to where the carefully wrapped Heart of War was leaned against his leg—"the Heart can feel his sword. They're calling to each other."

"Josef," Eli said patiently, "for the last time, you're not a wizard. You can't hear a damn thing that sword is saying."

"I don't have to hear him to know what he wants," Josef growled. "You're just mad you can't talk to him." Josef flashed Miranda a conspiratorial grin. "It's the only spirit we've found that won't talk to Eli."

"Who'd want to talk to a spirit that chose you, anyway," Eli muttered, reaching for his spoon to finish the last of his impromptu dinner. "He must have horrid taste."

"Enough," Miranda said, shoving Eli's bowl out of reach before he could take another mouthful. "We're wasting our time. What are we waiting for, anyway?"

A chorus of screams erupted from the kitchen, and Eli's face broke into an enormous grin. "That."

A crowd of cooks poured screaming out of the kitchen, followed by a thick plume of white smoke. The servants at the front tables started to panic, screaming "fire." The soldiers ran forward, shouting for order as the servants rushed the doors to the kitchen gardens. While the overwhelmed guards yelled and tried to keep people from trampling each other, Eli and Josef calmly got up and jogged toward the now unguarded door to the upper castle. Miranda watched the panic in shock for a moment and then stood up and stomped after the thief.

The main hall of the servant level was even more crowded than the dining room. Alarm bells were ringing up and down its length, and the smell of wood smoke and burning tar hung heavy in the hazy air. Servants seethed from the dozens of interconnecting hallways like ants out of an overturned hill, shouting and shoving as they rushed the exits. Eli let them surge past him, nimbly working his way upstream along the wall. Only when a platoon of guards carrying buckets appeared at the far end of the hall did he change course and duck down one of the small connecting corridors.

"I can't believe it!" Miranda whispered fiercely as they half walked, half ran down the narrow hall. "You started a fire just so you could get past some guards? Do you *ever* consider the consequences of your actions!?"

"We didn't start a fire," Nico's voice said calmly.

Miranda jumped and whirled around. At first, she saw nothing but the empty hallway filled with hazy smoke, dark except for the sputtering wall sconces set at wide intervals. Then, Nico appeared from the shadows a foot behind them, as if she had emerged from the wall itself, looking very pleased with herself.

Miranda refused to be intimidated. "What did you do?"

"Nothing bad," Nico said. "I just let the furnace know what I was, and now it's trying to burn down the castle."

"You deliberately terrified a fire spirit?" Miranda gasped. "That's horrible!"

Nico crossed her arms over her chest, her brown eyes perfectly calm. "I didn't terrify it. I introduced myself. It was the furnace's decision to try and kill me by burning everything. Don't worry, though; it's a slow, fat spirit. The servants will have no trouble holding it back, if they can get over their own panic."

"Don't you dare blame the furnace," Miranda said. "Spirits are panicky by nature, fire spirits especially. It's our job to protect them from things like this, not scare them witless."

"*Your* job, you mean." Nico turned away. "Don't assume that everyone thinks like you."

Miranda's face reddened, but before she could retort, Nico vanished into the shadows as suddenly as she had appeared.

"How does she do that?" Miranda said, crossing her arms over her chest.

"She's always been like that," Eli said, giving the Spiritualist a little push down the hall. "Didn't I tell you she didn't need a costume?"

Miranda shook her head and let him jostle her down the corridor. They had gone only a few steps when Nico popped back into view, making Miranda jump again.

"I forgot to tell you," she said to Eli. "Renaud is in the treasury. I overheard the valets complaining about it when I was getting in position. He's been in there since last night, apparently."

Miranda's eyes went wide. "The treasury? You're sure?"

Nico shrugged. "That's what I heard. Apparently, he's been spending all his time staring at a support pillar."

"Well, there's no accounting for taste," Eli said. "Maybe he's never seen one before. I don't think he got out much."

"You're sure it's a pillar?" Miranda's voice was pleading. "Are you sure you didn't mishear?"

"I don't mishear," Nico said flatly.

Miranda clenched her hands together. "Oh, dear."

Josef, who had been quiet all this time, stepped forward to block her way. He planted himself in front of the Spiritualist, looking down at her with a stony expression. "Why is a pillar bad?"

"I'll have to explain later," Miranda said, pushing past him. "We need to get to the—"

"No," Josef said, grabbing her arm. "You'll explain now."

He looked up and down the corridor. Behind them, in the main hall, servants were still running madly for the exits. Josef shook his head at the panic and marched Miranda in the other direction. He tried the first of several small, inconspicuous doors. When it opened, he shoved Miranda inside. Nico and Eli followed suit, cramming themselves into the small closet.

"What are you doing?" Miranda hissed, fighting Josef's hold.

"You haven't been open with us," Josef said, tightening his grip. "You were the one who asked for our help, Spiritualist. You don't get to string us along, telling us whatever you think we need to know. I'm not going a step farther until you tell us why Renaud being in the treasury is enough to make you go white."

Miranda briefly considered lying, but Josef's face was murderous in the dim light filtering through the warped cracks in the closet door. She swallowed against her dry throat and decided it was time to come clean.

"It's not like I was hiding it," she said, slumping against the back wall. "I just didn't think it would be an issue."

"Obviously it is," Josef said, releasing his grip. "Talk."

"Fine," Miranda said. "I wasn't just wandering through Mellinor when I found out you three had stolen the king. I was sent here by the Rector Spiritualis."

"Figures," Eli said. "That old windbag probably couldn't stand having a country in the Council that didn't buy into his Spiritualist mumbo jumbo."

"Ignore him," Josef said, cutting off Miranda's retort

before she could open her mouth. "Why did the Rector send you?"

Miranda shot Eli an icy glare. "We received a tip from Coriano that Eli was in this kingdom."

Josef arched an eyebrow. "Coriano works for you?"

"Worked," Miranda corrected him. "We couldn't let *someone*"—she glared at Eli—"continue to ruin our good reputation, so the Spirit Court paid Coriano to tip us off since he was following your trail anyway. Everything was fine until I got here. Then Renaud bought Coriano out from under us."

"That's the problem with mercenaries," Eli said. "They always live up to their name."

"Stop interrupting," Josef said flatly. "What about the pillar?"

Miranda shook her head. "When Master Banage sent me here, we didn't know the king was the target. He thought Eli was after an obscure wizard artifact that has been in Mellinor's possession since its founding, Gregorn's Pillar."

"Obscure?" Eli looked insulted. "Why would I want to steal something no one's heard of?"

"Gregorn," Josef said and frowned. "I've heard that name before."

"I'm not surprised," Miranda said. "Gregorn was Mellinor's founder, and, despite their current rhetoric, he was actually quite a famous, and quite a nasty, enslaver."

"What does Banage care about the pillar then?" Josef asked. "He's not an enslaver. Why would he want something that belonged to one?"

"To keep it away from other wizards who want to follow Gregorn's path," Miranda said.

"What's it do, then?" Josef asked. "Does it amplify powers somehow, or call spirits to you?"

Miranda began to fidget.

"I'm not actually sure," she admitted at last. "Master Banage never told me exactly. All I know is that it's bad news for everyone if a wizard gets his hands on it." Master Banage's exact words had been 'soul-imperiling danger for both the human and spirit worlds,' but after Eli's earlier comments, she didn't think they would appreciate the gravity of that statement.

Eli scowled at her. "I thought the Spirit Court was around to keep stuff like that under control."

"We do," Miranda snapped. "Why else do you think Master Banage sent me to keep the pillar from being stolen? I'm a fully initiated Spiritualist! I'm not exactly an errand girl."

"So why let it sit in Mellinor all this time if it's so dangerous?" Josef scratched his chin. "Seems awfully irresponsible."

"We're a neutral power!" Miranda threw up her hands. "We can't just waltz in and demand a country's national treasure! Besides, in case you forgot, Mellinor hates wizards. Gregorn's Pillar is perfectly harmless to normal people; so leaving it in a country where wizards are deported on sight seemed like an acceptable risk."

"Let me get this right"—Josef bent down to look her straight in the eye—"you think that Renaud, an enslaver, is trying to get this pillar, which is named after another enslaver, and is, in your words, 'bad news' if a wizard gets his hands on it." He arched an eyebrow at Miranda. "Don't you think you should have told us about this earlier?"

"I'm sorry!" Miranda sputtered. "I really didn't think

it was going to be an issue! Renaud grew up right above it, so I figured if he knew about the pillar at all, he would have gotten it years ago, before he was banished."

"He wouldn't have had access to it when he was a prince," Eli said. "The treasury vault can be opened only by the king's direct order."

Everyone turned and looked at him, and Eli took a step back.

"What? I did do *some* research on Mellinor. That was my first plan, actually—get Henrith to open the vault for me—but then I figured kidnapping would be much more high profile."

Miranda slapped her hand against her forehead. "Well," she said, "that clears things up nicely."

"Does it really matter?" Eli said. "I mean, our objectives haven't changed. Get Renaud, get the money, get away. The plan is still rolling smoothly. We'll just have to be more careful. Besides"—he rubbed his hands together—"sneaking into a treasury sounds much more profitable than sneaking into a throne room."

Miranda grunted, but she could think of nothing sufficient to counter all that was wrong with that sentence. Eli grinned and opened the closet door, spilling them out into the dark hazy hall.

"Look," Miranda said, balancing herself against the sooty wall, "even if you're right, and the plan is still valid, we don't know where the treasury is. Since we made it this far with only a spying rat for trouble, it's a safe bet Renaud doesn't have the Pillar yet, but if anyone recognizes us, we'll be up to our neck in guards and, shortly after that, enslaved spirits. We don't have time to wander around lost."

"So we'll ask someone." Eli smirked and pointed over her shoulder. "In fact, I think I've spotted someone who can help us."

Miranda whirled around, and her eyes widened in shock. Standing at the junction where their small corridor met the madness of the main hall, still as a statue with her hands pressed against her mouth despite the other servants pushing past her, was Marion. As soon as Miranda made eye contact, the girl rushed forward, and the Spiritualist barely had time to catch her breath before the librarian's hug crushed it out of her.

"Oh, Lady Miranda," she gasped. "I knew you'd be back! I knew it! The king's not really dead, is he?"

Miranda clutched the girl's shoulders awkwardly. "No, Henrith's alive. He's with Gin, and safe."

Marion looked up at her, eyes glowing with delight. "Really? Oh, thank goodness." She looked around at Eli and Josef. "Who are these? Reinforcements from the Spirit Court?"

"More or less." Miranda grinned, and Eli rolled his eyes. "Listen"—she pushed Marion back so she could look the girl in the eyes—"Marion, this is serious. We need to get to the treasury."

Marion nodded vigorously and grabbed Miranda's hand, pulling her to the end of the corridor. "This way," she said, turning down a tiny hallway Miranda hadn't noticed before. "With the main halls like that, it's faster to take the servants' passages."

Miranda nodded and resigned herself to being dragged. Eli took up position right behind her, with Josef bringing up the rear. As usual, Nico was nowhere to be seen. Marion led them through a maze of narrow halls and then down a flight of stairs. This led to more hallways and then more stairs, until Miranda could hardly believe all of this labyrinthine tunneling fit inside the same castle she'd bullied her way into only days before.

As they followed the twisting hall down yet another stair, something occurred to her, and Miranda looked over her shoulder at Eli. "How did you know it was Marion?" she whispered. "I never told you what she looked like."

"Simple," Eli whispered back. "Who else in this place would possibly be happy to see you?"

Miranda couldn't help but chuckle at the truth of that, and she turned her attention back to the stone hall as Marion led them past the turn-off for the prisons and down yet another narrow stair, heading deeper and deeper into the castle's foundations.

CHAPTER
20

M arion led them deeper than Miranda had imagined the castle could reach, down below the prison, below the foundations, and into the very heart of the stone that lay far below the fertile soil of Mellinor. Though the city was low lying, there was no sign of water here, no seepage over the years as one would expect to find this deep below the surface. Only the ancient, wooden support beams and the occasional fluttering light of the lamps broke the monotony of the smooth, dry stone as the narrow hallways and connecting stairs descended deeper and deeper into the earth.

Finally, at the base of the longest stairway yet, they reached a small wooden door.

"This is as far as I can take you," Marion said, turning to face them. "The treasury hall is just beyond here, but I've never been inside myself. Actually," she said and blushed sheepishly, "servants aren't even allowed past the prison, but I spent a lot of time memorizing drawings of the castle back when I was the Master Architect's assistant, before I got promoted to librarian."

"Well, thank the Powers for that," Eli said, smiling charmingly. "You've been a most effective guide, Lady Marion."

Marion's blush spread as Eli took her hand and guided her back toward the stairs. "I must insist that you return now. You've risked far too much helping us."

"It was the least I could do," Marion mumbled. She looked shyly at Miranda and dropped into a sudden, haphazard curtsy. "Thank you, lady. Good luck!"

She whirled around and scrambled back up the stairs as fast as she could go. Miranda watched her with a faint smile. Only when the girl's footsteps had safely faded away did she turn back to the grim task before them.

Josef had pressed himself against the wooden door and was peering through the gaps in the boards with one eye. Nico was crouched below him, peeking under the crack where the door met the floor, while Eli hovered impatiently behind them both. "How does it look?" he asked.

"Interesting," Josef said. He stepped aside so Miranda and Eli could have a look.

Miranda pressed her eye against the crack, and her breath caught in her throat. On the other side of the door was the treasury hall Marion had mentioned. It was much larger than Miranda had expected, roughly a hundred feet from end to end and wide enough for ten men to stand shoulder to shoulder. She knew that last bit for certain, because that's how they were standing. The corridor was absolutely packed with soldiers. They were standing at attention in tight rows running from wall to wall down the entire length of the carved hall. Each soldier carried a tall, wooden shield in one hand and an iron-tipped spear in the other. Bright torches hung from every bracket on the blackened walls, filling the entire corridor with light. At the end of the hall, almost hidden by the bristling spears and peaked helmets, the top edge of the iron treasury door was visible, a black spot in the dancing light.

"That explains why there were no guards outside," Josef whispered. "They must have packed the entire army in there. Even if we were invisible, we couldn't sneak through without shoving half a platoon out of the way."

Miranda bit her lip. "Nico"—she looked down at the girl—"couldn't you just do your, um, disappearing thing to get past them?"

"It doesn't work like that," Nico said. "It's too far to go in one jump. I'd have to land in the middle of them. Anyway, what would I do when I got there? You all would still be here."

"Well," Josef said, "I guess there's nothing for it." He walked back up the stairs a little ways and took hold of one of the wooden support beams. Bracing his foot against the stone wall, he dug his fingers into the wood and began to pull. The wood squealed under his grip, and the old stone crumbled. Josef pulled harder and, with a cracking sound, yanked the beam free of its anchors. Miranda gaped like a landed fish as the swordsman swung the six-foot beam over his shoulder like it was made of straw. The noise had drawn some attention. Shouted orders and the sound of shields slamming down filtered through the thin door. Josef, however, walked calmly down the stairs past Eli and the gaping Miranda and paused just in front of the door, beside Nico.

"Ready, girl?" he said.

To Miranda's amazement, Nico's pale face lit up in an enormous smile. "Always, swordsman."

"Wait," Miranda whispered. "What are you—"

Josef lifted his foot and, in a motion too fast for Miranda's eyes to follow, kicked down the door. Time slowed to a crawl as all the soldiers turned toward the sound, and for one endless, silent moment, no one moved. Then, Josef's wooden beam caught the closest soldier square in the chest, and the hallway erupted.

The soldiers surged forward, shouting and brandishing their spears. The alarm horns rang out deafeningly close, and the stone floor trembled under the pounding boots as the wave of armed men crashed into the small doorway. Josef swung his beam in huge arcs, sweeping soldiers off their feet and slamming them by the half dozen into the mosaic walls. He waded into the thick of them, the Heart of War securely strapped across his back, its leather disguise falling off in ragged chunks as it deflected strokes that would otherwise have landed in the swordsman's spine.

Miranda tried to run forward, but Eli's hands wrapped around her shoulders and flung her with surprising strength against the doorframe.

"Let me go!" she shouted. "That idiot's going to get us all killed!"

"Too late for that!" Eli shouted back. "He's already going. If you interfere, he'll have to watch out for you, and then he really will die." He eased his grip a fraction. "Trust him," he said. "Josef's the best there is."

Miranda wanted desperately to believe the thief, but at that moment a resounding twang cut through the battle as the archers in the back released a flight of arrows into the fray. She watched in horror as the arrows sailed over the crowd, almost scraping the smoke-stained ceiling before arcing downward straight at Josef's unguarded head. Right before the barbed tips landed, they vanished. Suddenly, Nico was there, standing on his shoulders, her enormous coat swirling around her like water, the arrows clutched in her bony hand. She tossed them aside just in time to knock the next volley out of the air, effortlessly shifting her balance to match Josef's swings, for the swordsman kept going as if she wasn't there. Josef was laughing, moving in long, rolling arcs down the chaotic corridor, the beam flying in front of him and the Heart guarding his back. Whenever he left an opening, soldiers of all sizes and builds would lunge for it, only to be caught by a well-aimed kick and then swept into the wall with the others as the beam came down.

Miranda watched in amazement, not bothering to fight Eli's grip any longer. "He's a monster," she whispered.

"Yes," Eli whispered back. "That's why the Heart of War chose him."

When Josef's path of destruction had almost reached the treasury door, Nico launched herself off his shoulders and began laying waste to the last few lines of archers, most of whom had dropped their bows and were frantically fighting with short swords. Nico moved between them like a shadow, jabbing each man twice between the ribs before he fell to the ground clutching his stomach, unable to do more than gurgle in pain. By the time she reached the end of the archer line, the remaining soldiers were fleeing in panic, stumbling down the hall as fast as they could and paying no attention to Eli or Miranda as the two stepped out of the shelter of the small stair.

The hallway was a mess. Soldiers lay slumped in moaning piles against the cracked stone walls, their bloody splashes obscuring the rolling mosaics. Still, while badly battered, almost all were alive and groaning pathetically as Miranda and Eli hurried past them. Josef sighed loudly, leaning the battered, bloody, but still intact wooden beam against the wall beside the treasury door. He was sweaty, dirty, and breathing hard, but he could have been plowing a field or digging a ditch for all Miranda could tell. There wasn't a wound on him. Nico was the same way, leaning against the wall with a satisfied grin.

"That," Josef panted, "was the best five minutes of this whole"—pant—"awful"—pant—"job."

"Glad someone's having fun," Eli said, rolling one of the unconscious soldiers away from the door. "Now, let's see if the reward was worth the mess."

He took a step back and looked up at the enormous iron door with a low whistle. "Impressive." He grinned wide. "Now I see why Renaud didn't just enslave his way in as a boy. Sandstorms are chaotic and stupid, easy to control if your will is stronger. But metal, especially thick, old metal like this?" He rapped his knuckles on the door's surface, making a strange, metallic echo down the ruined hall that only made him grin wider. "You'd use up all your energy just waking it up, never mind controlling it."

Miranda stepped forward, running her fingers over the smooth, cold iron. "Can you open it?"

If possible, Eli's grin grew wider still. "Who do you think I am?" he said, putting both hands palm down above the door's handle. Miranda snorted, but said nothing, stepping back to watch him work. A moment after Eli's hands settled on the iron, his expression changed from cocky to quizzical. He gave the door a push with his palms, and it swung inward with a faint scrape.

Miranda blinked in amazement. "I guess you're not all talk."

"High praise indeed," Eli said, stepping back. "I wish I could claim it, but that wasn't me. The door's unlocked."

Josef walked over to him and stared hard at the metal door, which was slowly drifting open under its own weight. "You realize," he said quietly, "this is probably a trap."

"We've been walking into a trap since we got here, most likely." Eli looked sideways at Josef. "You said so yourself."

Josef shrugged and picked up his beam again. "Too late to worry about it now."

"Let's get this over with," Eli said, and shoved the door as hard as he could.

The metal slab swung open easily, and an old, cold wind ruffled their hair. The light from the hall torches extended only a foot from the threshold. Beyond that, the treasury stretched out into flat blackness, without depth or end. Miranda took a tentative step forward, reaching out, but she felt no spirits, mad or otherwise. The groans of the soldiers outside faded as soon as she crossed the threshold, and the scrape of her boot was frighteningly loud in the sudden stillness.

All at once, Josef shuddered as if he'd been thrown into an icy pond. He stepped forward, staring determinedly into the featureless dark. "I know you're there," he said. "Come out."

His voice echoed in the darkness, the words repeating

over each other and then fading again. For a long moment, nothing changed. Then, a few yards in front of them, a match flared to life, illuminating a pair of eyes, one blue, one clouded silver.

"Hello, Josef," he said. "What took you?"

CHAPTER
21

Not whom you were expecting?" Coriano smiled and touched his match to the wick of a glass lamp that dangled from his hand. The light flared up, illuminating the empty walls that ran in a smooth arch until they disappeared into the darkness overhead, beyond the lamp's reach. Underfoot, the flame sent shadows scurrying across the stone floor decorated with the stained outlines of removed shelves and trunks. The makers of those stains were gone, however, leaving only dust, cobwebs, and occasional woodchips behind. By the time the lamp's flame steadied, it was painfully obvious that the heavily guarded treasury was completely empty.

Miranda stepped forward. "Where is Renaud?"

"Forget him," Eli said. "Where's the treasure?"

"Where is the treasure, indeed," Coriano said. "Did you know that, among bounty hunters, you're famous for your unpredictability, Eli? They never understand when I tell them how, in one aspect, you're steady as the sun.

Miranda would know best." He flashed her a cold smile. "I gave her the same advice as I gave all the others: If you want to catch Eli Monpress, simply put yourself between him and what he wants. Because his only constant is that, once he decides something is his, he's never able to let it go, not even to save his own skin."

"Then," Miranda said, "all those soldiers outside?"

"A necessary deception." Coriano tilted his head. "Anything less than a full guard and you might have guessed something was wrong. I even let that librarian wander around in the hope that she would take you to the small stair, just to make it seem really authentic."

Miranda's face went scarlet, but before she could open her mouth, Eli grabbed her shoulder.

"Well done, then," Eli said, pushing Miranda back and taking her spot beside Josef. "You've found me. However, you still haven't caught me."

"But it's not you I'm after," Coriano said. "It's the man who follows where you lead." A sudden flash of white cut the dark as Coriano drew his sword and aimed the point directly at Josef's chest. "Master of the Heart of War, we have unfinished business."

Josef brandished the dented, bloody support beam like a club in front of him, a broad smile breaking across his face. "Let's finish it, then."

"Are you mad?" Miranda grabbed Josef's arm. "Weren't you listening? Renaud could be claiming the pillar right now. We don't have time for pride fights!"

"If you're looking for the new king," Coriano said, "he's in the throne room. Back through the treasury hall and straight up the main stair four flights. The first door on the right will take you to the promenade hall, and you just follow the flags to the throne room itself. He's got the entire contents of the treasury up there on my advice, so I could set my trap and he could work on his pillar in peace."

Miranda's hands began to shake. "You're letting him work on the Pillar? Do you have any idea what that could mean?"

"No," Coriano said, "and neither do you. Does it matter?"

"Of course, it matters!" Miranda's voice echoed through the empty cavern. "You were there in the clearing. You should know better than most that the man has nothing but contempt for the spirits! If he gets that Pillar, there won't be a spirit in the world that can stand against him, and every spirit he conquers will go as mad as that sandstorm. Doesn't that mean anything to you?"

Coriano raised his white blade and brought the red-wrapped hilt to his lips. "The only spirit I care about is Dunea," he whispered, "my River of White Snow, and all she cares about is beating him." He pointed the tip of his sword at the hilt of the Heart of War poking over Josef's back. "Everything else is meaningless."

Miranda growled, but Josef stepped in front of her, his enormous back and the great sword strapped across it blocking everything else from view. The swordsman looked over his shoulder, and Miranda's blood went thin at the look in his eyes. Even when he had waded out into the sea of soldiers with nothing but a stick of building material, he hadn't looked as large or as deadly as he did now.

"Nico," he said. "Protect Eli and the girl." He turned back to face Coriano. "This is my fight."

A cold hand grabbed Miranda's and she looked down to find Nico dragging her out of the treasury.

"We'll meet you upstairs," Eli said, jogging after the women. "Don't lose."

Josef didn't answer, but Miranda saw him grin as he turned to face Coriano, the beam brandished before him. Coriano raised his white sword in greeting as the enormous treasury door drifted shut, obscuring them from view.

"We can't just leave him!" Miranda shouted, fighting Nico's grip. "Shouldn't we help? We could beat Coriano and go upstairs together!"

"You don't get it, do you?" Eli grabbed her shoulders and spun her around. "Do you think Josef's my servant? That I can just order him around?" He was breathing hard now, and his face was more serious than she had ever seen it. "'Do not postulate where you do not understand,'" he sneered, his voice warped into a biting mimicry of her own. "Maybe it's time you listened to your own advice, Spiritualist. Josef Liechten travels with me by his own choice. When he says 'This is my fight,' that's what it means. His fight, not ours to interfere with because it doesn't match what we want to do."

"But he's your friend!" Miranda shouted. "You can't just leave him to die! Coriano would have had him last time if Renaud hadn't released the storm. What makes you think he'll survive?"

"He won't lose." The absolute surety in Nico's voice struck Miranda like a hammer. The girl looked up at the Spiritualist, her enormous black coat twitching around her calm, pale face. "Josef's the strongest swordsman in the world," she said. "He won't lose to someone like Coriano and his arrogant white sword."

Miranda stared blankly, trying to think of an answer to that, but Nico was already gone, picking her way through the groaning soldiers and toward the stairs. Eli shot Miranda a look that dared her to say something more and started after the girl. Miranda took one last, long look at the treasury door. Then, with a heavy sigh, she turned and followed the other two through the ruined hall, past the splinters of the tiny servants' door where Josef had made their entrance, and up the broad main stair that led back to the upper levels of the palace.

After getting lost twice, they found the door that opened into the throne room's approach. The long hall had changed dramatically since Miranda and Marion had pushed their way through the crowd that had gathered to see Renaud ages ago. Black mourning banners hung from the vaulted ceiling in place of the Mellinorian flags, and the sconces on the walls burned low behind black shades. The edge of the newly risen moon was visible through the high windows, but the watery glass and high, swift clouds distorted into ghostly shadows what light the moon shed, leaving the lofty hall as gloomy as a cemetery forest. Eli, Miranda, and Nico crept along the wall, scurrying from fat stone pillar to fat stone pillar, but it soon became obvious that such precaution was unnecessary. The promenade hall was empty.

"Where is everyone?" Miranda said, stepping out into the dim light.

"Probably still fighting the fire," Eli said, cocking an eyebrow at Nico. "I really hope you didn't underestimate the situation. Henrith won't thank us for getting his throne back if the castle burns down."

"It won't." Nico glided silently through the gloom. "That furnace wasn't smart enough to manage anything as spectacular as burning down an entire castle."

"Comforting words indeed," Miranda said, shaking her head. "Come on. The throne room is this way."

They half walked, half ran the length of the long promenade. The golden doors to the throne room loomed large, glowing silver in the dim moonlight, and, as they discovered when they reached them, locked tight.

"Not even locked," Eli said, running his hands over as much of the ornate gold work as he could reach. "The doors themselves have been sealed somehow." He got down on his knees and tried to peer underneath, but the doors were set flush with the marble floor, without so much as a hair crack to look through.

"Nico," Eli said, stepping back. "If you would be so kind."

Nico nodded and shook her hands free of her bulky sleeves. Bracing her boots against the slippery marble, she slammed her palms against the metal and started to push. The doors groaned under the pressure and began to bow inward. Cracks sprouted in the carved gold, growing in cobwebby spirals as Nico pushed harder. With a soft, peeling crack, large sections of the gold began to flake off, revealing the dark metal beneath. The door squealed, and the marble under Nico's feet began to crack under the pressure, but the iron core of the doors beneath the soft gold did not budge. Nico gritted her teeth and pushed harder still, growling under her breath. The stone supports around the doors began to creak. Grit fell from the ceiling. Small showers of dust at first and then fist-sized bits of stone started coming down like hail.

"That's enough!" Eli shouted, ducking the falling rocks. "You're going to bring the ceiling down on our heads!"

Nico stepped back, panting. The doors, though mangled and dented with two Nico-hand-shaped craters, remained defiantly shut. Miranda bent down and picked up one of the larger flakes of gold leaf from the debris scattered across the floor. "The great, golden doors of Mellinor," she said and handed the piece to Eli. "Just a gilded fake."

"Gold is an impractical material for making doors, anyway." Eli crumpled the gold foil and deftly slipped it into his pocket. "Well," he said, "I wanted to be quick about this, but I guess there's no choice."

Nico stepped aside, and Eli took her place in the marble crater that had been smooth floor a minute before. He laid his hands on the dented metal and began whispering in the gentle tone Miranda had labeled his spirit sweet-talking voice. He was barely two words in when he jerked back, clutching his hand as if he'd been burned.

"We have a problem," he announced. "I can't talk to the doors."

"What's wrong?" Miranda picked her way through the rubble toward him.

Eli gazed grimly up at the twisted metal, shaking his hands vigorously. "They're terrified. So terrified, in fact, I'm surprised they're still standing."

Miranda looked at Nico, but Eli shook his head. "Not her. Demon fear is different, vindictive. This is enslaver work. Renaud's scared them shut."

Miranda raised her eyebrows skeptically and brushed her hands against the doors. As soon as her fingers made contact, white-hot pain shot up her arm. It went through skin, muscle, and bone and straight to the core of her spirit, and it was all she could do not to burst into tears. Her hands jerked away of their own accord, taking shelter in the cool, smooth cloth of her skirt. The burning remained, however, and with it an echo of terror so great that it made her legs watery. In the moment she touched the doors, one iron-clad command had overshadowed everything. It rang through the metal, greater than the fear and heavier than the pain, an unbreakable order: Don't move.

"That bastard." Miranda looked up at Eli, her face pale with fury. "We have to stop him. I don't care if he's after Gregorn's Pillar or not. Anyone who would do this to a spirit can't be allowed to live."

"For once, we agree." Eli reached up and began to unbutton his valet jacket, and then the white shirt underneath. "I hadn't meant to use this just yet," he said, "but I can't let Josef find us standing around, can I?"

He turned, and Miranda cringed before she could stop herself. His jacket and shirt hung open, revealing his bare chest. A series of angry red burns ran in a swirling pattern from his collarbone to just above his navel. Before she could ask what caused such an injury, the burns began to hiss. Smoke rose up from the marks in a white plume, curling into a cloud that smelled faintly of charred flesh. The temperature in the room began to rise. It was a pleasant, dry heat at first, but it increased exponentially with every breath Eli took. The ball of smoke above the thief's head blackened as the heat grew. Sparks flashed at its center, faintly at first, then more violently, until the cloud was popping like a greenwood bonfire. Despite the fire show happening less than a foot above him, Eli's face was calm and his eyes were closed, as if he were asleep. The cloud was as hot as a smelter now, and Miranda took a step back as the hissing and snapping reached a crescendo. With a final crack, a tremendous blast of hot air and smoke shot out of the cloud, and every lamp in the hall snuffed out at once.

For a moment, the world went black, and then bright red light, more intense than any fire, blossomed in the air above Eli. The light swirled and grew, blending smoke and fire to form feet, then legs. A broad-barrelled chest three times as tall as Miranda flashed in the darkness, growing muscular arms, boulder-sized fists, and shoulders like fiery mountains. Finally, with a new burst of heat, the remaining light condensed into an enormous flame-wreathed head whose pointed crown brushed dangerously near the peak of the hall's vaulted ceiling. Fully formed, the creature stretched languidly, sending a shower of sparks down around him. Red light rippled along the new-made muscles, tracing the intricate connections between limb and trunk as the creature's surface hardened from smoke and fire into red-hot stone. When it was done stretching, it tilted its enormous head down. Glorious, fiery swirls moved like weather fronts across its face as the great hinge of a mouth opened wide, dripping fire.

"Eli," it said. "It is good to see you."

Eli pulled his coat closed, covering his now unmarred chest. "You, too, old friend."

Miranda could not believe what she was seeing. The enormous spirit glowed like the heart of a smith's fire, but the solidity and weight reminded her of Master Banage's great stone spirits. The heat coming off it was more powerful than Kirik's at full burn, and the giant hadn't even done anything yet.

"A lava spirit," she said, not bothering to hide the amazement in her voice. "I've never met a wizard who could take one as a servant, not even Master Banage."

"You still haven't met one," Eli said. "Karon isn't a servant. He's my companion."

"But," Miranda gaped, "how do you control him?"

"I don't," Eli said, grinning. "I ask."

The enormous, burning spirit looked from Eli to Miranda, then back again. "You're keeping strange company these days," he rumbled.

"Only temporarily," Eli assured him. "Now, I was hoping you could do me a favor. I need these doors open."

Karon glared at the doors. "That's a powerful command they're under. I may have to kill them."

"At this point, that might be a mercy," Eli muttered. He looked at Miranda, whose distress was obvious, and he sighed. "Be gentle, if you can. The Spiritualists have always been a bunch of bleeding hearts."

Karon nodded and turned to the doors. Miranda could feel them shaking through the marble, still too scared to open even when faced with death. As the lava spirit stepped forward, Nico and Eli retreated behind one of the support pillars, and, a moment later, Miranda followed. The hall shook as the lava spirit positioned himself in front of the trembling doors. Karon pounded his fists together a few times, getting them white hot. Then, with a hiss, he slammed his glowing hands into the quivering metal. The doors screamed when he made contact, filling the air with the bloody stench of iron. Melting gold flowed in glowing rivers down the door's surface as the remaining scrollwork and flourishes dissolved under Karon's fire like marzipan dipped in steam. Karon ignored the wealth flowing around him and wedged his glowing fist deeper into the iron's screaming heart. At last, the terrified metal could hold no longer, and the doors began to slip away. Iron dripped like wax from Karon's fingers, falling in large, hissing black drops to splash against the stone floor. Back in the hall, Miranda huddled behind Eli, cringing away from the splatters of liquid metal and the smelter blast of Karon's heat. Her left hand clutched the empty finger where Allinu's ring normally rested. Never in all her life had she wished so hard for her cool mist spirit.

At last, the heat faded, and Miranda felt the thunderous stomp of Karon stepping back. She peeked around the corner. All that was left of the golden doors of Mellinor was a gaping hole, its melted edges bleeding liquid metal onto the blackened, cracked floor.

Karon looked over at Eli, who was admiring the wreckage from a distance.

"Good work," the thief said, nodding.

The lava spirit's face rippled in what Miranda guessed was a smile. Eli strolled forward, stepping without hesitation over the still-smoking metal. "Very good work indeed," he said, grinning up at Karon. "Now, if you don't mind, I'd like it if you could hang around a bit longer. I have a feeling I'll need your help again sooner than I'd like."

Karon nodded and squatted by the ruined doors, watching with intent as Eli stepped over the smoking threshold.

Beyond the circle of Karon's ambient glow, the throne

room was as dark as the treasury had been. Miranda stepped forward, squinting against Karon's glare, and, as her eyes adjusted, the room began to take shape. The first thing she noticed was that the royal banners that had lined the far wall were gone. So were the elegant lamps, chairs, and end tables that had once ringed the open room. In their place, the entire contents of the treasury—golden statues, jewelry, weaponry, overturned chests of embroidered silk, everything—had been stacked along the walls in sloppy piles. But most upsetting of all was what lay directly ahead of them. At the far end of the room, at the foot of the dais steps, the gilded throne of Mellinòr lay on its side, broken and splintered, as if it had been kicked off its perch. In its place, standing like a trophy at the top of the tall dais, was a squat, gray pillar.

CHAPTER
22

The two swordsmen stared at each other long after the sounds of the footsteps of the fleeing wizards had faded. Coriano held his white sword delicately in front of him, the blade shimmering with its own pearly brilliance. Brighter than the lantern at the bounty hunter's feet, the sword glowed like the moon in the dark, empty treasury. Josef kept his eyes even with it, letting them adjust to the light.

Coriano took an experimental step forward, but Josef's only response was to tighten his grip on the heavy beam and hold his ground. Coriano stepped back again, resting his sword wearily on his shoulder. "You can drop your oversized matchstick," he said. "I'm not going to roll over when you come swinging like those fools in the hallway. Draw your sword."

"You set all this up just to fight me," Josef said. "Well, here's your chance. Come when you're ready."

Coriano chuckled. "You think this is about you? Don't flatter yourself, Mr. Liechten. You are just the trappings.

You know what I'm after." His good eye flicked up and focused just above Josef's left shoulder, where the Heart of War's hilt waited. "Draw."

"The Heart is my sword," Josef said. "It chose me, so I'll decide when to draw. If you're so keen to cross blades with it, make this worth my while."

Coriano's eyes narrowed, and there was no hint of humor in his expression when he raised his sword again. "Have it your way."

Coriano lunged, and Josef raised his beam just in time to keep the white blade from burying itself in his neck up to the hilt. The sword cut through the solid hardwood like it was taffeta, and Josef was forced to duck as the swing carried over his head. But Coriano was waiting. As soon as Josef's head went down, the swordsman's knee hit him square in the ribs. The blow opened Josef's chest wound and sent him sprawling. He hit the stone floor hard and brought what was left of the beam up just in time to save his stomach from the next blow. The sword sliced clean through the wood again, but this time, Josef was prepared. At the split second when the white edge was buried deep in the beam, he twisted the beam. The blade caught, and Coriano's eyes widened as, with one enormous heave, Josef sent beam, blade, and swordsman hurtling through the air.

Coriano ripped his sword free and landed neatly. The beam clattered to the ground behind him, sending a shower of dust and splinters into the air. Josef struggled to his feet, clutching his chest, which was bleeding freely again. He drew his short sword and dropped into a defensive position.

"You can't be serious," Coriano said, sounding almost

annoyed. "You can't really expect to beat my Dunea with that metal hunk. She was made by Heinricht Slorn himself, the greatest master of Shaper wizardry the world has ever known. She was forged to be a killing blade in the hands of a master swordsman. This is her purpose, her nature, and you would face her with a sword so deep asleep, it doesn't even know which side its edge is on? Be reasonable, man. You won't be able to land a touch, much less a blow."

Josef grinned. "Only inferior swordsmen blame their swords, Coriano."

Coriano's eyes darkened. "We'll see."

He lunged again. Josef sidestepped, sliding his blade along the flat of the white sword, going for Coriano's knuckles. The older swordsman spun, and the white blade flew up to bite into Josef's left shoulder. Josef gritted his teeth and dropped to one knee, spoiling the blow and saving his tendon, but the shallow cut was enough. Pain shot down his arm, and he felt himself going off balance. The cut had sliced through the leather strap that kept the Heart of War in place, and the enormous sword's weight threatened to topple him. He twisted, slipping out of the harness before it could pull him to the ground. The Heart of War rang like a bell as it hit the stone floor, and the entire room vibrated with the deep, clear sound.

Josef didn't have time to see where it had fallen. Coriano's sword was coming again, a high blow aimed at his right shoulder. Josef dodged and swiped at the one-eyed swordsman's side, hoping to catch him off balance, but Coriano's white blade was there before Josef saw it move, and the top third of Josef's short sword clattered to the ground.

Coriano returned his sword to the ready position.

"We've been here before, Josef," he said calmly. "We both know how it ends. Pick up your true blade and fight."

Josef's downswing caught Coriano off guard. The jagged edge of the broken blade bit deep into the bounty hunter's leg, and only the older man's speed saved his artery from being cut clean through. Coriano danced away, sword flashing. Josef grinned and swung his stub of a sword, flinging an arc of Coriano's blood onto the dusty ground.

"One touch," he said.

Coriano didn't answer. He lunged with a snarl, and they began a complicated dance around the treasury. Coriano's blows fell lightning fast, and it was all Josef could do to dodge them. There were no wasted strokes in Coriano's style, every white flash was a killing blow, and only Josef's instincts, sharpened over years behind the sword, saved his skin from a new collection of holes. He blocked when he could, but the white blade whittled his sword to shavings. By the time they came around again to where the Heart had fallen, he was down to a chunk of hilt.

Josef was panting now, and even Coriano was looking strained. He was leaning to the right, favoring his uninjured leg, but even though the pain must have been blinding, the one-eyed swordsman never gave an opening. His sword flashed like a silver fish, and Josef gasped as the tip flew across his chest, leaving a burning trail. He stumbled, and the broken hilt flew out of his hand and clattered off into the dark. A hard kick followed the cut, and Josef found himself on his back again, gasping painfully, with Coriano standing over him. The swordsman's face was twisted in disgust. He laid his white sword against Josef's neck, where the artery pulsed, and the blade's light flickered.

"She's angry," Coriano whispered. "Angry enough that even your deaf ears should be able to hear her. All this time, chasing you through country after country, and when we finally catch you, this is all you can give us." He flicked his wrist, and the white sword's tip plunged into Josef's previously injured shoulder. "You're slow, and your guard is sloppy. You rely on gimmicks and refuse to fight with your full strength. Is this the master of the Heart of War?" He plunged his sword into Josef's other shoulder. "The greatest awakened sword in the world, with all of humanity to choose from, why did it choose you?"

The white sword slid down his blood-soaked chest, and Josef bit his tongue to keep from screaming.

"You are a waste of time," Coriano sneered, and, with a smooth thrust, he plunged his sword into Josef's stomach. When Josef struggled, Coriano looked him square in the eyes and twisted the blade, wedging it deeper. "You're not even worth dragging back for your bounty," he whispered, his voice sharp and deadly as the metal in Josef's flesh. "Lie here and rot, Josef Liechten."

He yanked his white sword out, and Josef couldn't stop the groan as his own blood ran hot and free down his sides and onto the cold ground. With a final disgusted look, Coriano turned away, casually wiping his blade on his sleeve.

He walked over to the Heart of War, still lying abandoned where Josef had dropped it. Its surface was ink black in Dunea's pearly light as Coriano knelt, running his fingers over the sword's dull, dented edge.

"Not a whisper," he murmured. "Not even a presence. Can this truly be the Heart of War?" He glanced over at Josef's prone body. "They say it was forged at the dawn of creation. The Heart of War is a legend that Dunea and I have dedicated our lives to finding, the greatest awakened blade, the ultimate test."

He reached out and grabbed the Heart's crudely wrapped hilt, but when he pulled, the sword did not budge. He scowled and pulled harder. The sword stayed completely still, as though it were part of the floor.

"The weight of a mountain," Coriano murmured, rocking back on his heels. "It is the real thing, the true Heart of War. Only the hand it chooses can lift it." He traced the hilt one last time, and the awe on his face faded. "How tragic that we should meet it now, when it chose so poorly."

He stood up, sliding the River of White Snow back into her sheath. "The Heart will lie here, then, until it chooses a new master." He looked sadly at Josef. "You, on the other hand, will be carted off and buried alone as a thief. A fitting end for the man who failed his sword and denied us our great ambition."

He shook his head and turned away, limping toward the treasury door. Josef lost track of the uneven footsteps' sound almost as soon as they began. The dim cavern was growing darker, and the cold stone pulled at him until he was as heavy and motionless as the floor itself. However, even as the sound around him faded, the mantra in his head grew stronger, one word echoing through his fading consciousness.

Move.

It had been there since he took the first blow, soft at first, easily lost in the heat of combat. Now, when things were still and his life was leaking out of him, it was deafening.

Move.

Move.

MOVE.

Josef closed his eyes. He had to be very close to death indeed to hear this voice. Finally, he answered. "I can't."

Get up, it shouted, loud enough to make him wince. He turned his head slightly. The Heart of War was barely a foot away. All he had to do was reach out, but his arm would not move.

Take me, the deep voice said. *Fight with me.*

"I can't," Josef said again. "How will I become stronger if I rely on you to win my battles?"

The strange voice sighed. *If you don't draw me, Josef Liechten, you will die here, and this pathetic weakness will be the height of your achievement.*

Slowly, his breath coming in short, shallow gasps, Josef moved his arm. Slowly, he dragged his hand across the stone floor, now damp and sticky with his blood. He reached out, one finger at a time, inch by painful inch, and gripped the long, crude handle of the dull, black sword.

Now—the Heart of War gave a satisfied sigh—*we can begin.*

Coriano had just reached the iron treasury door when he heard the scrape of metal on stone. He looked over his shoulder, and his good eye widened. At the center of the room stood Josef Liechten. His head was down, and his wounds were still bleeding sluggishly, but he was standing straight, in a fencer's ready position, and in his hand was the Heart of War.

Coriano turned and drew his sword. Dunea was quivering with anticipation, her light bright and eager, but the

Heart of War looked no different than it usually did, and Coriano felt a stab of disappointment.

"Is your blade still asleep?" he asked, circling. "All awakened swords gain their own light as they grow. I expected the Heart to shine like the sun, but you can't even manage that."

Josef didn't respond. He stood perfectly still, breathing deeply. This close to death, he could feel Coriano's sword—a sharp, cold, feminine, bloodthirsty presence. By contrast, the sword in his hand was heavy and blunt, but with that weight came the absolute knowledge that, when he swung, it would cut.

Coriano raised his sword. "If you disappoint me this round, swordsman," he said, sneering, "I'll take your head."

He sprang forward, aiming high to strike Josef's injured right shoulder. However, right before his blow landed, Josef moved. His actions were slow and deliberate, so different from his frantic dodges before. The Heart of War moved with him, following the curve of his blood-streaked arm. Together, they struck, forcing Coriano to change up in midstride, bracing Dunea with both hands to block the blow.

It was like being hit with a mountain.

Coriano flew backward, slamming into the wall. His ribs cracked like kindling, and only his instinctive reaction to tuck in his head saved his skull from shattering against the stone. However, before he could even process his body's reaction, Dunea's voice shot through the blinding pain, and he almost retched. The River of White Snow was screaming, her light undulating in wild patters across her blade, save for one section. Where the Heart had struck, the white steel had caved in. Coriano could not believe what he was seeing. Nothing he'd fought before had ever been able to scratch his awakened sword. He opened his spirit without hesitating, forcing his calm over her panic, forcing her to straighten out. She extended slowly, reasserting her shape. As she drank in his calm, he felt her spirit sharpen to a cutting edge. He looked up and found Josef waiting, still standing in the middle of the room, the Heart of War held loosely in one hand.

Coriano pushed away from the wall, forcing himself to ignore the pain. This was it at last, their shared ambition, a true duel between awakened blades. His palms were sweaty against Dunea's red-wrapped hilt as he took his ready position. This was what they had been training for. This moment was why they had chased Josef across half the known world. He held Dunea before him, and her light was nearly blinding. He'd never felt her so alive, so ready to strike. He brought his spirit as close to hers as he could and matched her killing instinct with his own, a musician tuning a chord to its true tone. When there was no more dissonance between them, he leveled her blade at Josef's chest and lunged.

He moved faster in that moment than he had ever moved before. With his spirit fully opened and roaring through him, his body felt as quick and weightless as sunlight. Only Dunea had weight, a heavy, killing quickness that could slice through bone, stone, and steel. Together, they were on Josef before he could have seen their movement, sword and swordsman moving as one to strike the larger man's heart.

Josef moved as if underwater, slowly and deliberately raising his blade. It was as though he lived in a different

world, where time was a physical thing, a sticky morass
between seconds that he swam through like a carp, faster
than sound, faster than light, and inexorable as gravity.
Even at his own blinding speed, Coriano could only
watch as Josef turned, set his footing, and lifted the Heart
of War to receive Dunea's blow. He saw it happen, and
yet Coriano could not change his strike. He could not
move fast enough.

There was a flash of blinding light when Dunea struck
the Heart, and Coriano felt himself falling. He hit the
ground hard, skidding across the stone until he came
to a stop several feet behind Josef. He lay still, unable
to breathe from the impact, and tried in vain to see
where he was. The room was suddenly very dark. For
a breathless second, he lay there in confusion, and then
he felt the warm slickness coating his stomach, and he
understood.

His hand was stretched out in front of him, still
clutching Dunea's hilt. Just above the guard, the white
blade ended in a ragged edge of torn metal. The rest
of the sword was in a dull, tangled heap a few feet in
front of him, and though he reached out to her with the
shredded remains of his spirit, the sword did not answer.
The River of White Snow was broken, and her light had
gone out.

Coriano's anguished cry echoed through the dark,
empty room, and Josef forced himself to turn. The Heart
of War's spirit was still coursing through him, and he had
felt it tear through the white sword and into Coriano's
chest as if his own arm had been the cutting blade.
Coriano was lying in a quickly spreading pool of blood.
His shoulders were shaking, and his hand still clutched

his sword's guard, the only part of the blade that was still snowy white. As if he knew he was being watched, Coriano forced himself to roll over. When his face came into view, his skin was as strained and white as his sword had been, marred only by the dark purple stain of his scar and a thin trickle of bright blood on his lip.

Josef could feel the Heart's power receding, but before he buckled, he forced himself to take a step forward. He plunged the dark blade into the stone floor and rested his weight against it. "You got your wish," he said, panting. "Was it worth it?"

Coriano's fingers tightened on the ruined hilt, leaving dark finger prints on the crimson silk. "No," he breathed at last. "Nothing is worth losing her." He brought the broken sword toward him, clutching it to his chest. "But it was the only end that could make us happy." He smiled. "Our souls will remember your name, Josef Liechten, and when we are reborn, we will hunt for you. Do not disappoint us…"

The last words were a hiss as Coriano's final breath left his body and he lay still, Dunea's hilt cradled against his chest. Josef watched as long as he could as the Heart's power faded. As it ebbed, the pain of his wounds came crashing back, and his heavy, tired body faltered under the impact. He slumped against the dull edge of his blade, fighting to breathe.

High above him, through the tons of stone, the castle began to quake.

CHAPTER
23

I see you've ruined my doors."

Renaud's voice slid through the darkness. Miranda jumped and squinted futilely against the lava spirit's light, but still she saw nothing. Only when Renaud turned his head could she see him clearly, standing on the dais by the pillar.

"They were ruined long before I got to them," Eli said, stepping forward. Karon bent down and glared menacingly through the warped remains of the doors, casting his fiery light over everything. Miranda and Nico walked under him to stand beside Eli.

"Step away from Gregorn's Pillar, Renaud," Miranda said.

"Well, well," Renaud said. "I told the lie myself, but I never thought it would turn into the truth. The Spiritualist and the wizard thief, working together."

"Your crimes dwarf his, at the moment." Miranda's eyes narrowed. "Give up, Renaud. There's no sandstorm to save you this time."

"I have no need for such childish ploys." Renaud turned back to face the pillar. "Not anymore."

"Stop!" Miranda shouted. "Listen to reason! Gregorn was the most feared enslaver who ever lived. He was not the kind of man to leave a boon for his ancestors. Whatever he left in that pillar will only hurt the balance between man and spirit that all life depends on, even yours, Renaud. If you use it, I guarantee the power you gain won't be worth it in the end. Step away, now!"

Renaud chuckled at her vehemence. "It's far too late for that, Miranda."

He shifted, turning toward Karon's light, and Miranda's eyes went wide. The enslaver's arms were buried in the pillar. Not just buried, eaten, up to his elbow. Where they met its surface, the pillar had corroded, leaving a black, gaping hole that glistened in the firelight like a rotten wound. As she watched, the pillar made a soft, wet sound, and another inch of Renaud's arms disappeared inside. Miranda covered her mouth, fighting not to be sick.

"Beautiful, isn't it?" Renaud sighed, gazing lovingly at the pillar's rotten surface. "Gregorn's greatest accomplishment lies just beneath this shell. Even now, the lineage of Gregorn in my flesh and blood is eating away at his barriers. When it is finished, Gregorn's legacy will be mine at last."

"You're mad," Miranda said, regaining her composure. "Anything Gregorn conquered as a wizard died with him long ago. What treasure could he have left you?"

"The only kind that matters," Renaud said calmly. "A spirit."

"Nonsense," Miranda scoffed. "No bond between

human and spirit, not even an enslavement, can last past the wizard's death."

"Ah, but you see," Renaud said as the pillar ate another inch of him, "Gregorn's not dead."

It took Miranda a few moments to find her voice after that pronouncement. Fortunately, Eli spoke for both of them.

"What do you mean 'not dead'? It's been four hundred years. You're kidding yourself if you think anything human can hold on that long."

"The human will is the greatest force in this world," Renaud said. "It can conquer any spirit, any natural force, even time, if only the wizard can master himself. Gregorn's will conquered a spirit powerful enough to raise Mellinor from the inland sea. A spirit so strong, so dangerous, that nations trembled at Gregorn's feet for three months before the strain of controlling the spirit finally destroyed his body."

"As it should," Miranda spat. "I hope that spirit crushed—"

"His body," Renaud said, cutting her off, "not his will. Our bodies, our shells are fragile. They age and die, but while we have will, we have life. Gregorn understood this in a way your Spirit Court, with all its self-censorship in the name of arbitrary *balance*, never could. When his flesh began to fail him, my ancestor used the last of his power to enslave the only human soul a wizard can control, his own."

"Impossible," Miranda said grimly. "You can't enslave yourself any more than you could lift yourself off the ground by grabbing your own shoulders."

"That is the blindness of your discipline," Renaud

sneered. "You Spiritualists are so quick to dismiss things, aren't you? So quick to say this is impossible, or that is impossible, and so, when the impossible happens in front of you, you're as blind and deaf as any human." He looked up at the pillar triumphantly. "Gregorn mastered himself and turned his own dying body into a pillar of salt, binding his spirit to this world. He left only one decree to his followers: form a kingdom around him and never let another wizard within its borders so that their spirits could not interfere with the delicate balance of his control."

Renaud leaned into the gaping, black blot that had now consumed over half of the pillar's surface, caressing it like a lover. "That's the real reason behind Mellinor's wizard ban," he whispered. "The reason why I was forced to grow up as a stranger in my own home, the reason I was banished, and the reason I returned. Everything in Mellinor grew from that one purpose: to protect Gregorn's control. Everything in this kingdom still serves her first king. Everything here exists so that this spirit who raised kingdoms and frightened nations, the spirit Gregorn gave up rebirth to gain, could never, ever escape him.

"That, Spiritualist," Renaud said, grinning cruelly, "is the true power of the human spirit, which you, with your rings and your self-limitations, will never reach."

Miranda trembled with rage, but before she could speak, Eli stepped forward.

"If you're so impressed by all this," he said casually, "why are you even here? If everything in Mellinor is in service to Gregorn, what are you doing to that pillar except undermining a greater wizard's work?"

"Taking what is mine," Renaud hissed. "I am Gregorn's

heir, the first wizard in the Allaze family since Gregorn himself." He thrust his hands deeper into the pillar, which shuddered and ate. "It is time for a new wizard king in Mellinor. Time for me to receive at last what my ancestor has held in trust for me for all these years. Together, we shall finish what Gregorn started. We will crush the trembling world into submission until every spirit waits on my demands and every wizard depends on my whim."

"Don't fool yourself!" Miranda cried, her voice shaking with barely restrained anger. "Gregorn isn't holding anything for you. A man who was willing to give up rebirth and sleep in a salt pillar for eternity just to keep a stranglehold on a spirit isn't the type to quietly pass on his legacy to a new generation. Even if that pillar eats you whole, Gregorn will never give that spirit to you!"

"Any other time you would be right, Spiritualist," Renaud said. "But what you don't realize is that, at this point, he doesn't have a choice." The enslaver looked at the place where his arms met the pillar, and his haughty smile became a mad grin. "After four hundred years, his soul has degraded so far past human, he's no better than the salt he's trapped in."

As he spoke, the black surface of the pillar began to bubble and hiss. Renaud laughed and plunged his hands in deeper. Then, with a sickening thrust, he threw open his spirit, and Miranda gasped as the black, sickening weight of his triumph-drunk will rolled over her.

The pillar groaned as Renaud's spirit crashed against it, stabbing into the black wound where his arms were buried and pressing down, forcing the hole wider. The black taint on the pillar's surface bubbled and hissed as Renaud forced himself in, using his spirit as a wedge.

The harder he pressed, the faster the dark stain spread, eating what was left of the pillar's knobby gray surface as rot from an infected wound devours a limb. With a final, triumphant stab of his spirit, Renaud's arms disappeared into the sucking maw. His head followed, then his chest and his legs until, finally, he vanished completely. The pressure of his opened soul still pounded through the room, but the man himself was gone, eaten by the pillar, which was now entirely covered in the slick, black rot.

The second the last inch of his heel disappeared into the pillar, a wailing scream cut through the air. Miranda slapped her hands over her ears, but it was no use. The spirit scream cut straight to the well of her soul. It was worse than the sound the sandstorm had made, for that had been many small voices and the effect had been broken up. This scream was one enormous, anguished cry that set her teeth on edge and brought tears to her eyes, but worst of all, worse than anything, was the ghost of a human voice behind it.

Black sludge began to pour off the pillar's surface, oozing from the hole Renaud left behind him and pouring onto the marble floor. It eroded the stone where it touched, hissing loudly as it washed down the dais steps, and the smell almost made Miranda vomit. The liquid stank of rotten meat, like open sewage on a hot day. The stench filled the room to bursting, until Miranda could feel it eating her skin.

"What is it?" she choked out, looking frantically at Eli.

"Gregorn," Eli said, his voice muffled by the handkerchief he'd covered his nose and mouth with. "Or what's left of him. Renaud's forcing him out."

The ooze from the pillar showed no sign of stopping. It flowed down the dais to pool on the floor. The stone floor hissed and cracked as the acid spread across it with frightening speed, and yet the pillar showed no signs of slowing. Above it all, Renaud's spirit hung like an iron weight, and the fearsome spirit wail went on and on—almost human, yet never stopping for breath. When the black pool reached the center of the throne room, Renaud's spirit jerked and the pool froze, quivering like a caught leaf.

"Gregorn," the enslavement boomed through Renaud's voice, sending enormous ripples through the black liquid. "Kill them."

The wailing scream spiked, and the black sludge began to boil. No, Miranda took several steps back; not just boil, grow. The pool was rising, bubbling up into an enormous mound of black slime between them and the pillar on the dais. It grew and grew, and as it grew, its screaming deepened, until there was nothing human in it at all.

Eli looked up at the quivering, putrid, acidic sludge that was all that remained of the world's greatest enslaver, and his face paled. "Well," he whispered, glancing sideways at Miranda. "You're the Spiritualist, how do we stop it?"

"I have no idea," she confessed. "I've never even heard of something like this."

High above them, the peak of the mountain of ooze had reached the highest point of the vaulted ceiling. When it touched the stone, it wailed again, sending a rain of acidic globs down on top of them.

"Wonderful," Eli said, dodging the spray. "Just bleeding wonderful." He sighed deeply, though Miranda couldn't imagine how he managed it, considering the stench, and he looked over his shoulder at the lava spirit, still waiting in the hall. "It's never easy, is it?"

"Easy is boring," Karon rumbled, stepping through the ruined doorway.

"I hoped that was what you'd say." Eli smiled. "Well," he said and turned back to the blob, "let's have some fun, then."

Miranda felt the lava spirit's answering laugh deep in her stomach. The castle shook to its foundation as Karon charged forward, his glowing stone feet cracking the floor with every step, and his flaming fist aimed straight at the center of the quivering pile of black liquid. The blob that had been Gregorn surged forward to meet Karon mid-way, and Eli, Miranda, and Nico dove for cover as the two spirits collided in an explosion of black steam.

CHAPTER
24

Miranda hunched over, gasping for breath. For once, Nico and Eli were right down on the floor with her, coughing and choking as the black steam burned their lungs. Eyes watering, Miranda looked up in time to see the thick, acidic clouds swirling off Karon's molten fist as the lava spirit prepared to swing again.

"Wait!" Miranda choked out, but the lava spirit didn't hear her. His fist slammed into the slick mound that had been Gregorn, but the blob barely flinched. Instead, it sucked in the blow, sending tarry tendrils up Karon's glowing arm, trapping the spirits together. Black steam churned around them as the spirits screamed together. Karon struggled against Gregorn's grip, but the more he fought, the tighter the black tar adhered. Finally, with a great, rumbling cry, the lava giant opened his enormous mouth and breathed a column of white-hot fire over both of them. The blob shrieked and pulled away, showering acid that immediately evaporated in the shimmering heat.

A fresh wave of black steam surged across the room, covering everything in a stinging, inky cloud.

"You have to stop him!" Miranda wheezed in the direction she'd last seen Eli. "If he keeps evaporating the liquid like that, we're going to suffocate before he can make a dent!"

Somewhere in the black clouds, Eli coughed a few words, and the roaring of Karon's fires stopped. Almost instantly, the clouds began to clear. Wiping her eyes furiously, Miranda squinted up to see Karon frozen in midswing. Eli coughed again, and the lava spirit nodded. Karon brandished his smoking fist one last time at the black blob and vanished in a great puff of ash, which blew back to Eli.

"What are you doing?" Miranda shouted, struggling to her feet as Eli closed his shirt over the reemerging burn. "I didn't mean get rid of him entirely!"

"Can't have it both ways!" Eli shouted back. "Watch out!"

Denied its target, the acid blob screamed louder than ever, sending a rain of black sludge showering down. Miranda, Eli, and Nico ducked as the fist-sized globs struck the wall behind them, and sank deep in the dissolving rock.

"He'll melt the palace into slag at this rate!" Eli shouted over the spirit's wail.

"We have to do something!" Miranda cried.

"You tell me!" Eli cowered as more acid spattered around them. "I'm out of good ideas!"

"I'd take a bad one, at this point!"

Still screaming madly, the mound of sludge shivered from base to tip. Suddenly, with a sickening, liquid snap, a torrent of black water began to pour out of its base. It was as if a dam inside the sludge had burst, sending a river of foamy, black liquid roaring across the floor straight toward them. It happened so quickly, Miranda couldn't do anything except watch in horror as the wave rushed at her. Only when the black tide washed over the piles of discarded treasure, dissolving the carved mahogany and precious metals in the time it took to catch her breath, did Miranda's instincts gain the upper hand on her fear. She spun around and dashed for the far wall, her feet skidding across the marble. As soon as she was close enough, she launched herself at the wall, and her grasping fingers caught the edge of a decorative niche. She hauled herself up, tossing over the stone bust of some Mellinorian king or other to make room, and pressed her body as far back into the crevice as she would fit. Eli followed her lead, climbing into the alcove next to hers.

"Nico," he shouted, "there's a shelf a bit higher up you could jump to."

But Nico didn't answer. Miranda peered over the lip of his hiding place. Several feet below, the girl was standing at the base of the wall, stoically watching the black tide as it rushed toward her.

"Nico," Eli said more urgently, leaning out of his crevice and thrusting out his arm. "Take my hand!"

"Josef told me to protect you," Nico said, not even looking at him.

"Don't be an—" He gasped and ducked as a black wave crashed against the wall, sending burning spray up the walls around them. Miranda turned away in horror as the black surge covered Nico's lower body, and waited for the scream.

But there was no scream, not even a pained gasp. Miranda turned back. Nico was standing in inky liquid up to her knees. Smoke rose in white plumes where the acid touched her, yet her posture was as calm as ever. She might have been wading in a warm river for all the attention she paid the black water eating at her legs.

At the center of the room, the black blob quivered, and the tide of black sludge receded with a sucking hiss. Miranda watched in spellbound horror as the girl's legs came back into view, bracing for the worst. However, while Nico's trousers, boots, and the hem of her coat were completely dissolved where the acid had submerged them, her pale skin was untouched, as were the heavy silver manacles she wore on her ankles.

Gregorn screamed in angry confusion as Nico took a step forward, her bare, uninjured feet moving through the sludge of the dissolved treasure in quick, light steps. As she walked, a soft, dry sound cut through the spirit's wailing. It sounded like dust blowing through grass, and it took Miranda a few seconds to realize that Nico was laughing. The girl hopped clear of the treasure detritus and stood before the screaming sludge spirit, tilting her head back so she could see all of him at once. When she spoke, her voice was full of that horrible, dry dust laughter.

"You think you can beat us with that?"

The black sludge froze in midshriek and hung there, quivering. Nico watched for a moment, and then she raised one bony hand to her throat, and the temperature in the room plummetted.

In one smooth motion, Nico tossed her coat to the ground. Without its bulk to hide her, she was skeletally thin. Her threadbare shirt was sleeveless, and her bony arms hung like cracked branches from a crooked trunk. Her silver manacles glowed with their own light, casting weird shadows across the acid-etched floor as she reached up to take off her hat.

"Nico . . ." Eli's voice held a warning, but if the girl heard him, she ignored it. "That stupid girl," he whispered.

Miranda didn't have to ask what he meant. Without the coat to hide her, the girl's aura was inescapable. Predatory menace rolled off her in waves, stirring Miranda's deepest instincts to run, to get out. But she could not move. Deep, irrational, primordial fear had turned the air to glue, snaring her soul like a rabbit under a wolf's paw. She could do nothing except cower in her alcove and watch, gasping in the acidic air and waiting for the threat to kill her or pass by. For the first time, she understood why all spirits fear a demonseed, and why Gin had been so adamant about killing the girl, no matter how small or controlled she seemed.

"Can't you stop her?" Miranda whispered through gritted teeth.

"Only Josef can stop her when she gets like this." Eli was pressed so far back in his alcove Miranda couldn't see him anymore. "You might want to get down," he whispered.

Nico stretched her arms out, flexing her shoulders. One by one, the thick manacles at her wrists, ankles, and neck popped open with a hard, metallic snap. Each time, the silver clung to her for a moment, screaming angrily, but even fully awakened metal can't fight gravity. The manacles hit the floor with a crash, cursing Nico all the way down. As soon as she was free of their touch, the small girl's posture changed completely.

The Nico who stood at the center of the circle of cast-off clothes and silver restraints was an entirely different creature than the Nico who had entered the throne room with them. Her thinness was no longer awkward, but deadly and cutting, like garrote wire. Her movements were languid as she dropped lazily into a stance, her newly freed hands flourished in front of her.

With a thin smile Nico stared up at the enormous sludge. Then the dim moonlight seemed to bend around her, and she vanished.

The sludge roared as shadows, blacker than any simple darkness, streaked across its surface, appearing and vanishing in an instant, like black heat lightning. It was nauseating to watch, but Miranda could no more look away than she could sprout wings and escape. Everywhere the shadow touched, a large section of acidic sludge vanished. It wasn't that it got knocked away, or that the creature was pulling it back. Where the darkness landed, that piece of the blob was simply gone. Within a few seconds, the acid spirit looked like a mouse-nibbled biscuit, and the fear in the room was suffocating. The stones were screaming, the unlit lamps were screaming, the gold-plated decorations, the remaining contents of the treasury, the glass windows, the air itself, *everything* in the throne room was screaming nonsense in a state of full panic. The voices stabbed Miranda's ears, filling them to bursting, but all she could do was press herself tighter against the screeching wall and watch wide-eyed as Nico winked into view, landing neatly at the center of the throne room.

Gregorn's sludge was about half the size it had been. It lay at the far end of the room, whimpering pathetically, but still protecting the dais as it had been commanded to do. Nico, on the other hand, looked healthier than Miranda had ever seen her. Her pale skin was flushed and glowing. Her body was no longer skeletal, but strong and supple. Her legs were longer and her torso more filled out. She also looked taller, a suspicion confirmed by the new gap between the hem of her shirt and the waist of her trousers. It was as if she'd aged ten happy, healthy years, and yet the freezing, predatory menace rolling off her was stronger than ever. She glided across the corroded stone, and the acidic sludge shrank back, but it would not give up its position in front of the dais, not even when Nico stopped a foot away from its trembling base.

"Nico!" Eli's voice was thin and strained, but the fact that he could speak at all was a miracle. "Don't do it, Nico!"

The girl ignored him. With a triumphant cry, Nico plunged her bare hand deep into the acid's center. If Miranda had named the spirit's scream a wail before, the cry it gave now reduced its earlier sounds to whimpers. Gregorn's spirit thrashed on the end of Nico's arm like a speared fish, slinging acid in huge arcs. But, despite its struggles, the spirit was shrinking. It was now not more than double the height of the dais. Then it was no taller than Gin, and still it was shrinking, its cries growing smaller and smaller. When the sludge was no larger than Nico herself, a new shape began to emerge. The black tar narrowed and separated, revealing long appendages. Ribs appeared at its center, and its peaked top became a rounded head. Two legs, barely more than tar over bone, appeared at the base, and shoulders like knives led to twiglike arms. Finally, the last of the sludge disappeared altogether, and Nico stood over the kneeling, black form of an old, skeletal man.

Wisps of hair still sprouted from his head, plastered down by black tar, and his face, his face was still human. Sunken eyes grayed over with cataracts looked pleadingly up at his conqueror. His cracked, black lips moved pathetically, but no sound came out. Black tears pooled in the hollows of the ancient enslaver king's cheeks as he looked up at her, his ruined hands rising slowly to grasp Nico's wrist where her hand was buried deep in his hollow chest.

With a final, cruel smile, Nico yanked her hand free, and what was left of Gregorn toppled to the ground. He made no sound as he fell, the last of his human features crumbling to dust even before they struck the pitted stone. Nico shook the dust off her fingers, and Miranda knew as surely as if she'd been standing over him herself that Gregorn's spirit was dead.

"Nico." Eli's soft voice made Miranda jump. She hadn't seen him leap down from his alcove, but the thief was standing a dozen feet behind the demonseed. Cautiously, he held out his hand, the largest of Nico's manacles, her neck piece, dangling from his fingers. "You did well," he said. "You did as Josef asked. Now it's time to come back to us."

The girl turned slowly, regarding him through slitted eyes that flashed in the darkness with their own flickering light. The room was deafeningly silent. Everything seemed to be holding its breath as Nico considered him.

"Come back?"

Her voice was different. The dry dust scrape that had been just a whisper before now completely overwhelmed her natural sound. It was so alien, so strange, that if

Miranda had not seen Nico's lips moving, she would not have been able to name the speaker as human. Nico took a step forward, moving with unnatural grace toward the thief until she was only a few inches from Eli's outstretched hand. Then, with casual cruelty, she reeled back and punched him.

Eli didn't try to dodge. He took the blow full in the chest, and it sent him flying backward. He landed with a bone-snapping crunch on the scarred marble, the silver manacle clattering off into the dark. The second he hit the floor, Nico was on top of him again with another of her gut-wrenching, light-bending jumps. She kicked the manacle out of his hand and grabbed the thief around the neck, lifting him off the floor. "Come back?" she hissed, glaring at him with eyes that opened wider than human eyes should. "To what? I see how you treat the girl. A weapon, a *servant*. Our kind do not serve, thief!"

"I'm talking to Nico, not you," Eli said coldly. "You're just an interloper, a deadbeat tenant. We treat Nico as a partner, which is far more than I can say for you, bug."

She roared at that, drawing her fist to hit him again, but before she could strike, there was a silver flash in the thin space between them. Nico screamed and flailed backward, dropping Eli on the ground. Breathing hard, the girl reached down and wrenched something out of her chest. She tossed it to the ground where it landed with a clatter, and Miranda recognized one of Josef's knives. Eli grunted and rolled over, another knife ready in his hands.

But Nico's white skin was knitting itself back together as Miranda watched, and she crept toward Eli like a hunting spider. "You treacherous thief," she hissed. "How dare you take his blades!"

"Ah-ha," Eli said, coughing as he sat up slowly. "So there is some Nico left in there." He tucked the second knife back into his sleeve. "Listen to me, Nico. This isn't the real you. You're human, Nico. Still human, even now. Josef didn't nearly die five times over rescuing you just to have it end like this, in this nowhere kingdom." He held out his hand, his face kind and pleading. "Come back to us."

Nico paused and stared at his hand, and for a moment, the inhuman light in her eyes flickered out. Then it was back brighter than before. She lifted her clenched fist, ready to bring it down on the thief's unguarded head, but before she could swing, a tremendous crash stopped everything. Glass exploded above them, and Nico looked up just in time to see the swirling mass of gray fur and knife-sharp claws crash through the high window right before it landed on top of her.

Miranda pressed her hands to her mouth. The relief mixed with fear was almost more than she could bear. "Gin!"

Gin had Nico in his mouth. He shook her fiercely before flinging her as hard as he could against the stone wall. Her impact cracked the marble, and she slumped to the floor, her limbs bent under her at unnatural angles. Gin bounded to one side, putting himself between the crumpled girl and Miranda.

"I came as soon as I felt her," he growled, never taking his eyes off Nico's motionless body. "I told you, didn't I? Demons can't be trusted."

Miranda jumped down from her alcove and ran to him, flinging herself face down into his swirling fur.

"The king?"

"Still hiding and safe enough," he said quietly. "Not that any of us are 'safe' at this point." He voice thickened to a snarl as Nico stirred. "Get the thief."

Miranda nodded and looked around for Eli. The thief was still on his back where he had fallen, coughing painfully.

She ran to help him. "Can you stand?"

Eli nodded and took her offered hand, groaning as she pulled him to his feet.

Gin gave a warning growl. Nico was stirring, her cracked limbs righting themselves as they watched.

"What do we do now?" Miranda said.

"We do what we should have done when this mess started," Gin said. "We kill her."

"The dog might be right," Eli whispered, his voice thin and pained. "At this point, without Josef, I don't know anything else to do. Every moment she spends like this, our Nico goes further away. But whatever we do, let's do it quickly, otherwise"—he tapped his foot on the acid damaged stone—"the castle will do it for us."

Miranda froze. Now that he'd pointed it out, she didn't know how she'd missed it. Now that Gin had injured the demon and broken the spell of fear, every spirit in earshot was awake and calling for blood. Every piece of the throne room, from the broken glass to the stones under their feet, rumbled with desperate anger. Showers of dust cascaded from the ceiling as the marble strained against its mortar. Even the support pillars were edging closer, preparing to break free and let gravity do the rest, even if it cost them their lives, if that's what it took to kill the demon.

With a sickening series of cracks, Nico sat up. She

stretched out her arms, and the joints snapped back into place. As she moved, the terrified dust flung itself off her, creating a low cloud that obscured her movements. Even so, Miranda could feel when Nico turned, feel the girl's regard sliding over her skin. Then Nico opened her eyes, and Miranda's blood turned to lead. The girl's eyes, which were too large to be human anymore, glowed with a steady, otherworldly light. They shone bright as candles through the terrified dust, brilliant but illuminating nothing. The rest of her face was lost in shadow, but Miranda could see clawlike hands scraping as the girl edged to the rim of her crater, and that was enough.

Nico moved along the wall, gathering herself for another leap, but Gin didn't give her the chance. He charged with a howl, barreling toward the demonseed. She snarled in answer and sprang to meet him, winking through the darkness faster than Miranda could follow. But Gin's sight was better than Nico's, and the ghost-hound's teeth caught Nico's arm just before she landed a killing strike on his skull. She whipped her other arm around and caught his jaw before he could bite down, stopping his momentum like an iron wall. Gin struggled against her grip, and Nico cackled, her terrible eyes narrowing to glowing slits. She slammed her feet into the screaming stone and lifted the ghosthound off the floor. Gin yelped in surprise as Nico swung him over her head and slammed him into the cracked wall where she had landed before. The hound rolled as he flew, landing on his feet. His paws barely touched the stone before he pushed off again with a roar, barreling straight for Nico. The demonseed had no time to dodge before the flat of Gin's head hit her square in the chest and the two of them

went flying in a tangle of shifting fur and snapping fangs.
But when they landed, Nico was on top. With a triumphant cry, she plunged her claws into Gin's back, and the
ghosthound howled. He fought her as hard as he could,
rolling and snapping, trying to knock her off, but her
hand was deep in his muscle, and he couldn't dislodge
her. Dark red blood flowed down his sides, matting his
fur and hiding his patterns. His movements grew slug-
gish, but he would not stop fighting, even when his legs
collapsed. Miranda's throat was raw before she realized
was screaming, though she couldn't make sense of her
own words, or if they were words at all.

Without thought or warning, her spirit flung itself
open, and Miranda's power roared to life. Spirit voices
shot through her, clearer than ever before, flooding every
sense until she could almost taste where one soul ended
and the next began. Without thinking, she swept her spirit
across them. The response was immediate. Every spirit
was desperate for action, desperate to fight the intruder.
A direction was all it took. She thrust her hand toward
the demonseed, and the spirits leaped forward, screaming vengeance. A volley of broken glass, stone, and metal
came from every corner of the throne room to strike Nico
wherever there was room to strike. The impact ripped her
hand free of Gin's back, and she toppled over. The marble
floor was ready for her. The moment she hit, the stones
sank beneath her, going as soft as clay at Miranda's command. As soon as Nico was mired, the stone surged over
her arms, legs, chest, and neck before hardening again,
pinning the demonseed to the ground. Miranda ran forward, flinging out her hand. The throwing knife that Nico
had flung away clattered across the tiles and leaped into

her grip. Miranda clamped her fingers on the hilt as she jumped, aiming the point to land deep in Nico's exposed throat.

But the blow never connected. The demonseed ripped her legs free of the stone at the last moment and caught Miranda in the chest. The Spiritualist grunted in pain as the new impact hit the old bruises, and she tumbled backward, cracking her head on the stone floor. Nico sprang to her feet, flakes of dead stone falling off her like dried mud.

"Stupid girl," she hissed, her eyes glowing like lanterns in her shadowy face. Her hand shot out, grabbing Miranda around the throat. Miranda struggled violently as Nico lifted her off the ground, but her head was ringing and the demonseed's grip was like iced iron against her skin. Nico pulled her close, close enough that Miranda could smell the strange, metallic stench of the girl's transformed skin. The demonseed's mouth curled into a sharp-toothed grin as she dangled Miranda from her outstretched arm, the Spiritualist's still kicking weakly as her air ran out.

"That's enough."

The deep voice cut clean through the spirits' clamor, leaving only silence in its wake. Nico froze, her lantern eyes flicking past Miranda to the tall figure standing in the ruined doorway, outlined by the falling dust.

Josef stood lopsidedly, Heart of War under his shoulder, like a crutch. Very slowly, he hobbled past Eli, who was still on the floor, clutching his ribs, past Gin, who lay motionless on the ground, and stopped right behind Miranda.

"Put her down."

Nico obeyed, and the Spiritualist landed in a heap on the shattered floor, coughing and clutching her throat. Neither the demonseed nor the swordsman paid her any attention. They stood face to face, Nico cowed and heaving, Josef still and calm. With great effort, he shifted his weight to his own feet and lifted the Heart of War over Nico's trembling body.

"Time to come home," he said, and he brought the sword down.

Miranda could barely breathe. She knew the Heart of War was an awakened sword, but that did not describe what happened next. As the blade connected with Nico's shoulder, the Heart of War's spirit opened like a wizard's. Miranda had never even heard of a spirit that could open its soul, yet the Heart's presence was doubling and doubling again, growing exponentially until it filled the hall with its oppressive, immobile weight. It was as if a mountain had fallen on the castle with the sword at its center and Nico beneath it. She crashed to the floor, and Josef followed her down, sinking to his knees.

With a shuddering sob, Nico started to shrink, the terrifying light in her eyes fading away. Her claws dulled into fingers, and her frame shriveled to skin and bones again. As she shrank, the aura of fear receded, and Miranda felt the spirits calming as the Heart of War's weight pushed them into a deep sleep. Only when the room was still did the Heart's spirit begin to pull back. When the mountain was just a sword again, Josef lifted the black blade and slammed it into the stone beside Nico's head. She was lying on the floor with her eyes closed, small and feeble again, as if nothing had happened. Josef slumped down the dull blade of his sword, resting on his elbow beside her.

"Stupid girl," he muttered, brushing the wild black hair out of her sleeping face with a gentle finger. He smiled and, his eyes rolling back in his head, fell forward to lie beside her, the Heart of War standing over both of them like a guard.

Miranda didn't realize Eli was moving until he crawled past her, Nico's silver restraints tucked under his arm. He pulled himself to her and began clamping the manacles back into place, a grim look on his face. "Gin's still alive," he whispered roughly, locking the silver ring onto Nico's neck. "Get him up and get them out of here." He nodded toward Josef and Nico. "We're not safe yet."

At this point it was meaningless to argue. Miranda climbed slowly to her feet and stumbled toward Gin's collapsed body, almost crying with relief when she saw his bloody chest rise and fall.

"Gin," she whispered, fisting her hands into his coarse fur. "We have to move."

The ghosthound's orange eyes cracked open, and he shifted just a little. "Gin." She shook him, blinking back tears. "Come on, mutt. We have to get you out of—"

"Leaving so soon?"

She had never hated Renaud's voice as much as she did at that moment. She turned slowly, putting her back against Gin's shoulder. On the other side of the throne room, still safe on its dais, the pillar waited. But, she squinted in the dim light, it was different now. All the black, rotten sections had vanished and, instead of its original dingy gray, the pillar's surface was now white and fragile as crusted snow.

A wave of spirit pressure burst out from the dais, and the room began to shake. Long cracks raced across the snowy surface of the pillar, and as they spread, the castle began to shake from its foundations. Showers of white dust poured down as cracks blossomed across the marble arches that held up the roof. Fissures sprouted on the walls, running like dust-bleeding capillaries from floor to ceiling as the stone spirits, already traumatized by multiple enslavements and a demonseed, finally started to lose their grip. Whole sections of wall began to come loose as Miranda watched, shattering the glass windows as the ceiling's weight began to shift.

Then, as suddenly as it had started, the shaking stopped. The room became deathly still, as though the world were holding its breath, waiting.

In the silence, the pillar split open.

CHAPTER
25

Gregorn's Pillar split cleanly. The crystallized salt fell away in two neat halves, dissolving into fine crystals that spattered like wet snow against the marble. Where the salt crumbled, watery light swelled in its place, blue and calm like the noon sun seen from the bottom of a clear lake. At the light's heart, casting long, dancing shadows across the ruined stone floor, was Renaud.

He stood at the center of the dais, the last of the salt falling around him, and across his shoulders, draped like the pelt of some mythic beast, was a glowing waterfall. It roared in a torrent over his shoulders and down his back, and then, just before it spilled onto the floor, it hit the wall of Renaud's open spirit and turned in midair. The water's own momentum forced it back up his chest and over his shoulder, where the cycle began again, an endless circle of water churning in furious anger. But no matter how it writhed and tossed, its flow was contained by the barriers of the enslavement. Renaud's control was

well entrenched, and the water could not break free even
enough to wet his clothes, which were completely dry
despite the flood rushing across them.

Renaud held out his hand and the water followed
his movements, charging down his arm to form a long,
thin spike at the tips of his fingers, which he leveled at
Miranda's head.

"That's two kings of Mellinor your little group has
murdered," he said. "Not to mention the destruction of
our throne room. I don't think anyone could object to
your execution, at this point."

"The only murderer here is you, Renaud," Miranda
hissed, clutching Gin's fur. "Release that spirit!"

Renaud chuckled, and the water flowing across his
shoulders roared even faster. "I don't think you want me
to do that. I see now why Gregorn was willing to die to
keep this spirit. He's barely awake, but just look what he
can do."

Renaud swung his arm, and the spike of water flew out
in an arc, striking the wall like a cannon shot. The stones
exploded outward, sailing into the night. Wind rushed in,
and Miranda ducked as a shower of rubble flew toward
her. When Renaud pulled back his hand, the entire north-
west corner of the throne room was gone, leaving a gaping hole where the wall had been.

The stones in the roof squealed, but with one of their
corner supports gone, it was a losing battle against gravity. One by one, they hurtled to the ground, cracking the
floor where they hit. Renaud cackled, and the water's
light flashed wildly around him, shifting from blue to
white to almost black in sickening confusion.

"Renaud!" Miranda shouted, putting her arms up in

a desperate attempt to shield herself and Gin from the falling rocks. "Enough of this! You're going to destroy everything if you keep this up!"

"And what do I care?" Renaud's voice trembled with the force of the spirit he held back. "Mellinor is mine to do with what I like!" He held out his hand again, and the water rushed over it in a fountain of white spray. "This is the heart of Mellinor," he shouted, raising the water high over his head. "Everything else is just an empty shell!"

As he clenched his fist, Miranda could hear the water's own deep voice, warped by the enslavement, screaming in frustration as it fought Renaud's hold. And as it screamed, the palace began to shake worse than ever.

"We have to get out of here!" Miranda turned frantically to Eli, trying to cover Gin's head as ever-larger pieces of ornamental stonework crashed down around them. "That idiot won't stop until he brings the whole place down!"

Eli looked up from where he was fixing the last of Nico's restraints, but whatever he'd been about to say was interrupted as a large chunk of stone arch landed not half a foot away from Josef's head, covering them all in a shower of grit.

"All right," Eli growled. "That's it."

The naked fury in his voice shocked Miranda out of her protective crouch, and she looked up just in time to see another, fist-sized stone hurtling toward Nico's unprotected shoulder. Eli caught it without looking and hurled it as hard as he could at Renaud's grinning face.

"Do you think this is fun?" he shouted. "Do you think this is a game? Is beating us so important that you'll bring down your own roof to do it?"

Renaud shattered Eli's stone with a flick of his hand. "Don't flatter yourself, Monpress. This was never about you. You and your collection of oddities were just in the wrong place at the wrong time when fate decided to hand me my birthright." He grinned maniacally. "Consider this my thanks, a throne room for your tomb, my way of repaying the unknowing kindness you did me."

The water hissed as he spoke, changing its flow as Renaud's triumph rippled through his wide-open spirit, subtly altering the shape of the enslavement. Suddenly, Miranda had an idea.

"You might want to watch your captive before you speak of kindness," she said, turning to face Renaud head on. "I don't know what that spirit used to be, but Gregorn died trying to control it." She smiled her most infuriating smile. "No matter what you say about birthrights, Renaud, you're no Gregorn. I give you fifteen minutes before the water breaks your soul and eats you alive."

"What would you know about control, girl?" Renaud thrust out his hand, and a wall of water surged down from the dais, rising over Miranda in a great wave. "You Spiritualists know nothing about control! You go on and on about balance, about our duty to the spirits, but we wizards are the ones with the power! The spirits obey *my* will, even one who bested Gregorn!" He was shouting now, his face scarlet. This close, Miranda could feel the chains of his enslavement vibrating with his rage, and the suspended wave he held over her head began to tremble. "Soon," Renaud crowed, "even you will learn that this is the proper balance! With the wizard on top, and the spirit below!"

"If that's the case," Miranda said and smiled at him

through the wall of water. "If you're so in control"—just a little more—"why is your shirt wet?"

Renaud's arm shot up to his shoulder. Sure enough, his black shirt was soaked through. He snatched his hand away, but not before a tremor of uncertainty fluttered through the enslavement that held the water captive. A tremor was all it needed. The wave roared in triumph and crashed against the enslavement's barrier. Renaud staggered and slammed his control down again. Then, with a snarl, he crashed the suspended wave down on Miranda's head.

The force of the water knocked Miranda off her feet. She spun in the freezing, dark water as the current batted her back and forth, crushing the air out of her lungs. Her chest burned as she tried desperately to hold on to what breath she could, but no matter how she struggled, the water would not let her go. It hadn't been enough, she realized as cold crept in. He'd regained his control too quickly. But even as she sank, she could still feel the echo of Renaud's uncertainty, and far below her in the icy depths, she felt a tremble of hope. As the water darkened around her, the last bubble of Miranda's breath drifted from her lips in the shape of a request. Deep at its heart, as far as possible from the iron walls of the enslavement, the water listened.

Eli was on the move as soon as the wave crashed down. Enslaver, king, Gregorn's heir, whatever he decided to call himself, Renaud was still human, and he could concentrate on only so many things at once. Eli didn't know what had possessed Miranda to taunt a man bent on destruction, but she had his full attention, and the thief was determined not to let the opportunity pass him by.

Using the water to keep himself out of Renaud's line of sight, Eli crept to the fallen ghosthound.

"Mutt," he whispered, poking Gin's side. "Wake up, mutt. Your mistress needs you."

The ghosthound was unresponsive. Only the shallow rise and fall of his chest showed that he was alive at all. Eli put a little more weight into his voice. "Gin, wake up. Miranda's going to die."

The ghosthound's breathing hitched as the spirit voice trembled through him, and one of his ears swiveled in Eli's direction.

"You are very forceful, aren't you, wizard?" Gin's voice was barely a whisper. "I'm an inch from death myself. If you have the energy to use your tricks, why don't you save her?" The ghosthound opened one enormous orange eye and focused its menacing gaze on Eli. "We both know you can."

The thief grimaced. "I'd like to, but the price of playing the hero isn't one I can afford right now. It's you or nothing, mutt."

"Not...quite..." Gin closed his eye, but one of his ears flicked toward the water, and Eli looked up.

Miranda's body hung limp at the heart of the wave. On his dais, Renaud was grinning triumphantly, but as the enslaver lowered the water to get a better look at her, the Spiritualist's head jerked up. She met Renaud's grin full on, and her spirit opened like a flower.

Despite having no bound spirits to resonate the power, Eli took a step back as her spirit washed over him. It filled the room, warm and strong as a desert wind. There was no fear in it, no doubt, only the practiced, controlled power of a master Spiritualist nearing the peak of her craft, and that power struck Renaud like a wave of lead.

The enslaver fell to the ground, unable to move. With so much power coursing through the room, Eli could almost see the outline of Miranda's fully opened spirit bearing down, not on Renaud himself, but on the channels of the enslavement, cutting away the banks that held the water spirit captive. Using the current's own ebb and flow, Miranda sawed the cutting edge of her soul against the prince's overstrained will. With every surge of Miranda's power, the feedback through Renaud's connection with the spirit slammed him into the floor, grinding him into the stone. Cracks began to appear in his enslavement, and the well-contained wave began to sprout leaks. Shouting in triumph, Miranda and the water pushed together one last time. Then, with an explosive crack, Renaud's control shattered, and water burst in every direction.

The wave holding Miranda splashed to the ground, and she landed on her back, soaked and gasping beside Gin. The ghosthound shifted his head so that his nose pressed against her heaving side.

"I told you before, thief," he said, looking at Eli as he nudged Miranda into a sitting position. "My mistress is no weakling."

Miranda looked at Gin in confusion, still coughing, but there was no time to ask what he was talking about. Renaud was still on the ground. Miranda's spirit had closed when she fell, but the effects on the enslaver didn't seem to be fading.

"What did you do to him?" Eli said, reaching down to help her up.

"Exactly what he did to me," she said, taking his hand and letting him pull her to her feet. "He's learning the ultimate difference between Spiritualists and enslavers. You see, *my* spirits serve me willingly, so when I'm knocked on my back from spirit feedback, *my* servants don't try and take advantage of the situation." Her face broke into a triumphant grin. "Renaud's may not be so considerate."

With a thundering roar, the water surged toward the dais. Renaud raised his head, his spirit swinging wildly as he tried to reassert his control, but nothing he mustered could stop the wall of furious water rolling toward him, growing larger and faster with each moment. By the time it reached the dais, the wave's crest brushed the collapsing roof. In a final act of desperation, Renaud threw the brunt of his power at it, stopping the wave for a moment at its peak. But the enslaver's exhausted, overextended will could not hold back the water's rage, and his soul crumpled. The wave crashed down with a scream, shattering the stone dais. Miranda got one last look at Renaud's body as the water tossed him up, his pale face contorted in terror as he plummeted head first back into the swirling water and disappeared beneath the waves.

The moment he hit, the whirling spirit light in the water vanished, plunging the room into total darkness. Miranda gripped Gin's fur, letting the ghosthound's heavy breathing be an anchor for her thudding heart. Slowly, her eyes adjusted, and the world began to reinstate itself. The wind whistled softly through the shattered windows and the gaping hole in the wall, peeking in to see what the fuss was about before quickly blowing away. From the darkness where Renaud had fallen came the gentle sound of flowing water, but Miranda could see nothing. The dim moonlight seemed to avoid that section of the throne room. The quiet stretched on and on, and, at last, Miranda took a tentative step forward. She jumped back immediately as something freezing and wet touched her foot. Shivering, she pressed herself against Gin's warmth and squinted into the darkness.

In the indirect glow of the moonlight, she could just make out a thin layer of water spreading out from the ruined dais. It ran past the fallen stones, over the ruined floor, and under Josef and Nico's bodies. Gin shivered when it touched him, and Miranda tore a strip out of her ruined skirt to try and stem the flow.

"We have to move," she muttered. "This water's like snowmelt. They'll die if they sit in it much longer."

"I think temperature is the least of our worries," Eli muttered, staring into the darkness where the dais had been.

Before she could ask what he meant, a flash pulsed in the darkness and warm, blue light blossomed through the room. Blinking the spots out of her eyes, Miranda turned toward the dais as well, bringing her hands up to shield her eyes. In front of them, floating above the pile of rubble that had been the royal seat of Mellinor, was a tall column of pure, clear water. It hung in the air as if weightless, spinning slowly. The light at its heart was blinding bright, like the glint on a far-off wave. Water poured from its sides like a fountain, rushing in little streams down the rocks to join the spreading pool that was quickly carpeting the entire room in clear, cold water. The turning column slowed, then stopped, and though it had no face, no distinguishing features, Miranda felt its gaze land on her.

"Wizard," the deep, deep voice shook the castle to its foundations, making little waves in the freezing shallows the throne room had become. "Thank you for freeing me from Gregorn's legacy. You have saved me from a life of madness and servitude, and I owe you a great debt. To show my appreciation, I will hold back my waters until you and your companions have escaped."

Miranda stared at the water, dumbfounded. "Hold back your waters?" She looked down at the shallow river lapping at her feet. "Spirit," she whispered. "Who are you?"

The castle trembled again as the water chuckled, sending little waves splashing against her calves. "I forget," he rumbled. "My imprisonment has been a long time by my reckoning, but how much longer is it for you humans, with your lives like mayflies? Very well, as another part of my thanks, I will give you my name." The pillar of water twisted and brightened until its light banished the shadows from the room. "I am Mellinor, spirit of the inland sea."

CHAPTER
26

The inland sea..." Miranda's voice wavered.

"All of this land was once my basin," the spirit rumbled. "From the foothills of the mountains to what is now desert, it was all mine. Until that man came." The water's light turned a deep, angry blue. "Though he trapped me deep in the cold stone and stinging salt, I remembered sunlight and moonlight, the wind on my waves, and the madness did not take me." His voice trembled, and the water began to flow more quickly. "Now, thanks to you, I shall feel the sun and wind again. I shall retake what was stolen, and, after so long alone, my waters shall lap against my shores once more."

"An inland sea," Miranda said again. She looked up at the brilliant spirit, shaking to her toes with something that had nothing to do with the freezing water covering her feet. Now she understood how this spirit could have over-powered even the great Gregorn, and why the famous enslaver had used his own life to keep it trapped. The pillar of water floating over the ruined dais was no common spirit that could be trapped in a ring or compressed into a ball. This was the glowing heart of a Great Spirit, one of the masters of the spirit world. Miranda swallowed against the lump in her throat. A Great Spirit who wanted its land back.

"Wait!" Miranda stumbled forward. "Great Spirit Mellinor, wait. Mellinor, that is, the kingdom Mellinor, which now lies in your basin, is home to thousands of people. Millions of spirits have made homes there since you were trapped four hundred years ago. If you reclaim your land, then all of those people and spirits will drown."

"And what concern is that to me?" Mellinor rumbled. "If it was not for that enslaver, those spirits would never have taken root here. They should be grateful for the time they had."

"I know Gregorn did you wrong," Miranda cried. "If I could undo your imprisonment, I would, believe me! But those people, those spirits are innocent! Please, you can't just drown them!"

"Do not tell me what I can and cannot do, wizard!" The spirit's deep voice was choppy with rage, and the column of water swelled into a breaking wave. "I take no more orders from your kind," the water roared, and Miranda braced for impact.

"Now, just a moment." Eli stepped in front of Miranda, hands in his pockets. His voice was bland and casual, but something in his tone was enough to stop the wave in midcrash. "Is that any way to talk to the Spiritualist who risked her own life to free you?"

The water retreated a bit. "And who are you to defend her?"

"Just a common thief who doesn't like the idea of drowning." Eli smiled. "But this girl here"—he slapped Miranda on the shoulder—"she teamed up with her enemies, disobeyed her orders, and stuck out her own neck, all to keep Gregorn's descendant from enslaving you. Now," he said, arching an eyebrow, "don't you think you should at least hear her out?"

The wave fell a bit, almost as if it was embarrassed. "Very well," it gurgled. "She may speak."

Eli nodded and nudged Miranda forward. For her part, Miranda was too shocked to do much besides gape.

"You can't talk to a Great Spirit like that," she hissed when Eli nudged her again.

"I just did," Eli whispered. "Now you'd better do your part, or we're all in the drink." He pushed her hard, and she stumbled out right in front of the wall of water.

She straightened up, squinting into the blinding light. The spirit loomed over her, and she wished more than anything she had not left her rings behind. Even if her spirits' powers were nothing to the sea before her, maybe they would at least have some idea how to talk to it.

"Great Spirit," she started shakily. "I know we have no right to prevent you from reclaiming your land, but if you could just wait a day or two, I'm sure we could move people and some of the spirits out of the way. Then you could reclaim your basin, and we could limit the loss of life."

She finished hopefully, smiling up at the glowing water. It did not respond. Miranda's smile faltered, and she began to fidget. "Of course, it might take some convincing to get people to—"

"Are you finished?" the great wave rumbled.

Miranda jumped. "More or less."

"Then I have heard you out. Your offer is unacceptable. I will not delay my freedom for the convenience of those who have profited from my imprisonment."

"Now hold on," Eli said, stepping up to stand beside Miranda. "If you're a Great Spirit, isn't it your responsibility to watch over the lesser spirits?"

The wave turned, angling the peak of its foaming crest directly at Eli's head. "What do you know of that, human?"

"I'm right, aren't I?" Eli said, staring up at the swirling water with his arms crossed over his chest. "I know your imprisonment was awful, but, enslaved or free, you're still a Great Spirit. Those animals and trees and all the rest living on what used to be your land, they're yours to guard just as much as the fish that lived in you when this was all sea. Even if things have changed, you can't just turn your back on them."

Without warning, the shallow water at Eli's feet geysered up, lifting the thief clear off the ground until he was level with the wave's crest.

"What would a human know of the pain of enslavement?" the spirit roared. "Who are you to lecture me when it was your kind who created this situation? You humans disgust me. You came from nowhere—blind, short lived, half deaf—and yet you were given dominion over the spirit world? Understand this, boy"—the geyser of water surged higher still, pushing Eli almost to the ceiling—"I take no more orders from your kind."

With a flick of his current, the great spirit sent Eli hurtling across the ruined hall. For a gut-wrenching moment, Eli flew silently through the dark. Then he struck the crumbling wall with a deathly thud and tumbled with a splash to the ground. Miranda held her breath, waiting for him to move, to breathe. But he did not stir. The ripples around him stilled, and Miranda felt her stomach turn to ice. Without thinking, or knowing what she could do if she reached him, she hurled herself forward, slipping and skidding across the wet floor. Before she had gone more than a few steps, a wall of water erupted, blocking her path.

She whirled on the spirit, eyes flashing. "You had no right!" she shouted. "Thief or not, he helped us, helped *you*." Her spirit roared open, stronger and brighter than it had ever been and sharp as a spear as she leveled it at the water's glowing heart.

"Come then, little girl," the wave rumbled, rising up. "If this is how your kind repays kindness, it's better I kill you like this than leave you to dirty my waters later."

"Miranda!" Gin howled, struggling to stand. "He's a Great Spirit, Miranda! Don't be an idiot!"

But Miranda's rage had taken her further than his voice could reach. With a roar, she hurled the sharpened edge of her spirit at the sea's glowing heart as the water at her feet erupted, covering everything in a great, white wave.

Eli lay on his back where he had landed, trying not to think. He tried not to think about the pain or the freezing water that soaked his lower body. He tried not to think about the waves of spirit power rolling over each other just a few feet away. He especially tried not to think about the frantic, desperate edge on the fiery spirit he had come to recognize as Miranda's, and what that kind of desperation meant for their odds of survival.

Worried about her? a familiar, silky voice whispered in his ear.

Eli started, sending a new wave of pain through his body. The sultry voice chuckled. *Such a pretty little wizardess, and so concerned for your safety,* she tsked in his ear. *These little dalliances of yours make me less inclined to help you.*

"It's not a dalliance," he muttered. "And I didn't ask for your help."

A thin, white line appeared in the air above him. It hung for a moment, shedding its ghostly white light in a surgical stripe across his chest. Then, with a sound like silk sliding through sand, a white hand reached through the cut in the air to cup his chin. Long, feminine fingers, whiter than moonlit snow, stroked his bleeding cheek, leaving a burning touch behind that was almost painful, yet never enough.

I rather like you this way, she murmured, tracing the bridge of his nose. *Broken and helpless. It reminds me of when I first found you.* That *time, you accepted me with open arms.*

"Time is a fickle master," Eli said, closing his eyes against the light. "He changes many things."

You're full of sayings today. The disembodied hand brushed past his lips and slid down his neck to his chest, tapping the gaping wound the stones had torn open when he hit the wall, just below Karon's burn. Eli sucked in a breath when she touched the ragged skin, and he felt her chuckle against his skin. *Your time is about to end, if you stay like this. Such a pity, I hate watching you squander my gifts.* Her white fingers moved in circles along his rib cage, tracing the bloodstains on his torn shirt. *Of course,* her voice slid seductively along his ear, *I could help you, if you asked nicely.*

Eli turned away. "Do what you want, Benehime."

She laughed gleefully as he said her name, and a second disembodied hand snaked through the white opening to join the first. Her palms slid over his open wound and, still laughing, she pressed down. Overwhelming pain lanced though Eli's body, darkening his vision and slamming his teeth together. It was as if every wound, bruise, cramp, and discomfort from the past twelve hours was happening again, only all at once, and amplified. He gasped and tried to jerk away, but Benehime's hands pinned him to the icy floor as surely as if he were nailed there. The pain went on and on, until he was sure it would never end and he would be stuck like this forever. Then, like the sun coming out from behind a cloud, it stopped. The pressure lifted from his chest and breath thundered back into his body.

As he lay on his back in the shallow water, gasping like a landed fish, Benehime's white hands moved to cup his cheeks. *Next time, I'll make you beg*, she murmured, trailing her burning touch across his skin one last time before drawing her hands back through the white cut in the air. *I will see you soon, my favorite star.*

The white line faded with her voice, leaving Eli staring at the empty air. It took a few moments more for her overwhelming presence to fade completely, and as his soul righted itself, he realized he could barely feel Miranda's spirit at all anymore.

Miranda was on her hands and knees in the water beside Gin's flank, panting. Her librarian's outfit was dirtied beyond recognition, and her pinned hair had tumbled in a wet tangle down her neck, clinging to her skin like red seaweed caught in the tide hole of her shoulders. She was soaked and shivering, her eyes dull and weary, but she was not beaten. They were huddled in a small circle, with Josef and Nico's heads propped on Gin's paws to keep them from drowning in the shallow water that rode in hand-high waves across what was left of the marble floor. The fact that Gin did this without complaining was proof enough of how serious the situation was. Two feet above them, held back only by the invisible bell jar of Miranda's open spirit, the wall of black water rippled in threatening patterns.

Mellinor surrounded them on all sides, his powerful current beating steadily against the thin bubble of Miranda's spirit. Each time the water crashed down, she felt her mind drowning under the endless, tireless power. Each time, it pushed her right to the edge of buckling, but each time she rallied and met the crash strength for strength, keeping their tiny bubble intact for another few seconds before the next wave hit and the struggle started all over again.

In the tiny space between the surges, the grim corner of her mind that could still think on things besides mere survival wondered why she bothered to resist.

She had done well, at first. After Eli went down, she'd been able to go blow for blow with the water for a little while. The great spirit was powerful, but his imprisonment had left him slow and weak. However, the longer he spent in the open air and moonlight, the more his power returned, and as he had gained strength, Miranda had exhausted hers. Slowly, inch by inch, the great spirit had pushed her back until he washed her under entirely. Now, trapped in a bubble with her air running out, it was all she could do to survive another wave. Of course, the grim corner muttered, just surviving wasn't winning. She wasn't even sure what the standards of victory were in a fight like this. Even if she had been stronger, more resilient, even if she hadn't let herself be trapped, her enemy was a great spirit of an inland sea. She could no more defeat him than she could defeat a mountain.

So why was she holding out, her doubt whispered. What hope was she trying to preserve? There was no help coming, no knight to ride to her rescue. Even if she could somehow get a message to the Spirit Court, Master Banage was the only wizard strong enough to have a chance against Mellinor, and he would never raise his soul against a great spirit, not even to save her. Hopelessness welled up in her chest, and Miranda choked back a sob, almost losing her rhythm as another wave crashed down. As she struggled to keep their last few feet of air intact, she couldn't banish the thought that, even if she did somehow get out of this alive, Master Banage would never forgive her for fighting a great spirit. Especially seeing as she was doing it to protect two bounty-carrying criminals and a demonseed. Perhaps it would be kinder to everyone if she dropped her shield and let the water carry them away.

"Just concentrate." Gin's gruff voice was frighteningly close to her ear, but the sound of his growl lovelier at that moment than any music in the world. "Great spirits may be old and flashy, but they're still spirits. The strength of their souls is limited by their physical form. Your strength, a wizard's strength, is limited only by your will. That's the secret I learned back on the steppes, when I first decided to follow you." He pressed his wet muzzle hard against the small of her back. "I will watch your back, mistress, so never let your will falter."

Miranda turned and clung to him, burying her face in the coarse fur of his long nose. "I will not let you down."

The waves pounded harder than ever against the shell, but Miranda met each one blow for blow, and no water got through. With every failure, Mellinor roared and foamed, his waters churning as he struck again and was again defeated.

But just as Miranda steadied herself into this new pattern, a surge of oddly familiar spirit power shot through the black water like an arrow, freezing everything with one word.

Stop.

The waves stopped. The water stopped. Even Miranda paused, pressing her hands to her mouth to keep from crying out. Even though the word had not actually been spoken, she would know that spirit voice anywhere. It was Eli.

CHAPTER
27

Like someone had opened a drain, Mellinor's waters poured away. Miranda's bubble shattered, and she toppled over, gasping at the fresh air. Mellinor's water was still ankle deep on the floor, but the spirit's attention wasn't on her any longer. The wave had reformed itself above the shattered dais, and all its attention was focused on the gangly figure standing at the far end of the room in a circle of shattered marble.

"What a pain," Eli said, running his hands through his wet hair. "We go to all this trouble, and the spirit at the heart of everything turns out to be an ungrateful jerk." He stepped out of the crater he'd made when Mellinor threw him and smiled up at the enormous wave. "It's time to go."

"I go nowhere, boy," the sea spirit hissed, pulling his water closer.

"We'll see." Eli's smile widened, and he opened his spirit.

The room changed. Every spirit, from the stones underfoot to the air overhead to the clothes on Miranda's body, was suddenly wide awake and focused on Eli like he was the only thing in the world. His open spirit was quick and airy as it raced through the throne room, but there was something different about it, something Miranda had never felt in a spirit before, wizard or otherwise. It felt like light. There was no other way of describing it.

Eli walked casually, seemingly oblivious that he was the object of so much attention. As he walked, the spirits made way. The dirt from the flood rolled aside when he came near, so did the fallen stones and the broken glass, making a clear path. Miranda watched in amazement as the room rearranged itself to make Eli's walk easier. Even the marble trembled as he stepped on it, not with fear, but with anxiousness, as if it wanted more than anything to make a good impression as he walked the last few steps to the crumbled dais.

Mellinor had shrunk to a wavering ball. He floated over the pile of stones flashing between nervous gray and deep blue.

Eli stopped when his boots were almost touching the shattered rock that had been the first step of the dais stairs. He put his hands in his pockets and looked up at the quivering water. "Now"—the word hummed with power—"I need you to get up."

It was not an enslavement, as Miranda had been bracing for. It was a request. Mellinor shivered, sending tall waves across his surface. "How is it possible?" the water whispered. "How was I allowed to toss you like that when you bore her mark? Had I but known, had you shown me..."

"None of that matters now," Eli said. "Just get up. You're ruining what's left of Henrith's throne room."

The remaining loose water leaped back into Mellinor's sphere, and the floating ball of water churned as the sea spirit tried to make himself smaller. The best he could manage was still twice Eli's height. He was about to try again when Eli's voice stopped him.

"That's good enough," the thief said. "Now, please understand that we are, in fact, very sorry all of this happened to you. You have every right to be angry at Gregorn and his descendants, but you need to understand our position. This kingdom"—he pointed toward the ruined windows where dawn was just beginning to tint the sky—"it's not yours any more. You need to move on."

The sphere of water spun slowly on its axis, its light muted to a deep, cold blue. "Where would I go? My home was here, my seabed and my fish. Without the land, I am nothing. A homeless spirit is no better than a ghost."

"You'll go where all water eventually goes," Eli said gently. "To the ocean."

"The ocean?" The light at the spirit's heart fluttered madly. "Not there. I'll die before I go there. You'll have to kill me first."

"Why are you so afraid?" Eli said. "All of your water has been through the ocean thousands of times."

"But he hasn't."

Eli sighed and turned to watch Miranda hobble toward them, clutching her sides. Her face was pale and exhausted, and fresh yellow bruises stood out stark on her pale, water-logged skin. Her eyes, however, were determined as she dropped to the ground beside the thief, breathing heavily.

"Water spirits flow in and out of each other," she gasped. "Rain falls and makes creeks that flow to rivers and, eventually, as you say, to the sea, but," she said and looked up at the slowly turning water, "a sea is more than the water that passes through it. Even the smallest creeks have their own souls separate from the water that fills them. You can't just blithely send that soul to fend for itself in the ocean."

"She speaks the truth," Mellinor rumbled. "The ocean is a hungry mass too large to have a cohesive soul of its own. As soon as I joined the waves, that mob of water spirits would tear me apart. They would split me into smaller and smaller pieces with each tide, and with every split I'd grow weaker and stupider, until I could no longer remember my own name."

Eli shook his head. "You'd still be alive."

"To what end?" Mellinor's light flashed wildly as the water heaved. "I'd be worse than a ghost. At least if I dry up here, I can die as myself, with my soul intact and entirely my own."

"Is that really what you would prefer?" Eli said.

The sphere bobbed in the approximation of a resolute nod. "If you won't let me have my land, yes."

Eli thought a moment, then nodded gravely. "Very well, we'll do as you ask."

Miranda looked up at Eli, horrified. "You can't just kill him."

"That's how he wants it!" Eli shouted, spinning to face her. "Were you listening at all? Why do you care, anyway? As I recall, he was trying pretty hard to kill *you* when I interfered."

"He's in this position because of us!" Miranda yelled

back. "If it wasn't for Gregorn, none of this would have happened. We have a duty to make things right!"

"Make things right?" Eli flung out his arms to take in the whole of the ruined throne room. "Miranda, look around! Do you really think the masters of Mellinor are going to be happy if we tell them that everyone in the country has to move? Do you think they'll even listen? Even if they did, how long would it take to get everyone safely out? A week? A month? What's Mellinor here going to do while he waits, hang in the air? He'll evaporate before the masters finish their committee meeting. You know as well as I do that a displaced spirit has two choices: find a home or die. I don't want the second option any more than you do, but there's no place for him here, and he won't take my compromise and go to the sea, so guess where that leaves us." Eli crossed his arms and glared down at Miranda. "He's made his choice, so, for once, can you put aside your Spiritualist dogma and just let the spirit be?"

Miranda pushed herself up, her fists shaking with fury. "I won't let you kill him."

Eli met her glare head on, and they stood that way for several moments, like children having a staring contest. Finally, when it was clear she wasn't going to back down, Eli flung up his hands.

"All right," he said. "If you're so concerned, *you* deal with him."

Miranda blinked; she hadn't expected him to turn this back on her. "I don't know what to do."

Eli made a series of frantic "you see?" gestures, which Miranda ignored. Instead, she looked down at her hands. They seemed so bare and fragile with only the one small ring on her pinky. She blinked hard, then blinked again, and her head shot up. "I could take him as a servant."

Eli stopped flailing and stared at her blankly.

"He could live with me," she said, pointing at the small ring. "Then he would have a home but no one would need to be displaced."

Eli's eyes flicked skeptically from her to her pinky finger and back again. "It's an interesting idea, but you can't keep him in that, you know."

She looked down at the ring in surprise. "What? Oh, no, not this one. I mean, it's empty, but there's no way even a fraction of his spirit would fit. Besides, I'm saving it. Look," she said and took a deep breath, "forget the ring. I'm not even talking about the ring." She pointed at her chest. "I could do what you did, with the lava spirit."

"Karon was an entirely different set of circumstances," Eli said, glancing up at the hovering water. "He was also much smaller."

"I'm not saying it would be the best living situation," Miranda huffed, "but I'm pretty sure it beats the rest of our alternatives."

Eli stoked his chin, considering. "I can't lie to you," he said, "it's an incredibly stupid, reckless idea that you'll probably regret. Still, I can't think of a technical reason it wouldn't work. Of course, in the end, it's not really up to us."

They turned to look at the spirit, who bubbled as he considered the idea. "Servitude to a wizard," he sloshed thoughtfully. "You'll forgive me if I'm skeptical about putting myself in a human's hands again."

"Well," Eli said, slapping Miranda hard on the back,

"I can't vouch for her character, but I'd bet money she beats dying here."

"True enough, wizard," the spirit rumbled. "I don't see as I have much choice in the matter."

"It must be by choice," Miranda said, ignoring her aching sides and straightening up to her full height. "I can only take servants who follow me willingly. However, it would be nothing like Gregorn's bond, I can promise you. As my servant, you would be subject to my command, but, in return for your service, I can offer you the Spiritualist's vow that I will never force you to act against your will or keep you if you wish to leave. I will never cast you aside for any reason, and, so long as I have breath, I will do my best to keep you from harm. I offer you power for service, strength for obedience, and my own body to act as your shore, but that is all I can give." Clenching her hands at her sides, she looked up at the churning water. "Is it enough, Mellinor?"

The water spun slowly on its axis, his light shifting softly as he thought. "It is enough, Spiritualist," the water said at last. "Your pledge is accepted."

The great sphere of water splashed to the ground. Mellinor rolled forward, forming a wave as he had before, but this time the water that engulfed Miranda was warm and gentle. It flowed up her body and snaked around her shoulders, pausing just a moment in front of her eyes, as though the spirit was weighing what he saw there one last time. Whatever the test, she must have passed, for the water rippled approvingly and, in one smooth motion, slid into her mouth.

Miranda tensed, eyes wide, as the spirit poured down her throat. From the moment she decided to offer her body as a vessel, she'd tried to ready herself for the feeling, but this was so wildly different from anything she'd ever experienced, all her mental preparations seemed laughable now that she was up against the reality. It wasn't like her other spirits. Those had felt like gaining a new limb or a close confidant. This was like gaining a new soul.

Mellinor's power surged through her body as the sea poured into her, filling every hidden nook, every fold of her spirit, even the ones she hadn't been aware of until that moment. It filled the well of her soul to overflowing, and still the water came. As the spirit's strength went on and on, she realized at last how small and pathetic her earlier attempts to fight him had been and how much he had been holding back as he tried to batter her into submission. A wave of regret surged through the water, and she instinctively forgave him everything. All that they had done wrong was pooled together now, one great ocean of fears and regrets that threatened to swallow her. Yet Mellinor's reassurances buoyed her up, and she realized that he was just as much a part of this as she was. They were horse and rider now, servant and master, spirit and human. Unequal, yet the same.

When she opened her eyes at last, she found herself on her back with no memory of how she'd gotten there. Her body ached at every joint, and yet, it all seemed so far away. Time moved in fits and starts. It should have been dawn by now, she was sure, but the throne room was darker than before. She felt a pressure under her shoulders, and she lolled her head back to see Eli crouched over her, his face closed and thoughtful. He had his arms hooked under hers and was dragging her across the floor.

Miranda started to wonder where he was taking her, but then her drifting attention was caught by the wonderful sound that filled the air.

"What is that noise?" she whispered, or thought she whispered. It was hard to be sure. She wasn't quite clear yet where she ended and Mellinor began, but Eli seemed to understand.

"Rain," he said, laying her down beside Gin. "Not even your belly could hold all that water, so I sent what was left to putter itself out."

She nodded languidly. It all seemed very sensible. "Where are you going now?"

"If I told you, it would be no fun at all." Eli smiled. He reached into his jacket and pulled out something white and square, which he tucked into Miranda's skirt pocket. "Sleep well, little Spiritualist," he said, standing up with a wink. "I'm sure we'll meet again."

Miranda nodded peaceably and closed her eyes. Within seconds, everything but the lovely sound of the rain had fallen far away, and she slipped easily into a deep, dreamless sleep.

CHAPTER
28

Miranda woke slowly, her mind rising like a bubble from her deep sleep. Below her, Mellinor was still sleeping, his currents deep and calm at the bottom of her awareness. She let him be and drifted upward, the dandelion fluff of her thoughts coming and going on their own time. Everything felt wonderful, like she was floating in a warm, lavender-scented cloud while someone played music in the distance. She winced, off-key music. Unbearably off key. Her thoughts began to thicken into consciousness, falling into place while worries filled the cracks between them. Suddenly, she wasn't quite as comfortable. She hovered for a moment on the edge of sleep, fretting, and finally decided that if she was awake enough to fret about waking she might as well go all the way. At least then she could stop the awful music.

She opened her eyes to find herself buried at the center of a large feather bed. An elderly maid dozed in a chair by the bed's foot, her soft snores stirring the dust motes that hung suspended in the honeyed sunlight pouring down from the high windows. The awful music came from behind a large folding screen, which split the already small room in half. Miranda shifted experimentally, and she jumped as something heavy rolled across her chest. With some effort, she freed one of her hands from the tightly tucked sheets and groped clumsily across the comforter. After a few uncertain moments, her fingers closed around a soft leather pouch filled with the heavy, familiar shapes of her rings. An incredible feeling of relief rushed through her, and she sighed contentedly. At the sound, the sleeping maid leaped from her chair.

"Lady," she clucked, shuffling across the thick carpet to pull the sheets tighter. "Please do not move."

"Is she awake?" an excited voice called from behind the screen. There was a shuffle, and then King Henrith came bounding into view, a handsome but sloppily tuned tenor vikken dangling from his left hand. His cheeks and neck were wrapped in white bandages and there was an angry gouge across the bridge of his nose, but otherwise he looked quite well compared to the last time she'd seen him. The maid backed away reverently as he approached, and Miranda sank a little deeper into the bed.

"I was hoping you'd wake up during one of my visits," the king said, grinning. "Of course, I haven't been able to visit very often. Things have been busy, but I did think you'd enjoy some music." He held up the poor vikken by its strings. "How did you like my—"

"It was lovely," Miranda cut in. "How long have I been like this?"

"Well," the king said and scratched the top of his chin, which was the only section of his beard that wasn't covered in bandages. "Three days, I think. Really, it feels longer."

"Three days?" She clutched her ring bag. "Eli is gone, I take it?"

"Yes," Henrith said, sounding annoyed, "and all the loose gold with him, what wasn't melted to slag, anyway. Honestly, I don't think we could have expected better. I was more distracted by the state of the room and, of course, you and my brother. We thought you were dead as well, but your beast told us that you were merely suffering from exhaustion, so I asked one of the girls—"

"Gin told you?" Miranda sat up in a rush, but the pain that shot through her skull at the movement sent her right back down again.

"Well, he didn't tell us exactly." The king sat down on the nightstand. "One of the other wizard chaps spoke with him."

"Other wizards..." Miranda closed her eyes. This conversation was veering rapidly in directions she didn't think her battered mind could handle right now. "I'm sorry," she muttered. "Could you start over? From the beginning, please."

"There's not much to it," the king said. "They arrived right after I did. That night, when the shaking started and your dog ran off, I just couldn't stay put. I kept hearing these awful sounds. It was like the forest itself was trying to get away from something."

Miranda remembered the terrifying aura of Nico's uninhibited powers and shuddered. The king didn't seem to notice.

"I decided it was time to stop hiding, so I made my way back to the castle only to find everyone out in the yard because of a fire in the kitchens or some such. The kitchen staff had it well in hand, but with all the noises from the throne room and the stories the wounded soldiers were telling, no one wanted to go back in." The king chuckled. "Nobody believed I was who I said at first. It took me a good hour to convince them I really was their king, and then it was another two hours after the water stopped pouring out of the castle before I could get together a group bold enough to go inside and see what all the fuss was about.

"I'm still not quite clear on what happened," Henrith said, frowning. "But the wizards showed up about half an hour after we found you and just sort of took charge." He gave her an amused look. "It's funny, after four hundred years without them, Mellinor's suddenly up to its neck with wizards."

"These wizards," Miranda said, reaching into her leather bag, pulling out the thick, gold loop of her Spirit Court signet, "do they wear rings like me? Are they Spiritualists? How many are there?"

"That's the strangest thing," Henrith said, adjusting his bandages. "They wore no rings, and they didn't say anything about the Spirit Court. The serious fellow who leads them said he was with the League of Something or Other."

Miranda froze. "The League of Storms?"

"Yes! That's the one!" Henrith grinned. "There were more than fifty at the beginning—seemed to pop right out of thin air, gave us quite a fright, I can tell you—but most vanished again after an hour or so. Now there are maybe eight or nine. Still, they're doing a great job fixing the damage Renaud did to my throne room, and at no expense to us, so I'm inclined to let them be. Though I would like to ask you for your version of what happened that night. The doctors demanded we take it slowly so as not to risk your... Where are you going?"

Miranda had swung her feet over the edge of the bed and was shoving her rings back onto her fingers. "Thank you for your hospitality, my lord," she said in a rush. "The Spirit Court will not forget such kindness, and I will of course be happy to relate what happened in the throne room, but I can't afford to waste any more time in bed."

"Are you sure you should be getting up?" Henrith said, eyeing her suspiciously. "The doctors still aren't sure what's been wrong with you."

For a moment, Miranda considered trying to explain the dangers of opening one's spirit for prolonged lengths of time, especially to such an extreme degree as she had, and then accepting a new spirit on top of that. However, seeing the concerned look on Henrith's face, she opted for something less explanatory and more understandable.

"It's just exhaustion," she said, sliding to the edge of the fluffy mattress while ignoring the increasingly urgent calls from her muscles that standing would be a very bad idea. "I was a bit overzealous with my abilities. Luckily, I recover quickly."

Henrith arched an eyebrow at her but didn't say anything as she took a deep breath and, gripping the heavy bed frame like a lifeline, hauled herself to her feet. It hurt every bit as much as she'd expected, but she firmly ignored the pain and set about looking for something more substantial than a woolen nightgown. Fortunately, some thoughtful servant must have anticipated this, and a delighted smile spread over Miranda's face when she saw her riding suit, freshly laundered and mended, laid out on the dresser under the window. Using the heavy furniture to support her sleep-weakened legs, she hobbled along the wall to the dresser. When she picked up her jacket, something white tumbled out of the pocket and landed on the thick carpet by her feet.

"Ah," the king said. "We found that with you, in the pocket of the librarian's uniform you, um, borrowed. It looked important, so I told them to keep it here for you."

Miranda bent down and picked up the rectangular object. It was an envelope. She turned it over. Stamped at the center of a large glob of green sealing wax was a fanciful, calligraphic *M* that she recognized all too well. However, what caught her breath was the name written across the fold in neat, precise capitals.

"Etmon Banage," she read, frowning in confusion. What in the world could that thief have to say to her master? She slid her thumbnail under the wax, but, right before it cracked, she thought better of it. No matter the source, opening the Rector Spritualis's private mail was not a wise career move. Squishing her curiosity, she tucked the unopened letter back into her coat pocket and reached instead for her freshly pressed shirt. She draped it over her arm and turned around, looking at the king expectantly.

He looked back at her, smiling pleasantly, and showed no signs of leaving.

"Thank you for your concern, Majesty," she said pointedly. "I really do appreciate it, but I've had my time to lie about. I must do my duty."

"Fine, have it your way." The king sighed sullenly, tucking the vikken under his arm. "Just don't blame us when you get sick again. I'll wait for you in the garden."

She dropped a half curtsy as he walked back behind the screen. She heard the footman greet him, and then the scrape of the door as he left. When it closed, she gave herself a little shake and, with the maid's stony assistance, began the painful work of getting dressed.

Fifteen minutes later, Miranda was dressed and on her way to the throne room. She probably should have gone to meet Henrith in the garden first, but the League of Storms took priority over just about everything, even courtesy. She felt ten times herself again back in pants with her rings and Eril's pendant in their rightful places. Her spirits were in an uproar, both at being left behind and at the new interloper they could feel through Miranda's skin. She sent a warning thread of energy down her arms, and the ruckus quieted instantly. Miranda felt guilty forcing them down after everything that had happened, but dealing with the League of Storms was not an activity that bore distraction.

She paused at the end of the corridor and smoothed over her hair with her fingers one more time. When she was satisfied that she looked as collected and competent as she could make herself without a mirror, she turned the corner into the promenade hall and stopped dead in her tracks.

The throne room looked nothing at all as it had when she'd last seen it. The marble floor was smooth again, with no sign that it had ever been scoured by the acidic soul of a dead enslaver. The colored-glass windows were unbroken, filtering the sunlight into colorful streams that played across the gracious golden fixtures and delicate ornamental stonework, all of which was back in its proper place. The roof had been restored to its original graceful arch, and the walls were smooth and straight again, as though they'd never been broken. Only the great golden doors were immune to this miraculous repair. They hung sadly from their hinges in a cascade of melted gold and iron slag, just as Eli's lava spirit had left them.

Men in austere black coats were standing in pairs over the few remaining spots where the damage was still apparent. Most of them seemed to be lost in deep contemplation, studying the last bits of wreckage as if the shattered stones were works of art. As she watched, one of them waved his hand, and a cracked stretch of wall righted itself before her eyes.

"Should you be up, Lady Spiritualist?"

Miranda jumped at the voice, and she turned to see a handsome middle-aged man in a long black coat standing a few feet behind her with a polite smile on his face.

"My apologies," the man said and held out his gloved hand. "I did not mean to frighten you. I am Alric, deputy commander for the League of Storms."

Miranda took his offered hand firmly, keeping her eyes locked on his face. This was not the time to show weakness. "Miranda Lyonette."

"Ah," he said, smiling, "Master Banage's young protégé."

"How unfair," Miranda said, taking back her hand. "You know who I am, but I've never heard of you, Sir Alric."

"The League lives to serve, lady. We have no need to make a show of our achievements." He smiled as he spoke, but the thin-lipped expression did not reach his blue eyes. "Now"—he took her arm and began walking her toward the throne room—"to business. I was hoping you would wake up before we finished our work. I have several questions I'd like to ask you about the night all this unpleasantness occurred."

Miranda nodded. "You want to know about the Great Spirit."

"Of course not," Alric said. "That's your realm, lady, not ours. Our interest lies in the one called Nico." He stopped, and his grip on her arm tightened. "You know what she is, of course." He smiled at her. "Tell me, then, why did you let her escape?"

Miranda stepped back, putting some space between them. "It was my duty to see to the welfare of the spirits first," she said, keeping her voice steady and neutral. "Considering the extraordinary circumstances that night, I judged her to be the lesser threat."

"The 'lesser threat'?" Alric chuckled. "I sincerely doubt that."

As he spoke, his pleasant smile took on a sinister tint and, despite the warm sunlight, a shiver ran down Miranda's spine. Suddenly, she was uncomfortably aware of just how powerful a wizard the man standing in front of her was.

"That night," Alric said, "the demonseed inside the girl awakened, correct?"

"She did change," Miranda said, choosing her words carefully. "But things were happening very quickly, and I have no experience with demons. Some of your members must have been close by, since you arrived in Mellinor in such a timely fashion. Surely you can ask one of them."

"The League can move quickly when it needs to," Alric said. "And seeing how every spirit within a hundred miles of this place was in a screaming panic on the night in question, we felt it necessary to move very quickly indeed. Thus, imagine our surprise when we arrived and found not only no demonseed but no spirits that would tell us where it had gone. I was hoping you could shed some light on the subject."

"I've told you what I know," Miranda said coldly. "She changed, and my ghosthound was injured trying to subdue her. However, one of Eli's companions was able to bring her under control, and she changed back."

"Awakened demons don't just 'change back.'" Alric leaned closer. "Isn't there something else you'd like to tell me?"

"No." Miranda glared stubbornly.

Alric's blue eyes grew colder still, but before he could speak, a man's voice called his name from the throne room.

Miranda jumped at the low, rumbling sound. Alric gave her a final warning look before turning on his heel and marching back into the throne room where the man who'd called him was waiting. The man was standing at the center of the sun-drenched hall and was wearing the same long black coat as all the rest, but Miranda was positive he hadn't been there when she'd arrived—there was no way she could have missed a man like that. He was enormously tall, close to seven feet, and every inch of him—the ready tenseness of his broad shoulders, the lightness of his boots on the stone, the clenched hand on the hilt of his long blue-wrapped sword—spoke of a man who lived for one purpose: to fight. To fight and win.

He turned as Alric approached, and his silver eyes flicked to Miranda for only a moment, but a moment was enough. She felt blinded by the intensity of his attention, the sheer weight of his focused gaze, enough to make her lungs falter. She hung on his look, pinned like a fly, until his eyes flicked down to Alric, and the air came thundering back.

Without a word, she turned on her heel and fled. Her spirits were wide awake, yet oddly silent, their attention buzzing against her shaking fingers. She shoved her hands in her pockets and walked faster. So that was the Lord of Storms. For the first time, she understood why Banage had been so adamant about leaving demon matters in League hands. The silver-eyed man did not look like someone who took well to having his affairs meddled in. She almost felt bad for Eli and Josef. If the Lord of Storms himself was here looking for Nico, it was only a matter of time before they found her. Alric had said that awakened demons don't go back to sleep and, whatever Josef's sword had done, Miranda believed him. She shuddered, remembering the flickering glow of Nico's lantern eyes. Despite Eli's pleas, she didn't see how something like that could ever go back to being human. Hopefully, the thief and the swordsman would have enough sense to give her up quietly when the Lord of Storms came, or there wouldn't be enough of them left for her to catch, much less bring back to Banage.

That thought nearly made her sick, and she put the whole affair out of her mind. Whatever horrors were yet to happen, it wasn't her problem anymore. That thought cheered her up immensely, and she threw open the door to the stables with remarkable gusto for someone who'd spent the smaller half of a week in bed.

Gin was where she knew he would be, sprawled at the center of the stable yard, eating a pig. The stains on the cobbles around him spoke of many such meals, and she stopped at the edge of the walkway, putting her hands on her hips with a mock glare. "Are you eating them out of house and home?"

"Nice to see you, too," Gin mumbled between chews. He licked his chops and rolled to his feet. Miranda winced when she saw the long, still-healing gash that ran across his shoulders, interrupting the flow of his undulating patterns.

"It's not as bad as it looks," he growled when he saw her expression. "I'm not made of paper, you know."

Miranda walked over and reached up to scratch behind his ear. "I'm glad to see you doing so well."

"So am I," Gin said, but he leaned into her scratching. "So, where now?"

"Home," Miranda said. "I have to let Master Banage know what happened, especially now that the League's involved. I think our Eli hunt is going to get a bit more hairy from here on."

"If Banage lets us keep going," the hound said. "League nonsense aside, Eli still got away with the increased bounty and more than eight thousand in loose gold. Banage isn't going to be happy about that part, and he's not the forgiving type."

"Let's cross that bridge when we reach it," Miranda said, giving him a final pat. "Finish your pig, we're leaving as soon as I find where they put the rest of my things."

They left that afternoon, after Miranda said good-bye to Marion and paid her respects to the king. Henrith was in a bit of a panic when she found him, for the league members had left just a few minutes before, vanishing as mysteriously as they had appeared.

"It really is too much," he said, slumping down in his chair. "First we have no wizards, then we have too many, and now none again."

"It doesn't always have to be that way," Miranda said, sipping the tea he had insisted she try before leaving. They were sitting in the rose garden behind the main castle, just below the throne room's windows. It, like the rest of the palace, had been repaired, but here and there the plants were bent at odd angles where the falling stones and overflowing water had crushed them. Deep inside her, Mellinor shifted uncomfortably at that thought. Miranda sent a warm reassurance before setting her cup down and meeting Henrith's dejected gaze. "The Spirit Court would be delighted to send a representative. We might not be as flashy as the League, but no country was ever worse off for having a Spiritualist."

"I think I may take you up on that offer," the king said thoughtfully. "After all, of all the wizards who've tromped through my kingdom over the past week or so, you're the only one who did right by us, and we won't forget that."

"Your Majesty flatters me," Miranda said and smiled. "Perhaps I can do you another good turn. I'm going home to Zarin to give my report to the Rector Spiritualis. Master Banage is a powerful man, and he might be able to convince the Council of Thrones to throw out Mellinor's part of Eli's bounty. I think coercion of a monarch counts as extenuating circumstances enough to justify a slight bending of the rules."

The king set down his teacup. "I appreciate the offer, but it won't be necessary. After all this ruckus, I think thirty-five thousand is the least we can do to reward the person crazy enough to catch Eli Monpress." He smiled broadly. "I hope, lady, that it will be you."

"I'm not sure if that's a compliment," Miranda said, laughing. "But I shall do my best, all the same."

In the end, he gave her three bags of the tea to take with her. She bundled them into her pack, along with the generous store of sandwiches, fruits, nuts, and bread from the palace kitchens, and secured the lot across Gin's lower back. Then she climbed into her spot right behind the ghosthound's ears and let him put on all the show he liked as they bounded over the gates and out of the town. Once on the road, she was careful not to comment when he set a slower pace, and if she made them take more breaks than they usually did, Gin didn't mention it. So, in this casual way, they crossed the borders of Mellinor and followed the trade roads north and a little east toward Zarin, the wizard city at the heart of the world.

Far to the west, on the other side of Mellinor, Eli was having a harder time of things.

"I give up," he said, turning his back on the deep, fast river he had spent the better part of an hour trying to convince to pull back its waters long enough for them to cross.

"Why don't you just give it an order?" Josef said from his perch on the enormous bag of gold. "Worked well enough on the big lake spirit back there, why not a river?"

"It was a sea spirit," Eli growled. "And that was totally different." He turned his scowl toward Nico, who was sitting on the ground beside Josef drawing patterns in the sand with a split twig.

"This is all your fault, you know," he said, pointing at her. "If you hadn't been so careless and ripped your coat to shreds, the river would have no idea what you are, and we would have been safely across thirty minutes ago. Now it thinks we're part of some vast, demonic conspiracy and is looking for a way to drown us."

As if to prove his point, the river chose that moment to splash several rocks onto the shore, which landed in the sand inches from Nico's bare knees. Eli shook his head and glanced forlornly upriver. "Nothing for it, we'll have to find a bridge and cross like normal people. Fortunately, I think there's one in our direction."

"Our direction?" Josef scratched his chest where the bandages poked above his shirt. "Where are we going, anyway?"

"Isn't it obvious?" Eli said. "We can't get anything done with Nico in that condition. We're going to get her a new coat."

"A new coat?" Josef cocked an eyebrow at the wizard. "Is that all?"

"Yes," Eli said, starting up the sandy bank. "So make sure you don't lose any of that gold. If we're lucky, we'll have just enough to pay for it."

"We've got enough gold to purchase a fully stocked villa and the noble title to go with it!" Josef said, kicking the bag with his boot heel. "What kind of coat are we buying?"

But Eli was already a good distance ahead, digging through the maps in his shoulder bag and muttering to himself. Josef rolled his eyes and stood up. With a grunt, he heaved the bag of gold onto his back and balanced it on the flat of his sword while he tied it in place. Then, with the Heart of War secured over one shoulder, and the bag of gold tied across the other, he tromped down the bank after the thief. Tossing down her twig, Nico stood and followed, fitting her small, bare feet into the swordsman's large tracks. Every few minutes, the river would send a new volley of rocks at her, which she dodged easily, never taking her eyes off Josef's back. She stayed less than a step behind him the whole way, one thin hand clutching the tattered remains of her coat and the other stretched out in front, her long fingers resting on the cutting edge of the Heart of War's blade.

acknowledgments

To my parents for raising me; Lindsay for finding me and giving the most wonderful advice; Matt for being my champion; and Devi and everyone at Orbit for taking a chance, thank you.

Last but not least, thank you Steven. You are, and always shall be, the original Eli.

extras

orbit

meet the author

Rachel Aaron was born in Atlanta, GA. After a lovely, geeky childhood full of books and public television, and then an adolescence spent feeling awkward about it, she went to the University of Georgia to pursue English literature with an eye toward getting her PhD. Upper-division coursework cured her of this delusion, and she graduated in 2004 with a BA and a job, which was enough to make her mother happy. She currently lives in a '70s house of the future in Athens, GA, with her loving husband, overgrown library, and small, brown dog. Find out more about the author at www.rachelaaron.net.

interview

Have you always known that you wanted to be a writer?

Yes and no. I've always wanted to tell stories, but I went through several mediums before settling on writing. For a long time (all through middle and high school) I wanted to write and draw manga. Unfortunately, my artistic talent never matched my ambitions. In the end, I'm really glad I went with books. I feel that I've been able to tell a much larger story in far less space through writing than I ever would have managed with panels. Plus, no one makes fun of my drawings anymore.

When you aren't busy writing, what are some of your hobbies?

I'm a total nerd. I play video games and read as much fantasy and manga as I can get my hands on. I also have a horrible adoration of trashy television, particularly reality police shows. You can learn so much about human behavior watching a drunk, shirtless man trying (and failing) to bluff his way out of a ticket.

Who or what inspires you in your writing?

I draw inspiration from all over: things I read, things I watch, daily life, the usual places. One of my favorite things to do is to take something I already love, say, a clever confidence scheme executed by a charming thief, and add magic. This can be a great kick-off for all kinds of stories. Then there are the ideas that just come to me while I'm doing something else, like why are girls always riding giant cats? How about a giant dog? All of these ideas get sorted through and picked over and the best go into my novels, whether they look like they'll fit or not. I've actually had some of my best plot twists emerge while trying to shoehorn in yet another cool idea. Sometimes it seems like a lot of bending around just for some extra razzle-dazzle, but those "Oh, cool!" moments are what make fiction, especially genre fiction, so much fun.

How did you develop the concept for The Spirit Thief?

It started, very appropriately, with Eli. He wasn't even my idea at first, but a character concept from one of my husband's old Dungeon and Dragons buddies, a thief whose goal in life was to be worth one million gold. I loved it, I couldn't get it out of my head. A thief actively trying to make his bounty higher? Why would he do that? What would he be like? Thus, Eli came into my life and started talking to this door. It was all downhill from there.

Everyone else went through several pretty radical iterations before settling into their current roles. For example, Miranda was originally Eli's thief rival. That lasted about a chapter before I realized this woman was way too duty bound to ever steal anything. After a few more tries, she settled in as the cop to Eli's robber, and the Spirit Court emerged from my need to give her a backing organization. It was a great fit and I've never been happier to be wrong about a character. Josef, on the other hand, was a last-minute addition. He came into being because I needed someone to carry the Heart of War, making this one case where the sword truly did choose its wielder on every level. It had excellent taste, and I'm very happy with the cast I ended up with.

As for the concept of the book itself, it evolved naturally. After all, I had a thief and a cop, now I needed a crime, and what better crime than kidnapping a king? But, since nothing can ever go smoothly, the king had to have a dastardly brother waiting in the wings. Once I figured those bits out, the novel found its own way.

When you began writing, did you set out to write a series, or did it just happen organically?

I tried to fit it all into one book. Really, I did. I'd read on all these publishing blogs that no brand-new writer can sell a series, so I was determined *The Spirit Thief* would stand on its own. I even tried to convince my then soon-to-be agent it was a stand-alone book. He didn't buy a word of it. Finally, I admitted it was the first book in a series and everything went much more smoothly. I may have been the author, but the book was a thing of its own by that point. I could no more have made it a stand-alone work than taught it to wash the dishes. Sometimes, you just have to call a duck a duck.

Eli's magical power—having the ability to talk to the spirits of inanimate objects—is something rather new and exciting. How did you derive the idea for this?

As I've mentioned, I'm a nerd, and one of the nerdy things I do is make up magical systems. I have tons of them lying around waiting for a story, but this particular one seemed tailor-made for someone whose main super-power is talking people (and now objects) into doing what he wants. I've always loved the idea of talking things. Not just swords or items of great importance, but silly, normal things like pots and fireplaces. I wanted to create a world where everything could talk back to you, if you could listen, and also one where humans weren't looked on terribly favorably. We're a pretty scrubby bunch, after all. I'm sure my couch doesn't approve of me.

Do you have a favorite character? If so, why?

Eli, of course! He's hands down the most fun to write. Josef is a close second, because I adore straight-talking swordsmen, followed by Gin, as he's just a straight-talking swordsman of another (shifting) color. I also have an extremely soft spot in my heart for Miranda. She tries so hard.

What's in store for Eli and his crew in the next novel,
The Spirit Rebellion?

Eli and company had it relatively easy in Mellinor, but
now they're headed out into the larger world where
things get more complicated. After all, as Eli never
misses the chance to point out, he's worth a lot of money
now. Money attracts attention, and attention makes even
simple heists much more dangerous. To keep his hide
intact, Eli's going to have to play his cards much closer to
his vest…Too bad subtlety isn't one of his strong points.
Meanwhile, Miranda has to deal with the fallout from the
fact that, not only did she fail to catch Eli in Mellinor,
she actually ended up helping him. Let's just say that her
homecoming to the Spirit Court isn't as warm and cheery
as she's used to.

*Finally, what has been your favorite part of the publish-
ing process so far?*

The feedback, definitely. Back when I was first writing
The Spirit Thief I would give it to my friends and family
to read, but I always had a hard time believing them when
they said they liked it. I thought, oh, they're only saying
that because they have to or because they don't want to
hurt my feelings. But then I started submitting my novel
to agents, and even though I got a lot of rejections, I also
got requests for more pages. Then I got a letter from my
current agent's assistant, the wonderful Lindsay Ribar.
She'd read the first few pages of *The Spirit Thief* and
wanted to see more. Now, anyone who's ever tried to
do anything with publishing, or with any competitive

creative work, can understand the elation I felt at this. Here was a person, an exceedingly busy person with no reason to give me the time of day, wanting to read what I'd written. A publishing professional who'd picked me up out of the slush pile, out of the hundreds of other pages from hundreds of other authors, and liked my words enough to write me an e-mail asking for more. That's a fantastic feeling.

I still had a long way to go after that, of course. The novel you hold in your hands is the product of the hard, dedicated work of many wonderful, book-loving people, both on my agent's side and from Orbit. Without their feedback, time, and attention, *The Spirit Thief* would never have become what it is. That's the part of publishing that never loses its sparkle, the fact that these wonderful people are willing to pour their time and attention into my silly little story about a thief who talks to doors. Every time I think about it, I feel humbled and elated all at once, and also determined to do my part to deliver the best stories I possibly can. That feeling of working together and being part of a team is definitely my favorite part of the publishing process.

introducing

If you enjoyed THE SPIRIT THIEF,

look out for

THE SPIRIT REBELLION

The Legend of Eli Monpress Book 2

by Rachel Aaron

PROLOGUE

High in the forested hills where no one went, there stood a stone tower. It was a practical tower, neither lovely nor soaring, but solid and squat at only two stories. Its enormous blocks were hewn from the local stone, which was of an unappealing, muddy color that seemed to attract grime. Seeing that, it was perhaps fortunate that the tower was overrun with black-green vines. They wound themselves around the tower like thread on a spindle, knotting the wooden shutters closed and crumbling the mortar that held the bricks together, giving the place an air of disrepair and gloomy neglect, especially when it was dark and raining, as it was now.   •

Inside the tower, a man was shouting. His voice was deep and authoritative, but the voice that answered him didn't seem to care. It yelled back, childish and high, yet something in it was unignorable, and the vines that choked the tower rustled closer to listen.

Completely without warning, the door to the tower, a heavy wooden slab stained almost black from years in the forest, flew open. Yellow firelight spilled into the clearing, and, with it, a boy ran out into the wet night. He was thin and pale, all legs and arms, but he ran like the wind, his dark hair flying behind him. He had already made it halfway across the clearing before a man burst out of the tower after him. He was also dark haired, and his eyes were bright with rage, as were the rings that clung to his fingers.

"Eliton!" he shouted, throwing out his hand. The ring on his middle finger, a murky emerald wrapped in a filigree of golden leaves and branches, flashed deep, deep green. Across the dirt clearing that surrounded the tower, a great mass of roots ripped itself from the ground below the boy's feet.

The boy staggered and fell, kicking as the roots grabbed him.

"No!" he shouted. "Leave me alone!"

The words rippled with power as the boy's spirit blasted open. It was nothing like the calm, controlled openings the Spiritualists prized. This was a raw ripping, an instinctive, guttural reaction to fear, and the power of it landed like a hammer, crushing the clearing, the tower, the trees, the vines, everything. The rain froze in the air, the wind stopped moving, and everything except the boy stood perfectly still. Slowly, the roots that had leaped up fell away, sliding limply back to the churned ground, and the boy squirmed to his feet. He cast a fearful, hateful glance over his shoulder, but the man stood as still as everything else, his rings dark and his face bewildered like a joker's victim.

"Eliton," he said again, his voice breaking.

"No!" the boy shouted, backing away. "I hate you and your endless rules! You're never happy, are you? Just leave me alone!"

The words thrummed with power, and the boy turned and ran. The man started after him, but the vines shot off the tower and wrapped around his body, pinning him in place. The man cried out in rage, ripping at the leaves, but the vines piled on thicker and thicker, and he could not get free. He could only watch as the boy ran through the raindrops, still hanging weightless in the air, waiting for the child to say it was all right to fall.

"Eliton!" the man shouted again, almost pleading. "Do you think you can handle power like this alone? Without discipline?" He lunged against the vines, reaching toward the boy's retreating back. "If you don't come back this instant you'll be throwing away everything that we've worked for!"

The boy didn't even look back, and the man's face went scarlet.

"Go on, keep running!" he bellowed. "See how far you

get without me! You'll never amount to anything without training! You'll be worthless alone! WORTHLESS! DO YOU HEAR?"

"Shut up!" The boy's voice was distant now, his figure scarcely visible between the trees, but his power still thrummed in the air. Trapped by the vines, the man could only struggle uselessly as the boy vanished at last into the gloom. Only then did the power begin to fade. The vines lost their grip and the man tore himself free. He took a few steps in the direction the boy had gone, but thought better of it.

"He'll be back," he muttered, brushing the leaves off his robes. "A night in the wet will teach him." He glared at the vines. "He'll be back. He can't do anything without me."

The vines slid away with a noncommittal rustle, mindful of their role in his barely contained anger. The man cast a final, baleful look at the forest and then, gathering himself up, turned and marched back into the tower. He slammed the door behind him, cutting off the yellow light and leaving the clearing darker than ever as the suspended rain finally fell to the ground.

The boy ran, stumbling over fallen logs and through muddy streams swollen with the endless rain. He didn't know where he was going, and he was exhausted from whatever he had done in the clearing. His breath came in thundering gasps, drowning out the forest sounds, and yet, now as always, no matter how much noise he made, he could hear the spirits all around him—the anger of the stream at being full of mud, the anger of the mud at being cut from its parent dirt spirit and shoved into the stream, the contented murmurs of the trees as the water ran down them, the mindless singing of the crickets. The sounds of the spirit world filled his ears as no other sounds could, and he clung to them, letting the voices drag him forward even as his legs threatened to give up.

The rain grew heavier as the night wore on, and his progress slowed. He was walking now through the black, wet woods. He had no idea where he was and he didn't care. It wasn't like he was going back to the tower. Nothing could make him go back there, back to the endless lessons and rules of the black-and-white world his father lived in.

Tears ran freely down his face, and he scrubbed them away with dirty fists. He couldn't go home. Not anymore. He'd made his choice; there was no going back. His father wouldn't take him back after that show of disobedience, anyway. Worthless, that was what his father had written him off as. What hope was left after that?

His feet stumbled, and the boy fell, landing hard on his shoulder. He struggled a second, and then lay still on the soaked ground, breathing in the wet smell of the rotting leaves. What was the point of going on? He couldn't go back, and he had nowhere to go. He'd lived out here with his father forever. He had no friends, no relatives to run to. His mother wouldn't take him. She hadn't wanted him when he'd been doing well; she certainly wouldn't want him now. Even if she did, he didn't know where she lived.

Grunting, he rolled over, looking up through the drooping branches at the dark sky overhead, and tried to take stock of his situation. He'd never be a wizard now, at least, not like his father, with his rings and rules and duties, which was the only kind of wizard the world wanted so far as the boy could see. Maybe he could live in the mountains? But he didn't know how to hunt or make fires or what plants of the forest he could eat, which was a shame, for he was getting very hungry. More than anything, though, he was tired. So tired. Tired and small and worthless.

He spat a bit of dirt out of his mouth. Maybe his father was right. Maybe worthless was a good word for him. He certainly couldn't think of anything he was good for at the moment. He couldn't even hear the spirits anymore. The rain had passed and they were settling down, drifting back to sleep. His own eyes were drooping, too, but he shouldn't sleep like this, wet and dirty and exposed. Yet when he thought about getting up, the idea seemed impossible. Finally, he decided he would just lie here, and when he woke up, *if* he woke up, he would take things from there.

The moment he made his decision, sleep took him. He lay at the bottom of the gully, nestled between a fallen log and a living tree, still as a dead thing. Animals passed, sniffing him curiously, but he didn't stir. High overhead, the wind blew through the trees, scattering leaves on top of him. It blew past and then came around again, dipping low into the gully where the boy slept.

The wind blew gently, ruffling his hair, blowing along the muddy, ripped lines of his clothes and across his closed eyes. Then, as though it had found what it was looking for, the wind climbed again and hurried away across the treetops. Minutes passed in still silence, and then, in the empty air above the boy, a white line appeared. It grew like a slash in the air, spilling sharp, white light out into the dark.

From the moment the light appeared, nothing in the

forest moved. Everything, the insects, the animals, the mushrooms, the leaves on the ground, the trees, the water running down them, everything stood frozen, watching as a white, graceful, feminine hand reached through the cut in the air to brush a streak of mud off the boy's cheek. He flinched in his sleep, and the long fingers clenched, delighted.

By this time, the wind had returned, larger than before. It spun down the trees, sending the scattered leaves dancing, but it did not touch the boy.

"Is he not as I told you?" it whispered, staring at the sleeping child as spirits see.

Yes. The voice from the white space beyond the world was filled with joy, and another white hand snaked out to join the first, stroking the boy's dirty hair. *He is just as you said.*

The wind puffed up, very pleased with itself, but the woman behind the cut seemed to have forgotten it was there. Her hands reached out farther, followed by snowy arms, shoulders, and a waterfall of pure white hair that glowed with a light of its own. White legs followed, and for the first time in hundreds of years, she stepped completely through the strange hole, from her white world into the real one.

All around her, the forest shook in awe. Every spirit, from the ancient trees to the mayflies, knew her and bowed down in reverence. The fallen logs, the moss, even the mud under her feet paid her honor and worship, prostrating themselves beneath the white light that shone from her skin as though the moon stood on the ground.

The lady didn't acknowledge them. Such reverence was her due. All of her attention was focused on the boy, still dead asleep, his grubby hands clutching his mud-stained jacket around him.

Gentle as the falling mist, the white woman knelt beside him and eased her hands beneath his body, lifting him from the ground as though he weighed nothing and gently laying him on her lap.

He is beautiful, she said. *So very beautiful. Even through the veil of flesh, he shines like the sun.*

She stood up in one lovely, graceful motion, cradling the boy in her arms. *You shall be my star*, she whispered, pressing her white lips against the sleeping boy's forehead. *My best beloved, my favorite, forever and ever until the end of the world and beyond.*

The boy stirred as she touched him, turning toward her in his sleep, and the White Lady laughed, delighted. Clutching him to her breast, she turned and stepped back through the slit in the world, taking her light with her. The white line held a moment after she was gone, and then it too shimmered and faded, leaving the wet forest darker and emptier than ever.

CHAPTER
1

Zarin, city of magic, rose tall and white in the afternoon sun. It loomed over the low plains of the central Council Kingdoms, riding the edge of the high, rocky ridge that separated the foothills from the great sweeping piedmont so that the city spires could be seen from a hundred miles in all directions. But highest of all, towering over even the famous seven battlements of Whitefall Citadel, home of the Merchant Princes of Zarin and the revolutionary body they had founded, the Council of Thrones, stood the soaring white spire of the Spirit Court.

It rose from the great ridge that served as Zarin's spine, shooting straight and white and impossibly tall into the pale sky without joint or mortar to support it. Tall, clear windows pricked the white surface in a smooth, ascending spiral, and each window bore a fluttering banner of red silk stamped in gold with a perfect, bold circle, the symbol of the Spirit Court. No one, not even the Spiritualists, knew how the tower had been made. The common story was that the Shapers, that mysterious and independent guild of crafting wizards responsible for awakened swords and the gems all Spiritualists used to house their spirits, had raised it from the stone in a single day as payment for some unknown debt. Supposedly, the tower itself was a united spirit, though only the Rector Spiritualis, who held the great mantle of the tower, knew for certain.

The tower's base had four doors, but the largest of these was the eastern door, the door that opened to the rest of the city. Red and glossy, the door stood fifteen feet tall, its base as wide as the great, laurel-lined street leading up to it. Broad marble steps spread like ripples from the door's foot, and it was on these that Spiritualist Krigel, assistant to the Rector Spiritualis and bearer of a very difficult task, chose to make his stand.

"No, here." He snapped his fingers, his severe face locked in a frown even more dour than the one he usually wore. "Stand here."

The mass of Spiritualists obeyed, shuffling in a great sea of stiff, formal, red silk as they moved where he pointed. They were all young, Krigel thought with a grimace. Too young. Sworn Spiritualists they might be, but not a single one was more than five months from their apprenticeship. Only one had more than a single bound spirit under her command, and all of them looked too nervous to give a cohesive order to the spirits they did control. Truly, he'd been given an impossible task. He only hoped the girl didn't decide to fight.

"All right," he said quietly when the crowd was in position. "How many of you keep fire spirits? Bonfires, torches, candles, brushfires, anything that burns."

A half-dozen hands went up.

"Don't bring them out," Krigel snapped, raising his voice so that everyone could hear. "I want nothing that can be drowned. That means no sand, no electricity, not that any of you could catch a lightning bolt yet, but especially no fire. Now, those of you with rock spirits, dirt, anything from the ground, raise your hands."

Another half-dozen hands went up, and Krigel nodded. "You are all to be ready at a moment's notice. If her dog tries anything, *anything*, I want you to stop him."

"But sir," a lanky boy in front said. "What about the road?"

"Never mind the road," Krigel said, shaking his head. "Rip it to pieces if you have to. I want that dog neutralized, or we'll never catch her should she decide to run. Yes," he said and nodded at a hand that went up in the back. "Tall girl."

The girl, who was in fact not terribly tall, went as red as her robe, but she asked her question in a firm voice. "Master Krigel, are the charges against her true?"

"That is none of your business," Krigel said, giving the poor girl a glare that sent her down another foot. "The Court decides truth. Our job is to see that she stands before it, nothing else. Yes, you, freckled boy."

The boy in the front put down his hand sheepishly. "Yes, Master Krigel, but then, why are we here? Do you expect her to fight?"

"Expectations are not my concern," Krigel said. "I was ordered to take no chances bringing her to face the charges, and so none I shall take. I'm only hoping you lot will be enough to stop her should she decide to run. Frankly, my money's on the dog. But," he said and smiled at their pale faces, "one goes to battle with the army one's got, so try and look competent and keep your hands down as much as possible. One look at your bare fingers and the jig is up."

Off in the city a bell began to ring, and Krigel looked over his shoulder. "That's the signal. They're en route. Places, please."

Everyone shuffled into order and Krigel, dour as ever, took the front position on the lowest stair. There they waited, a wall of red robes and clenched fists while, far away, down the long, tree-lined approach, a tall figure riding something long, sleek, and mist colored passed through the narrow gate that separated the Spirit Court's district from the rest of Zarin and began to pad down the road toward them.

As the figure drew closer, it became clear that it was a woman, tall, proud, redheaded, and riding a great canine creature that looked like a cross between a dog and freezing fog. However, that was not what made them nervous. The moment the woman reached the first of the carefully mani- cured trees that lined the tower approach, every spirit in the group, including Krigel's own heavy rings, began to buzz.

"Control your spirits," Krigel said, silencing his own with a firm breath.

"But master," one of the Spiritualists behind him squeaked, clutching the shaking ruby on her index finger. "This can't be right. My torch spirit is terrified. It says that woman is carrying a sea."

Krigel gave the girl a cutting glare over his shoulder. "Why do you think I brought two dozen of you with me?" He turned back again. "Steady yourselves, here she comes."

Behind him, the red-robed figures squeezed together, all of them focused on the woman coming toward them, now more terrifying and confusing than the monster she rode.

"What now?" Miranda groaned, looking tiredly at the wall of red taking up the bottom step of the Spirit Court's tower. "Four days of riding and when we finally do get to Zarin, they're having some kind of ceremony on the steps. Don't tell me we got here on parade day."

"Doesn't smell like parade day," Gin said, sniffing the air. "Not a cooked goose for miles."

"Well," Miranda said, laughing, "I don't care if it's parade day or if Master Banage finally instituted that formal robes requirement he's been threatening for years. *I'm* just happy to be home." She stretched on Gin's back, popping the day's ride out of her joints. "I'm going to go to Banage and make my report." *And give him Eli's letter*, she added to herself. Her hand went to the square of paper in her front pocket. She still hadn't opened it, but today she could hand it over and be done. "After that," she continued, grinning wide, "I'm going to have a nice long bath followed by a nice long sleep in my own bed."

"I'd settle for a pig," Gin said, licking his chops.

"Fine," Miranda said. "But only after seeing the stable master and getting someone to look at your back." She poked the bandaged spot between the dog's shoulders where Nico's hand had entered only a week ago, and Gin whimpered.

"Fine, fine," he growled. "Just don't do that again."

Point made, Miranda sat back and let the dog make his

own speed toward the towering white spire that had been her home since she was thirteen. Her irritation at the mass of red-robed Spiritualists blocking her easy path into the tower faded a little when she recognized Spiritualist Krigel, Banage's assistant and friend, standing at their head. Maybe he was rehearsing something with the younger Spiritualists? He was in charge of pomp for the Court, after all. But any warm feelings she had began to fade when she got a look at his face. Krigel was never a jolly man, but the look he gave her now made her stomach clench. The feeling was not helped by the fact that the Spiritualists behind him would not meet her eyes, despite her being the only rider on the road.

Still, she was careful not to let her unease show, smiling warmly as she steered Gin to a stop at the base of the tower steps.

"Spiritualist Krigel," she said, bowing. "What's all this?"

Krigel did not return her smile. "Spiritualist Lyonette," he said, stepping forward. "Would you mind dismounting?"

His voice was cold and distant, but Miranda did as he asked, sliding off Gin's back with a creak of protesting muscles. The moment she was on the ground, the young, robed Spiritualists fanned out to form a circle around her, as though on cue. She took a small step back, and Gin growled low in his throat.

"Krigel," Miranda said again, laughing a little. "What's going on?"

The old man looked her square in the eyes. "Spiritualist Miranda Lyonette, you are under arrest by order of the Tower Keepers and proclamation of the Rector

Spiritualis. You are here to surrender all weapons, rights, and privileges, placing yourself under the jurisdiction of the Spirit Court until such time as you shall answer to the charges levied against you. You will step forward with your hands out, please."

Miranda blinked at him, completely uncomprehending. "Arrest? For what?"

"That is confidential and will be answered by the Court," Krigel responded.

"Powers, Krigel," Miranda said, her voice almost breaking. "What is going on? Where is Banage? Surely this is a mistake."

"There is no mistake." Krigel looked sterner than ever. "It was Master Banage who ordered your arrest. Now, are you coming, or do we have to drag you?"

The ring of Spiritualists took a small, menacing step forward, and Gin began to growl louder than ever. Miranda stopped him with a glare.

"I will of course obey the Rector Spiritualis," she said loudly, putting her hands out, palms up, in submission. "There's no need for threats, though I would like an explanation."

"All in good time," Krigel said, his voice relieved. "Come with me."

"I'll need someone to tend to my ghosthound," Miranda said, not moving. "He is injured and tired. He needs food and care."

"I'll see that he is taken to the stables," Krigel said. "But do come now, please. You may bring your things."

Seeing that that was the best she was going to get, Miranda turned and started to untie her satchel from Gin's side.

"I don't like this at all," the ghosthound growled.

"You think I do?" Miranda growled back. "This has to be a misunderstanding, or else some plan of Master Banage's. Whatever it is, I'll find out soon enough. Just go along and I'll contact you as soon as I know something."

She gave him a final pat before walking over to Krigel. A group of five Spiritualists immediately fell in around her, surrounding her in a circle of red robes and flashing rings as Krigel marched them up the stairs and through the great red door.

Krigel led the way through the great entry hall, up a grand set of stairs, and then through a side door to a far less grand set of stairs. They climbed in silence, spiraling up and up and up. As was the tower's strange nature, they made it to the top much faster than they should have, coming out on a long landing at the tower's peak.

Krigel stopped them at the top of the stairs. "Wait here," he said, and vanished through the heavy wooden door at the landing's end, leaving Miranda alone with her escort.

The young Spiritualists stood perfectly still around her, fists clenched against their rings. Miranda could feel their fear, though what she had done to inspire it she couldn't begin to imagine. Fortunately, Krigel appeared again almost instantly, snapping his fingers for Miranda to step forward.

"He'll see you now," Krigel said. "Alone."

Miranda's escort gave a collective relieved sigh as she stepped forward, and for once Miranda was in complete agreement. Now, at least, maybe she could get some answers. When she reached the door, however, Krigel caught her hand.

"I know this has not been the homecoming you wished for," he said quietly, "but mind your temper, Miranda. He's been through a lot for you already today. Try not to make things more difficult than they already are, for once."

Miranda stopped short. "What do you mean?"

"Just keep that hot head of yours down," Krigel said, squeezing her shoulder hard enough to make her wince.

Slightly more hesitant than she'd been a moment ago, Miranda turned and walked into the office of the Rector Spiritualis.

The office took up the entirety of the peak of the Spirit Court's tower and, save for the landing and a section that was set aside for the Rector Spiritualis's private living space, it was all one large, circular room with everything built to impress. Soaring stone ribs lined with steady-burning lanterns lit a polished stone floor that could hold ten Spiritualists and their Spirit retinues with room to spare. Arched, narrow windows pierced the white walls at frequent intervals, looking down on Zarin through clear, almost invisible glass. The walls themselves were lined with tapestries, paintings, and shelves stuffed to overflowing with the collected treasures and curiosities of four hundred years of Spiritualists, all in perfect order and without a speck of dust.

Directly across from the door where Miranda stood, placed at the apex of the circular room, was an enormous, imposing desk, its surface hidden beneath neat stacks of parchment scrolls. Behind the desk, sitting in the Rector Spiritualis's grand, high-backed throne of a chair, was Etmon Banage himself.

Even sitting, it was clear he was a tall man. He had

neatly trimmed black hair that was just starting to go gray at the temples, and narrow, jutting shoulders his bulky robes did little to hide. His sharp face was handsome in an uncompromising way that allowed for neither smiles nor weakness, and his scowl, which he wore now, had turned blustering kings into meek-voiced boys. His hands, which he kept folded on the desk in front of him, were laden with heavy rings that almost sang with the sleeping power of the spirits within. Even in that enormous room, the power of Banage's spirits filled the air. But over it all, hanging so heavy it weighed even on Miranda's own rings, was the press of Banage's will, iron and immovable and completely in command. Normally, Miranda found the inscrutable, uncompromising power comforting, a firm foundation that could never be shaken. Tonight, however, she was beginning to understand how a small spirit feels when a Great Spirit singles it out.

Banage cleared his throat, and Miranda realized she had stopped. She gathered her wits and quickly made her way across the polished floor, stopping midway to give the traditional bow with her ringed fingers touching her forehead. When she straightened, Banage flicked his eyes to the straight-backed chair that had been set out in front of his desk. Miranda nodded and walked forward, her slippered feet quiet as snow on the cold stone as she crossed the wide, empty floor and took a seat.

"So," Banage said, "it is true. You have taken a Great Spirit."

Miranda flinched. This wasn't the greeting she'd expected. "Yes, Master Banage," she said. "I wrote as much in the report I sent ahead. You received it, didn't you?"

"Yes, I did," Banage said. "But reading such a story and hearing the truth of it from your own spirits is quite a different matter."

Miranda's head shot up, and the bitterness in her voice shocked even her. "Is that why you had me arrested?"

"Partially." Banage sighed and looked down. "You need to appreciate the position we're in, Miranda." He reached across his desk and picked up a scroll covered in wax seals. "Do you know what this is?"

Miranda shook her head.

"It's a petition," Banage said, "signed by fifty-four of the eighty-nine active Tower Keepers. They are demanding you stand before the Court to explain your actions in Mellinor."

"What of my actions needs explaining?" Miranda said, more loudly than she'd meant to.

Banage gave her a withering look. "You were sent to Mellinor with a specific mission: to apprehend Monpress and bring him to Zarin. Instead, here you are, empty-handed, riding a wave of rumor that, not only did you work together with the thief you were sent to catch, but you took the treasure of Mellinor for yourself. Rumors you confirmed in your own report. Did you really think you could just ride back into Zarin with a Great Spirit sleeping under your skin and not be questioned?"

"Well, yes," Miranda said. "Master Banage, I *saved* Mellinor, all of it, its people, its king, everything. If you read my report, you know that already. I didn't catch Monpress, true, but while he's a scoundrel and a black mark on the name of wizards everywhere, he's not evil. Greedy and irresponsible, maybe, and certainly someone who needs to be brought to justice, but he's nothing on an Enslaver. I don't think anyone could argue that defeating Renaud and saving the Great Spirit of Mellinor were less important than stopping Eli Monpress from stealing some *money*."

Banage lowered his head and began to rub his temples. "Spoken like a true Spiritualist," he said. "But you're missing the point, Miranda. This isn't about not catching Monpress. He didn't get that bounty by being easy to corner. This is about how you acted in Mellinor. Or, rather, how the world saw your actions."

He stared at her, waiting for something, but Miranda had no idea what. Seeing that this was going nowhere, Banage sighed and stood, walking over to the tall window behind his desk to gaze down at the sprawling city below. "Days before your report arrived," he said, "perhaps before you'd even confronted Renaud, rumors were flying about the Spiritualist who'd teamed up with Eli Monpress. The stories were everywhere, spreading down every trade route and growing worse with every telling. That you sold out the king, or murdered him yourself. That Monpress was actually in league with the Spirit Court from the beginning, that we were the ones profiting from his crimes."

"But that's ridiculous," Miranda scoffed. "Surely—"

"I agree," Banage said and nodded. "But it doesn't stop people from thinking what they want to think." He turned around. "You know as well as I do that the Tower Keepers are a bunch of old biddies whose primary concern is staying on top of their local politics. They care about whatever king or lord rules the land their tower is on, not catching Eli or any affairs in Zarin."

"Exactly," Miranda said. "So how do my actions in

Mellinor have anything to do with some Tower Keeper a thousand miles away?"

"Monpress is news everywhere," Banage said dourly. "His exploits are entertainment far and wide, which is why we wanted him brought to heel in the first place. Now your name is wrapped up in it, too, and the Tower Keepers are angry. Way they see it, you've shamed the Spirit Court, and, through it, themselves. These are not people who take shame lightly, Miranda."

"But that's absurd!" Miranda cried.

"Of course it is," Banage said. "But for all they're isolated out in the countryside, the Tower Keepers are the only voting members of the Spirit Court. If they vote to have you stand trial and explain yourself, there's nothing I can do but make sure you're there."

"So that's it then?" Miranda said, clenching her hands. "I'm to stand trial for what, saving a kingdom?"

Banage sighed. "The formal charge is that you did willfully and in full denial of your duties work together with a known thief to destabilize Mellinor in order to seize its Great Spirit for yourself."

Miranda's face went scarlet. "I received Mellinor through an act of desperation to save his life!"

"I'm certain you did," Banage said. "The charge is impossible. You might be a powerful wizard, but even you couldn't hold a Great Spirit against its will."

The calm in Banage's voice made her want to strangle him. "If you know it's impossible, why are we going through with the trial?"

"Because we have no *choice*," Banage answered. "This is a perfectly legal trial brought about through the proper channels. Anything I did to try and stop it would be seen as favoritism toward you, something I'm no doubt already being accused of by having you brought to my office rather than thrown in a cell."

Miranda looked away. She was so angry she could barely think. Across the room, Banage took a deep breath. "Miranda," he said. "I know how offensive this is to you, but you need to stay calm. If you lose this trial and they find you guilty of betraying your oaths, you could be stripped of your rank, your position as a Spiritualist, even your rings. Too much is at stake here to throw it away on anger and pride."

Miranda clenched her jaw. "May I at least see the formal petition?"

Banage held the scroll out. Miranda stood and took it, letting the weight of the seals at the bottom unroll the paper for her. The charge was as Banage had said, written in tall letters across the top. She grimaced and flicked her eyes to the middle of the page where the signatures began, scanning the names in the hope she would see someone she could appeal to. If she was actually going to stand trial, she would need allies in the stands. However, when she reached the bottom of the list, where the originator of the petition signed his name, her vision blurred with rage at the extravagant signature sprawled across the entire bottom left corner.

"Grenith Hern?"

"He is the head of the Tower Keepers," Banage said. "It isn't unreasonable that he should represent them in—"

"*Grenith Hern?*" She was almost shouting now. "The man who has made a career out of hating you? Who blames you for stealing the office of Rector out from under him? He's the one responsible for this 'fair and legal' accusation?"

"Enough, Miranda." Banage's voice was cold and sharp.

Miranda blew past the warning. "You *know* he's doing this only to discredit you!"

"*Of course I know*," Banage hissed, standing up to meet her eyes. "But I am not above the law, and neither are you. We must obey the edicts of the Court, which means that when a Spiritualist receives a summons to stand before the Court, no matter who signed it or why, she goes. End of discussion."

Miranda threw the petition on his desk. "I will not go and stand there while that man spreads *lies* about me! He will say anything to get what he wants. You know half the names on that paper wouldn't be there if Hern hadn't been whispering in their ears!"

"*Miranda!*"

She flinched at the incredible anger in his voice, but she did not back down. They stared at each other for a long moment, and then Banage sank back into his chair and put his head in his hands, looking for once not like the unconquerable leader of the Spirit Court, but like an old, tired man.

"Whatever we think of Hern's motives," he said softly, "the signatures are what they are. There is no legal way I can stop this trial, but I can shield you from the worst of it."

He lowered his hands and looked at her. "You are my apprentice, Miranda, and dear as a daughter to me. I cannot bear to see you or your spirits suffer for my sake. Whatever you may think of him, Hern is not an unreasonable man. When he brought this petition to me yesterday, I reacted much as you just did. Then I remembered myself, and we were able to come to a compromise."

"What kind of compromise?" she said skeptically.

"You will stand before the Court and face the accusations, but you will neither confirm nor deny guilt."

Miranda's face went bright red. "What sort of a compromise is that?"

Banage's glare shut her up. "In return for giving Hern his show, he has agreed to let me give you a tower somewhere far away from Zarin."

Miranda stared at him in disbelief. "A tower?"

"Yes," Banage said. "The rank of Tower Keeper would grant you immunity from the trial's harsher punishments. The worst Hern would be able to do is slap you on the wrist and send you back to your tower. This way, whatever happened, your rings would be safe and your career would be saved."

Miranda stared at her master, unable to speak. She tried to remind herself that Banage's plans always worked out for the best, but the thought of sitting silently while Hern lied to her face, lied in the great chamber of the Spirit Court itself, before all the Tower Keepers, made her feel ill. To just be silent and let her silence give his lies credence, the very idea was a mockery of everything the Spirit Court stood for, everything *she* stood for.

"I can't do it."

"You must do it," Banage said. "Miranda, there's no getting out of this. If you go into that trial as a simple Spiritualist, Hern could take everything from you."

"It's not certain that Hern will win," Miranda said,

crossing her arms over her chest stubbornly. "Tower Keepers are still Spiritualists. If I can tell the truth out in the open, tell what actually happened and show them Mellinor, let the spirit speak for himself, there's no way they can find me guilty, *because I'm not.*"

"This is not open for debate," Banage said crossly. "Do you think I like where this is going? This whole situation is my fault. If you had another master, this would never have grown into the fiasco it is, but we are out-maneuvered."

"I can't just sit there and let him win!" Miranda shouted.

"This isn't a game, Miranda!" Banage was shouting, too, now. "If you try and face Hern head-on, you will be throwing away everything we worked together to create. You're too good a Spiritualist for me to let you risk your career like this! You know and I know that you are guiltless, that your only crime was doing the right thing in difficult circumstances. *Let that be enough.* Don't fool yourself into thinking that your fighting Hern on this will be for anything other than your own pride!"

Miranda quaked at the anger in his voice, and for a moment the old obedience nearly throttled her with a desperate need to do what Master Banage said. But Mellinor was churning inside her, his current dark and furious, his anger magnifying hers, and she could not let it go.

Banage must have felt it, too, the angry surge of the great water spirit, for she felt the enormous weight of his spirit settle on top of her as the man himself bowed his head and began to rub his eyes with a tired, jeweled hand.

"It's late," he said quietly. "A late night after many

long days is no time to make weighty decisions. We'll pick this up tomorrow. Maybe after a night's rest you'll be able to see that I am trying to save you."

Miranda's anger broke at the quiet defeat in his voice. "I do see," she said, "and I am grateful. But—"

Banage interrupted her with a wave of his hand. "Sleep on it," he said. "I've given orders for you to be under house arrest tonight, so you'll be comfortable at least. We'll meet again tomorrow for breakfast in the garden, like old times. But for now, just go."

Miranda nodded and stood stiffly, mindful of every tiny noise she made in the now-silent room. As she turned to leave, she stopped suddenly. Her hand went to her pocket and fished out a white square.

"I'd almost forgotten," she said, turning back to Banage. "This is for you."

She laid the envelope on his desk. Then, with a quick bow, she turned and marched across the great stretch of empty marble to the door. Pulling it open, she plunged out of the room and down the stairs as fast as her feet could carry her.

Banage watched the door as it drifted shut, the iron hinges trained after centuries of service to never slam. When the echo of her footsteps faded, Banage let go of the breath he'd been holding and let his head slump into his hands. It never got easier, never. He sat for a while in the silence, and then, when he felt steady enough to read whatever she had written him, he let his hand fall to the letter she had placed on his desk.

When he looked at the letter, however, his eyebrows shot up in surprise. The handwriting on the front was not Miranda's, and in any case, she never addressed him as "Etmon Banage." Curious, he turned the letter over, and all other thoughts left his mind. There, pressed deep into the soft, forest-green wax was an all too familiar cursive *M*.

Banage dropped the envelope on his desk like it was a venomous snake. He sat there for a few moments staring at it. Then, in a fast, decisive motion, he grabbed the letter and broke the seal, tearing the paper when it would not open fast enough. A folded letter fell from the sundered envelope, landing lightly on his desk. With careful, suspicious fingers, Banage unfolded the thick parchment.

It was a wanted poster, one of those mass copied by the army of ink-and-block spirits below the Council fortress. An achingly familiar boyish face grinned up at him from the creased paper, the charming features older, sharper, but still clearly recognizable despite more than a decade's growth. His mocking expression was captured perfectly by the delicate shading that was the Bounty Office's trademark, making the picture so lifelike Banage almost expected it to start laughing. Above the picture, a name was stenciled in block capitals: ELI MONPRESS. Below the portrait, written in almost unreadably tiny print so they could fit on one page, was a list of Eli's crimes. And below that, printed in tall, bold blocks, was WANTED, DEAD OR ALIVE, 55,000 GOLD STANDARDS.

That's what was printed, anyway, but this particular poster had been altered. First, the 55,000 had been crossed out and the number 60,000 written above it in red ink. Second, the same hand had crossed out the word WANTED with a thick, straight line and written instead the word WORTH.

"Eli Monpress," Banage read quietly. "Worth, dead or alive, sixty thousand gold standards."

A feeling of disgust overwhelmed him, and he dropped the poster, looking away as his fingers moved unconsciously over the ring on his middle finger, a setting of gold filigree of leaves and branches holding a large, murky emerald as dark and brooding as an old forest. He stayed like that for a long, silent time, staring into the dark of his office. Then, with deliberate slowness, he picked up the poster and ripped it to pieces. He fed each piece to the lamp on his desk, the heavy red-stoned ring on his thumb glowing like a star as he did so, keeping the fire from spreading anywhere Banage did not wish it to spread.

When the poster and its sundered envelope had been reduced to ash, Banage stood and walked stiffly across his office to the small, recessed door that led to his private apartments. When he reached it, he said something low, and all the lamps flickered, plunging the office into darkness. When the darkness was complete, he shut the door, locking out the smell of burnt paper that tried to follow him.

CHAPTER
2

Eli Monpress, the greatest thief in the world, was strolling through the woods. His overstuffed bag bounced against his back as he walked, and he was whistling a tune he didn't quite remember as he watched the late afternoon sunlight filter through the golden leaves, bringing with it a smell of cold air and dry wood. So pleasant was the scene, in fact, that it took him a good twenty paces to realize he was walking alone.

He stopped on his heel and spun to see Josef, his swordsman, sitting twenty paces back in the middle of the path with Nico, Josef's constant shadow, sitting beside him. Beside her, Josef's famous sword, the Heart of War, stood plunged into the hard-packed dirt, and beside it lay the enormous sack of gold they'd liberated from Mellinor's sadly destroyed treasury. Despite the fine weather, none of them looked happy.

Eli heaved a dramatic sigh. "What?"

Josef stared right back at him. "I'm not taking another step until you tell me exactly where we're going."

Eli rolled his eyes, this again. "I told you before. I told you this *morning*, we're going to see a friend of mine about getting Nico a new coat."

"I didn't ask what we were going to do when we got there." Josef folded his arms over his chest. "I asked you, *where are we going?* We've been walking vaguely north for almost a month now, and since yesterday we've been walking in circles around the same four miles of woods. This is the second time today we've passed that beech tree, and I'm tired of lugging your ill-gotten gains." The sack of gold jingled as his large fist landed on it. "Admit it," the swordsman said, giving Eli a superior sneer. "You're lost."

"I am not." Eli threw out his arms, taking in the scant undergrowth, rocky slopes, and slender, white-barked trees of the small valley they were in the middle of climbing out of. "We're in the great north woods, which the Shapers call the Turningwood, and the Council of Thrones doesn't have a name for because we left the Council maps a week ago. Specifically, we are in the Thousand Streams region of the Turningwood, a name you might appreciate, considering all the valleys we've had to climb through. Even more specifically, we are in the northeast corner of the Thousand Streams, where the streams are slightly less numerous. A little farther north and we'd be in the foothills of the Sleeping Mountains themselves, and a little farther east and we'd hit the frozen swamps on the coastal plain. So, as you see, I know exactly where we are, and it is exactly where we are supposed to be."

Despite such a grand display of navigation, Josef did not look impressed. "If we're where we're supposed to be, why are we still walking?"

Eli turned and started up the hill again. "Because the house of the man we are looking for isn't always in the same place."

"You mean the man isn't always in the same place," Josef said, making no sound of following him.

"No." Eli panted as he reached the crest of the valley. "I mean the house. If you don't like it, complain to him."

"*If* we ever find him," Josef said.

Eli shook his head and started down the other side of the hill, wishing that the swordsman would apply his stubbornness to something useful, like being a perfect gold carrier, or finding them something tastier than squirrel to eat. By the time he'd reached the bottom of the next valley, Josef had still not crested the ridge of the one before. Eli grimmaced and kept walking, though more slowly and with one ear out for the sound of jingling gold, which would tell him if this was just a Josef bluff or if he was actually going to have to go back and push the man up the hill. Fortunately, the decision was rendered moot when he took another step forward and found nothing but air.

He yelped as the world spun upside down and sideways. Then, with a sharp pain in his ankles, it stopped, and he found himself hanging high in the branches of a tree. Blinking in surprise, Eli looked down, or up, depending, and saw he was strung up by his ankles in the branches of an large oak. That much he'd been prepared for, but how he was hanging took him by surprise. Instead of ropes, a knot of roots with dirt still clinging to them bound his feet, ankles, and lower legs. They moved as he watched, creaking with a sound very much like snickering. He was still staring at the roots and trying to figure out what had just happened when he heard Josef come over the hill. Eli craned his neck and started to yell a warning, but it was too late. The second Josef was off the rocky ravine, a snaking cluster of roots erupted from the ground and grabbed his feet. The swordsman flew into the air with a lurch and came to rest neatly beside Eli.

"Well," Eli said. "Fancy meeting you here."

Josef didn't answer, he just scowled and bent over, wiggling his foot. There was a flash, and a long knife dropped out of his boot before the roots could tighten. The swordsman caught it deftly an inch from Eli's face and bent over, reaching for the closest root.

"I wouldn't do that," Eli said, glancing up, or down. "It's a bit of a drop."

Josef followed his gaze. The ground swung dizzyingly a good thirty feet below them, but the drop was made even longer by the enormous hole the roots had left when they'd sprung. Josef shook his head in disgust and stuck the knife into his belt. "I thought you were friends with trees."

"For the last time, it doesn't work like that," Eli said. "That's like saying, 'I thought you were friends with humans.' Anyway, don't be a grouch. We've found it! This is the Awakened Wood that guards the house."

Josef sighed. "Wonderful. Fantastic welcome. Is your friend always this friendly, or are we a special exception?"

Before Eli could answer, a woman's voice interrupted.

"Eli Monpress." The words were heavy with laughter. "I wouldn't have thought we'd catch you."

Both men craned their necks. Directly below them a tall, young woman in hunter's leathers stepped out from behind the tree they were dangling from, a smug smile on her tan face. She was very young, not more than sixteen, and lanky, as though she hadn't quite grown into her limbs yet. She crossed her long arms over her chest and stared at them as though daring Eli to try and talk his way out of this one. Eli opened his mouth to oblige her, but he never got the chance. From the shadows behind the girl, a pair of white, thin hands in silver manacles shot out and closed around her throat. The girl's eyes bulged and she dropped to her knees as Nico flickered into sight behind her.

"Release them," Nico said in a dry, terrifying voice. "Now."

"No, Nico!" Eli shouted. "She's not going to—"

The rest of it was lost in the girl's roar as she ducked and tumbled forward, using Nico's own iron grip to take the smaller girl with her, slamming them both into the ground with Nico on the bottom. As soon as she was on top, the girl elbowed Nico hard in the ribs. Nico gasped, and her grip faltered. The girl shot up, rolling gracefully to her feet. When she turned around, she had a long, beautiful knife in her hands, the blade glowing with its own silver light.

Nico was back on her feet in an instant, and for a breathless moment the two watched each other. Then the girl in the hunting leathers shook her head and slid her knife back into the long sheath on her thigh.

"I begin to understand why you needed that coat," the girl said, not taking her eyes off of Nico. "Let them down, gently please."

The tree made a sound like a disgruntled sigh and lowered its roots, releasing Eli and Josef just a little higher than would have been a safe drop. The men landed hard in the dirt, and while Josef was on his feet almost immediately, Eli took a bit longer to get his breath back.

"Hello, Pele," he coughed, trying to discreetly determine if his back was broken. "Always a pleasure."

Pele arched an eyebrow. "Can't say I feel the same." She glared at Nico, who was still watching her from a crouch. "Must you always bring such trouble?"

PS 3601.A27 S65 2010